Heart of the Fae

ALSO BY EMMA HAMM

The Otherworld

Heart of the Fae

Veins of Magic

The Faceless Woman

The Raven's Ballad

Bride of the Sea

Curse of the Troll

Of Goblin Kings

Of Goblins and Gold

Of Shadows and Elves

Of Pixies and Spells

Of Werewolves and Curses

Of Fairytales and Magic

Once Upon a Monster

Bleeding Hearts

Binding Moon

Ragged Lungs

and many more...

HEART
OF THE
FAE

Visit author online at www.emmahamm.com

Cover by: Natasa Ilincic

Editing by: Amy Cissell and Juliette Cross

For the little girls who
played with faeries
in the garden.

Keep playing with them.
You never know when they might be real.

TIREE
MULL
Iona
TÍR NA NÓG
INNER HEBRIDES
TÍR FO THUINN
ISLAY
HY-BRASIL
'PHANTOM ISLAND'
ARRAN
IRELAND
Bangor
scriobhai

LL &
RWORLD
Cuan
na Merrows
Tír na nÓg
Caisleán Seelie
Chathair an
Tsolais
Hy-Brasil
Cathair na
Corcha
Foraoise Draíochta
Unseelie
Caisleán
Unseelie

Glossary of Terminology

TUATHA DÉ DANANN - Considered to be the "High Fae", they are the original and most powerful faerie creatures.

SEELIE FAE - Otherwise known as the the "Light Fae", these creatures live their lives according to rules of Honor, Goodness, and Adherence to the Law.

UNSEELIE FAE - Considered the "Dark Fae", these creatures follow no law and do not appreciate beauty.

DANU - The mother of all Tuatha dé Danann and considered to be an "earth" mother.

MACHA - An ancient Tuatha dé Danann who is known as one of the three sisters that make up the Morrighan. Her symbols are that of a horse and a sword.

REDCAP - A troublesome faerie, frequently found in gardens harassing chickens.

WILL-O'-THE-WISPS - Small balls of light that guide travelers into bogs, usually with the intention for the humans to become lost.

BROWNIES - Friendly, mouse-like creatures who clean and cook for those who are kind to them.

PIXIE - A winged faerie whose face resembles that of a leaf.

CHANGELING - Old or weak faeries swapped with human children, usually identified as a sickly child.

GNOME - Generally considered ugly, these small, squat faeries take care of gardens and have an impressive green thumb.

DULLAHAN - A terrifying and often evil faerie who carry their heads in their laps.

HY-BRASIL - A legendary isle which can only be seen once every seven years.

MERROW - Also known as a Mermaid, merrows have green hair and webbed fingers.

BOGGART - A brownie who grows angry or loses their way turns into a boggart. They are usually invisible, and have a habit of placing cold hands on people's faces as they sleep.

POOKA - A faerie which imitates animals, mostly dogs and horses.

KELPIE - A horse like creature who lives at the edge of a bog. It will try to convince you to ride it, at which point it will run underneath the water and drown the person on its back.

SELKIE - A faerie which can turn into a seal, as long as it still has its seal skin.

PROLOGUE

Once upon a time in a hidden land beyond human reach, there lived a king and queen of the Seelie Fae. They desperately desired an heir to the throne, but had not been blessed with children. In his frustration, the king journeyed across the sea to the cursed home of the Unseelie.

He made a deal with an ancient crone, half spider and half woman. If she would give him a child, then he would bring peace to their lands. The crone was pleased and promised when he returned to his wife, she would bear him a child.

The Queen carried not one, but two children. Twin boys, both heirs to the throne.

Many years passed. Their lives were filled with light and love. They had forgotten that the Unseelie do not make deals without payment, and stopping a war paid for one boy.

Not two.

Their first-born son grew into a warrior. His blade was unstoppable, his aim always true, his speed lightning quick. Their second born son grew into a scholar. He knew every whisper on the wind, every lie and story, every bit of knowledge that made the kingdom run smoothly. The King and Queen were certain the brothers would rule the Seelie Fae together.

They had not seen the jealousy growing within their youngest son's heart, nor had they seen the doubt growing in the eldest.

In a fit of rage, their youngest son buried a blade in his brother's back. The wound was superficial and might have healed if it hadn't revealed a nightmare.

Their son, their perfect first born, was flawed. Gemstones and crystals grew out of the wound, marring his strong body, and marking him unfit to rule their kingdom. Embarrassed and appalled, they did the only thing they could.

Banishment.

The disgraced prince was sent away to a phantom isle which could only be seen once every seven years. He begged his family to allow him to remain, but they had no pity for the man who had hidden his true nature.

The first-born son of the Seelie King faded into myth, then legend.

Then nothing at all.

Chapter 1

Blood covered her hands. The metallic smell burned her nostrils and overwhelmed her senses. Although she'd finished the surgery an hour ago, she still saw the gaping wound, the splayed open flesh, and the iridescent shimmer of the blood beetle feasting upon sinuous muscle.

Sorcha sat on the back stoop with her hands dangling off her knees. The chickens pecked at her soft leather shoes; the jabs helped to ground her. This weightless feeling always happened after a long, grueling attempt to extract a beetle.

"Shoo," she whispered. One chicken shook its head, feathers ruffled in displeasure. She was certain the nasty redcap rode one of them. The faerie was secretive in his pranks, and likely thought she couldn't see him, but Sorcha always caught glimpses out of the corner of her eye. "There are tastier things than my feet."

She tapped her foot against the ground. The chicken clucked loudly and beat its wings against her legs, rushing to the other side of the pen. Even though Sorcha fed them every morning and night, she would bear the brunt of their anger.

Chickens were vindictive little things.

"Sorcha!" a feminine voice shouted. "Get back in here!"

She stood, wanting desperately to dust off her skirts but knowing she would only smear blood on them. To waste new fabric would be the worst kind of sin. She stared down at the blood flaking off her hands, lips pressed in a thin line.

"It will have to do," she muttered.

Their three-story home was at the edge of town, the only suitable location for a brothel. The stone walls were sturdy and clean, and the wooden roof free of rot. It was by no means elegant, but it was suitable for its purpose. For Sorcha, the cobblestone steps felt like stairs to the gallows.

Sorcha dunked her hands into a bucket of clean water near the door. Her sisters had meant it for cleaning, but if they wanted her to rush, then they needed to make the trek to the river once again.

She scrubbed her hands together, tainting the water with blood. It turned as red as the muscles in her father's back that had been revealed when she pressed her blade deeper…

"Sorcha!"

Snapping out of her stupor, she wiped her hands upon the plaid wrapped around her waist. A breeze pushed red curls in front of her gaze, obscuring her vision. She huffed out an angry breath and shoved them back.

There was blood caked underneath her nails.

"I'm coming!" she shouted, pushing open the door.

The room beyond was still. Papa's room was always quiet, but now it was silent as a tomb. Sorcha prayed every night it would not become one.

She knew how to prevent children from being conceived, how to birth a child, and all the ailments that might come after for both mother and babe. She had guided countless women through the trials of labor and treated many a croupy cough.

But she wanted to be a real healer. Her soul yearned to do more, to set bones and find cures for diseases. Shelves of books lined her bedroom, each containing detailed notes for every herb, every technique to heal, even the right faeries to beg for help.

It was a shame the faeries had stopped listening a long time ago.

Trophies of Papa's travels decorated the walls of his room. A bear pelt covered the stone floor, a dark wood desk contained all his notes and a balancing scale to count his coins. His pallet bed covered almost the entire back wall, heavy curtains shrouding him from Sorcha's view.

"Sorcha, his fever is back," her sister said.

She rushed to his side.

Rosaleen was the youngest in the brothel and innately kind. The longer she stayed here, the quieter she would get. Kind people never lasted in this profession. They were either lucky, and some nobleman took them as a mistress, or they disappeared forever.

Rosaleen's heart-shaped face was pale with fear. She had tied her blonde ringlets with a leather thong, but a few escaped to bounce with her movements.

Such a pretty little thing would surely capture a nobleman's favor. Or a soldier's, at the very least. What man wouldn't want a mistress such as her?

Sorcha pressed her hand against Papa's forehead and tsked. "We completed another treatment, and I thought rest would stave off another fever. I'm sorry, I was wrong. Can you get him hot water, please, Rosaleen?"

"Will it help?"

"It will. A spot of tea fixes a great many things," Sorcha lied. He wouldn't heal tonight, in a fortnight, or even in a year. He wouldn't heal at all. But Rosaleen was a delicate creature and lying eased her worry.

Sorcha watched her sister rush from the room with a troubled gaze.

"Good riddance," Papa coughed. "They fawn over me as if I'm already dead."

"They're worried," Sorcha replied with a smile. "And they have a right to be."

"There will be another man to take my place. A business like this won't be empty for long."

"But will he be as kind? Will he be as understanding?"

"I am neither of those, and the girls shouldn't expect another man to be."

Sorcha helped him sit up, her hand sturdy and strong behind his back. She remembered him as a tall man, broad and capable of taking on the world. He had thrown men out of this establishment without breaking a sweat. Now, he was skeletal. Each inhalation rattled and exhalation wheezed. His hands shook, and his eyes remained unfocused.

While he caught his breath, she plucked at the bandages and poultice packed around his ribs. "How does it feel?"

"Sore," he grumbled. "Damn beetles are always moving."

"At least we got rid of another hive mother."

Papa snorted. "It's something, but it won't save me."

No, it wouldn't.

A blood beetle infection was a death sentence, and no one had figured out how to cure it. They came from the skies. Swarms of green locusts, so beautiful the villagers wore their wings as jewelry in the first year. Then, they laid their eggs inside people. There was no catching up with them after that.

Sorcha sighed and laid her hand over one of the many bumps on Papa's back. The beetles lived underneath the skin, eating flesh from the inside out. They multiplied while feasting slowly upon their hosts, but at least they didn't spread until they exhausted their food supply.

Sorcha had figured out a way to extract them. She cut through skin, muscle, and sinew, carefully pulling the beetles out from behind. She then burned them and buried their ashes. It was the only way she could be certain they wouldn't fly off and infect someone else.

The bump underneath her hand shifted.

"I felt that one," Papa huffed. "How long do I have girl?"

"A few more months. I've been trying to keep up with their reproductions, but your body won't take this much trauma for long."

"That's what I thought."

The door eased open and Rosaleen poked her head through. "Can I come back in now?"

Sorcha rubbed Papa's back. "Yes, come on in. Can you pour the water in a cup for me, please?"

Pottery was scarce at the brothel. No one wanted to sell household objects to prostitutes, so they made do with what Sorcha received as trade from her midwifery. The mangled clay cup was lopsided, but it held water without leaking.

She packed yarrow into the cup and gave it a swirl. "Here you go, Papa. Drink up."

"Is this that bitter tea you keep making me drink?"

"It keeps the fever down and helps stop the bleeding."

"I don't like it." He sipped and made a face. "I think you're poisoning me."

"I think you're being a child. Drink it all—" she paused. "All of it, Papa. And then go back to sleep."

He grumbled, but laid back down on the bed without too much of a fuss. Sorcha drew the curtain so the light wouldn't disturb him.

Rosaleen stared at her. The weight of her gaze was like a physical touch. There wasn't much for Sorcha to say. She didn't want to ruin their happiness—and income—by giving a date to their father's death. They needed to stay strong, and later they could grieve.

She tucked her little sister under her arm and guided her from the room. "What's the matter little chick?"

"I'm worried about Papa. Aren't you?"

"You let me worry about him. I'm the healer, aren't I?"

"Midwife."

The word stung.

"I'm doing more than the healers would. They'd be bloodletting him when the beetles already do that. He doesn't need any leeches. He needs the beetles removed."

"They're still not listening to you?"

The sisters walked into the kitchen and main living space for the women. When they first moved to this city, only the family had lived in this building. Their Papa was a born businessman, and he set his sights on expanding their clientele. Now, there were thirteen women living and working under their roof.

The twins snuggled up near the fire, their heads pressed together as they shared secrets. Sorcha's herbs hung from the ceiling to dry for later use. A worn table stretched from end to end, two benches serving as seats. They stored a cauldron in the back room and brought it out for supper to hang over the fire.

Briana, the eldest of their sisters, swung the opposite door open. Masculine laughter and shouts echoed from the front of the house. "Rosaleen, you've a customer out front."

"All right," she squeezed Sorcha's waist. "I'll be back later. You'll be fine without me?"

"You worry too much," Sorcha replied. "Go on then. Make some money."

As the tiny blonde skipped past, Briana gave Sorcha a measured stare. "You're keeping yourself busy today, I hope? There's a long line of appointments, and I don't have time to watch over you today. You'll fend for yourself if you're sticking around."

Sorcha had never been like her adopted sisters. Her witch of a mother taught her too many things and her young mind had absorbed the information. Sorcha had more uses than whoring, Papa used to say. People paid more for healing than they did for bedding. And besides, no one wanted to risk laying with the devil's spawn. Papa never thought she was a witch or cursed, but she was whip-smart.

He made the decision for her to walk the path of a healer. From that day forward, she dedicated herself to helping others and tried to avoid the same fate as her mother. The acrid scent of burning flesh was seared into her memory.

Sorcha ducked her head and nodded. "I'll be at the guild meeting most of the day and then need to stop by Dame Agatha's."

"That poor woman is pregnant again?"

"Seems so."

Briana tsked. "That man needs to give her a break, or she'll go to an early grave. Speaking of, I'll need you to restock our own stores. We can't have any children running around."

"Of course. On the way back, I'll gather more mealbhacán, but the wild carrot tastes awful."

"I don't care what you gather, or how bad it tastes. Just make it useful."

Briana must have had a difficult client, Sorcha mused. Or perhaps it was the teeming mass of energy behind her. Men always grew excited on the Solstice.

She raced up the rickety wooden stairs, trying not to make eye contact with any of the male customers below. They lived in a large city, and most people knew her. She wasn't in the market for entertaining.

"Sorcha! When are you going to let us love you like we love your sisters?"

Only when she crested the first flight of stairs did she pause and lean over the railing. The long tangled mass of her hair hung over the edge. "Oh, Fergus. Someday you will make your wife jealous with talk like that."

"She knows I'm loyal to her!"

Briana stood behind the man, waving her hands frantically.

Right. Sorcha wasn't supposed to insult the customers, or they'd leave. She puffed out a breath that stirred the red curls in front of her face, conceding. "I'm a healer, Fergus. I don't partake in your festivities, but a man certainly can dream!"

He let out a hearty laugh, his cheeks stained red. "Ah, and dream I do, my lovely lass!"

She raced up the rest of the stairs. Her skirt whirled in an arc behind her, the blue plaid fluttering with her movements. The last thing she wanted to hear was that Fergus, of all men, dreamed of her.

They all slept on the top floor, away from the rooms where they brought clients. A place they could call their own was important. However, the more women they brought into their family, the less room they had.

Sorcha didn't work in the brothel, so her room was the smallest. It had once been used as a storage closet, but now held a small cot and stacked chests. Books, herbs, and all manner of magical objects were scattered around the room.

The first chest creaked as she opened it. She reached into the dark depths, her fingers skimming over well-worn objects, until she closed her fist around her greatest treasure.

Her mother had passed down her knowledge along with sacred objects. Many feared Paganism—considered it the work of the devil. They named those who practiced it witches. Sorcha knew better.

She pulled out a stone carved with a white dove. Pressing it to her lips, she whispered, "Good morrow, Máthair."

Not a day passed when she didn't miss her mother's laughter, her calloused hands, and the scent of cinnamon in her hair. She hadn't been a witch, just a healer who knew how to ask favors of the Fae.

Sorcha dropped the stone back into the chest and picked up a ceramic pot. Her mother had lovingly painted tiny flowers all around the edges, each stroke created with care and precision. She measured out a small bit of sugar and scooped it onto the windowsill.

"Share a taste of sugar with me," Sorcha said, "in celebration of our dutiful work."

Like her mother, Sorcha respected the old ways and the Fae. She believed in them where others did not. Her room was always clean, and her books always neatly packed away. All without Sorcha touching a single item. The brownies took care of her, and she took care of them in return.

She scooped up her medical notes and tucked them into a bag she slung over her shoulder. Patting her hair, she gave up on tying it back. The nest of curls would be free before she made it to the guild.

Tugging hard on her bodice, she pressed her hand against her chest. A hag stone—bored through with natural holes by running river water—hung around her neck. Another gift from her mother, so she could always see through the glamour of magic.

She turned and made her way back down the stairs.

Rosaleen was already exiting her room, closing the door gently behind her. Her hair stuck up in all directions, like a dandelion puff. She glanced over her shoulder and shrugged. "I wasn't expecting that one to be so quick. He paid for a half hour, so I suppose he can sleep it off."

"Someone new?"

"He wouldn't say who he was. Looks like a nobleman. His clothes are too fine to be working class."

Sorcha pulled up her sister's sleeve which was dipping dangerously low on her shoulder. "Fancy catching this one for good?"

Rosaleen blushed. "Oh, he's much too fine looking for me."

"And you're a rare beauty. He would give you a good life, away from working so hard."

"I couldn't leave all of you."

"None of us would think less of you for it. You'd be safe, well-fed, and you could visit. If he's kind, think about it."

"He was certainly kind," Rosaleen tucked a strand of hair behind her ear. "And I can appreciate a man who doesn't take much work."

Sorcha chuckled and touched a finger to Rosaleen's chin. "Think about it, little chick. Go get yourself cleaned up."

"The tea is downstairs?"

"Ask Briana. There's a few tonics left, and I'll bring back more."

They walked down the stairs together, giggling as Rosaleen told stories about the customers she'd already had that day.

"Will you be gone long?" Rosaleen asked as they reached the ground floor.

"Briana's asked that I make myself scarce. There's a lot of customers, and I don't need to be underfoot."

"We might need you if anyone gets too rowdy."

"The men don't pay for healing anyways. I'd rather find customers who will at least trade."

"Not Dame Agatha?" Rosaleen's eyes glinted with mischief.

"You were listening!"

"Just through the grate while he was getting ready. I haven't heard a single rumor about Agatha being pregnant again, so what are you really going to do? Are you hiding a man?"

"Not everything is about men, Rosaleen." Sorcha lifted her bag and pawed through it. "I'm just visiting the shrine, that's all."

"I thought you were done with the faeries?"

"No one can be done with faeries. They will always be there, and someone has to leave offerings."

They had argued about this since they were children. Papa and his girls lived in the city where people had forgotten their ties to the land. Sorcha had grown up on the moors. She knew will-o'-the-wisps by name and had spied on goblin markets. She left offerings for brownies and whispered secrets to the Tuatha dé Danann.

If she had never seen these things, she might have questioned whether faeries were real.

Shaking her head, she pushed her way through the crowd of men in the front room. Briana hadn't been wrong. They were unusually busy, even for this time of year. Perhaps someone had spread word of the mysterious brothel filled with golden women.

Rumors said that Papa's daughters came from a line of goddesses. They were all unnaturally pretty with milk-pale skin and heart-shaped faces. Their full lips were always red and didn't leave berry stains on men's skin. Loose blonde curls never needed a hot iron, and they were graceful as dancers.

There were some who wondered about their odd duck of a sister. In comparison, Sorcha was a startling red rose among daffodils. She was taller than her sisters with waist-length red hair and tight-ring curls that billowed around her like a cloud. Freckles dusted her skin from the top of her head to the tips of her toes. And everyone found her slightly pointed ears to be unnerving.

Faerie touched, the villagers used to say. Her mother must have had a changeling child she refused to give back. Or perhaps that was just a sign she was touched by the devil, like her witch of a mother.

Whatever the reasoning, Sorcha was odd, strange, unusual.

She pushed past the last man and stepped out onto the streets. A horse and buggy waited out front, the emblem of an eagle painted on its side in gold. She reached into the pocket of her dress and pulled out a small shriveled apple.

Soft velvet lips plucked the fruit from her palm, and the horse nickered with happiness.

"You'll be waiting for a while, my friend," Sorcha said with a grin.

"Hey, woman!" A whip cracked over her head. "Ain't nobody ever told ye not to touch a stranger's horse? Get out of here."

She ducked away and disappeared into the crowd.

It was market day. The teeming mass of people all seemed to have something to sell. Unwashed bodies pressed against her, but all she could smell was fish, meats, and fresh fruit.

"Eggs for sale!"

"Flowers for your lady?"

"Fabric in every color!"

Sorcha kept her bag close to her side and tried not to make eye contact. She didn't need any trouble from the suspicious villagers who made the sign of the cross when she passed. Stalls lined the streets with food, billowing cloth, even jewelry from the far reaches of the land. Some vendors she recognized. Others she did not.

A minstrel played his flute, filling the square with a jaunty tune. Sorcha recognized the song and covered her grin. The words were highly inappropriate. His hat on the ground overflowed with coins, so others must have appreciated the jest as much as she.

He winked at her when she placed a single coin with the others.

A woman selling dried herbs caught her arm and pressed a small jar of honey into Sorcha's palm. "For Danu."

"I will leave it in the forest," Sorcha tucked it into her bag. "For anything in particular?"

"Good health."

Nodding, she continued to push through the crowds of people. It wasn't the first time someone asked for a blessing. They weren't willing to follow the old ways themselves—too risky—so they'd ask Sorcha to leave them for her. If she was caught, she'd be burned at the stake by the same people who handed her gifts to take to the Fae.

A few others passed her bits and pieces to leave as offerings. A small packet of sugar, a dried bunch of lavender, a tiny jar of fresh cream. Little things that the faeries appreciated and might leave blessings for in return.

That was the deal with faeries. Their favors could not be bought or bribed. One had to continue leaving gifts and someday, maybe, the faeries would gift them a blessing.

Another woman grabbed Sorcha's arm and pulled her away from the crowd. A dirty kerchief covered her head and a moth-bitten brown dress hung from her thin frame. "My daughter won't stop crying. She's screaming the nights away, and my husband plans to leave her on the hill tomorrow night saying she's a changeling. Is there another way?" Her swollen eyes brimmed with tears, cheeks scrubbed raw and nose stuffed.

Sorcha patted her hand. "Bring her to the river and hold her in the water. No need to put her underneath it, just her legs will do. If they look the same, then she's no changeling. If they look like birch branches, then you know you're housing a faerie under your roof."

"The river?"

"Faerie magic doesn't work under flowing water and the glamour will break. If she's no Fae, then bring her to the brothel. I'll have a good look at her and see if I can give you something to help her. And you, get some sleep."

"Bless you, lady. We have nothing to pay you."

"I don't ask for payment. Leave an offering for Danu when you can and apologize for blaming her children for your child's illness."

The woman wrung her hands. "And if it is a changeling?"

Sorcha frowned. "Then you'll leave it in the woods and hope they bring your child back."

She pulled away and continued her journey with a troubled mind. Many families thought their sickly babe was a changeling, but rarely was it true. There hadn't been a changeling in this area for as long as she could remember.

Yet, offerings to the Fae had diminished in the past years. With the blood beetle plague, the rising of other religions, and more outsiders in their lands, faerie stories faded into myth.

The people forgot the shrines. Cattle and lye tainted the holy waters. Many people didn't leave cream and sugar on their doorsteps. No one remembered the old ways, and they were paying for that.

Sorcha shook her head. She hoped it wasn't a changeling. Often, the Fae swapped out children for a reason. It was an unwanted, ugly babe, or it was an ancient faerie who needed a quiet place to die. Neither of those were a fair trade for a human child, and leaving it on a hill didn't result in gaining their child back. The faerie would die alone on the hill, cold and unwanted once again.

But it was the only solution she knew.

She tried not to let her eyes linger upon the shadows at the edges of the street. Families cast out the infected from their home. The fear of spreading the blood beetles giving way to panic. She couldn't stop her eyes from searching for them at the edges of the crowd.

Her gaze caught on a painfully thin man. He scratched at a bulge on his cheek which shifted every time he touched it.

Sorcha shivered and hurried along her way.

The Guild building loomed at the end of the street. It looked nearly as impressive as the church. Imposing and tall, the walls stretched so high she had to shade her eyes to see their peak. One of the more prestigious patrons had paid for full stained glass windows. On one side, a healer looked down at her with disapproving eyes. On the other, a priest held his hands solemnly before him.

Taking a deep breath, she hiked the bag higher on her shoulder. Noblemen worked here, their fine velvet clothing easily ruined by her dirty touch, their jewelry blinding her with its opulence. She was not a welcome visitor.

She walked up the steps, counting each one as she went. By the time she reached thirty, she was at the front doors.

"This time will be different," she told herself. "They will listen to you. You'll make them."

Sorcha pushed the doors open and stepped onto the marble floors. Her footsteps echoed, those closest to her glancing up at the intrusive sound. She didn't let herself meet their gaze. She knew from experience their expressions would turn to shock and then anger. How dare a woman tread among their favored kind?

Confidently striding to the end of the building, she halted in front of a bespectacled man peering at ledgers. He didn't look up.

She cleared her throat.

"What is it this time, Sorcha?"

"I've come to speak with the healers' guild on the matter of blood beetles."

He didn't argue. They'd fought enough battles that minstrels should sing of their war. He lifted a hand, sighing. "Third hall on the left."

"Thank you."

She told herself to stay calm. Yelling at these men would only make them dig their heels in further, and she wanted to help. The blood beetles weren't going away, but maybe, just maybe, she could help the infected survive longer.

Her stomach rolled.

There wasn't any reason to be afraid. They couldn't lock her up or call her a witch. That would mean admitting they believed in magic, and these were men of science. The worst that could happen was that they would laugh at her.

It shouldn't bother her as much as it did. Her pride had always been a personal weakness, and one she had yet to tame. Sorcha wanted them to say she was right. Just once.

She pushed the door open and stepped into the hall.

A group of men gathered around a body laid out on a long table. A blanket draped over the dead man's legs, but that modesty seemed unnecessary when they had his rib cage cracked open.

"Gentlemen," she called out, "another blood beetle victim?"

The man standing at the head of the table raised his gaze. "Sorcha. I thought we threw you out last time."

"You did. And yet, here I am again. I have information on extracting the blood beetles I thought you might find helpful."

"I doubt anything a woman has to say would be helpful."

The room was as cold as his voice. She swallowed her anger and stilled her shivers. "I have taken detailed notes, as you requested last time, including drawings of my findings. As you have one of the afflicted before you, I would be happy to perform a live demonstration."

"Child, I appreciate your dedication, but you were never formally trained. We have no need for a midwife's opinions over the domain of men."

"Are women not afflicted as well?"

"I fail to see how this improves your argument."

"You dismiss me because I cannot understand the domain of men. However, it also affects the domain of women. According to your logic, I would understand that far better than you."

He sighed, bowed his head, and braced himself on the table, clearly taking measured breaths. "Sorcha. I should not have to explain this to you."

"What is there to explain? I have information that may be useful. You should listen."

Their collective gaze burned. She had known they wouldn't want her in the same room while they studied. It still frustrated her beyond reason.

"Why won't you listen to me?" she asked. "It's not a difficult thing to do. I am certain you can hear me as none of you are so advanced in age that I must shout."

Her eyes strayed towards the corner of a room where a handsome man stood. Geralt. His ink-dark hair glinted blue in the strong light trickling through the glass ceiling. His lips quirked to the side in a smirk, and his cobalt eyes sparkled with humor. Supple breeches hugged his well-shaped thighs, a white linen shirt billowed at his elbows, and a green brocade vest hugged his broad chest.

He swaggered forward. "If I may, gentlemen?"

Sorcha held in her snort of displeasure. She had been the one speaking, yet he did not direct his question towards her.

The doctor removed his glasses and snapped his handkerchief in the air. He pressed it against his nose, as if Sorcha brought with her a rancid stench, and waved his hand. "Please do."

"Sorcha," Geralt said as he strode forward. "It's not that we don't value your opinion, we certainly do. It's just that we are very busy and on the brink of great discovery."

"That you can remove the beetles? I've told you this every time I've come here."

"No. We have found a way to prevent them from breeding within the human body."

She ground her teeth together, so hard her jaw creaked. "That's impossible."

"It's not. I understand how badly you want to help us, and we appreciate it. But I am begging you," he held his hands clasped before him. "Give us more time. More uninterrupted time."

"I don't have time," Sorcha growled. "And neither do the rest of our people. The blood beetle plague gets worse with every season. You and your fellow doctors hole up in this room day after day, and you never find any kind of resolution. You take bodies like you're one of the Dullahan. All for nothing!"

Her shouts bounced off the high ceiling and struck the men like falling arrows. Some had the decency to flinch. Others remained stoic. Geralt's eyes narrowed upon her, and for once, Sorcha thought she had finally angered him.

The spark of fire disappeared.

"We are doing the best we can," the cajoling tone returned to Geralt's voice. "You are the bravest, most daring girl I have ever met. I appreciate your tenacity." His hand pressed against her spine and turned her from the room.

"I'm not leaving yet, Geralt. I can at least watch the examination. Perhaps I might have—"

"Sorcha," he interrupted. She could feel each finger burning through the fabric of her dress. "Perhaps you can explain why you don't have time to wait? I would like to offer my help."

"I don't want your help."

"But I want to give it. So please, walk with me."

She peered over her shoulder at the body. "If they would just listen, for once in their stubborn lives, I might be able to teach them something!"

"Not today, lovely. Not today."

He propelled her from the room with such ease Sorcha wondered if he had cursed her. More likely he was overpowering her. Geralt stood a head taller and didn't mind using his greater weight to his advantage.

There was little else she could do. Sorcha wanted to stay but would only make a larger scene if she did. Perhaps someday they would let her linger, even in the corner or in the shadows.

But she was just a midwife, and therefore, a lesser being.

Geralt leaned down, his lips brushing her ear. "Now, what is wrong with your father?"

"You know what's wrong with him. He's infected."

"I know he's infected, but you've never used him as an excuse before. What has changed?"

"It's progressed."

Geralt nodded at another nobleman. The other did not return the gesture. Old blood rarely acknowledged new riches. "How far?"

She stopped in her tracks. "Why are you even asking? You don't care how he fares."

"Of course I care." He pressed a hand against his chest. "I have always cared, Sorcha."

Everything was spiraling out of control. Her gut clenched and her fingers curled into fists. "This is not why I am here, Geralt. I'm not having this conversation with you in the middle of the Guild."

"Then let us walk outside."

"We've talked this through so many times. Enough!" Her exasperated shout echoed. Men stopped in their work and glanced towards them.

Her face turned bright red, the ache a weakness she resented. The last thing she needed was for these men to think she was hysterical. She already shouted enough.

Sorcha ducked her head and marched towards freedom, reminding herself to stay calm and composed.

"Sorcha!" Geralt called after her.

She rushed forward, bursting through the front door, and jogging down the steps. He caught up with her. The harsh tug of his hand on her arm would leave bruises.

"Would you at least listen to me?"

"I think I've heard it enough times." She shook herself out of his grip and rubbed at her bicep.

"You would have everything you desire," he said as she walked away. "You'd have a home, a husband, children."

"Is that what I'm supposed to want?"

"A man who adores you. Who whispers poetry in your ear every night and devotes himself to your happiness."

It sounded so good that she paused. He spoke of a life every woman desired. A loving relationship with a man who supported her every whim and passion. But she knew Geralt well. He wanted to believe he was that man, yet his eyes lingered upon the curves of other women. He drank more than he admitted, and above all else, he wasn't as good as he thought.

"I desire a useful man. One who can help us in our hour of need." She glanced over her shoulder. A curling red lock brushed across her face in the stiff breeze. "Words are of no use if no one is left to hear them."

"You want me to be the hero?" His jaw tightened before he growled, "I can't save everyone."

"No, you cannot. You're not a healer. You pay to be in that room among the brightest minds to satisfy your morbid curiosity," she lashed out. "Why won't you believe me when I say I can help?"

"You are a woman! What help could you provide?"

There it was. There was the anger, the red rage she saw so rarely. He buried his temper deep inside until it boiled over his edges.

"My sex doesn't change how much I know."

"You're naturally weak. You cannot help that, and we all understand. Why can't you?"

She drew herself up, squared her shoulders and gripped her plaid. "I am not weak because of my femininity. I do not look down upon you for not knowing how to birth a child or the right way to guide a woman through her first menses. Perhaps you should ask yourself why you feel the need to look down upon me."

A crowd gathered around the edges of her vision. This wasn't the first time she had screamed at a man in the street. Or a woman for that matter. She gritted her teeth.

"You can't change the world, Sorcha."

"I would if I could." She turned away from the town, from the villagers hiding smirks, from confused, handsome Geralt.

CHAPTER 2

A crash shook the entire kitchen. Clay plates rattled, and a mug fell to the floor, shattering with an echoing clatter. The shutters slammed against the stained-glass windows with thunderous bangs.

The brownies flinched. They lifted their pointed, furred faces towards the ceiling. Nervous chuckles floated in the air with the bubbles from their dishes.

Oona, the only pixie in the kitchen, lifted her violet gaze and sighed. "The master's angry tonight."

"He was angry last night and the night before that!" The gnome walking into the room could look a sheep in the eye. His face was eerily similar to a bowl of mashed potatoes, with winged eyebrows always drawn down in an angry frown. He waddled to Oona and dumped a basket of flowers on the table. "For dinner."

"Thank you, Cian. Are you bringing the master his supper tonight?"

"That grumpy thing up there? Howling like he plans to tear the whole castle apart? I will not, under any circumstances. He's been too angry lately. The boy can go hungry."

"He has a right to be angry."

"No one has a right to be angry for that long."

Oona turned, lavender wings fluttering in the air. High arched eyebrows lifted even higher. The leaf-like fan of her forehead vibrated in anger. She shook a long finger at Cian, the extra digit giving her tsking weight. "You know as well as I why that man is angry. His own brother banished him here. His twin! After trying to kill him, more than once, need I remind you."

Cian crossed his short arms over his wide chest. "I have never felt bad for a king, and I don't plan to start now."

"Not a king." She shook her head. "A man who might have been king, if circumstances were different. Those he loved betrayed him, hanged him, and sent him to this isle with us. The least we can do is bring him supper."

"You bring it to him, then. I don't need to get thrown across the room like last time."

"He wouldn't dare."

"Few would," Cian nodded. "You're a frightening woman, pixie."

"And don't you forget it." She reached out and rapped him on the head with a wooden spoon. "Now, where is the master's dinner?"

He blushed, the red color highlighting on the peaks of his wrinkled skin. "Didn't get him one."

"Cian!"

"What? I told you I wasn't bringing him dinner!"

"There's not enough time to find him something to eat," she huffed. "And what do you think I'm going to do? Bring him pollen and honey?"

"Why can't he eat what we do?"

"Because he's a direct descendant of the Tuatha dé Danann. You think they eat like us?"

Oona spun and frantically searched the kitchen for anything she could bring to their howling master. He wasn't a picky man. He rarely ate at all, but he couldn't eat flowers, and he certainly couldn't drink only cream.

She ended up with her hands full of bread, honey, and milk. It was the best she could do although it wasn't likely to cool his anger.

Oona blew out a breath which stirred the petals of her hair, then marched from the kitchen.

The stone steps to the master's quarters always made her nervous. No railings prevented her from falling straight down the center. Looking down the stairs, she gulped. The fall would kill her, so she was certain to tread carefully while making her way to the master's quarters.

The peak of the tower opened to a walkway suspended over open air. Wind whistled past her ears. The vines in her hair turned to whips striking against her cheeks and neck.

She strode across the walkway while holding her breath. A stone door blocked the master's side of the castle from everyone else, protecting them from his rage.

Oona placed her shoulder against the door and grunted as she pushed.

Sounds of shattering glass and splintering wood filled the room beyond. Her hands shook as she traversed the broken landscape of furniture and vases. The master had gone through his seating area and beyond into his bedroom.

She paused a moment and stared at a crooked painting. The Queen stared down from the wall with a soft smile on her face. Now, three ragged strips were missing. The sagging canvas warped her face along the sliced edges.

"Master has never harmed you before," she whispered to herself. "What happened tonight?"

The sounds of the master's wrath silenced at her words. He'd heard her.

Oona took a deep, steadying breath, and walked towards his bedroom. She tentatively pushed the wooden door open with her toe, holding her breath.

"Master?" she asked.

"Go away."

She peered into the dim light. The curtains hung over the windows, covered in dust, and tied down at the bottom to hold them tight. Shadows formed around a four-poster bed with one post snapped in half. She could make out his dresser, the chandelier swinging on the ceiling, even where his rug began. But she could not find him.

A bell rang in her mind. It warned her to leave and not let him lure her into his darkness. To preserve her own life and let him go hungry.

Her heart said the opposite.

She lifted her hand, snapped her fingers, and a warm faerie light danced in the air.

"There you are," she said. "I could hear you from downstairs and grew worried. You did quite a number on the front room."

"Go away, Oona."

He huddled beyond the bed, folded in on his great height until he was little more than a ball. His face turned away from her light as he always did when he saw her.

Not for the first time, she wished he would look at her without prompting.

"Master," she shook her head and marched to his dresser. "What have you done with your cloak?"

"I didn't think I would have visitors."

"Well, we share a castle. There's more of us than there are of you. What would you have done if the will-o'-the-wisps wandered up here to clean?"

"Frightened them away."

She reached into the top drawer and pulled out one of his many hooded cloaks. "Frightened them away. They already tremble when you walk past. Do you want them to run?"

"They should."

"I don't."

"You find no value in your own life."

Oona tsked. "That's cruel and unlike you. What happened, Eamonn?"

The glow from her faerie light reached him. He lifted a hand to cover his face and the other to reach for the cloak. "Not now."

"Yes, now." But she gave him the hood, watching the silk trickle from her fingers like black water. "You can't keep breaking furniture. We have a limited supply. Shipwrecks don't wash up every day."

He pulled the cloak over his shoulders as if his muscles had stiffened. Oona knew better. Once he lifted the hood over his face, she knelt on the floor.

"Don't—"

She didn't listen. She reached out and pressed her hand against his.

"What happened?"

Eamonn turned his hand, letting her fingers dance over his palm which now held an open wound. "Another careless mistake."

"Oh, master. It's just a cut."

"You know it's more than that."

She glanced down, peeling her hand back from his. His flesh had parted from the meaty muscle of his thumb in a diagonal to his pinky. No blood welled from the wound. Instead, sparkling violet and blue crystals grew in the golden glow.

The wound would never heal again.

Oona curled her fingers over the disfigurement. "It's not as bad as the others."

"No, but it is a reminder of what I am."

"You are our king."

"I am an abomination and a pathetic excuse for Seelie royalty."

She linked her fingers through his. "Those are your brother's words, not yours. You are not ugly, nor are you deformed. In every way that matters, you are a Seelie Fae."

"Except physical perfection. I can never be king."

"Rules like that were meant to be changed. It isn't right that you're here and he's sitting on your throne."

Eamonn pulled away. He rose with creaking knees to his massive height. Oona was not a small pixie, but the Tuatha dé Danann were giants among men. The hood covered his face, and his hands glimmered in the light. His entire body was a geode cracking open with every slice to his flesh.

"Leave," he growled.

"Are you going to be all right alone?"

He turned his back on her. "I always am."

With a breaking heart, Oona solemnly left the room. She was careless on the stairs and nearly tumbled to her death before she made it back to the kitchens. Tears streamed down her cheeks.

Cian peeked in through the garden door. "What's he done now?"

"Nothing. He's done nothing but chosen to be alone."

"Ah, good riddance. All he'd do is break things down here. I like my garden the way it is."

He disappeared, and her heart stung as if she had swallowed something bitter. She looked up at the ceiling and shook her head. "He shouldn't be alone. He doesn't deserve to be alone."

Chapter 3

A branch launched back and smacked Sorcha across the face. She flinched, another twig pulling at her hair until she whimpered. She paused and tried to untangle herself, huffing out a breath.

The trees held fast, tangling her curls around their thin branches and twisting at her scalp. Her plaid stuck on the lower branches, and her arms were held down by vines.

"I don't want to let go of my anger," she growled. "It's healthy! No man should tell me what to do."

Anger rose again at the memories. Even her tromp through the woods hadn't cleared the red haze obscuring her vision. How dare he suggest she still her tongue, and then follow up those words with yet another suggestion of marriage? He must be mad.

"Let me go!" she grunted. "I'm calm."

Another harsh tug made her wince.

Sorcha sucked in a slow breath. Her cheeks puffed as she exaggerated the movement. "See? I'm not angry and won't desecrate this place with my…" she paused and grimaced. "With my trivial issues."

How had she forgotten? This was a sacred place, a haven for all who needed it, and here she was waltzing in wearing anger like a cloak upon her shoulders.

She hung her head in embarrassment. "My sincerest apologies. I will not make the same mistake again."

The trees groaned their approval. She shook her head and her hair slid from the confines of branches and leaves. The curls bounced against her cheeks, untangled and smooth. Her dress fell heavy against her legs, her plaid swaying with the sudden movement.

Her lips tilted in a soft smile. "I have learned your lesson, Danu, and I will remember it."

Nudging a branch aside, she stepped into the clearing. Green moss carpeted the ground all the way to the stones piled in the center. An artist had carved a triskele long ago; the three linked swirls faintly glowed on the granite. Water bubbled in between the mounds, smoothing the stones into perfect spheres.

She felt the warmth of the Fae here. The lingering effects of magic and nature made the tips of her pointed ears heat.

She pulled the bag off her shoulder and placed her offerings upon the stones. "Great Mother of old, I bring you gifts from those who seek your favor. Aileen, Eithne, and Nola leave honey, lavender, and sweet mead." As she spoke, Sorcha placed her hand upon each item. "I have brought you my mother's pin. It sparkles in the sun and reminds me of this place. I would like to leave it if it pleases you."

A warm breeze spiraled around her. It lifted her hair and teased the end of her nose. Dust motes danced and butterflies stirred into motion. Their wings flashed brilliant colors as the sunlight played across them.

Danu was pleased. Sorcha tilted her head towards the sun and let its heat soothe her soul. Although she was here, in her favorite place, dark thoughts still shoved to the forefront of her mind.

There were too many things to worry about. The blood beetles. Papa. Geralt. Her sisters. The list went on and on until she was drowning.

"Danu," she whispered, "my mind is troubled. I do not seek help, as I know you cannot always give it, but if there is a spare moment of your time... listen to my fears."

The air in the glen stilled as though something or someone was leaning forward in anticipation.

Encouraged, Sorcha sank to her knees and dug her hands into the moss. "The blood beetle plague is spreading ever faster. My own father has contracted the infection. I have the knowledge to extend his life, but I cannot stop him from dying. I fear I am only prolonging the inevitable.

"My sisters will not last long without his guidance. The man who takes his place will be unlikely to view them as people. I do not wish for them to lose their business or their home. They have done what it takes to survive here in the city. There is no shame in their profession, but there will be many who seek to take advantage of us in our father's absence.

"The Guild members refuse to listen. They sit in their ivory tower and poke at dead bodies while so many people die. They have gone so far as to say that because I am a woman, I do not have as much knowledge as them. I do not have the patience, nor the endurance, to continue. I will say something foolish or headstrong, and they will never listen again.

"Please, great mother of all and protectress of the Tuatha dé Danann, hear my plea for help."

Sorcha leaned down and pressed her forehead against the soft moss. She held her breath as she waited, but expected no response. No matter how many times she cried out for help, the Fae always ignored her.

It wasn't in their nature. Even the Seelie court was fickle, their rules keeping them strictly away from humans. The Tuatha dé Danann were separate from those rules. They were the beginning and the end, the start of all Fae. But that didn't mean they liked humans any more than their brethren.

Her heart thundered in her ears. Was that a giggle in the forest? Unlikely. Although, if it was, perhaps the Fae were listening.

She waited until her knees ached and her back screamed for relief. The moss turned cold beneath her fingers, the water glimmering in bright droplets upon her nails.

"Please," she whispered again. "Just this once, please, listen to me."

A branch cracked. That was no giggle, nor was it caused by the wind. Sorcha's spine tensed further, and she squeezed her hands in the moss. Could it be possible? Could this be the moment Danu finally answered her?

Loud thuds echoed nearby, the pawing of a large creature she could not see. Sorcha flinched. The breeze picked up. Its heat scorching along her shoulders and whistling in her ears.

"Women do not belong on their knees, child."

The voice sliced through her consciousness like a well-sharpened blade. It was the rustling of leaves, the gong of sword striking shield, the crunch of teeth biting through an apple. Sorcha's hands began to shake as she pushed herself up onto her elbows and lifted her gaze.

Her eyes caught upon hooves that sparkled and faded into human feet. A swath of rich green fabric tumbled down atop them. The tail of a golden belt lashed out and settled against rounded hips.

The woman was tall. So tall she rivaled the surrounding trees. Her mane of red hair hung heavy to her waist, the color so vivid that Sorcha's eyes burned. Harsh angles defined a face not delicate, but strong. Verdant eyes glowed as she stared at Sorcha.

"Are you hard of hearing, girl? Stand up."

Sorcha stood, albeit slowly. "You aren't Danu."

"Astute for a woman so willing to bow."

The pieces fell together. The sound of stamping hooves, the red hair, the triskele carved into the stones. Sorcha's brows drew together. "You're Macha, aren't you?"

"And you're at my shrine."

Every muscle in her body seized. There were many myths regarding Macha, and all claimed she was dangerous. A sister to the Morrighan, Macha was known for her strength on the battlefield. She would paint woad upon her skin and hack through any man who stood in her way. The fanciful tales claimed she had a steed made of fire and trapped dead men's souls within her blade.

"I meant no disrespect," Sorcha said as she dropped her gaze. "Please accept my sincerest apologies. I will leave."

The blade at Macha's waist shone sunlight into Sorcha's eyes. Lifting a hand, she held her breath and stepped backward. Each step brought her closer to freedom and the promise of life. This was no kind Fae before her.

"I did not give you permission to leave, human."

Sorcha winced. "What would you have me do?"

"You asked for help. I'm interested in providing it."

"I—" It was bad luck to not accept a Fae's favor. Except this didn't feel like a gift. This felt like an offer which would require a price. "I don't make deals with faeries."

"Yet you came to what you thought was my mother's shrine? You begged for a favor just moments ago, but nothing is free. Here I am, Sorcha of Ui Neill. Ask your favor of me, and perhaps I shall be kind."

Her mind raced through the details she remembered of this Tuatha dé Danann. Macha was a war Fae, but also was known for protection. She had once been a kind and motherly figure before mankind tried to kill her and her babe.

There was a small chance that Macha would help. Sorcha was a strong woman, capable, and frustrated by the limitations men placed upon her. Her frustrations would call out to a faerie such as this.

None of this guaranteed safety. In fact, Sorcha might argue the exact opposite was more likely to happen.

Faeries weren't trustworthy creatures.

"I wish to stop the blood beetle plague," she said. "If there is a way to save my father, to prevent other deaths, I would like to know it."

"You are a smart girl. No promises, no questions, just a statement I cannot interpret in any other way." One of Macha's brows lifted. "I like you."

"I did not come here to beg for help from the Fae. Nothing comes without a price, and I have very little to give."

Macha's gaze turned stormy, and she strode towards Sorcha. Closer and closer she came, growing ever larger until they stood toe to toe. Sorcha's neck ached as she tilted her head. The faerie was easily seven feet tall and her hair made her seem even larger. The cloud of color sparked with static electricity.

"You want something that you are incapable of without help. You have to ask for it, Sorcha. Ask for my assistance, and I will give you all you desire."

"I don't know your price."

"And you won't until we strike a deal."

Sorcha sucked in a deep breath. Their chests brushed, a zing of magic traveling through her and sparking at the points of her ears.

"Will you provide a cure for the blood beetles?"

A soft sigh brushed across Sorcha's face and smelled of crushed grass. "Yes, I will. And I will do even more. So long as you are on this journey to find your cure, your father will remain alive."

Sorcha thought she might faint. "Papa?"

"It is the least I can do. I am sending you on a quest, little human. Far from your homeland, from your family, from everything you know. Centuries have passed since I last saw the cure you seek. Even I am uncertain where it lies, although I have my suspicions."

"If you don't know where it is, how am I supposed to find it?"

"There are others who know." Macha cupped Sorcha's chin, her hand so large it touched both pointed tips of her ears. "You will start by finding my children. Their names are Cormac and Concepta. Use their knowledge wisely."

"You want me to find two faeries? Here?"

"They were banished from the Otherworld and remain in yours."

"Glamoured or invisible?" Sorcha asked.

Macha's hand clenched, squeezing Sorcha's jaw until her eyes watered. "Glamoured to look as you do. They will appear as nobles, but they should be the only twins living in the same manor. Find them, and you'll start your journey."

"What do I say to them?"

"That I asked you to find them, and that they owe me a favor. Tell them what you seek. They will guide you."

Sorcha wasn't so certain that was the truth. Two unknown Fae who owed a favor to a Tuatha dé Danann? Her breakfast rose dangerously high in her throat.

Air filled her lungs as Macha stepped away. The myths had not prepared her for the cold gaze of a Fae. She wanted to flee from that angry look. What had she done? Had she somehow insulted this faerie of war before she had even started?

"Thank you," Sorcha said, "for my father. He has suffered for far too long."

"I care little for human life, but I can see how important it is to you. As such, it is my pleasure."

Though it made her sweat to ask, Sorcha swallowed hard and murmured, "What is your price?"

Endless possibilities unfolded before her. The Fae might ask for a child, for Sorcha's life, or something as simple as an unnamed favor.

She wasn't certain how much she was willing to pay. Many faceless infected people may not be worth a life enslaved. But for her father? He had saved her from begging, took her out of the slums and into the city, gave her a life.

How could she say no?

Macha bent and dipped her fingers in the holy water of the shrine. She licked the droplets and smiled. "You will endure hardship, pain, and perhaps even death. I will enjoy watching your struggles as payment."

"What kind of quest are you sending me on?" Sorcha heard her own voice as though underwater. Distorted and slow, it echoed back upon her.

"One that benefits the both of us," Macha replied. "You get your cure. I get my children back."

"What does the cure have to do with your children?"

"Nothing at all. But in finding your cure, I trust you will bring my children back to Tír na nÓg."

"The land of youth?" Sorcha stumbled over the words. "The Otherworld?"

"I am growing tired of explaining my decisions to you. Leave now, or I will run you out of this shrine and rescind my offer."

Sorcha scooped up her bag and spun on her heel. She could not risk the Fae changing her mind. This was a chance to save her father! To save everyone.

At the edge of the clearing, she paused. One foot crossed the threshold of the shrine and into the forest beyond. The other remained in the enchanted glen.

She looked over her shoulder at the faerie who watched her with calculating eyes. Macha reclined on the mossy ground, her fingers playing in the burbling water of her shrine.

"Why are you doing this?" Sorcha asked one last time.

"I, too, have been at the mercy of men, more times than I wish to recount. My mother would tell you the best way to answer them is to remain steadfast, quiet, and continue doing the right thing." Macha's eyes flashed brilliant green. "I am not a woman, but sword and shield. I will carve my own path, or I will force others to create it for me."

"What does that have to do with me?"

Their gazes met and Macha smiled. "You are the same, little human. They tell you time and time again you are a pool of still water. Yet, we both know underneath the surface a tempest rages. I will enjoy seeing your claws grow."

Unsettled, Sorcha plunged into the forest. Branches pulled at her clothing and tugged at her hair. She did not let them hold her. This was no longer a safe place, no longer a haven.

Her breath sawed out of her body in ragged gasps. She had made a deal with a faerie. What had she been thinking? Such a contract was binding.

What if she didn't find the cure? Sorcha stumbled out of the forest and fell onto her hands and knees near the carriage road. Had she agreed to go on a wild goose chase for the rest of her life? Would she spend eternity searching for an impossible thing?

She couldn't breathe enough air. It stuck in her throat and made her chest ache. Her ribs expanded, her mouth opening and closing as she tried to breathe.

Logically, she knew this was a panic attack. Some part of her mind recognized her imagination carrying her away from sanity. Her body did not recognize this, vomit rising from her stomach.

She coughed as she expelled her breakfast violently. Mucus hung in streams from her nose and mingled with the drool dripping from her lips.

What had she done?

"Inhale, Sorcha," she muttered. "One breath. Two breaths."

In and out, she counted every heartbeat and movement of her lungs. Birds chirped in the trees nearby. Twenty-seven chirps before they stopped. Carriage wheels creaked and stones crunched under their weight.

Her fingers curled in the soil. She would be all right. There was a cure. There had to be a cure, because faeries couldn't lie.

Now it was up to her, as it always had been, to save her people. Her family. She could find the one thing that would save them all and kill the blood beetles. Her life had meaning again, other than just being the midwife who serviced both a brothel and the entire town.

"Is that Sorcha?" The sound of the carriage paused. Hooves stamped the ground, making her flinch. "Sorcha, darling, what are you doing?" —the voice was familiar—"It is not safe to be on the road in the twilight hours."

"Dame Agatha. It is so good to see you again."

"Well, I should hope it would be under better circumstances than finding you on the side of the road! Get up, child."

The words were too similar to the faerie's. Panic fled to the back of her mind, resolve and purpose taking its place.

A red carriage had paused in front of her. The wheels gleamed with gold paint, along with the emblem of a rose. A delicate flowered curtain was drawn back from the small window and framed Dame Agatha's aged face.

"How are you feeling?" Sorcha wearily asked her least favorite patient.

"Well, I was just about to call upon you, Sorcha. I have exciting news!"

"You're to be blessed with a child?"

"Again!"

"Again," Sorcha repeated with a sigh. Her lie had been the truth after all. "Congratulations are in order, then. I suppose you'll be stopping by the brothel soon?"

"Oh goodness, no, I'll need you to come to me."

Dame Agatha had never come to the brothel for any of her treatments. She considered their home to be a den of miscreants and thieves, no matter how many times Sorcha assured her it was the safest place in Ui Neill.

She wiped her mouth on a sleeve, trying her best to ignore the acidic taste of vomit on her tongue. "This is not your usual carriage, Agatha."

"Oh goodness, no. A dear friend loaned this to me. I'm going to visit them! Certainly, you've heard of the MacNara twins. Lovely folk."

Sorcha froze. "Twins?"

"Oh, you haven't heard of them yet? They are new to this area, but the nicest family you'll ever meet. So giving! So progressive."

She glanced towards the forest. "Thank you, again, for making this easy on me."

Movement stirred branches nearby. Sorcha thought she saw a flash of unnatural green and the glint of fiery hair.

"Agatha? Might your friends have need of a midwife?"

"Well, I don't see why not. You know I love having you meet my friends, Sorcha. Not your sisters, of course. I'm certain you understand why. But do come with me! It will be so refreshing to have a new face at these boring social gatherings."

Sorcha looked down at her earth-stained dress and the dark stain of vomit on her sleeve. Her sisters would be far more presentable, even after a hard day's work. It was a shame Agatha would never realize that.

"It would be my honor, Agatha." Sorcha stepped onto the footrest and opened the carriage door. Black cushions and waxed wood covered the interior of the impressive carriage.

"You can tell me what you think of names for this newest little one."

"Ah, how many is it now?"

"Nine, child. You should know. You've delivered them all!"

"Right," Sorcha said as she settled onto the seat across from Agatha. "My apologies, I lost count at seven."

"Truthfully, so did I. What do you think of Derval?"

Chapter 4

Their carriage ride was dreadfully boring. Sorcha kept a smile plastered on her face and showed more teeth than was necessary. Agatha continued to prattle on without caring if anyone was listening. By the time they reached the stately manor of the MacNara twins, Sorcha was certain they had debated every name under the sun.

She was ready to get out of this cramped space. The scenery passed by at a slower pace than Sorcha could have seen if she was walking. The company turned out to be less than agreeable, and the destination could not live up to the promised entertainment.

But she would be a fool to not take this opportunity while it lasted.

They slowed to a stop, and the driver struck his hand against the ceiling. Sorcha opened the carriage door and stared up at the splendorous home. White marble gleamed in the splashed pink of the setting sun. The house was four stories high with rare glass windows. Twin staircases rose from the ground, meeting in a half circle that led to the red front door.

"My goodness," Sorcha whispered.

"It is quite a sight, isn't it?" Agatha said as she stepped out of the carriage. "They are impressive people with more wealth than they need. If they continue spending it on such things, I say let them keep it! Give us plebeians more sights like this." She winked. "It does a body good to see real beauty."

Normally, she wouldn't agree. But the stately manor might change her opinion if it was as beautiful on the inside as it was on the outside.

Agatha smoothed a hand down the silk of her gown, which was an unusual choice for visiting nobles who were partial to velvet and fine embroidery.

Did the other woman know the twins weren't human?

Tentatively, Sorcha asked, "Agatha, why are you meeting with the MacNara twins?"

"Oh," she lifted a hand and fanned her face. "They invited me to their manor, so of course I said yes. It's good to meet one's neighbors."

"They are hardly our neighbors, Agatha. They live half a day's ride from us."

Sorcha noted the way Agatha's eyes slanted to the side. The other woman pressed a hand against her throat as though she might still the pulse fluttering there. "Can you keep a secret, dearest?"

"Yes," Sorcha said, but she already knew what Agatha would say.

"The gossips aren't always right, but it's said the MacNara twins have some… gifts. I know in my progressed age that having a child will be difficult. But I already love this one as much as the rest, and I want it to survive."

"You want to make a deal with them."

"It's not a deal with the devil, my goodness! They're blessed."

"They're faeries, Agatha."

A measured stare filled the silence, stilling Sorcha's bitter tongue. "They are not faeries, Sorcha. There's no such thing as faeries, but there are blessed people."

Blessed? Sorcha wanted to smack some sense into the woman. Faeries were not blessed creatures hailing from the Heavens. They were earthen spirits making deals which required payment. Why couldn't Agatha see the truth in these thinly veiled secrets?

For all she wanted to get started on this journey, Sorcha didn't want Agatha's life to hang in the balance. They shouldn't stay here. Surely, the cure could wait until the new babe arrived. The thought left a foul taste upon her tongue.

"It's a bad idea to make deals with things you don't understand," Sorcha said. "Perhaps we should go."

"Nonsense. We've made it this far, and I refuse to turn back." Agatha lifted a hand when Sorcha opened her mouth. "I won't hear any more of it, Sorcha. I've made my decision. You can come with me or not, though I will feel sorely abused if you do not come with me. I invited you, and here you are. I've never known you to be a woman who goes back on her word."

So, she was frightened to go on by herself. With a lifted brow, Sorcha reached out and took Agatha's arm. "All right. Let's go."

The unrecognizable footman stayed with the carriage. As the women crested the stairs, the hair on Sorcha's arms lifted. She glanced over her shoulder at the footman who had eerily not moved in the slightest.

"Sorcha?" Agatha asked.

"Everything is fine." At the last possible second, Sorcha swung the hag stone around her neck into her hand. She lifted it to her eye and blinked.

He sat perched upon the carriage with natural grace, his long legs covered by fine, black cloth and a stately jacket pressed into crisp folds. She might have thought him human if he hadn't been missing his head.

"Dullahan?" she whispered.

She dropped the hag stone and rushed after Agatha who was already entering the MacNara estate. The inside of the building was as stunning as its exterior. White walls gleamed with gold filigreed wallpaper. A grand stairwell of white marble and light gray swirls spiraled from the ground floor and higher.

A butler greeted them and draped Agatha's pale blue cloak over his arm in a swath of color. His mustache twitched when Sorcha walked through the door, her slippers trailing mud across the pristine floor.

"Sorcha, isn't it lovely?" Agatha's voice echoed in the room. "They are gracious hosts to allow us entrance to such a grand palace."

"Hardly a palace," she responded. Although the home was beautiful, it was lacking a certain human touch. There were no portraits, no artwork, nothing but blank walls and empty space. In fact, it looked as though no one lived there at all.

The butler grunted his disapproval.

"Agatha, please don't go anywhere without me." Sorcha glanced around nervously.

The Dame's heels clicked upon the marble floors. Sorcha's own feet remained silent. Her leather slippers hardly touched the ground as she raced to the other end of the room. Snagging onto Agatha's sleeve,

Sorcha steered her back towards the foyer.

"Dearie, you're far too concerned about my well-being. I may be in the delicate stages of pregnancy, but I assure you, I have carried many a child to term."

"I remember, Agatha."

They passed by the stairs just as a voice slithered through the air. "And who, may I ask, are you?"

The overwhelming scent of oranges filled the air. Sticky and sweet, it coated her lungs with citrus.

Sorcha glanced up at the head of the stairs. A woman stood there, far too beautiful to be human. Unbound golden curls fell in waves to her waist. A red silk dress caressed her body as she shifted, the deep V between her breasts leaving little to the imagination. Gold chains laced across her body, dipping down her torso, and framing her shoulders.

"Oh, my," Agatha murmured.

Sorcha swallowed hard. "Agatha, perhaps you should tell her why we're here."

"I know why the old woman is here," the MacNara twin said. "What I don't know is why you're here."

"I invited her." Sorcha felt the Dame tremble. "I assumed your hospitality would stretch farther than just my presence."

"You were wrong." Concepta's hand curled around the railing of the stairwell. "But you have done it, nonetheless. I'll speak with your friend alone."

Agatha spluttered, "Well, I never. She is my companion. You must not separate us."

"Ivor, please show our guest to the blue room."

"I absolutely am not leaving without Sorcha." The butler walked up and placed his hand against Agatha's spine. "Take your hand off me, sir! Sorcha? Sorcha."

"It's fine, Agatha," Sorcha replied. "I don't mind meeting with Lady MacNara. Please rest your feet in the blue room. I'm certain Ivor won't mind providing you with tea and biscuits."

The unimpressed stare the butler gave her suggested that he had not, in fact, planned on providing tea and biscuits. Sorcha narrowed her eyes.

He sighed. "It would be my pleasure, Dame Agatha. Please follow me."

They filed out of the room. A flash of silk was the last bit of her wayward patient she might ever see.

Sorcha sighed again. Faeries were proving to be even more difficult than the stories had claimed.

"Well?" Concepta asked from above. "Are you coming or not?"

"Are you in a rush, Fae?" she asked as she made her way up the steps. "One might think an immortal would be more patient."

The faerie bared her teeth. "And one might think a weak little mortal would know how to watch her tongue."

Sorcha reached the top of the stairs and shrugged. "I've never been good at that."

"You should learn." Concepta lunged forward, anger turning her eyes from crystal blue to raw amber. Sorcha gasped as the faerie's hand wrapped around her throat, gripping the other woman's wrists, but unable to break free. Concepta shoved her backward until Sorcha's spine hit the wall with a harsh crack, her eyes losing focus as pain bloomed behind her eyes.

She blinked. There was something off about the faerie's face. It twisted and warped in anger, shimmering with sparkling light in one moment and lined with rage the next.

The snarl that tumbled from Concepta's mouth wasn't human. Guttural and raw, it vibrated in Sorcha's ears.

"You reek of my mother, human." Concepta's lips brushed Sorcha's ear. "Are you another of her pets? What foul poison have you come to spread?"

Black spots crept at the edge of her vision. Her mouth gaped open, and a wheeze escaped her lips.

"If you cannot speak, I'm afraid I'll have to tell my mother you died without ever delivering her venomous message."

Sorcha pushed her thumbs into the sensitive tissue of Concepta's wrists. The pressure points allowed her the barest breath which she used to whisper, "Your favor."

The faerie's eyes widened. "What did you say?"

The grip upon Sorcha's throat lessened enough for her to cough and gasp, "Your mother said you owe her a favor."

"And she's using it for a little human?" Concepta shook her head. "Good guess, but not very believable."

"She said you knew how to cure the blood beetle plague."

"She said what?"

"Faeries can't lie," Sorcha rasped. "I know this as well as you. Tell me how to cure it."

Concepta released her and backed away. Her laughter sounded like hammers striking metal. "Oh, this is a pleasurable thing. You simply must meet my brother. He will like you."

There would be bruises on her throat. Delicately, Sorcha probed the muscles of her neck. They throbbed as if a noose had tightened across her airways. Faeries were strong, she noted, far stronger than any human.

She coughed. "Please."

"Yes, yes." Concepta waved a hand in the air. "Fine, then. Come meet my brother first. He'll want to know what's going on."

Was this it? Would she finally be able to save her father? Hope raised its head, filling her chest to the brim with happiness as fragile as a dandelion seed. It couldn't be this easy.

Could it?

The image of her Papa, skin moving with beetles, propelled her forward. The hallways were blank sheets of paper. White walls, white floors, gold filigree but nothing that suggested anyone lived here.

"Is this a new home?" she called out.

"No."

"Do many faeries live here?"

"Yes."

Odd, but Sorcha could see the sense in it. What faerie would decorate a human home with images of their family? A headless portrait would look out of place if not simply morbid.

She kept a hand around her neck as they twisted through empty room after empty room. A breeze trailed by. The distinct outline of a hand tugged at her gray skirt, pulling her forward.

Twin doors stood open at the end of the hallway. Beyond that, an oasis grew. Vines tangled from a ceiling which looked like a giant birdcage. Hydrangeas bloomed and filled the air with their sweet scent although they were not in season. An ornate fountain spewed mist into the air, white lilies twirling at its base. Brightly colored fabric spilled across the ground and was dotted with pillows.

People laid out upon the cushions. They held jeweled goblets in their hands, red wine pouring down their cheeks and onto their chests. Harp music gently wafted on the breeze from a musician in the far corner.

A man stretched near the fountain. His sculpted chest was bare to the sun, skin slicked with oil and well-tanned. Silk pooled around him, pants or skirt she could not discern. Red rubies wrapped around his throat and dangled on his forehead from a golden headpiece. A chain hung from his ear to a piercing in his nose.

The tingling sensation of magic pricked her skin. Sorcha clutched the hag stone at her neck.

"I wouldn't do that if I were you," Concepta said.

"Why not?"

"You don't know what kind of Fae live here, little human. If you peer into our world, you will run from this place screaming."

"As you are Macha's children, I assumed you were of the Seelie court."

"You know very little of our kind. Seelie or Unseelie is not a breed." Concepta flicked a glance towards her. "It's a choice, whether you want to follow the rules or you don't."

She watched as the faerie picked her way through the lounging people. She draped herself across the fountain next to her brother and dangled her fingers in the water. Sorcha thought she looked very much like her mother. It didn't seem like a safe observation to voice.

"Brother," Concepta said. "I brought you a gift."

"You know I dearly love gifts," Cormac murmured. "But human playthings break so easily."

His gaze felt like a physical touch upon her skin, lingering on the swells of her breasts and the apex of her thighs. A slow smile spread across his face, teeth stained green by the viscous drink he nursed.

"I am not here for your entertainment," Sorcha replied. "I was sent by your mother."

"And Concepta didn't kill you yet? You must be a very impressive warrior."

"I am no fighter, Lord MacNara. Macha said you owe her a favor and I am here to collect."

He tsked. "Oh, sister, this is boring. Take her away."

How could he say that when he hadn't even listened? The glee in Concepta's unnatural eyes suggested she had known this would happen.

Her father needed her. Her sisters needed her. Gods above, the entire world needed help, and Sorcha had the rare opportunity to do so!

The faerie woman moved to stand up, but paused when Sorcha flinched forward.

"Wait!" Sorcha shouted so loud that even the music stopped. "I was told you know how to cure the blood beetle plague. I will do anything for your knowledge."

Cormac leaned forward and pointed a jeweled finger at her. "Anything?"

It was a sharp question, capable of slicing through flesh and bone. Was she willing to do anything?

"Yes," she said firmly. "Anything."

Concepta trailed a finger down her brother's arm. "I told you she wasn't boring."

"We're going to help her?"

"Yes."

"Even against our better judgment?"

"We have better judgment?"

Their hands met and fingers intertwined. "It's against the rules, sister."

"I like to break rules."

"It will cause trouble."

"For us?"

"There are always ripples."

Concepta lifted their hands and pressed a lingering kiss against his knuckles. "Then we will ride the waves they cause. I think this one will be worth the trouble if she succeeds."

"What makes you think she can?" Cormac cast a disbelieving glance at Sorcha. "She's just a slip of a girl."

"I am strong," Sorcha interjected. "I have brought countless children into this world. I know the cruelty of man first-hand, and I fear very little. There is much for me to lose if you don't help me."

The words seemed to catch Cormac's interest. He canted his head to the side and asked, "Like what?"

"My father."

He snorted. "My father was a king among mortal men, and he did little for me. Try again."

"My sisters. They live with my father, and if he dies of the blood beetle plague, they will become ill as well. I will not watch them die."

"You love your sisters?"

"More than I can say."

"In that, we see eye to eye." He released his hold upon Concepta's hand to trail his fingers through her golden curls, dragging a thumb across her lips. "Fine, we will help you."

"You know how to find the cure?"

"Our mother does not lie. We know how to cure the blood beetle plague."

Her heart stopped. The relief surging through her veins made her knees weak. "How?" she whispered. "Please tell me how, and what I need to do."

"Oh, it's not as simple as just telling you. We don't have the cure. We only know where it is."

"Is it an object?"

"In a way," Cormac chuckled. His sister laid her head in his lap, then kicked her feet into the air. "The cure comes in the form of a person, at least for you."

"A person?"

"One simple being whom you will return to us."

Concepta rolled to her side. "You'll bring him back to the mainland, and then you'll have your cure. Eventually."

"Why would I bring a person here? What does that have to do with the blood beetle plague?"

"You don't need to know the information. All you need to do is travel to Hy-brasil."

"The cursed isle?" Sorcha blinked. "It can only be seen every seven years. I don't have time to wait seven years!"

"Then it's lucky for you that the time to see that isle is actually..." Concepta looked up at her brother. "Now?"

"In a few weeks."

"In a few weeks," she repeated. "And then you can see the isle. You can get our faerie, by whatever means necessary of course. Bring him back, and you'll have your cure."

Sorcha shook her head in confusion. "You're not making any sense. Do you have the cure or not?"

"We do."

"Then why aren't you giving it to me now?" She huffed in frustration. "Your mother said you owe her a favor."

Concepta's eyes sparked yellow again. She lifted herself into a crouch upon the stone lip of the fountain. "Are you saying I'm a liar?"

"We both know faeries can't lie."

"My mother's favor saved your life. You owe us another, which means you will bring back that pathetic excuse for a Prince! And if he screams or cries when he sees me I will bite off his tongue with my teeth."

A harp string snapped. Sorcha startled at the sound and turned to see all inhabitants of the room had fled. The musician was the last, the fabric of her dress caught on her own instrument.

Sorcha's teeth chattered against each other. "What are you going to do to him, if I bring him back?"

"That is none of your concern," Cormac said. "Do we have a deal?"

She was making too many deals with faeries all in one day. Her gut screamed that this was a bad idea. Macha was one thing. The revered Tuatha dé Danann valued female life and strength. These two? Some thread in their mind had unraveled, leaving gaping holes where insanity grew.

She watched Concepta crawl into her brother's lap and stroke the flat planes of his chest.

"She will say yes," Concepta said.

"Will she?"

"She can't let go of a future where she is the 'hero.' So many people have told her 'Sorcha, you are just a woman. You cannot do what you think you can do.'"

"Humans are idiots."

"Humans are more than idiots. They are good only to feed the earth when they die."

Sorcha swallowed. "I don't want to hurt anyone."

Concepta's head snapped around, glaring over her shoulder with cat-like eyes. "You've hurt people your entire life. A stillborn child you couldn't save, a screaming pain-filled night of a woman who did not desire a babe, a changeling you left near the woods."

"I did what I had to do. I have never killed anyone."

"But you will. Someday, everyone does. Whether by choice or not, we're all killers. It's far past time for you to accept that."

Sorcha straightened her spine. She was no murderer. If this woman wanted to prove something with her cruel words, then all she managed to do was set Sorcha's resolve. If she had to choose between an unknown man and her family, Sorcha would always choose her family.

"All right. I'll bring him back."

"Alive," Cormac added.

"Alive and well. I will convince him to return, and I won't force him."

Concepta giggled. "You can try. I don't think he'll come back at all. Still, it will be fun to know someone is bothering him. You'll leave now."

"Excuse me?"

"Now."

Ivor the butler appeared at her side. Sorcha squeaked when he grasped her arm. She stared down at the normal human hand and couldn't shake the feeling that there were only three fingers touching her bicep.

"Wait!" she cried out. "I have to say goodbye to my family."

"You're boring me again," Cormac grumbled. "We said you will leave now."

"I need my things."

"What things? You won't need things where you're going."

"Personal items, clothing, a promise that I'll return. I cannot leave without letting them know where I am going."

Ivor pulled at her arm.

"Stop it!" Sorcha screamed and raked at his hand with ragged fingernails. "Let go of me, you brute. Have some pity. I don't want my sisters to think I'm dead!"

Cormac lifted a hand. "Wait."

The butler froze, and she heard the jarring cough of his breath.

"Say that again," Concepta ordered.

"I don't want my sisters to think I'm dead." Tears burned in Sorcha's eyes. "They'll worry about me, and I cannot abide that."

Cormac trailed his hand along his sister's jaw, caressed his hands down her flushed skin, and followed the V of her silken dress. She smiled and closed her savage eyes. "We will allow you to say goodbye. We know the rarity of a blood bond and cherish the love that blooms between siblings."

The pull on her arm returned, and Sorcha did not look back upon the twisted twins who had freed her. She had a chance to do something right and help those in need.

As she stumbled down the steps, Ivor shoved her into the carriage with Agatha who was pale as snow.

"Are you all right, my dear?" she asked.

"No," Sorcha replied. "But, I think I will be. We're going home."

She glanced out the window and watched the rolling green hills become a blur. The faerie carriage sped towards the city with unnatural speed.

Chapter 5

Briana huffed as she followed Sorcha. "You can't leave!"

"I have to, and I already told you why, so please stop trailing along behind me. I have to get my things."

"You haven't even told us where you're going." Briana's voice thickened with unspoken emotion.

"I don't know where I'm going."

The Dullahan coachman had brought her straight to the brothel. He didn't speak, and she wasn't about to lift the hag stone to her eye again, but she understood his quick gestures. She didn't have a lot of time to make her goodbyes.

It was easier that way. Her sisters were prone to hysterics, especially when they weren't getting what they wanted. Sorcha had been their crutch for a long time.

Although they were all close, she was the one they went to in times of struggle. That meant she heard all their secrets, their stories, their gripes about each other and the life they lived. She kept them all safe, childless, and made certain every bruise or scrape healed. They weren't likely to admit it, but Sorcha was an integral part of their lives.

She would miss them so much.

Briana snatched a nightshirt out of Sorcha's hands. "Absolutely not! I'm not blind. You show up in some fancy carriage with a coachman, a coachman, and then you think I will believe you're off to cure the beetles? Sorcha! If you wanted to go off with some well-to-do nobleman, you know we'd be happy for you. Why are you lying?"

"I'm not lying."

"There you go again. Is it Geralt? Is that why you don't want to tell us?"

Sorcha scooted past Briana and stuffed another skirt into an oversized pack she could carry over her shoulder. It was better than smacking her sister in the face. "I can't believe you would even suggest I would accept Geralt's proposal!"

"He's rich. He's got plenty of land, and he's obviously in love with you, though I can't understand why he's still wasting his time when you so clearly won't come to your senses."

"I'm not marrying Geralt." Sorcha grabbed an armful of her journals and dumped them into the bag with her clothing.

"Why are you taking those?"

"I might need them."

"You can come back for them. Surely whoever you are going to see will let you come home? We don't mind letting you keep this room." Briana let out a frustrated grunt and ran her fingers through her hair.

She wanted to keep the room, too. There were so many memories within these walls. Sweet and cherished moments where her sisters had shared secrets and weathered nightmares.

Sorcha devoured all the details she could find. The marks on the door where she'd kept track of Rosaleen's growth. The flowerpot on the windowsill, now empty, because Briana had insisted the plant would grow back. The carved trunk her father had worked so long on, even though it looked more like scratch marks than the whale he said it was.

Life had a strange way of pulling her away from here. Every moment of her life, she had spent rushing away to faerie glens and leaving offerings. Now there was a chance to see the Otherworld in person, and she was so frightened to leave.

"Briana, I love you. I don't know if I've said it enough, but I do."

Her sister's face creased in worry. "What are you doing? What choice have you made, Sorcha? You can trust me."

"I already told you," Sorcha brushed her hand along Briana's cheekbone, memorizing the shape of it. "The faeries offered me a deal to cure the beetle plague. I won't see Papa die."

She left her sister in the room and lumbered down the stairs. The pack was too heavy for her, but she refused to let any of it go. The books were important. Every herb, every poultice, every bit of her mother's teachings was in those books. Where she went, they went.

Three flights of stairs felt like a full day's hike. Heaving the pack to the floor, she quietly made her way to Papa's room.

Knocking, she called out, "Are you awake?"

"For you, always."

Sorcha smiled, blinking back the tears welling in her eyes. She slipped into her father's room and closed the door behind her. Shadows hid the salt tracks on her cheeks.

"You're leaving," he said.

"You heard?"

"How could I not? Your sister was screeching like a banshee."

She settled onto the edge of his bed. "You always said at least one of us was a changeling child."

"Yes, but I always thought it was you."

"I made a deal." She blurted the words out and let them hang in the air between them. "There wasn't another way. The Guild won't listen to me, you're getting worse, and the beetles are spreading. Someone had to do something, Papa."

"And that someone had to be you?"

"Are you so surprised?"

He pushed himself up onto his elbows, gray-streaked hair plastered to his skin with sweat. This was the reason why she would risk her life. This man, who had given up so much to give her a chance.

Papa slicked his hair back, huffing out a tired breath. "I woke up this morning, and the beetles were worse than ever. I coughed up blood for the first time, and I know what that means. I didn't tell you because I didn't want you to worry. Then, this afternoon, they stopped moving. I don't know why. I don't know how. But they stopped and my first thought was that you had something to do with it."

A tear slid down her cheek. "Papa—"

He lifted a hand. "I'm not finished. I didn't raise you for the beginning bit of your life, but I saw a good girl when I met you. I never met your mother, but she obviously raised you right. The others are spoiled, vain, cruel to each other. You have never been like them. I knew from the moment you set your heart on curing me, you would find some way to stop this. I'm glad it's you. I'm sad you must leave me to do it, and I hope you didn't trade your soul for my old life. But I will stand by you if this is what you want."

"Oh Papa," she choked as she threw herself into his arms.

She hadn't done this since she was a little girl. It was far more difficult to fit in his lap now that she was full grown, but she tried her best. He rubbed her back as she fought back tears.

"It's not a shameful thing to want to save your family, Sorcha."

"They think I'm running away to be with a man. As if I would leave you? Them? I love you all too much to leave without good reason."

"And they love you. It's why they're so upset."

"What am I going to do without you?"

He chuckled. "I imagine you'll do just fine. Do you know where you're going?"

"You believe me?" She lifted her head from his shoulder. "You don't think I'm crazy or lying?"

"You've always seen faeries, Sorcha. I thought you were crazy when you were little, but then I started noticing things myself. Tiny hands used to tug your hair all the time. You stayed the night with Rosaleen, but your dresses were all perfectly pressed and folded on your bed. Strange things happen around you, child."

"Most would say I'm a witch." She wiped at her eyes, catching the salty tears upon her fingertips.

Papa shook his head, the deep grooves in his forehead standing out in stark relief. "You're no witch any more than your mother was. Faeries are picky who they choose to help, so I'd say you're lucky. Not cursed."

She didn't want to let him go. She wanted to stay curled up against his chest forever, or until he stood up as a strong man again.

Her chest heaved with silent sobs. “I don’t know what I’m doing, Papa. Is this the right thing to do?”

“Does it feel like it?” He tapped her chest. “In here?”

“Yes.”

“Then it’s the right thing to do, and family be damned. You’ll return to us someday, I’m certain of it.”

She wasn’t. Sorcha had a sick feeling deep within her belly that this was the last time she’d see him. Her hands shook as she cupped his cheeks.

“Goodbye.”

He pressed his palm against the back of her hand, holding it against his heart. “Goodbye, sweet girl.”

If she stayed for a moment longer, she would never leave. She threw herself from the bed in a whirlwind of movement and rushed out the door.

“Sorcha?” Rosaleen called. “Sorcha, are you really leaving?”

“Tell the others I love them!” she shouted and scooped up her bag.

The front door slammed behind her so hard the shutters shook. The Dullahan started, a bland expression on his face.

She tossed the bag into the carriage and lunged in behind it. Her fist slammed against the roof.

“Go!”

The whip cracked, an unnatural sound of creaking bone. Tears fell freely down her face as the carriage raced away from the brothel. Her sisters poured out of the house, their shouts echoing in her ears for miles down the road.

What had she done? Saying goodbye made her want to shatter into a thousand pieces. But a deal was a deal.

Sorcha had never been away from home. She'd only been alone once in her life, for three full days after her mother's corpse had stopped smoking. Those were dark memories. Thoughts her mind had hidden, so she wouldn't dwell upon the past.

Now, she'd be alone for an undetermined amount of time. Would she handle it well? Her heart felt like it was going to jump out of her chest. Short breaths expanded her lungs. Swirls of darkness blinked in front of her eyes.

She focused on the landscape flying past. They headed towards the sea, and she hadn't been to the ports since she was a girl. Her father had specifically avoided setting up a brothel near sailors. He said they were too frequent customers who never paid their debts. It was easier in a city where rich men might find their way down a dark alley.

Rolling green hills calmed her mind. Stone walls bisected the fields, built to remind everyone where their land was. Each stone glistened with moss, worn with age, touched by hundreds of passersby. White dots of sheep speckled the land.

Every now and then, they would pass over a stone bridge. Streams ran underneath them, housing trolls and goblins for the night. Sorcha could almost feel them, hidden in their hovels under the ground.

These emerald lands had always called out to her. This wasn't just a field. It wasn't just grass and sheep. This was home.

She pressed her head against the side of the carriage. The jolting movement thumped her skull against the wood every now and then, but even that didn't dull her torment. The land rooted her in the now, in the moment, in everything that wasn't the loss of her family.

She would see them again, Sorcha told herself. Even if it took years to get back.

Lush fields gave way to small homes with cultivated gardens. Then cobblestone paths snaked through the towns which grew larger and larger as they reached the ocean. She could smell salt and brine upon the air.

The carriage slowed as it passed through throngs of people in ragged clothes. Women with scarves over their heads avoided meeting her gaze, and men in moth-eaten wool leered at the carriage. Sailors who had seen better days wandered the docks, and farmers with dirt-streaked cheeks peddled their wares. Children snuck their hands into pockets for even the smallest of coins.

The wheels clattered as they passed by another brothel. Sorcha didn't recognize any of the women hanging out of the windows, but there was something in their haunted eyes that chilled her to the bone. These were not prostitutes looked after by a kind man. Run down, exhausted, and used, their bodies told the sad story of their lives.

Some part of her, equally chilled, wondered if that could be her future. Eventually, her skills wouldn't be necessary for the brothel, or they would find someone who would do the same things without the burden of room and board. Where would she go? There were no jobs for women like her. No husbands for a woman favored by the Fae.

She leaned back against the soft cushions of the carriage and refused to look back outside.

The ocean breeze coiled through her window, tangling in the loose strands of her hair. She could smell the fish, the seaweed, the salt of the ocean, and the sweat of men. She could hear the crashing waves as if she had put a seashell to her ear, but this was the real thing. These waves were just outside. All she had to do was lean forward one more time. Haunted eyes stared back at her, even though her eyes were closed.

"I will not become them," she whispered.

The carriage wheels squealed as they lurched to a halt. The Dullahan pounded the roof of the carriage, silently demanding she leave.

Sorcha let out a long, steadying breath. "You can do this, Sorcha. You've done harder work before. All you have to do is step outside this carriage."

She curled her hand around her pack. Her fist clenched hard until the leather straps dug into her palms. Courage was never an easy thing to find even when necessary for survival.

The door banged open, and the Dullahan stared at her with dull eyes.

"Yes, I know," she said. "Give me a moment, please."

"It's time for you to go." His lips moved, but his voice came from his hands.

Sorcha shivered. The last thing she needed was a reminder that the man standing before her was actually headless, and that he was holding said head to speak with her.

"Where am I to go?"

"Find the ship with the yellow belly. It's Fae marked, and will take you to Hy-brasil."

"And when exactly is the isle visible?"

The Dullahan narrowed his fake eyes. "You have six days."

"Is that doable on a ship?"

"I'm no sailor, girl. Ask the captain."

He held out his hand for her to take. Sorcha couldn't force herself to touch him. The sparkle of malevolence in his gaze made her nervous, and she wondered if he would make her touch his head.

She leapt from the carriage on her own, shouldering the heavy weight of her pack with a sigh. "Thank you for the safe journey."

"You thank me for following my masters' orders?"

"Well, yes." She tucked a strand of hair behind her ear. "You may have been following orders, but you didn't pause overly long and it wasn't too bumpy of a ride. I didn't even get sick along the way. For that, I have you to thank. Not your masters."

His face twisted in confusion. "You are a strange human."

"You're not the first to say that. Oh," she shook her head. "I almost forgot."

Sorcha reached into her pocket and pulled out a small jar of honey she had neglected to leave at the shrine. In the rush to leave her home, she hadn't put it back in the kitchen where it belonged.

Now, the golden liquid felt wrong to keep. She held it out to the Dullahan with a soft smile. "Thank you."

"What am I supposed to do with this?" He held the jar close to his waist for his real eyes to look at.

"I don't know. It's a gift. Do you like honey?"

"I'm not the kind of Fae that likes honey."

"Then gift it to another, or enjoy it on your morning bread." Sorcha shrugged. "It matters little to me."

She walked past him, but noted the strange expression on his face. If she didn't know any better, Sorcha would have thought he was wistfully inspecting her gift. The Dullahan weren't known for their kindness. They announced death to all those who crossed their paths and cracked whips made of human spines.

Perhaps he'd never received a gift, she thought as she glanced over her shoulder.

Sorcha lifted the hag stone to her eye as he turned the carriage around. The candles still flickered inside, skulls grinning in decoration, the beautiful wood fading to stretched skin. Creaking wheels revealed human thigh bones spinning round. And the Dullahan himself, head seated in his lap with lips stretching from ear to ear, was staring back at her.

She lifted her hand in farewell just to have the satisfaction of seeing his confusion one last time.

The crowd swelled around her. People from all walks of life wandered the docks this afternoon. They drifted through the waves of people as a boat surfed upon the waves.

Colors and sound assaulted her senses. Vibrantly dressed women called out to her. Men shouted in the distance to raise the sails and hoist the anchors. A fish flopped on the ground where a woman hammered its head until it stopped moving. She moved onto the next while another woman sliced open its belly.

Sorcha's stomach lurched. Turning away from that side of the street, she struggled to make it to the docks. That was where she would find the captain. It had to be.

"Excuse me, sir?" she touched a man's shoulder. "Where might I find a ship with a yellow belly?"

"Why are you asking me?" he looked her up and down. "I don't give out charity to the likes of you."

"Charity?" Her mouth gaped open as he walked away from her.

Sorcha tried many times to find someone who could point her in the right direction. Women tried to hire her for work. Men mostly ignored her as if she didn't exist. One man even made her stand in front of him and shout to get his attention.

None of them wanted to point her towards a ship marked as the Dullahan had claimed. Did it not exist? She wanted to stand on a railing and scream. Someone in this gods forsaken port town must know where a ship with a yellow belly was!

The sun dipped low on the horizon and Sorcha gave up.

Weary and discouraged, she dropped her pack on the last dock and let it hit the wooden plans with a loud thunk. Heaving a sigh, she sat and swung her legs above the water.

"I just want to find a ship with a yellow belly," she moaned. She slumped forward and held her head in her hands. "It can't be that hard to find."

But it was. No one wanted to help her. Everyone's eyes were suspicious, and they thought the worst of her without asking who she was, why she was here, or what purpose she had in life. Why would people do that?

Her small sheltered town seemed so far away. Its people were backwards and dimwitted, but they were kind. She missed it already, and it hadn't even been a full day.

Sorcha sighed and tugged on her hair. "You can't give up. Too many people are relying on you."

She couldn't force herself to move. Her legs were aching from walking the docks all day. Pinpricks danced across her shoulders and spine from the heavy weight of her pack. Blisters seared the bottoms of her feet.

She might want to continue, but her body was telling her no. There was no possible way for her to get up and keep going. She hadn't even found a place to sleep.

"A stunning thing like you must charge a pretty penny for a night."

Her mind drifted for a moment. Would it really be that bad to entertain what her sister's had done for years? It seemed horrible in her mind, to give up her body for a few coins and a warm bed. But they didn't seem to mind.

No. She couldn't do it. She wasn't as strong as her sisters.

"Far too much for you," she retorted. Sorcha bared her teeth angrily and glanced up at the sailor staring down at her.

Dark hair and eyes blended into the night sky. A full beard masked most of his expression, although the gleam of teeth suggested he might be smiling. Dreadlocks pulled the rest of his hair away from his face.

His broad shoulders and chest were bare, and she imagined he was quite cold. A pelt of hair covered him from neck to dark pants. He wasn't wearing any shoes.

Sorcha's lips pursed. "Far too expensive."

"I wouldn't judge a book by its cover, sweet thing. Just how badly do you want somewhere warm to sleep?"

"Not that bad." She jerked her pack close to her side. "In fact, I'll go find a place myself. Thank you for reminding me it's growing dark."

"You sound like you aren't from around here, so let me tell you a few things. The docks aren't safe at night. Even for whores."

"I'm not a whore."

"Why else would you be on the docks? Respectable women stay up there," he pointed towards the candle light of the city. "The rest come down here to play with the likes of me. You look tired, hungry, and travel-stained. You either are a whore, or you will be soon enough."

Sorcha felt as though she needed to defend herself, or at least the title of whore. "My sisters run a successful brothel in Ui Neill. I don't take kindly to a man making less of their profession. And as for your knowledge," she struggled to her feet, "I'm looking for a particular ship. I need to travel far from here."

"A passenger?" he chuckled. "Sweetheart, you have to lie better than that."

"I am not lying. I was told to find the captain of a ship painted yellow and that he would take me to where I need to go."

"What do you want with the Saorsa?"

She smiled, the name was fitting. "The ship is named Freedom?"

"Who are you?" The man crossed his arms over his chest and frowned at her. "The Freedom doesn't take passengers."

"I'd think that would be the captain's decision."

"I am the captain."

The words echoed in Sorcha's mind. It couldn't be. Him? She looked him up and down. "You don't look like a captain."

"Have you ever seen a captain before?"

"No."

"Then you're a rather poor judge, aren't you?" His feet slapped against the dock as he turned away from her. "Oh, and by the way, being polite to a captain is a good start."

Sorcha stared at his back in shock. That was the captain? He couldn't be serious. She hadn't just ruined her chance at getting to Hy-brasil without even asking him if he'd take her?

She licked her lips and shouted, "The MacNara twins sent me!"

The captain froze. "Excuse me?"

"The MacNara twins sent me to ask you for safe passage. I need to go to Hy-brasil, and they said you are the only person who can get me there."

The moon floated in the air behind him, outlining his figure with silver. "They were right, but I'm not going to the phantom isle."

"You're my only option. I have to go, and I need you to take me. I cannot apologize enough that I was rude, but it's imperative I go."

"You can't even see the isle."

"You can in six days," she said. "The Dullahan told me. Please."

He turned back towards her and crossed his arms. "What are you paying?"

"I have nothing to give."

"Anything in that pack?" He pointed at her bag.

"Personal items, mostly journals. I'm a healer. I can help in any way while aboard."

Hope blossomed. He was sizing her up as though she was a person, not just a piece of meat. That had to mean something. Perhaps he would take her.

At this point, Sorcha would swim to the damn isle if it meant progress.

A caw startled her. Sorcha flinched and looked at the sky. Outlined in darkness and stars, a raven called out again.

"I thought those only flew during the day," she whispered.

"Damned Fae," the captain grumbled. "All right. Fine. Onto the ship with you, but you will help the entire trip. And don't you forget what I've done for you."

"I won't service your men on the trip. I'm to have my own quarters."

"You'll be sharing mine," he grunted as he walked away from her. "Having a woman on board is bad luck enough. I'll be keeping an eye on you."

Sorcha grabbed her pack and swung it over her shoulder. Blisters be damned, she would make it to this ship. "My name is Sorcha. What's yours?"

"Manus."

"The great?" She grinned. "It's an apt name for a captain."

"Now you're complimenting me?" He glanced at her once she

caught up. "Women are so damned difficult to understand. One minute you're blistering my ears off, and the next you're calling me after some historical figure."

"You didn't know the name Manus means great?"

"It's a name. Who knows what their name means other than themselves?" He must have noticed the pout of her lips, because he added, "What's yours mean?"

"Radiant," Sorcha said with a soft smile.

Manus growled again and pointed at a ship out to sea. "That's mine."

"How are we to get there?"

"By boat."

"I don't see any other ships."

"You ever been to the sea?" he said, lifting a brow. "You take a rowboat to the ship, and then we'll climb aboard."

One more thing she had to do, and then she could rest. Sorcha took a deep breath. This man could be lying to her. She certainly couldn't see the bottom of the ship to determine if he was telling the truth.

"Okay," she said. "Show me the way."

Chapter 6

Sorcha rolled to her side, eyes stuck together with sleep, her mouth dry. A scratchy blanket covered her legs and the overwhelming scent of tallow candles made her sneeze. She rubbed at her nose. The slight movement made her stomach roll.

"Oh, right," she muttered. "I'm on a ship."

She hadn't been bothered last night by the constant movement of waves. She'd been too tired to even notice there were men staring at her when the captain brought her aboard. Her pack was handed off with little complaint, and she didn't even ask where the captain would sleep. She face-planted onto the cot and propriety be damned.

Her stomach clenched hard, and her throat seized up.

"Ugh," Sorcha moaned as she burped. The ocean was making her entire body rebel now.

It took surprising effort to swing her legs over the edge of the cot. The whole time she held onto her mouth as though the effort would keep the bile in her stomach down. Another burp rocked her body forward. Bile burned the back of her throat.

Shaking her head violently, she lunged from the cot and pulled at the door. The fine details of the room didn't matter. The soft, polished statues stared with vacant eyes as she fled from the room and slammed her pelvic bone into the railing.

Vomit streamed out of her mouth and down the side of the ship. Sorcha hadn't thought there was anything left in her stomach. She didn't remember eating anything at all yesterday, but she couldn't stop the vomit.

"Ach, you didn't even have the decency to hit the water."

She recognized that voice. Her cheeks stained red, and she wiped at her lips. "I've never been seasick before. I apologize if I ruined your ship."

The man swaggering towards her didn't look at all like the captain she remembered. Tall and lean, he looked more like a pirate in a book.

Gold hoops swung from his ears. His hair and beard were so dark they gleamed blue in the sunlight. Richly tanned skin glistened with sweat like polished bronze. He had traded his worn pants for a fine cotton shirt tucked into a wide belt above tight black breeches. Knee-high boots—the leather folded over at the top, covering his knees—cracked against the deck of the ship as he strode towards her.

Sorcha was tongue-tied.

"Manus?"

"Don't recognize me, pretty thing?" His sleeves billowed as he lifted his arms. "A far cry from how we met, yes?"

"Very," she agreed. "I can hardly believe it's you."

He smiled, teeth flashing brilliant white against the dark tan of his skin. "Ah, that is the greatest compliment you might have given. You found me in a rather compromising position last night."

"One you are not proud of?"

"I'd never say I wasn't proud. Though you might have thought I was whoring, with good reason considering the words I said, I was actually visiting the one woman who's stolen my heart." He winked at her blush. "She is the only creature who can stand me. Sequestered on the land because the sea refuses to be her mistress, at least safely. I understand why my ladies fight over me, but, alas, I cannot choose between them."

The dramatic rendition of his life dissolved Sorcha's remaining seasickness. Her weak smile bolstered her strength, and she pushed herself away from the railing. "I'm certain they both miss you when you're gone."

"Neither of them miss me overly much, but it's kind of you. If you're feeling better, I ask that you join me in the center of the ship."

Sorcha's brows furrowed. "Why?"

"The ocean isn't a safe place, sweet thing. We're sailing into Fae waters, and I'd hate for you to be snatched up by a murúch."

"There are merrows here?" Sorcha flinched away from the railing.

"It's why the ship is painted yellow," Manus said. He walked towards her, slid an arm around her shoulders, and pulled her away from the railing. "Come, let me show you."

He reached into his pocket and placed a single sprig of heather on the railing. "A gift for the lovely ladies who guide my ship to safe waters."

Sorcha held her breath. She had always known faeries to take gifts that were offered, but they were always glamoured. Her gifts had disappeared. Running water erased the effects of magic, and she wouldn't need to use her hag stone to catch a glimpse of the Fae here.

A hand reached up from the edge of the ship. Impossibly pale, its long fingers were joined together by iridescent webbing. Rainbows sparkled upon the merrow woman's hand as she reached for the purple sprig. She was gentle as she pinched the blossom between her fingers and took it over the edge of the ship with her.

Sorcha's breath released in a great gust of air. "Was that?"

"It was."

"But the ship is so tall!"

"We put slats on the edge so they can climb it."

"Isn't that dangerous?" she asked. "Won't they drag you down into the ocean?"

"Myths aren't always the truth, Sorcha. We bring them gifts, and they give us safe passage. My men know the rules. If they wish to marry, then the marrows must be willing."

She blinked, surprised that anyone honored the Fae as she did. He read her expression well. The grin on his face was decidedly pleased as he sauntered away.

Free from watchful eyes, Sorcha lunged back to the railing. She squeezed her hand upon the polished wood and stared down into the waves.

A woman clutched the side of the ship, her wide dark eyes staring back at Sorcha with shock. Hair as green as seaweed tangled down her back in wet strands. She held the sprig of heather in her webbed hand. They blinked at each other until the merrow gave her a wide sharp-toothed grin and flipped off the ship. The bright flash of a green tail waved in the sunlight, splashing into a wave with one final twist.

Sorcha's knees went weak. A merrow. A real merrow had been so close she might have touched her. No hag stone had limited her vision.

No glamour had hidden her true form.

Breathless, she tangled her hands in her hair and spun towards Manus. "That was a real merrow!"

"I know," he said with a chuckle.

"No. Manus that was a real merrow."

"I saw her as well, sweet thing."

"That was a faerie, without a glamour, and she wasn't even frightened of me!"

He tilted his head back and boomed with laughter. "Ah, I was right to bring you aboard. I know a faerie lover when I see one. Come with me, Sorcha. I have something special to show you."

Manus wrapped an arm around her shoulders when she reached him. The weight steadied her against the gentle sway of the ship. It was massive in her eyes. The deck teemed with twenty men, all rushing from one end to the other. White sails snapped in the wind and stretched taut to guide them across the waters.

They stepped up to the bow and stood behind the masthead. Sorcha leaned against the railing to peer at the wooden woman's face.

"Is this a faerie?"

"It is," Manus replied. "So we always remember who has given us this gift, and who guides us in safety."

"You are close with the Fae, then?" Few people would admit their ties to magic. Faeries were viewed as a superstition and believing in them to be child's indulgence.

"No one is close to the Fae. I deliver items for them. And sometimes people, like yourself."

"People? What do the Fae want with people?" Sorcha hadn't heard this particular secret before. She'd read every book there was on the Fae and spoke at length with anyone who had experiences with them. No one had ever said the Fae requested people be brought to them.

"There's always something here and there. A famous musician, an artisan," he cast a glance in her direction, "a midwife."

She stiffened. "How do you know that?"

"I carried you and your things to my room last night. I deserved at the very least a peek at your belongings."

"That's a terrible thing to do."

"You could have been an assassin, sweet thing. I protect my men and my ship."

Sorcha couldn't blame him for that. She would've done the same thing if a strange man walked into her brothel. It still felt like a violation of privacy.

She tugged at the hag stone around her neck. "What did you look at?"

"Just a few of the journals. As soon as I realized you were a healer, I let the rest be."

"You didn't take anything, did you?"

"Of course not." He looked offended. "I am neither thief nor pirate. What would I have stolen from you that the sea cannot give?"

Sorcha released the breath she held. The sea rolled, shaking the boat with one great lunge. Sorcha held onto the railing and stared into the dark waters where a shadow moved. "What was that?"

"That was what I wanted to show you," Manus said. "Have you ever heard of a guardian before?"

"Like a surrogate parent?"

"Like the species."

Sorcha raised a brow. "No."

He moved to stand behind her, lifting a hand above her shoulder and pointing towards the horizon. "When the Fae mark a ship, it is guided not just by merrows. A guardian is assigned to the boat. They are half woman, half whale. Their twisted features are terrifying. They can rip a man in half just with their hands."

"You're joking."

"I'm not. They guide our ships towards the Otherworld and ensure nothing else comes with us."

She wanted to shiver, but his hand was on her shoulder. He would know she was frightened. That was exactly what he wanted. Pulling her leg like this was cruel.

"I don't take kindly to men trying to scare me," she said. "I don't believe you."

"You should. The guardians are a very real threat, and it is my suggestion that you stay away from the water until we get to your destination."

Sorcha shook her head. "Which is?"

His hand shifted slightly to the left. "Do you see that?"

How could she have missed it? Mist and storm clouds created a wall in the middle of the ocean. A bolt of lightning cracked through the sky, and although they were too far to hear the thunder, she swore she could feel it.

"We're going there? Why?"

"Because that is the only way into the Otherworld," he said as he walked away.

"Hy-brasil is not in the Otherworld!" Sorcha shouted.

"It's on the border, darling. And you have to get close enough to see it."

She wanted to reach out and punch him. Or grab onto his dreads and toss him overboard. Guardian.

Sorcha snorted, but walked away from the railing. The last thing she needed was another scary story in her head. She had grown up with the Dullahan, trooping faeries, changeling children, and all other manner of frightening Fae.

Grumbling, she skirted her way past sailors on their hands and knees scrubbing the deck. They were eerily silent in their work. Their eyes followed her all the way back to the captain's cabin where she shut and locked the door.

Now that the seasickness had subsided, she got a good look at his quarters. And what stunning quarters they were.

"A four-poster bed?" she muttered. "What need does a man have of a four-poster bed out to sea?"

It wasn't very large, hardly enough room for two people, but it took up a remarkable amount of space. A wooden red desk was shoved in the corner. It didn't look like anyone used it at all. There were no papers, no inkwells, nothing to suggest that Manus ever sat at the desk.

Sorcha peered underneath it.

"No chair?" she muttered. "Of course it would be for decoration only."

Brown sheepskin covered the floor, soft against her bare feet. She curled her toes in its thick wool.

Someone pounded on the door. Whirling on her heel, she called out, "I'm not taking visitors!"

"Good!" Manus shouted back. "We're going to be heading straight for the eye of that storm. It's moving away from us, so we're going to put some effort in to catch it. Stay in the cabin! I don't need you falling overboard."

Her lips curled as she mimicked him. "I don't need you falling overboard. It's a good thing you're helping me captain, or I'd have half a mind to trip you into the ocean!"

A chuckle echoed through the door, growing quieter and quieter until it disappeared.

Sorcha huffed and crossed her arms over her chest. She should feel tired, but the long night's sleep was plenty. One might think that a sea captain would have an entertaining room, but there was little here.

Where was the treasure? The maps of wondrous places? At least trophies from all the places he had traveled. The man had a Fae-marked ship, for heavens sake.

She gritted her teeth and rummaged through her pack. There was one thing that always settled her mind, no matter where she was.

Soft vellum covered the worn leather journal. Its parchment paper curled at the edges, darkened with age and brittle with age. She lifted it to her nose and inhaled.

It still smelled like her. No matter how many years her mother had been dead, her books still smelled like her. Aged paper, lavender oil, sunshine, and the faintest hint of clover.

As always, tears pricked her eyes.

"I miss you," she whispered against the journal's spine. "I left Papa yesterday, and I hope it was the right decision. You always told me to be brave and kind. I think that's what this journey is for."

She turned the page and lost herself into a naturalist's recounting of healing. She read of teas which could stop bleeding, setting bones, cleaning wounds, walking a woman through every step of pregnancy. Sorcha's mother had unimaginable knowledge that she wrote down every moment she could.

It would never be enough. She would always want to devour her mother's words and wished she could remember her voice. Ten years was enough to forget many things about a person.

If Sorcha tried very hard, she could remember the way sunlight turned her mother's rosy hair to fire. How Sorcha had spent hours counting the freckles on her mother's arm when she had been ill. But she couldn't remember the tone of her voice, the whispered stories, or what she sounded like when she told her daughter "I love you."

Sorcha sniffed and blinked away tears.

Shaking her head, she patted the journal and placed it back inside her pack. "You'll stay there," she whispered. "Safe and sound."

Slapping wings smacked against the porthole of the ship. Sorcha flung herself back against the bed and stared at the giant raven poking its head into her room.

"Excuse me?" she gasped. "Who are you?"

It cawed at her, cocking its head to the side and staring at her with a single yellow eye.

"No," she said as she rose to her feet. "Absolutely not. I do not need a feathered friend in this room with me."

The raven didn't listen. It hopped from the porthole down onto the desk.

"No!" Sorcha said again.

She flapped her hands at it. There wasn't anything to shoo it away with, and now it might be too late. Ravens were intelligent, but she wasn't certain it could fly out the porthole. If she scared it into the air, then she might never get it back down. She eyed its wings.

"You're mighty and quite large," she said. "I think if you were flying that your wings would hurt me."

It tilted its head to the other side and jumped one hop towards her.

"Ah," she gasped. "Please don't do that."

The raven hopped backwards.

"No," Sorcha shook her head. "Don't do that either."

The raven froze and met her gaze.

"Can you understand me?"

It squawked at her.

Overwhelmed again, Sorcha tried to back away from it. Her heel caught on the edge of a rug, and she tumbled hard onto the floor. The bang of her tailbone hitting solid wood made her wince just as much as the sudden lightning bolt of pain.

The raven lifted its wings as though it might fly into the air.

"No!" Sorcha lifted one hand, the other rubbing firmly at her bottom. "I'm fine. Please just stop."

It seemed to hesitate, wings still poised for flight.

"Really, I'm fine. I just didn't expect you to understand me. Are you the captain's?"

The raven's reaction was immediate. Its wings snapped down at its sides, its head rose from its feathers to an impossible height, and it croaked angrily at her.

"Did I insult you?" she asked. "I apologize. This is the captain's quarters. It's not that big of a stretch."

However, talking to a bird and expecting to be understood was a stretch. They were unnaturally intelligent, so it wasn't all that surprising that it reacted to her words.

She narrowed her eyes. "Am I making this up in my head? Yesterday, I was safe in my family's brothel, and now I'm hurtling towards the Otherworld. Or can you really understand me?"

It flapped its wings.

Sorcha rolled onto her knees and achingly rose to her feet. "I'm losing my mind. First, I make a deal with a faerie. Then I think ravens can understand me. What's next? Guardians are actually real?"

She snorted at the thought. The captain was trying to frighten her into staying in her cabin and away from his men. She understood that he might want her to stay out of the way, but he could have done it in a much more sensible way.

The raven croaked again and hopped towards the porthole. It pecked at the wood, the harsh thumps repetitive and strangely intentional. Between each jab, it would turn its head to stare at her.

Was it trying to get her to go to the window? She took a few hesitant steps forward. If the bird could understand her, did it want her to look outside?

"I'm losing my mind," she said.

Sorcha inched by the raven, keeping an eye on its movements in case it lunged at her. The bird stayed very still. She hooked her elbows on the edge of the porthole and leaned out.

The ocean waves didn't quite reach the window, but the salt spray misted her cheeks. The sun had set while she'd read. The moon spread its rays across the waves, turning them silver and frothy white.

It was beautiful. Untamed and wild, the ocean was the last bit of the world which remained a mystery. A wave crested against the ship, and the splashing water sounded like music.

"It's hard to believe such a place is so dangerous," she whispered.

She reached a hand towards the next wave. Sea water splashed, bitterly cold and bracing. Bubbles caught between her fingers and popped as she lifted them towards her mouth. She licked the salt from her skin with a soft chuckle.

"See?" she glanced over her shoulder towards the raven. "It's not all that dangerous."

A soft thump against the side of the ship startled her. She looked down into the black waters but could see nothing in their depths.

Sorcha narrowed her eyes and leaned further out the porthole.

Something in the darkness shifted. She couldn't see what was there, or where the movement came from, but the murk changed.

She scooted even farther out the porthole, her hands braced against the side of the ship.

In the darkness of the ocean, within arm's reach, an eye blinked—larger than a dinner plate and black as night. She could see it now. The entire impossible length of the creature stretched out larger than the ship.

Sorcha's mouth gaped open. Her fingers turned to claws. The guardian's head alone was larger than a horse! It was faintly human in shape, but its skin was ghostly pale and speckled. Its mouth was a large gash that spread across its face nearly to the ear canals on both sides of its head. Hair grew in a mohawk from the peak of its skull and stretched so far into the waves that Sorcha couldn't begin to guess its length.

It blinked its eye again. Lips stretched into what she hoped was a friendly smile, and Sorcha heard the thump again. The creature's long spindly finger was stroking the side of the ship. It paused at the top of the yellow paint and then traveled underneath the boat.

A soft whine escaped Sorcha's lips.

"Okay," she whispered. "I'm going back inside now. Please don't flip us."

She didn't want to startle the guardian, so she moved inch by inch until she fell onto the floor of the cabin. Only then did she allow herself to hyperventilate and shake her hands in the air. When did she lose feeling in her hands? Her heart beat so fast she thought it was rising into her throat.

"It's real," she whispered over and over again. "It's really real. That exists in the oceans. I'm never going swimming again."

The raven bobbed its head and made a sound like laughter.

"You stop it. You didn't see that thing."

The raven didn't stop laughing, even when Sorcha threw a pillow at it.

With all the new sights, and the rocking of the ship, Sorcha was certain she wouldn't sleep again. Nightmares would keep her awake. The possibility of the future would keep her awake. There was no possible way that she could slip into the endless night. But she did, and her mind did not plague her with dreams.

Chapter 7

The ghosts of his past walked with Eamonn across the ramparts of the castle. They tugged on the cloak wrapped around his shoulders, tangled in the high peak of his braid, clutched at his wrists and pulled him back towards the gloom.

He shook his head, trying to toss aside memories like water shaking from his skin. He was not so lucky. His mind held him captive and replayed old memories from his childhood.

His father stared with eyes cold and unfeeling. The blade in his hand glinted in the glaring sunlight that traveled up the sharp edge to the point. It swung down, slicing across Eamonn's face and spraying blood across the battlements.

His mother turned away from the sight. His brother's smirk scalded into his memory and branded his mind.

Memories were his prison. Torment his penance for years of foolish attachments and familial trust.

Storm clouds rolled overhead. Slate gray and heavy with moisture, they threatened lightning and thunder that would last for days. The weather grew angry with him. Together, they would rage against each heartbeat—each breath—that kept him alive.

He dug his fingers into the cracked stone of the barely waist-high wall that was the only barrier between him and a hundred-foot fall. In his youth, he would have feared cutting his skin. Now, he listened to the scrape of crystals cutting into granite that crumbled under his clenched fist.

A low rumble of thunder rocked the isle of Hy-brasil. Far below the castle walls, tiny dots of sheep and faeries scattered towards the safety of caves. They would wait out the sky's anger there. Perhaps they would build a fire, drink mead and whiskey, and tell stories from their youth.

All while their master stood upon the highest tower and roared at the sky.

Eamonn heard a voice just like his own on the wind. Deep like the thunder, but even more dangerous—his twin brother's voice.

"This was your doing," Fionn said. "You are responsible for all their suffering and the suffering of hundreds more. You made me do this, Eamonn, and now we all pay the price."

He shook his head. "I did not choose this life. I did not force your hand."

The wound upon his throat throbbed, and the geodes in his neck cast violet light upon his fists. He still felt the biting rope, fraying at the edges, and swaying in the breeze.

He released the catch of his cloak, and let it fall to the stones. It fluttered in the wind, stretching out as though it were cloth wings.

Leather leggings hugged his thighs. The sewn strips dipped into craters of geodes and grew taut over peaks of pointed crystal. No shirt covered his bare chest, allowing the wind to whistle through the valleys of disfigurement. Abdominal ridges rose above the line of his pants, the bumps of his ribs bisected by gashes of violet wounds. His left shoulder was almost entirely gemstone, the large chunk limiting his movement. Spindly veins of opal traveled across his chest, down one thick bicep, and stretched to follow the line of his spine.

The deepest wound wrapped around his neck. The perfect circle was two fingers wide and created a hollow valley of jagged crystals. It deepened his voice to a gruff rasp.

Like his shoulder, veins of opal sliced across his face. Two twin lines started above his eyebrow and at the peak of his temple. They cut across his eye, skipped only at the opening of his mouth, and met at his throat. The crystal at his lips limited his speech and caused him to speak from one side of his mouth, giving him a permanent sneer.

He shaved his head on both sides, leaving only the top to grow freely. He wore it in a braid, letting it swing to the middle of his back. The golden hair was the last bit of beauty he had left.

Eamonn had once been the most desired Seelie man any woman had ever seen. The strength of his body, the legends of his battle prowess, and the startling blue of his eyes had wooed many to his bed.

The memories of beautiful women turning away when they saw his true form and the nightmare he had become plagued him.

He walked to the end of the rampart, and let his toes hang over the edge. His eyes drifted shut as the wind brushed his cheeks. It whistled through the crystals and sang a song only he could hear.

He may not be dead yet, but the time was nearing. Soon, soon he could let go.

"Master," Cian's voice cut through the raging storm within Eamonn's head. "If you planned on jumping, you'd have done it a long time ago."

"Leave."

The gnome never listened. Eamonn could hear his footsteps as he padded down the ramparts.

Cian cleared his throat. "Now it seems to me you're frightening the pixies in the gardens. They're staring up like your body is going to come crashing down on them any minute, and I need them collecting the pumpkins before the storm starts."

"Make them gather in the rain."

"Their wings will get wet, and we both know how difficult they are when they have wet wings. So why don't you take a few steps back and stop their trembling." Cian paused, and then added, "Or jump off and save us all the trouble of worrying."

The gnome had such a way with words. Eamonn shook his head and held out a hand. He kept his back turned towards Cian, knowing most of the damage to his body was reflected on his chest and face.

"My cloak," he grunted.

"I've seen you before, boy. There's no need to hide."

"My cloak, Cian."

He knew they all had seen him. Eamonn had accidentally strayed too far from his tower many times. The pixies had caught him washing in the waterfalls. The brownies found him in the training grounds. They were all stuck on the same isle. There weren't a lot of places for him to hide.

None of this meant he felt comfortable around them. His disfigurement was a disgrace to the royal line. The truth was branded into his mind after they hung him for seven days. Old wounds like that cut to the quick and rarely healed.

Cool fabric met his outstretched hand. Eamonn's eyes drifted shut for a moment, thankful that the gnome had followed orders. He would never say it. There was no purpose in congratulating someone for doing what they were told.

He swirled the cloak in a wide arc and settled it over his shoulders. Heat enveloped him with unwelcome arms. Eamonn hated the cloak. He hated hiding, but this had become his existence. He was no longer the handsome man he once had been.

"Storm's coming," Cian said as he walked up to Eamonn's side. "And you're still standing at the top of your castle leaning over an edge that could crumble at any moment."

"Would it be such a loss?"

"No. We'd get along just fine without you, but I'd have to dig a new hole in the garden, and I hadn't planned on doing that until next spring."

"Ever so gentle, Cian."

"I don't have to be gentle with you. The warlord prince of the Seelie Fae should have thicker skin."

Eamonn twitched the edge of his cloak over his newly mangled hand. "That was a long time ago."

"Take one step back, and I'll tell you who I was before I came here."

"I know who you were," his toes curled over the edge. "Gnomes have always been good thieves. You stole from the wrong person and pay your penance here. Hy-brasil was and always will be a prison. Nothing more."

Cian planted a hand firmly against the base of Eamonn's spine. The sudden touch made him lock his muscles holding himself in place without twitching or revealing the sudden shock that raced through his veins. The gnome did not push, nor did he pull. He kept his hand against Eamonn's back relaxed but threatening.

"I was no common thief. I stole to make a living and feed my family. Your people view gnomes as little more than slaves. We work in your gardens, feed your people, while the rest of us go hungry. My children went to bed with their stomachs aching, and my wife withered away into nothing. I stole a single piece of bread from the kitchens of a lowly Seelie lord. For that, they banished me here—never to see my family again."

Eamonn remained silent. He knew the Seelie court was corrupt. It had been his desire to change those ways, even as he fought in the wars that upheld them. He had not been the king, however, and had little power to change anything then. Now, he never would.

His silence spurred Cian on. "I don't like you, Tuatha dé Danann. Not because of what you've done here, or even who you are, but for what you stand for."

The hand against Eamonn's spine flexed. His own hands slowly curled beneath the cape. If Cian pushed, Eamonn could catch himself on the half wall. He would need to have faith that the castle wouldn't crumble under his weight.

"I lost everything I ever had, because your people consider themselves above everyone else. It was a damned piece of bread, and I was banished from the Otherworld like I'd murdered someone. I wanted to feed hungry mouths, to get paid for the work I did. And look what happened to me!"

Eamonn felt the slightest nudge against his back.

"You got nothing to say to that?" Cian growled.

"There is little I could say which would change your mind."

"You're right. There's not."

The hand against his spine withdrew, and the gnome backed away. Eamonn straightened and squared his shoulders. He would not bow. He would not yield. Though he was a disgraced prince, he might have been king of these people.

He would not break.

Cian's feet struck the ground in hard echoes as he returned to the door which led to the rest of the castle. Creaking floorboards fought with the thunder. He stopped at the door and turned.

"You know," the gnome's words flung into the night like sharp assassin blades. "If you weren't such a prick, I might respect you. You don't even flinch."

"I fear nothing and no one. Leave, gnome, before I throw you from the tower instead."

The door slammed shut. A bolt of lightning sizzled through the air and struck the top of the tower. Thunder crashed so loud the pixies in the gardens below screamed and fled in terror.

Throughout it all, Eamonn stood silent and unmoving.

Long ago, he had been a pillar for his people. They called his name as he rode through the streets. They threw flower petals at his feet in hopes he might look upon them. Now, they ran in fear.

He tilted his head back and let his rage roar at the coming storm. He poured all the feelings of neglect, anger, fear, and self-hatred into the sound. It purged his blackened soul.

Eamonn twisted away from the edge of his castle and fell to his knees. Staring down at his ruined hands, he set his resolve towards living. He would begin his work again, turn his mind and passion towards saving his people in whatever way possible. Storms like this always brought shipwrecked cargo. He would wait to see what his people would find upon the rocky shore.

Death would wait a while longer.

Chapter 8

Less than a week at sea, and Sorcha was ready to kill herself. She held onto the railing and breathed through her nose. In and out. Slow and intentional inhalations, or she would vomit again.

Manus tried to make her eat, but she couldn't keep anything down. Even the ale tasted like bile. It exited her body as fast as she could drink it.

The ship coasted over a very large wave and crashed down the other side. Turning green, Sorcha moaned and leaned over the rail again. Watching the waves didn't help, but what else was there? Waves upon waves, that was it.

Her vision blurred. The muscles of her stomach clenched, trying to force out what wasn't there. She'd emptied her stomach of everything but thin bile hours ago. Now, dry heaves threatened to kill her.

The part of her brain which was a healer screamed she needed water. Not ale. Not whiskey. Water. Fresh, clean water that would hydrate her body. There was so much water surrounding them, and none of it was safe to drink. She licked her dry lips and wished for death.

"Sorcha! I need you away from the railing."

She lifted her head and tried not to shake. "Can't do that, Captain."

"Now!"

"I can't," she whispered. "I can't even move."

A wall of dark skin and beaded hair stalked towards her. "When I give you an order, girl, you best be following it. Get up."

"No."

"Get up!"

Sorcha leaned over the edge of the railing and prayed to whatever gods were listening. Take her now. Make it end. She didn't care how. If only she could stop throwing up for just a few moments, she would consider herself blessed.

Manus grabbed the back of her skirt and yanked her up. Her knees shook, muscles quaked, body bowed as she retched.

"Enough!" he shouted. "We are sailing directly into that storm I showed you, and I will not have you wrapped around the railing. The Fae wanted you in Hy-brasil, and that is where you are going. Now get back to my quarters!"

He released his hold, and she fell onto her hands and knees. "If I could stand to be in that room with that horrible raven then I would be there!"

"Raven?" Manus shook his head. "Damned thing can't leave well enough alone. I don't care who's sharing the room with you. You will be out of sight until we are through the storm."

"Why can't I stay on deck?" She looked up at him, eyes wide and skin pale. "I'll stay out of the way. The fresh air helps."

"I'm sure it does, pretty thing. But that storm is going to hit us hard. Waves will crash right over the deck, and at least in the cabin you can hold onto the bed. Make sure you grip the posts tight. Don't let go until I come for you."

He held his hand out for her to take. Sorcha eyed it as though it were a snake which might bite. Going back in that cabin would make her vomit even more violently than before.

But she didn't want to end up in the ocean during a storm either. Sighing, she slapped her hand onto his. "I hate the ocean."

Manus chuckled. "So many people do. She's a cruel mistress, and a temptress when she wants to be."

"A tempest you mean?" she asked while stumbling to the cabin.

"That, too, but it's unlikely we'll see a tempest while out here."

"What do you call that storm then?"

He opened the door and shoved her through. "I call that a widow maker. Stay safe."

Manus slammed the door so hard the floor quaked. The raven flapped its wings, slapping them against the table in anger.

"Yes," she murmured. "I agree. The man is charming, but he's also rude."

The ship tilted at a drastic angle. The entire frame shook with the impact of the bow hitting the water. Swearing, Sorcha tripped and landed on her hands and knees again.

"Apparently, he wasn't joking," she muttered.

Standing proved impossible as the ship rocked back and forth. Moaning with seasickness and fear, she crawled to the bed. Her hands fisted in the dark blankets which slid off the frame rather than pulling her up onto it.

Sorcha curled her fingers around a post and hauled herself up. Her stomach heaved again. There was nothing to vomit, but she still leaned over the edge of the bed.

Another great wave tossed the ship against the hard walls of the ocean. Sorcha's pack thumped against the wall, and a stone weight on the captain's desk fell onto the floor with a heavy crack.

She squeezed her eyes shut and hugged a pillow to her chest. There was nothing she could do but wait out the storm. She couldn't go out on the deck and help, she didn't know how. There were no men who needed healing, not yet. All she could do was follow orders and stay out of the way.

It went against every fiber of her being not to help, but she should stay where she was.

She heard the shouts before the ship rose, straight as a tree. She clutched the posts of the bed and whispered prayers.

"Please," she called out. "I do not wish to die so far from my homeland, from my family, from the earth. Faeries of the water and sky, help us."

The raven took flight, cawing its agitation and anger. The ship shifted again and landed hard on the waves which seemed to turn to stone. Sorcha screamed.

One of the posts snapped with a harsh crack. The wooden piece went flying into the air, tossed by the waves and their uncontrolled jouncing. Someone hit the door to the cabin hard, the frame vibrating with the man's weight.

Sorcha reached out her arms. "If we're going to die together, I might as well name you. Bran!"

The raven's head snapped towards her, as if it recognized the name.

"Come here!"

The ship rolled again, and the man leaning against the door shrieked as thunderous water ripped him away. Sorcha watched the handle rattle and whispered a prayer for the man to remain on the ship. Anything to keep them all safe.

Bran darted towards her as the ship crested another wave. Sorcha reached out an armand held him close to her chest. One hand gently stroked his breast feathers, the other clutched the nearest post and held on for dear life.

"I didn't think I would die like this," she whispered, treating the raven as her confessor. "I always thought it would be at the stake. Rumors called my mother a witch. She spoke with the faeries and kept the old tales alive. Because of that, they burned her. I still remember every moment of it."

She pressed her face against his back. Bran tilted his head and tucked his beak against her throat.

"I'm not a witch. I'm not odd, or frightening, and I don't have any knowledge that can't be learned. Nothing will ever stop me from believing in faeries or leaving them gifts because they were here first. We need to take care of them, because they take care of us in return. Not for payment, but because they are kind and good and everything humans have lost. And because even as I'm hurtling toward my death, I can't stop thinking about them."

The ship shuddered and froze. Sorcha listened to the groaning wood, the rivers of water splashing off the sides, and the pounding rain striking the deck. They had stopped moving.

A great deafening cry vibrated the entire ship. The high-pitched screams of men joined it. Sorcha realized with horror that the guardian had grabbed the ship in her mighty hands. She could imagine the wide split mouth gaping its terrifying scream, the thin pale hands clutching the Saorsa as if it were a child's toy.

They were going to die.

She closed her eyes and breathed in a slow, deep breath. She had failed on the very first leg of her journey. But then again, this had been an impossible task from the start. The Fae didn't want her to find the cure to the beetle plague. They wanted to watch a theatrical attempt by a foolish human girl who had trusted them too easily.

Hands slapped against the side of the ship. Tiny scratching sounds which were too small to be the guardian's massive fingers.

Sorcha peeled open one eye, clutched the raven tight to her chest, and glanced at the porthole.

Green hair snaked through the opening, and dark eyes stared back at her. Rainbows danced across the merrow's fingers as she reached through. When their gazes caught, the merrow paused and cocked her head to the side.

The raven struggled, squawking angrily until it wiggled free. He snapped at the air with his beak and flew towards the merrow.

"What?" Sorcha muttered.

Were they not going to die? Bran grumbled at the merrow who tilted her head to the other side. She reached out and brushed a long finger down the raven's beak, and then released the edge of the porthole. Her green tail shimmered as she pulled herself further up the ship.

"Are we saved?" She could hardly believe she uttered the words.

The angry look Bran cast towards her was answer enough. They were being saved by the very creature she was so terrified of. Now, she understood why it was so important to have a guardian in faerie waters.

Sorcha placed her hand against a post and rose on rubbery legs. She had barely been able to walk on the ship before the storm. Now, she didn't trust her balance at all. Her hands were shaking, and she feared the guardian would drop them. She didn't want to end up back in the water after that experience.

Carefully, she made her way towards the door. Manus's voice echoed in her head. Do not go outside. Don't open the door. Stay inside the cabin where it is safe.

Yet, she also heard the screams of his men. She heard the thumping crash of bodies landing against solid wood and the rushing waves of water cresting over the deck. There were people who needed healing.

It didn't matter that she was afraid. Fear was a beast she could conquer as long as she could save just one life. This was what she was born to do.

Sorcha tugged hard on the door which resisted her movements. She threw her weight into the backwards motion and inched it open, bit by bit.

Men slumped all across the deck. Some had piled across each other, moaning and rubbing their wounds. Blood slicked her door, a red handprint catching her eye.

Merrows dragged themselves up the sides of the ship and across the deck. A few had curled around sailors and were gently patting their cheeks. They didn't speak. Instead, they hummed their concern. Their voices were deep and calming.

Sorcha stumbled towards the nearest sailor and dropped to her knees. "Where does it hurt?"

"Everywhere," he groaned.

"Where is the worst?"

He gestured towards his chest. Sorcha reached forward without hesitation and ripped his shirt open. A bright bruise already formed, purple and angry.

She danced her fingers over his ribs and watched his reactions. He flinched from the tenderness, but didn't respond overly much to her prodding of the bones. There was the slightest of groans when she palpated his stomach. Sorcha hesitated and did it one more time. She didn't feel any swelling from internal bleeding, but the number of bruises was concerning.

"Are you having trouble breathing?"

"Leave me, girl."

"Answer the question, sailor. Can you breathe?"

Another hand touched hers. Webbed fingers spread across the bruising of the man's chest and gently pulled Sorcha's hands away.

Sorcha stared in fascination as the merrow wrapped herself around the sailor. The long green tail twined through his legs and down to his calves. Her chest pressed against the man's spine and her iridescent webs glowed as they smoothed across his skin. She placed her chin on his shoulder, humming the deep base of the merrow song.

"Sorcha," Manus said. "Come with me."

She looked up at the captain's hand he held towards her. "What's happening?"

"I told you the Fae take care of us. Now, come on."

Manus's hand was just as cold as hers. He pulled her up and held onto her elbow when she swayed. "Were you injured?"

"No."

"Good."

He pulled her towards the bow of the ship. She glanced over her shoulder, watching more merrows swarm over the railings. Two dragged a man up from the ocean. They slammed him down on the deck so hard that Sorcha winced, but the hard strike made him cough up the seawater in his lungs.

They were not just saving the survivors, she realized. Three more merrows pulled up another man and laid him gently on the desk. They rocked back and forth over his body, keening their grief.

"They mourn the dead?" she asked.

"Of course, they do. We work with them, and we will mourn theirs before we set sail again."

"They had casualties?" Sorcha glanced around, trying to find the merrow bodies.

"You won't see them on the ship. Merrows turn to sea foam when they die. It's a cruel death, but it's better than letting sharks eat them."

Sorcha swallowed hard. "I'm sorry to hear they lost loved ones."

"Well, I lost good men as well. Feel sorry for the lot of us."

She blinked and looked up at him. His cheeks were red and splotchy, his eyes casting glares in her direction even as he propelled her forcefully towards the end of his ship.

"Are you angry at me?" she asked.

"I never should have taken this foolish mission. The journey to Hy-brasil is dangerous, and I was fully aware of that."

"And that is my fault?"

"You asked to come here, freckles."

Sorcha jerked the arm he held. "How dare you blame this on me? I did nothing wrong!"

"You made a deal with the wrong faerie." He thrust her towards the bow of the ship and the wooden Fae staring off into the skyline. "I lost good men because of you. I won't blame you for their deaths, but I'm damned well getting you off this ship."

She stumbled, catching herself hard against the railing. The storm was subsiding, though the waves still churned with uncontrolled anger. She couldn't see anything in those secretive waves, the water dark and foreboding.

The island was within sight. Tall cliffs framed one side and led down to a rocky shore. A castle loomed over the small isle, crumbling towers and decaying wood structures giving the land an eerie, abandoned feel. It looked like a better abode for ghosts than people. Certainly not faeries.

"Hy-brasil?" she asked.

"You wanted to go to the island. There it is." His feet struck the deck hard as he walked away.

"Wait!" Sorcha spun. "How am I supposed to get there?"

"That wasn't part of our deal. As you can see, I have enough to worry about here."

"Can I borrow a rowboat at least?" She raced after him and caught the edge of his sleeve.

"Borrow? How are you going to bring it back? Swim to the isle if you need to get there so badly, freckles, or stay on the ship and return with us. I don't care."

"You want me to swim to that isle?" Sorcha jabbed a finger at Hy-brasil. "Do you even know what's in the water here? You said this was the gateway between the Otherworld and ours, so how many more faeries are there? We can both be certain I won't find just merrows!"

"Then stay on the ship, and I'll bring you home."

He whirled on her. His chest rose and fell in exaggerated rage while his hands opened and closed. Sorcha narrowed her eyes. He wasn't just angry at her. He was frightened. The storm had cost him much, and he was second guessing coming here at all.

They had to go back through the storm, she realized. This wasn't about the initial danger, but that they had to turn around and do it again. Maybe it would be easier returning to the human world, but she doubted it.

He would lose more men. More merrows would die. And she was pestering him with ferrying her over to the island which had caused all this trouble in the first place.

Sorcha released her anger with a soft sigh. "I understand, Manus. I do. But I need to bring my things with me, and they cannot get wet."

"I never said I'd ensure the safety of personal items."

"They're my mother's books," she called out as he turned away from her again. "They're the only thing I have left of her, and I will not let them go."

He hesitated. She watched his shoulders lift in anger, and then curl forward in defeat. "You're set on going, then?"

"I have no other choice. You know that as well as I. The faerie punishment for backing out of a deal is worse than a swift death at sea."

"I have a charm which will help your pack stay dry. It was a gift from a selkie, and I expect to have it back someday."

Sorcha twisted her fingers together. "I will do my best to return it once this is all over."

"I won't hold my breath."

Manus motioned for one of his sailors, the most mobile of the bunch strewn across the deck like autumn leaves. The raven burst out of the captain's quarters, its cry echoing as it launched into the air. She watched him stretch his wings and fly towards the isle.

Apparently, the raven was traveling to the same place as Sorcha. She turned her gaze to the land mass and suppressed a shiver. There was something about that place which felt wrong.

The air was too still. The ocean didn't crash against the rocks, but sluggishly avoided touching the land. Even the elements had forsaken Hy-brasil. There was more to the phantom isle than the legends sang, and Sorcha was afraid to find out what.

She braced her feet as the guardian gently set them down. The ship remained steady, bobbing as if there had never been a storm. Sorcha wished she could forget as easily as the Saorsa had.

Footsteps marked the return of the sailor who held her pack at arm's length. He held it far out in front of him, the pack dangling from his fingers as if he didn't want to touch her.

Sorcha recognized that expression. It was the same look her mother had been given for months before they burned her. They blamed her for every bit of bad luck. A neighbor's cow died, a child caught a cold, the well ran dry, all were the markings of a witch who had cursed the town. Sorcha's mother had been the one they chose to burn.

She snatched her pack out of the man's hands with a muttered curse. "I didn't call the storm, you imbecile. Give me that."

The sailor flinched away from her.

Good riddance. He could be frightened of her if that helped him make sense of the storm, but she wasn't about to let him treat her like a witch. Sorcha was a good person. She would have healed them all if the merrows weren't here.

She swung the pack over her shoulder and held her hand towards Manus. "The charm?"

He pulled a small bag from his pocket. The burlap was completely dry. Not even a single drop of water clung to its checkered pattern.

"This will do. Stick it in your bag and swim as fast as you can."

"Will the charm wear off?" She stuffed the small bag in her pack between her most precious books.

"It's unlikely to wear off. And freckles? A word of warning: where there are merrows, there are merrow-men. They'd like a pretty thing like you to stay with them, and most of their wives are here with us. No one will be able to stop them if they get ahold of you."

"Thank you," she gritted through clenched teeth.

He didn't stay to watch. Manus left to tend to his men, while she stood on the precipice of another decision. The water was another dangerous part of her journey. The ocean had yet to be kind, and its inhabitants were likely even worse.

Her eyes strayed to the haunted isle that had spawned straight from her nightmares. Hy-brasil, the phantom isle spoken of in legends and myths for centuries. Many believed it was a utopia, a place where men of highest intelligence and scholars of world renown were sent.

It looked like a ruin.

She carefully hoisted herself up on the railing and balanced with a sail rope in her hand. This was it. There was no going back once she jumped off this ship and landed in the waters below.

Papa's eyes swam in front of hers. His painfully thin body, the grating cough that kept the others up at night, the dangers of what might happen should she fail and he die. The beetles would infect her sisters next; they were the nearest food source. The families nearby might also fall. And she wasn't there to help prolong their lives.

Sorcha lifted her foot to hang in the salty air for a moment before she took a deep breath and leapt off the edge.

She hit the water with a stinging slap. Her skirts billowed up into her face and tangled with the long strands of her hair. The pack weighed her down, pulling her towards the bottom of the ocean with surprising ease.

Bubbles erupted from her mouth as she pumped her arms. Fabric tangled around her feet and trapped them. She couldn't kick. She couldn't breathe.

Frowning in concentration, she almost didn't notice the movement in the depths. Calm yourself, she thought. Calm was the only way to deal with the Fae. Panic would only lead to poor decisions.

She let her body relax although her lungs burned. Salt water stung her eyes when she opened them. Sorcha glanced down and held in a gasp when she saw red eyes staring back at her.

Deep at the bottom of the ocean, the merrow-men waited. They lacked the necessary tails to keep up with their brides. Instead, they had legs like a human man. Green scales covered their bodies which were hard with muscles. Gills and fins popped up with little rhyme or reason, giving them a grotesque appearance. But it was their faces that disturbed her the most.

Large fish-like mouths gaped open as they inhaled her scent in the water. Jagged teeth lined their gums. Their eyes bulged when they realized it was a human woman in their realm. Frilled fins fanned out around their faces and evil grins spread wide.

One curled his fist around a trident and pushed off the ocean floor. He was swimming towards her. His webbed feet made him a much more effective swimmer, and her own pack was steadily dragging her to the bottom.

Sorcha wouldn't let that happen. Determined, she reached down and ripped the bottom of her skirt. Two great, heaving pulls split the fabric down each side. It wasn't much, but it was enough.

Her legs now freed she swam with all her might. Muscles burned, lungs screamed, eyes watered, but she eventually broke through into the sweet air.

She gasped in breaths that shocked her lungs. There wasn't enough air in the world to satisfy her cravings, and every inhalation tasted metallic. She rolled onto her back—still sucking in air—and kicked towards the isle.

The merrow-man was still coming, she reminded herself. She couldn't rest just because she could breathe. It was time to swim. Once she made it to the island, she could rest.

Only then.

When she finally caught her breath, she rolled onto her stomach and lifted her arms above her head. One arm at a time, one kick at a time, counting under her breath each stroke that drew her closer to Hy-brasil.

She couldn't stop for even a moment, or the pack would drag her under the water. Her stomach churned from too many dips beneath the waves. A belly full of salt made her more nauseous, but there wasn't even bile left to vomit.

She'd seen no sharks, but the stories said she wouldn't until it was too late.

Above her head, the raven circled. Its caw snapped her eyes open as she paused for a moment to breathe.

"Bran?" she whispered.

Again, the corvid's cry jolted through her body.

"Right," she muttered. "I have to swim."

The isle grew closer and closer, even as the sun began to set and the ocean turned red. She could make it if only she swam a little… bit…more.

Her feet touched land.

A sob lurched her body forward. She slipped underneath a wave, but it didn't matter that she couldn't see. All she could taste was salt but there were rocks and sand beneath her feet. She didn't have to swim anymore, and she didn't have to lose her mother's journals.

"Thank you," she whispered as she pulled herself onto the jagged shore. "Thank you so much."

She curled her fingers in the sand and mud. The grit digging into her nailbeds made even more tears stream down her cheeks. She had made it to the phantom isle through storms, giant whale creatures, and merrow-men.

Sorcha had really done it.

She laughed through the tears and rolled onto her back. The stars twinkled in the night sky. They were so beautiful. The land was so beautiful.

It no longer mattered that there was a mysterious castle looming overhead. It didn't matter that ghosts likely traversed with silent feet all around her. She wasn't swimming anymore, and the ground didn't move here.

Letting out a ragged breath, her eyes drifted shut. Just for a moment, she told herself. She could rest for a moment before she had to get back up and find the Fae the MacNara twins wanted.

Stars danced beneath her eyelids as she settled into the sand.

Chapter 9

Cold air brushed her skin. Sorcha rolled to her side, murmuring in her sleep. Gritty sand touched her face and sucked into her lungs as she snorted awake.

She bolted upwards, scratching her nose with frantic hands. She coughed out sand and brushed dried salt off her cheeks. Her skin burned, raw and dry. Her lips cracked as she inhaled, blood leaking into her mouth and stinging her swollen tongue with the taste of iron.

Where was she? Her gaze danced over worn stones and bits of driftwood.

"Right," she whispered. "The boat…the storm…the swim."

Sorcha tucked her knees to her chest and hugged them close. There would be no more tears. She couldn't afford to lose her sanity; there was too much left to do.

Her mind settled, and she glanced around. What had awoken her?

Something snorted to her left. The muscles of her back seized, and she slowly turned her head.

A smooth, whiskered face blew air at her again. The seal's eyes were large and dark, surprisingly friendly. The warm air smelled of fish and rotten seaweed mixed with the musky scent of her newfound friend.

At her movement, the seal slapped a flipper against its belly and chortled.

"Oh," she said in surprise. "Hello."

It leaned in close and snorted at her again. When she flinched back, it let out another coughing laugh and rolled onto its back. Each smack against its side caused blubber to wiggle.

"Aren't you a funny little thing?" Sorcha wasn't certain it was so "little." The seal was already larger than her, and she was certain it wasn't full grown. Its long whiskers tilted up at her words.

It snorted at her one more time then turned to leave. Its body vibrated as it lurched across the shore, slipping into the water with more grace than it exhibited on land.

A thought sparked. "Are you a selkie?"

The only response was a quiet chuckle as the seal sank beneath the water.

Her muscles screamed in protest as she rose to her feet. The long muscles of her thighs seized, and her toes pointed as the arch of her foot clenched.

Sorcha whimpered. The pain was excruciating, but she couldn't stay on the sand. Stinging sunburns already covered her cheeks and arms. If she stayed out any longer, she would blister.

Water. She needed water. Her lips cracked as she opened them and wheezed out a breath.

She continued making soft sounds of discomfort as she pushed herself upright. She waved her arms for balance and settled. Coughing, Sorcha nodded her head.

"Step one, standing. Accomplished."

Her feet seemed so far away. She furrowed her brows and looked at her toes. When had she lost her left shoe?

Right about the moment a merrow-man had pointed his trident at her with a dangerous gleam in his eyes. She groaned and held a hand to her head. The headache pounding behind her eyes nearly sent her to her knees.

"Who is that?" a feminine voice asked.

"I don't know. She must have washed up from a shipwreck."

"That never happens."

"How am I supposed to know then? Banishment is the only way to get here, but faeries can't banish humans."

The second voice was far more masculine. Nasal and harsh, it made the pain behind her eyes spike higher.

"Please," Sorcha whispered. "Do you have any water?"

"Can she hear us, Cian?"

"Humans can't hear us when we're glamoured. She's hallucinating."

Sorcha stepped forward towards the sound, searching for the owners of the voices. "I can hear you. I came to Hy-brasil to speak with a faerie who lives here."

A scoff echoed across the stones. "There's plenty of faeries around here, human child. But there aren't many who will talk to you."

"Excuse me?" She blinked. "I need to talk to a Tuatha dé Danann who resides here. The MacNara twins sent me."

"Well, that changes things," the feminine voice said. "We might help you with that."

"We absolutely will not!" The other voice, Cian, was the male. "The master will have our heads, and I've gone toe to toe with him too many times. I will not be part of this."

"Please," Sorcha stepped forward and stumbled on a stone. She landed hard on her knees, crying out when the jagged rocks tore through her tender flesh.

"Look at her, Cian. We can't just leave her here."

"Don't be saying my name! Leaving her here is exactly what we'll do. We're not helping a human. Don't touch it! Woman, you'll be the death of me. She might be ill."

"But—"

"No buts! Stop helping people so much and think of your own hide. Humans don't belong here. Let it slip back into the water and forget about it."

Sorcha touched the gaping wound on her knee. Blood dripped from the torn flesh, already scabbing over, and encrusted with salt and sand. "Her," she whispered. "I am female, not an it."

"Could've fooled me," Cian grunted. "You look like something I'd scrape out of the ocean and toss to the side. Good luck making it to the castle."

Footsteps pattered across the granite stones. They were leaving. She gasped and stumbled to her feet, bracing her legs wide for balance. They couldn't leave, not yet.

"Wait!" she called out. "Please, wait!"

A blast of air heralded the approach of a Fae. Warm lips pressed against her ear and the feminine voice whispered, "I'll take care of you if you can make it home. One foot in front of the other, dearie."

The faerie presence vanished.

Sorcha lifted one leg and placed it before the other. She was unsteady, weak, and drained, but determined. Each movement splintered through her body in needles of icy pain.

"My body will not stop me," she whispered.

The longer she moved, the more her muscles loosened. Pain turned to ache, ache turned to exhaustion. She relaxed, and the fog cleared from her mind.

The haunting isle revealed tiny details of beauty she had not seen from the ship. The rocky shore was hazardous, true, but there were also small sparkling barnacles stuck to the stones. A pathway hewn into the side of the cliffs led up to emerald fields similar to her home.

And why wouldn't it be similar? This was still Ui Neill, she reminded herself. A mirrored reflection, but still the same structure of land and earth. The Otherworld was not so different from her own.

She hefted herself up on the first rock and caught her breath. Tiny purple flowers poked out between her fingers. The sun reached its peak, the heat causing mist to rise from the surrounding fields. It wasn't natural to see clouds this time of day, but there they were.

Sorcha pulled herself up on jutting stones and the marked pathway until she stood at the top of the hill.

Green filled her vision near to bursting. It was overwhelming to see such beautiful landscape. Her heart clenched and her fingers curled. Rolling hills covered in the most vibrant grass she had ever seen stretched as far as the eye could see. White dots of sheep lifted their heads every so often, smaller lumps of wool leaping through swirls of white fog.

Above it all, the castle loomed. The high peaks of towers looked like swords striking the gods.

Ravens flocked overhead. Their screams reminded her why she was here and how far she had come. She paused, hands on her hips, and lungs heaving.

"Not much farther now, Sorcha," she said to herself. "Then the real job begins."

Gravel crunched beneath her feet as she marched towards the castle. Her skin itched as if there were hundreds of eyes watching her journey. She supposed there could be. Fae were invisible to humans, and there were many on this isle.

She couldn't envision this as a prison. It was far too beautiful, too plentiful, too…human.

Skittering sounds of running feet rushed past her. Sorcha rocked forward with the force, her skirts stiffening with sand and salt. Her tangled hair stuck to her face as she whipped around.

No one. Not a single person stood around her, but she could feel the crowd. Hands tugged her clothing and grazed across her arms and pack.

She swallowed. "Thank you for your hospitality. I need to make it to the castle. Could you help me?"

It was a shot in the dark. The Fae standing around her might not want her to go there. They might want to toss her over the edge of the cliffs and wipe away all traces of humanity. Sorcha wouldn't blame them. Humans were rarely kind to the Fae.

Instead, gentle hands cupped her elbows and encouraged her to lean against them. The sores on her feet were so painful, she didn't hesitate to accept the invisible support. Tears pricked her eyes at their kindness.

"Thank you," she whispered. "I cannot thank you enough."

They helped her fly. Her feet skimmed the ground as they carried her towards the castle. The front door used to be red, the paint peeling from the top. Golden rivets tarnished with age were lodged around the frame, and a bronze lion held the knocker in its mouth.

Light filtered through the cracked door. She stooped and peered through the broken wood. An empty room stood beyond. White sheets covered the furniture, and cobwebs stretched from ceiling to floor.

Sorcha stuck a foot out and nudged the door open. Its groan echoed through the room and bounced up the grand staircase leading to the second story. A cobweb drifted on the air where she had torn it from its place on the door.

"This is the castle of Hy-brasil," she whispered. Sorcha reached up and caught the cobweb, transferring it and the spider to the wall. "Sorry."

Twitching her skirts to the side, Sorcha stepped into the castle with wide eyes. Dim light caught upon dust motes, turning the room to starlight.

"She made it," a familiar voice grumbled.

"I did," Sorcha replied. "You're Cian, are you not?"

"Humans aren't meant to know our names. I didn't give you that, ungrateful wretch."

"But I have it now, and I made it to the castle."

"With help."

She shrugged. "Does it matter? I'm here all the same, and now I would like to speak to the Tuatha dé Danann."

"The master isn't taking visitors."

There was a faint outline of a short figure in the shadows of the stairwell. Dust had settled upon his shoulders, far too round to be human and shuddering in anger. Sorcha narrowed her eyes on him and committed the little details to memory.

"I'm afraid I cannot give him that choice. Bring me to him."

"I'm not your errand boy."

"Then tell me the way." Sorcha put steel into her voice. She willed sharp edges into the words, so he would have no choice but to obey.

The Fae man grumbled. "If you think that will scare me—"

"It should," she interrupted. "You don't know me, gnome. You take a great risk in underestimating me."

She threw the words out in hopes her memory served true. Gnomes were short, squat creatures with round bodies and rolls of fat. The dust settling revealed a body type very similar to that.

Cian shivered and tossed the dust back into the air. "Good guess."

"Tell me the way to your master."

"What will you give me in return?"

"I will make no more deals with the Fae!" Her shout hurt her ears. "Now."

"Up the staircase then, girl. Keep going straight to the throne room. You can't miss it."

"Throne room?" She coughed in surprise.

"What, did you think the master would be in his receiving room? The throne room, girl. You want to see the master so bad? Perhaps you should prepare for what you will meet."

She refused to look towards him. Clothing stiff, body aching, face burning from sun and salt, she ascended the stairs with her head held high. She would not break nor would she yield.

Sorcha resolved to be stronger than she had ever been before. Stronger than when she helped her first patient's child into the world. More capable than when her father fell ill, and her sisters needed her to be the stable one. More brave than the first time she cut into a stranger's body and pulled out beetles hoping they wouldn't turn and attack her.

The Fae would not look at her with pity. The master was even less likely to give her any kind of clemency. She would need her wits about her. Sorcha knew convincing a Fae to leave this isle would be nigh impossible.

But she had to try.

The staircase led to more ancient stones. One wall had crumbled to dust revealing a room filled to the brim with tattered paintings. She didn't pause, although her curiosity piqued.

At the end of the castle, another stairwell descended. Chandeliers covered in cobwebs dripped spiders instead of gems. The white marble floor had once been a remarkable sight. Now, cracks ran like rivers through a canyon, marring the once opulent surface.

Stairs led up to a dais covered by moth-eaten gray fabric. The throne loomed in the darkness, outlined by antlers and horns jutting out in all directions. Sorcha could only see heavy boots leading up to thick, muscular legs. Shadows blanketed the rest of him.

The Tuatha dé Danann was a man.

"I have journeyed across the sea, through hardships and storm, to make a deal with you, m'lord." She hesitated before the throne, unsure whether she should continue.

His boots shifted. A heel nudged enough to reveal a perfect footprint in the dust. How long had he sat there? Had he been waiting for her?

"I no longer make deals with humans."

There was something wrong with his voice. It was the grating edge of rock against the bones of the earth. It scratched down her spine and made her palms tingle. She gasped.

"The MacNara twins sent me, and they said you would—"

"The MacNara twins?"

"Yes, m'lord. They said you would help."

"Did they? Perhaps they mistook me for someone else."

"I—" she stuttered over her words. "A-are you connected to the human world at all? Do you know what's going on out there?"

"I have no concern for human strife."

She gathered bunches of her stiff skirt into her fists. "We're suffering from a blood beetle plague. We cannot survive if we do not have the cure, and the MacNara twins said they would help if I brought you back to them. I beg—"

"I see little begging," he growled.

Sorcha's mind whirled. He wasn't letting her finish! How could she beg if he wouldn't give her the chance to speak?

"The blood beetles eat humans from the inside out. We cannot stop them on our own, and I need you to—"

"Need?"

"Yes!" she exclaimed. "Need. There is no other way to find a cure. The twins promised me that all I have to do is bring you back—"

"They lied." The shadows bunched and coiled.

"Fae cannot lie."

"Then they twisted the truth. I can tell you now, girl, the MacNara twins do not have the cure for the blood beetles. Now go."

Her chest clenched in horror. They had to have the cure. She hadn't traveled all this way only to discover that the faeries had tricked her.

"Go?" she repeated. "Where will I go? This is an island!"

"I don't care where you go. Hy-brasil is no place for one such as you."

Had she failed? He remained in the shadows, barely moving except his damned foot that created more mysteries than it solved. Sorcha only knew his voice grated on her nerves, his imperious nature made her palms itch to smack him, and his refusal to help suggested he was a heartless creature with no care for others.

How dare he?

"My family will die if I do not find this cure."

"You are so concerned over death, I wonder if you have any other thoughts in your head."

Sorcha's mouth gaped open before her cheeks flushed bright red with anger. "Do you have any concern over the welfare of others?"

"Little for those who threaten my staff."

"The gnome at the door?" She swung an arm wildly in the direction from whence she came. "He is one of the rudest, most foul creatures I have ever met! I will not apologize for my tone nor my words."

"Humans rarely have any sympathy for the Fae. Yet, you seem to think I owe you a boon for…what? Existing?"

"Are you so cruel you cannot feel even the smallest amount of sympathy for my people?"

The damned boot she had been staring at shifted again. A surge of triumph straightened her spine.

"I am known for my cruelty. And, it seems, so are you," he growled.

"Your judgment is cast quickly for a man who will not even show his face."

"The sight of my face is not one for the faint of heart."

"Then you willingly admit to being a coward and a boor?"

"A coward?" His voice deepened, slicing through the darkness and cracking against the stone. It shook her ribs and vibrated through her body. "You dare accuse me so?"

"I dare much for the well-being of my family." Sorcha's voice shook with righteous indignation but she shivered in fear.

The shadows quaked, and the drapes around the throne billowed as he stood up…and up…and up.

Her brow wrinkled in worry as she stared at his great height. Good lord, how big was he?

A cloak concealed much of his figure. Like great leathery wings, the dark fabric billowed as he stepped down the stairs towards her. Each measured step clunked hard. The cracked marble creaked.

He didn't have to rush towards her to intimidate. The sheer size of him made her shiver in apprehension. Broad shoulders, trim waist, and a hood covering his head were all she could make out, even at this close distance. Sorcha held her breath and stood her ground.

She would not show fear.

He stopped only when his toes were a hair's breadth from hers. Sorcha stared into the darkness of his hood, her head barely reaching his biceps. She set her jaw and squared her shoulders. Whatever he would say could not be worse than their previous words.

"You know very little of me, human." His breath brushed her hair, carrying the scent of mint and citrus.

"I can confidently say I find your morals, and thusly your character, to be abhorrent."

"On what are you basing these accusations?"

"You have forced your servants to call you master. You hide your face and intimidate a visitor seeking help. And then, you go so far as to refuse to provide aid to those who need it. Those, sir, are the facts upon which I judge you."

"Have you no care nor discretion for your own survival? You berate a creature of superior strength!"

"Superior? Sir, I find you lacking in every sense of the term."

His aggressive way of arguing made her think she had gotten through his thick hide, but she had been wrong.

His spine straightened, and his shoulders squared. The cloak drew tight across his chest and he stepped away from her. He took the air with him, stealing it from her lungs, as a blast of cold air pushed her back, such was his anger.

"Go," he said.

"I have nowhere to go," Sorcha repeated. "If you would stop being so stubborn—"

She didn't think. She reached out, grasped ahold of the cloak he wore, and yanked.

The fabric slid from his shoulders and revealed his horrific face.

Light speared across the misshapen form. Multiple marks gouged the flesh from his cheeks, forehead, and chin. She might have forgiven a scar, for they suggested heroic deeds. Even a birthmark or disfigurement from childhood could have been easily overlooked. But this?

Open wounds had turned to fissures in the stone of his face. Crystals grew from them, some violet, some precious gems, and a hint of color-changing opal, all jutting from his flesh and tainting whatever humanity he may have once held. They stretched far up the sides of his head, shaved other than a crop of hair at the top.

He might have been a handsome man once. His jaw was square, his lips full, and his eyes a piercing blue that stared straight into her soul.

Sorcha gasped as she met his gaze. Ice froze her veins and fear made her teeth chatter. And yet, warmth bloomed deep in her belly. His eyes were beautiful, expressive, and filled with so much pain.

"What happened to you?" she whispered.

He lunged towards her. With a gasp, she threw her hands up to cover her face. She knew that look. Sorcha had grown up in a brothel. The desire to strike a woman was easy to recognize in a man's expression.

He didn't hit her. Instead, his hand wrapped around her wrist with a punishing grip. Stone bit into the sensitive flesh, and she whimpered.

"Is this what you wanted to see?" he growled, so close to her face that their noses touched.

"I meant no disrespect."

He didn't give her even a moment of respite. He dragged her from the throne room so quickly she slid across the floor until she got her bearings. Only then did she jog to keep up with him.

Sorcha yanked on her arm. "Let me go!"

"No."

"Let me go, I said!"

"I heard you." His voice rumbled down the hallway and sent footsteps skittering.

"Where are you taking me?"

"You argue that you cannot leave this cursed isle, then insult me in the next breath. So, princess, I am taking you to your room."

"Room?" She dug in her heels, forcing him to drag her. "Is there a decent available room in this spider-ridden ruin?"

His fingers squeezed the delicate bones of her wrist, making her gasp in pain. "Are you afraid of spiders?"

"I'm afraid of very little."

"Good."

Sorcha winced as his shoulder struck the broken door. No wonder it had cracked nearly in half. The man treated himself like a battering ram rather than a person.

Stones dug into her heels as he yanked her outside, but she refused to yelp. He did not get the satisfaction of knowing the journey was just as painful as his stony grip.

"I can walk without you dragging me!" she shouted.

"I can hear without you screaming."

He picked up speed, then she couldn't speak anymore. Her breath tasted like blood as her lungs worked overdrive to keep up with him. The straps of her pack dug into her shoulders and arms. Her feet grew numb as the skin scraped off, and still he dragged her towards the opposite end of the isle.

By the time they reached his destination, she was ready to fall over. Dehydration and hunger weakened her mind and body.

He pointed to a small hut in what appeared to be a moor hanging on the edge of the ocean. Mist swirled across the swamp and moss.

"Your new abode," he growled.

Sorcha forced her eyes to narrow, to take in the details that her mind wanted to ignore. The hut hovered over the water on stilts and stretched out into the bay. Heather grew up to the salty water, crumbling and dying at the edges.

The hut's image wavered, as though she were looking through hot air. Runes appeared etched into the wooden walls and along the ramp leading to it. She suddenly understood the blinking lights hovering in the air near it.

"That's a hag's hut," she said.

"Astute. You should be right at home."

"Those are incredibly dangerous for anyone who does not practice magic. I cannot stay there."

"You can, and you will."

He grabbed her arm again, swinging her around onto the ramp and shoving her shoulders for good measure. He waved a hand in the air. Glimmering light rose from the ground into the sky.

Sorcha lurched forward and hit an invisible wall.

"What did you do?" she croaked as she slammed her fists in the air. "What did you do!"

"I'm keeping you here. Survive, human. Eventually, I might listen to your inquiry."

He turned and walked away.

Sorcha nearly choked on her own tongue. He walked away? He left her with the most dangerous of evil magics behind her, and then just walked away?

"How dare you?" she screamed. "Don't leave me here! You cannot!"

He could, and he did.

She pressed her hands and forehead against the shield he placed at the edge of the dock and sighed. There was no possible way she would even attempt to stay in that hut.

Sorcha turned and glanced at the runes which kept blinking in and out of sight.

"Think. What are your other options, Sorcha? How can you fix this?"

She scanned the surrounding area, stepping towards the edge of the ramp to peer into the water. White glowing eyes blinked back at her.

"Not the water then," she murmured. "So…um…"

The runes on the door glowed a bright red, but were dulled to a rusty hue from the splatter of aged chicken blood. Sorcha recognized the arcing patterns upon the wood.

"The hard way it is."

She secured her pack on her shoulders and stepped up the ramp. The hag stone between her breasts slid free. She pressed it to her lips, then held it to her eye and watched the spells melt away.

It was a relatively simple protective curse. There were parts of her mother's books which spoke of pagan rituals. This spell she recognized from the pages of a black book she never should've read.

Her fingers itched to try out what she had learned, to dismantle the circles drawn by witches of old. However, such aged curses were useful. Now she could be certain there was at least one place on the isle she was safe.

Sorcha reached out and dragged her finger straight down the first rune. The second, she traced the circles and lines without hesitating. And the last, she turned her hand in the air as though she twisted a doorknob.

A harsh crack echoed in the air, and the door swung upon.

Without the hag stone, the interior terrified her. Eviscerated chickens hung from the ceiling in various states of decay, their blood covering the floor until it shone as if polished, and here and there, startlingly white feathers made downy islands in the gore. Human skulls decorated the walls with candles inside them, making the eye sockets glow. Knives, hatchets, and scythes hung on wall brackets while chains dangled above them.

Through the hag stone, the room was entirely different. Although it was a small, single room hut, it was a home, albeit dusty. A dining room table with one place setting was in one corner. Dried fruit balanced in the center, mummified with age. There was a desk in another corner piled high with papers and adorned with ink wells. A small, but quaint bed was against the farthest wall below a window shining in the moonlight.

Sorcha swallowed hard and steeled her nerves.

"Faeries of this household, I mean no disrespect. I am a weary traveler who searches for a place to rest my head. This home is safe, it is warm, and I vow I will touch nothing which is not mine. If your hospitality stretches so far as to gift food and drink, I will assist in cleaning this household."

For a moment, she heard nothing. Silence rang as loud as her words. She could only hope she had not offended whatever brownies or redcaps remained.

She twisted her fingers and listened. Her patience was rewarded. Soft chirping sounds heralded faerie movement. Pattering footsteps started towards her, and she felt the slightest of nudges against her thigh.

Looking down, she saw that a line on the floor had smudged.

"Salt?" she whispered. Or at least something similar. The white powder now held a fingerprint in it, marring the smooth line.

When she looked back up, the room was no longer frightening nor haunted. It was merely a room to the naked eye.

"Thank you," she said. "Your kindness knows no bounds. I will honor the words I spoke before entering."

She made her way to the bed and dumped her pack on the ground. Her back groaned with the movement, balance shifting with sudden lightheadedness. She wasn't done yet.

Her hands knew where the small jar of sugar was, even if her mind wasn't entirely functioning. Sorcha rummaged through her pack and came up with the tiny clay jar. It always paid to have some kind of gift for the Fae. She'd learned this lesson time and time again until her pockets were always full.

For good measure, she also snagged a tiny coin. The dim moonlight gleamed off the edges, for she had polished it many times over. Sorcha called it her lucky coin, and it seemed appropriate to give away now.

"I will share what little I have with you," she murmured. "They are small, but I believe I may find more tomorrow. Not as payment, I know your ways."

Chairs screeched as she turned, rocking as they thumped onto the floor. Sorcha blinked at the table now clean of all dust and removed of dirty plates.

"Well, you didn't have to go through all that trouble."

A mug appeared out of thin air and plunked onto the table.

Sorcha was stunned. She wanted to hold the hag stone to her eye just to get a look at the hidden faeries. They couldn't be more terrifying a sight than their master.

"You are too kind," she breathed. "I will leave my things above the fireplace. Please enjoy them, and I'm sorry there's not more."

Hardly five strides carried her to the other end of the hut. She leaned, blew the dust off the hearth, and set her items down. The brownie in her small room at the brothel liked to climb. She always hid little gifts in the rafters just to give it a reason for adventure.

They were naturally curious creatures, something she always respected about them. Brownies, although sometimes a nuisance, were helpful. They wanted to do everything they could, and when they couldn't, lost their minds.

Her brow furrowed. She hoped that wasn't what she was dealing with here. House brownies easily turned to boggarts if they didn't keep busy. And the room had been dusty…

She turned. "Are you brownies?"

There was no response.

"It will not make me think ill of you. It's merely easier for me to know what you might like in the cupboards. The brownie at my home was fond of honey, but I met a boggart once, and he was much fonder of fresh bread."

The cup on the table tilted.

Sorcha smiled. "A boggart then. I'll do my best to steal something from that nasty Tuatha dé Danann's kitchen. We'll have this place shining, and then I'll bake fresh bread, as long as you don't pull the covers off me."

She watched the mug dance back and forth. Apparently, that was the correct thing to say.

The soft swishing sound of her skirts lulled her senses into a stupor. Sorcha stumbled to the bed and fell face down. It didn't matter that cobwebs tangled in her hair or that the layer of dust was so thick it bounced with her and then returned to the mattress. She was so exhausted, she could even sleep through the boggart placing clammy hands on her cheeks as it checked to make sure she was alive.

She slept for the rest of the afternoon, through the night, and well into the morning. However, it felt only a few seconds until she was blinking her eyes at the dappled sunlight shining through the hut window.

Blinking, she groggily realized that a soft sound had awakened her. Tapping, like a spoon against ceramic, although that couldn't be right. She remembered very clearly that she was in a hag's hut which had seen better days. Even the boggart couldn't have gotten a tea set in such a short amount of time.

Sorcha sat straight up in bed, the tangled mat of her red hair sticking out at odd angles. The room had completely changed overnight. The dust and dirt was piled in a corner, the floors revealed to be rich warm wood. The furniture gleamed and the fireplace was scrubbed clean of all grime and smoke stain.

Something clinked again, drawing her attention to the kitchen table near another window. Two chairs framed it, one currently occupied by a short woman with a mop of white hair. An aged, though clean, kirtle touched the floor. Tiny pink flowers decorated the pale fabric, and must have been hand-painted. Her white hair smoothed into a large bun, but strands of frizzy curls had freed themselves.

The strange woman set her spoon on the saucer and sipped at her tea.

Sorcha blinked. "Am I still in Hy-brasil?"

"I believe so. If I'm in Hy-brasil, then you must be here, too." The strange woman had a nice voice. Comforting, like that of a warm blanket on a chilled autumn day. It was familiar although Sorcha couldn't put her finger on why.

Large, brown eyes watched her every movement as Sorcha fiddled with the blanket covering her legs. "I don't remember tucking myself into bed."

"Oh, I assume that was the boggart, dearie. Although, I'd say she is well on her way back to brownie now, thanks to you."

"Thanks to me?"

"You gave her something to do, and that's all brownies want."

Sorcha's mind raced, and realization dawned on her like a hammer. "You're the voice I heard on the shoreline. You were with that gnome!"

"It's a good memory you've got there." The woman set her teacup down and smiled. "You can call me Pixie."

"Is that what you are?"

"It is. Are you surprised?"

"I've never met a pixie before," Sorcha said as she gathered the blankets at her chest. "It's an honor, ma'am."

Pixie chortled, the laugh booming out of her chest and shaking the table. "Oh, but you are a sweet little thing! So polite. Boggart, I think you were quite right. She's a fair treat in this horrid place."

"Boggart? Is she here?"

"Of course, dearie. She doesn't want you to see her yet. She came all the way up to the castle, a rarity I might add, to tell us how pleasant you were. You've made her happy giving her something to do and a place to clean. Losing her hag was a terrible blow."

"I—" her head was spinning. Sorcha couldn't keep up with what Pixie was saying, let alone the strange turn this adventure had taken. "I apologize if this seems rude, Pixie, but what are you doing here?"

Pixie sat up straight, setting her cup down so hard the saucer chipped. "How presumptuous of me! Dearie, if I have frightened you in any way, do allow me to apologize. I've come to take you up to the castle, get you some tea, and then..." Her nose wrinkled. "Perhaps a bath if you are amiable?"

"I can honestly say that would be appreciated."

Sorcha pushed the covers back and stretched her aching spine. The pain of her journey had dulled to a persistent stiffness, but it was significantly better than before. Her skin still felt like it was covered in a thin layer of filth, and her hair didn't move when she shifted. Sorcha winced, she needed a bath as soon as humanly possible.

She looked down and frowned. "Who changed me into my underthings?"

"Boggart, dearie. Had quite the time of it as well. You're much larger than she."

"Yet another thing I need to thank you for, Boggart. I'll be sure to cook two loaves of fresh bread for us tonight."

A faint squeak from the corner radiated delight.

Sorcha hobbled towards her pack. Muscles screamed as she bent down to find clothing, so much that a soft whimper escaped her lips.

"Oh, there's enough of that," Pixie grumbled. "We'll throw a cloak over you, and you'll be covered to decency. We don't have the same ridiculous restraints as humans. A body is a body."

"And a body grows chilled," Sorcha pointed out. The idea of leaving without having to tie up the back of her gown sounded lovely. Usually her sisters helped, and she had little reason to change clothing on a ship full of men. Here, she would need help.

"A body will last until it's stuck in the bath."

"I suppose you're right," she stood up only to groan again. "But I still need to find something to wear."

"We have plenty, dearie." Pixie stood up and hopped towards her, surprisingly spry for a woman who looked so old. "Let me help you put your cloak on. It pins at your throat now, doesn't it? There. It's lovely. We'll get you warmed up and fed in a moment!"

Pixie planted her hands on Sorcha's shoulder blades and shoved. For a glamoured being, her strength was impressive. Before Sorcha could blink, they were already outside and moving down the ramp.

Why was it that faeries dragged her around so much? Sorcha's eyes watered in the bright sunlight. "What time is it?"

"Mid-day, dearie. You've been asleep for some time."

"It was a long journey," she said.

"I imagine it would be! Coming from the human world all the way here. You're a brave little thing and polite."

"No braver than the next person." Sorcha tried to focus on the words, staring around her at all the new sights. There were people everywhere. Men and women, dressed in clothing styles from a hundred years ago or more, but still people. They tended the fields, drove herds of sheep out of their pens, laid in the grass, and pointed out clouds to each other. "Are these all faeries?"

"Indeed, they are."

"Why didn't I see them yesterday?" A man walked past them and doffed his shepherd's hat. Sorcha nodded back politely and tugged her cloak tighter around her waist.

"We tend to be shy around humans. One never knows how they will react. Boggart was adamant you were kind, so the others were less hesitant to be seen."

"Word travels fast around here," Sorcha mused.

"It certainly does."

Another man walked past them, his eyes lingering too long upon the gap at the bottom of the cloak which revealed the delicate lines of her ankle bones. Sorcha blushed, and Pixie smacked the back of the man's head as he passed.

"Cretin," Pixie muttered. "No respect for the womenfolk. Those selkie men need to be taken to task."

"That was a selkie?" Sorcha spun to stare at his back. He glanced over his shoulder and winked at her.

"We're not on a tour. Attention back towards the castle, please."

"But—"

"No buts! You aren't meeting a selkie today, or ever, if I have my say."

Sorcha furrowed her brows. "Are they dangerous?"

"To a person's sanity."

"He didn't seem all that bad."

"None of them do." Pixie guided her around the back to the castle, nudging her this way and that until she opened a small wooden gate. "The Fae are notoriously interested in humans. Far more than we should be, I might add. Stay away from faerie men, and you'll be much happier."

Sorcha stepped into the garden beyond the gate and inhaled the sweet scent of growing herbs. It was too early in the year for any plant to be bearing fruit, but tomatoes hung swollen and bright red. Basil spiced the air with a heady flavor while carrot tops tickled her toes.

"This garden is beautiful," she whispered.

"I'm sure Cian will be pleased to hear that."

"The gnome?" Sorcha skirted around a patch of turnips. "Cian is a gardener?"

"Most gnomes are. They're good at it, too. The earth listens to them, you see, and that makes it a lot easier. Come on!"

Sorcha glanced up and realized she'd fallen behind. Pixie was holding open a plain brown door framed by gray stone. Steam billowed out in hot, rolling waves.

"Where does that lead?"

"To the kitchens, dearie."

"I didn't see the kitchens before."

The cobblestone floor was cold against the soles of her bare feet. She curled her toes and held onto the door frame. The scent of pastries, bubbling stew, and strong tea made her head swim. Her stomach clenched in hunger.

Three women puttered around the kitchen. One leaned over a large cauldron, tasting the soup within. Another kneaded dough into a familiar shape while the last ducked behind a curtain. Trickling water striking a basin rained through her senses.

"Come on, dearie," Pixie said. "We'll get you all cleaned up, and then fill that belly of yours."

Sorcha tiptoed around the curtain and gaped at the large metal tub beyond it. "This is too fine for the likes of me."

"Nonsense. There's nothing better than bathing in hot water. In you go."

"I would be fine in a stream—"

"In."

The steely order had Sorcha unclasping her cloak. The fabric fell to the floor with a heavy thump, followed by her white underdress.

"Should I even be here?" she asked. The hot water stung the scrapes on her knees but made her muscles loosen their tight knots. She hissed her pleasure as the steam coated her face.

"Why shouldn't you be? Lean forward, and I'll get your back."

It had been a long time since someone helped Sorcha bathe. She remembered her mother scrubbing vigorously at her dirt-streaked skin. She was always red for days after her baths. In contrast, Sorcha's sisters were far less vigorous when she moved in with them.

"Your master didn't seem keen on having me linger," she said as the sponge slid over her skin.

"Yes, I heard he was rather…harsh with you."

She snorted. "Harsh is one way to describe it."

"He's a good man, but he has a temper."

"Was that his temper? I thought he was merely a brute, leaving little to make a good impression."

Pixie grabbed another bucket of water. "The master can be difficult, but don't let first impressions sway you. If you judge him harshly, he'll do the same for you. Hold your breath."

Water cascaded over her head and down her shoulders. Sorcha stared into the muddy water while clumps of earth swirled with her movement. Bubbles popped, releasing the scent of lemon into the air.

"Have you known him long?" Sorcha asked. The haunting vision of his marred face and electric blue eyes rose in the water.

"For as long as he's been alive. The master was a handsome child." Pixie paused. "And is still a handsome man."

She wanted to disagree. The words were on the tip of her tongue to say he wasn't handsome at all, that his exterior matched his interior, but she paused. Sorcha had always been quick to judge others. Perhaps now would be a good time to practice patience.

"I couldn't say," she said. "He didn't seem interested in helping me. That didn't add to his appeal."

"Help you? Whatever could the master help you with, dearie?"

Pixie moved behind the tub and tugged Sorcha backwards. Her spine hit the warm metal, and a soft sigh slipped from her lips. The weight of her hair slid out of the water and dangled to the floor. A slight tug suggested Pixie planned to work all the snarls into smooth curls.

"My people are dying," Sorcha said. "A plague is sweeping across our lands, and I can't cure it. No one can. Our doctors are baffled, our herbalists are stumped, and even the mystics shrug their shoulders and say the gods are angry. There is nothing to be done."

"And our master?"

"I was sent here by other Tuatha dé Danann. They said if I brought him back they would give me the cure. My father is dying, and my sisters are likely to grow ill afterwards. I had to do something."

The rasp of the brush lulled her senses. Her eyes drifted shut as the comforting rhythm reminded her body she had endured a significant journey.

"I'm sure if you told the master all that he'd help."

"He's already said no, but he doesn't know how determined I am."

"It's a good trait to have."

"Is it?" Sorcha laughed. "Perhaps I could bring you home with me, and you could tell my neighbors that. They only put up with me, because I'm a healer."

"A healer?" the Pixie's voice sparkled. "We don't have one of those."

She wanted to reply, but her muscles were so relaxed that all she could manage was a quiet murmur. The bath was exactly what she needed, although she hadn't known it before. Every ache disappeared. Every worry dissolved. She focused upon the repetitive movement of the brush, and let her mind quiet.

All good things came to an end. Eventually, the water chilled, and Pixie made it to the top of Sorcha's head.

"Come now, let's get you dressed." Pixie passed a gentle hand over Sorcha's head.

Tears pricked and water blurred the edges of Sorcha's vision. She hadn't expected to find people who were so genuinely good-hearted. It was nearly her undoing.

"Thank you," she whispered and stood. The water sluiced off her body, pouring in waterfalls from her breasts, lingering in the valleys of her hips.

Pixie tsked. "You need to gain weight, dearie. You're positively thin."

"I'm not from royalty. I'm working class."

"That doesn't make a difference to me. Come here."

The towel in Pixie's hands snapped as she held it out. Another strange moment. No one dried Sorcha off after her bath except herself. Even her mother had let Sorcha wrap herself in a towel before scrubbing her hair.

The soft towel dragged over every inch of Sorcha's body with expert precision. Pixie didn't hesitate as if she had done this her entire life.

"Pixie?" Sorcha asked. "What did you do before you came to Hy-brasil?"

The other woman hesitated for a moment. "I was a lady's maid to the most beautiful of Seelie women."

"Who?"

"The Queen Neve, of course."

"Queen?" Sorcha let out a long breath through her teeth. "That's a high-ranking position."

"Queen usually is."

"No, I mean the Queen's maid. That must have been an incredible experience. I envy you."

Pixie looked at her with shock in her eyes and burst into laughter. "Dearie, you are a delight! I have never in my life had anyone envy me for being a maid." She laughed so hard that she handed the towel to Sorcha. "High ranking for being a Queen's maid. The thought!"

With a soft smile on her face, Sorcha finished toweling herself dry. "It's a rather remarkable position, you must admit."

Twisted shadows danced behind the blinds and between the maids drifting through the room. Sorcha tilted her head to the side and watched the wings, feathers, and misshapen forms revealed by their shadows. They likely weren't aware she could see their true forms.

She hoped, someday, they might walk without the glamour in place. Their fear was warranted. Humans didn't react well to strange creatures. Sorcha refused to believe she would recoil from their appearances.

That would require she stay. She shook herself. Staying on this island wasn't a part of the plan, and she had to believe the Tuatha dé Danann would at least listen. Her journey was of great importance. He had to see reason.

"Pixie?" she called out. "Where is your master today?"

"Training in the yard, I would suspect. That's where he usually is."

"Training?"

"Oh, yes," Pixie said as she returned. She held a pale green gown in her hands, the swath of fabric nearly touching the floor. "He's a very impressive warrior, although I'll let him tell you those stories. I believe this will look lovely with that hair of yours."

She reached out and traced a finger across the dress. Velvet, the material of nobility.

"I cannot wear this," Sorcha said. "I'll ruin it."

"No one else is wearing it. You might as well ruin it or the moths will."

Yearning flooded through her, sparkling at the ends of her fingertips as she reached for the gown. She'd never worn such fine fabric before. The brothel prided itself on providing well-groomed, beautiful women to its customers, but the velvets were saved for her sisters when important clients came to visit. Sorcha had always worn wool and cotton.

Her fingers trailed over the fabric, pulling it into her arms. "Thank you."

"I enjoy decorating pretty things, dearie. Now put that on, and we'll get you some food."

Sorcha dragged the dress over her head and tied the towel along the wet length of her hair. Someone had set up a feast on the table. Fresh fruit, vegetables, lettuce, and bread overflowed their bowls. A jug of cold water sat within easy reach.

She fell onto her seat and stared in disbelief. "This is for me?"

"Well, it's not much," Pixie sniffed. "But it must do for now."

"This is more than I ever would have asked for. You should have sent me on my way with an apple."

"We have better hospitality than that. Eat up."

Sorcha shoveled food into her mouth and gulped glass after glass of water. Her stomach could rebel later. This was more food than she'd seen in weeks. The water tasted like the first snowfall.

When her belly ached and her throat closed at the thought of more, she pushed her plate back and sighed.

"I hate to be more of a bother," she began, "but do you have extra flour and butter? I'd like to make bread for Boggart, but have no supplies."

"For Boggart?" Pixie repeated. "Brownies prefer honey, dearie."

"She's not a brownie anymore and seemed very excited about bread."

"I suppose that hut has a kitchen, doesn't it? All right, then. We'll give you enough to stock your kitchen, and then you won't be a bother here."

The faeries filled her arms with everything she could need. So much food that Sorcha needed a pack which was quickly produced and stuffed to the brim.

They were kind and gracious almost to the point of suspicion. Sorcha's brows drew together as she left the kitchen with a shaking head. It made little sense for them to change their minds so quickly. One day they were invisible, and the next, they were making friends? It all seemed rather odd.

"What are you doing here?" The grumpy voice behind her was familiar.

Sorcha turned and met the gaze of Cian, the gnome. Not the glamoured human, not the invisible voice, but the short, squat gnome. Rolls of fat poured into the vague shape of a face. Two eyes, a nose, and a wide split mouth on pasty pale skin, all underneath the wide brim of a brown hat. He had shoved himself into clothing, buttons threatening to pop off under the stress. He wore no shoes, because his toenails were so long they curled into the ground.

"Cian," she said with a hesitant nod.

"You don't even have the good sense to run screaming?"

"I have your name. Why would I scream?"

"Gnomes are frightening creatures. We used to eat humans."

"'Used to' is the operative phrase there, I imagine," she said as she nudged the fence gate open with her hip. "Thank you for reminding me that not everyone here is as kind as the faeries in the kitchen."

"Brownies. They always want to take care of something. They'll smother you to death if you let them!"

She had come to the same conclusion. The gate slammed shut behind her, and she skirted back down the lane towards the hag's hut.

The faeries were kind, but almost too kind. She didn't remember the stories about brownies, but fully intended to put Boggart to good use. Plying someone with bread for information was easy enough, though perhaps a bit devious.

It would work out best for them both in the long run. She needed more information, and Boggart was the perfect person to ask.

Chapter 10

"She asked for what?" Eamonn's voice echoed in his chamber.

"The ingredients for bread, master."

"She didn't ask for the bread itself?"

"No. She said she wanted to bake the bread for Bronagh herself."

He leaned back in the high chair of his desk. Steepling his fingers, he pressed them against his lips. "Why would she want to do that? The boggart is hardly something to waste her time on."

"Perhaps she considers Bronagh worth her time, master."

He hadn't thought of that. Boggarts and those of the lesser Fae were traditionally beneath the Tuatha dé Danann. Their jobs were clear. Slaves, footmen, sometimes maids if they were pretty enough. Never in his life had he seen anyone take the time to treat them with respect.

The suggestion that the human cared was ridiculous. She had been so furious, charging into his throne room like she owned the place. Her eyes spat fire, while her words seared his pride. He refused to believe her as kind as Oona thought.

There was a warrior in her.

Oona bustled behind him, cleaning every inch of his quarters. She was good at that. He had never seen another pixie so willing to do a maid's job. She was the best, and the only acceptable maid to bring with him to this cursed place.

He much preferred the pixie without her glamour. The old woman's disguise grated on his nerves. Pixies were lithe creatures, with a cap of flower petals instead of hair. Hers was a pale dusky lavender, matching the shimmering wings she wore draped around her shoulders.

"Where is she now?" he asked.

"The same place as last night. The hag's hut."

"She went back?"

"Without complaint, I might add."

Eamonn leaned forward and pressed his elbows against the desk. "Why?"

"To cook bread for Bronagh."

"Yes, but why else? There has to be a reason."

Oona sighed. She crossed around to the front of his desk and knelt before him. "You will hurt yourself trying to understand the human. You know full well it's impossible."

"I cannot accept that as truth."

"Then you will go mad. Let it go, master. Some things you will never understand."

He couldn't let it go. He closed his eyes and saw her flashing green eyes. Emeralds and rainforests hid in her gaze, equally dangerous and cutting. It was strange he would remember her eyes, since the rest of her was unimpressive.

No self-respecting Seelie would ever entertain royalty while looking like they rolled in a pig's pen. The woman had been disgusting. Seaweed stuck in her hair, clothing wrinkled and smudged with dirt. One foot bare, the other covered by a threadbare slipper.

Yet, she'd held herself with the grace of a queen.

Perhaps that explained how she'd bewitched him. She was an enigma, an oddity, a strange creature who made little sense. She shouldn't exist, and yet, here she was.

"No human has ever come to Hy-brasil, have they?" he asked.

"Not that I know of, master."

"So how did she get here?"

"I wouldn't know. It's not my place to question how people arrive, only to take care of them when they do."

He snorted. "Cian made quite the impression."

"That was my fault," Oona winced. "I said his name in front of the girl. I didn't think she could hear us while we held our glamours, but somehow she did."

"He's angry at you?"

"When is he not?" She stood up from his floor and scowled at him. "You're stalling. What are you going to do about her?"

"Who?" Eamonn lifted an eyebrow and leaned back in his chair. For good measure, he lifted his booted feet onto the desk.

"Stop teasing me! It's bad for my health. You know full well who I'm speaking of. She's a nice little thing, and it's not settling well with me that you were so rude."

"Did I ask for an opinion?"

"No, but I'm giving one. She is the sweetest little thing that has washed ashore in nigh two hundred years. You need to apologize to her—" Oona lifted a hand when he opened his mouth, "—apologize, and then invite her to stay here. It's not safe to live in that hut."

Eamonn wanted to fly across the table and strangle her. Apologize? To that miscreant who shouldn't be on this isle to begin with? He had more things to worry about than the feelings of a silly little girl.

Memories of his brother flashed through his mind. His throat tightened as it had when the noose cinched tight across his Adam's apple. The gems at his neck cast a dim glow across his clasped fingers.

Oona made a soft sound of distress and looked away. "I meant no disrespect, master."

"I'm certain you didn't. You have always been one of my favored servants, and for that I spoil you. Do not make me regret that."

She bowed and turned to leave. He met her gaze as she hesitated by the door. "Master, if I may be so bold, perhaps we no longer wish you to see us as servants. We see you as family, my dear, and someday we hope you'll see us the same."

Her skirts swirled as she raced from the room.

He frowned. Was that how his people saw him? As a mysterious figure who cared little for them?

Long ago, when he was young and drunk on the idea of power, he had thought that way. Eamonn stood, clasping his hands behind his back as he wandered to the portrait of his mother. Her golden hair fell straight without a single strand out of place.

He remembered her like this. Always perfect, no matter what the situation. Even when they hanged him.

"What would you do, Mathair?" he murmured. "The girl is a problem.

A distraction."

She was the last thing he needed. There were only a few more months to prepare. Even then, he wasn't certain if he would manage. Eamonn walked a path leading only to death.

But a fair, red-headed lass haunted his steps. She had only been here for one night, and already he had not slept. What more would she do?

"Perhaps she is a witch," he said. "A temptress sent by my brother to ensure I never return home."

The thought was likely. Fionn would do anything to keep the Seelie throne.

Growling, Eamonn spun on his heel. Long legs carried him to a wall carved with the image of a great bird. He pressed his palm against a loose stone, pushing hard until the wall gave and revealed a crystal embedded within the structure. Gem touched gem, and the wall shifted.

Beyond, a room glowed, filled to the brim with Fae artifacts. Magic swirled in the air. It danced upon his skin, skittering across the crystals of his face and neck. He was not cursed; Eamonn had tested that immediately once the affliction made itself known. But magic enjoyed touching him all the same.

Brushing the dust motes aside, he reached for a small handheld mirror. Carved roses twined from the handle and bloomed at the top. He thought it rather frivolous. Magical objects always were.

"Show me the red-headed lass." He leaned forward and breathed on the glass. The mirror swirled with mist and cleared. No longer reflecting the room, it revealed to him the interior of the hag's hut.

"What?" he growled. "There must be trickery here."

That was not the girl who had marched into his throne room with anger burning her cheeks. The beauty spinning in circles looked more like a Fae lady.

Her hair, which he remembered as matted and soiled, spun around her in a wide arc. Curls bounced with her movements as she hopped from side to side, arms held as if a partner swung her around. The green velvet dress hugging her curves spun in a perfect circle as she twisted and turned.

He recognized that dance. The humans practiced it at Beltane. The women bent and swayed with lively music.

She danced alone. Her hands clapped in time to music that did not play, and the smile stretched across her face spoke of pure glee.

Eamonn's lips quirked to the side. She was a horrible dancer. Far too bouncy, no control over her limbs or facial expressions, and obviously untrained. Yet, there was still something compelling about her joy.

"This is not the muddy creature with the personality of a shrew," he murmured. "What other secrets do you hold, little human?"

The mirror heard his request, and the image shifted closer as the woman stopped dancing. Her ears were slightly pointed, he realized.

"Curiouser and curiouser."

The burning need in his stomach expanded, blossoming into a full-blown red haze of want and desire. He had to find out more about her. Where she came from, why she was here, what her plans were.

Eamonn brushed aside the wonderment of how she was raised, who had taught her the secrets of the Fae, and why her ears were tipped with faerie points. These were frivolous things which held little weight. They weren't important.

She wasn't important.

And yet…he lifted his head and shouted, "Oona!"

The pixie hadn't gone far. He heard the door open and her voice call out, "Yes, master?"

"Invite her to dinner."

"Master, she requested privacy tonight."

"What?" He dropped the mirror and strode into his parlor. "She said what?"

"She requested that Bronagh and she have a quiet evening to get to know each other."

"Why?"

Oona shrugged. "I would imagine she wishes to rest after her long journey."

"No, she's too smart for that." Eamonn couldn't imagine she didn't have some kind of plan. She was far too dedicated to her cause. Perhaps he was thinking too much like a warrior, and not enough like a man. "How much does Bronagh know about the castle?"

"As much as anyone, I would imagine. She used to live here."

"Would she remember many of its secrets?"

"Maybe?" Oona blinked and twisted her hands together. "You don't think the girl has any ulterior motives? Master, she's been very kind."

"Even the kindest of people can be coy. And clever. I would like to be certain she isn't plotting anything sinister."

Oona threw her hands up in the air. "She's the least sinister person I've ever met!"

"And that would make her an incredible spy, wouldn't it?"

He lifted an eyebrow and reached for his cloak. He would find out just how dangerous this woman might be. Although his people might think him indifferent, they were all he had.

With an embellished swirl, the cloak settled upon his shoulders, and he strode across the battlements.

Chapter 11

"You see, Boggart, it's rather easy to make bread," Sorcha said as she kneaded the dough into a rough shape.

The answering squeak made her smile. It wasn't a very supportive squeak, nor did it sound as if the faerie believed her. No matter. The bread would taste wonderful.

Homesickness overwhelmed her as the smell of flour and baking bread filled the small hut. Her sisters loved fresh bread, and Sorcha always made certain it was ready for them at the end of the night. They never wasted a scrap. The scent made the brothel feel more like a home rather than a workplace, and giggles had lifted their spirits to the rafters for hours every night.

She missed them more than anything else. Her eyes drifted towards the moon peeking through the window, and she sent a silent good night to her siblings.

All her hopes and wishes lifted into the air and drifted out to sea. She prayed they were healthy and happy. She hoped Rosaleen had taken up that kind nobleman and now lived in wealth and comfort, and Briana remembered to relax. Sorcha made the sign of the cross over her chest and breathed her worry into the moonlight.

"Please keep Papa alive."

She couldn't force those things to happen, not from here. Sorcha resorted to wishes and dreams. Perhaps the Tuatha dé Danann would hear her and see that her family would think kindly upon her choices.

A squeak interrupted her thoughts.

"Oh?" Sorcha turned and placed a hand on her hip. "And just what is that supposed to mean?"

Boggart still refused to speak although Sorcha was certain it could. Soft chirps were its only form of communication, and it remained glamoured.

Sorcha scanned the hut, trying to find whatever had made Boggart speak. The bread was over the fire, but it wasn't burning. No bugs had come in through the open window. The fire was roaring at the correct rate and wouldn't run too hot.

Nothing was amiss. Sorcha shrugged and shook her head. "I'm sorry. I don't know what you're trying to tell me. This would be easier if you would speak."

Another squeak, much louder than the first, echoed in the room.

"I don't know what you want, Boggart."

Multiple squeaks came from the creature who shimmered into view. Boggart dropped its glamour and revealed its true form. Skinny, wrinkled, and lightly dusted with white fur that smoothed over bare breasts, she resembled an albino rat. Her head hardly reached the top of the bed.

She pointed a knobby hand at the door. Sorcha noted that Boggart's fingertips were bulbous before glancing where she pointed.

"The door?"

A crashing boom rocked the wooden frame, bending the wood inwards. Sorcha flinched. Her hip struck the clay pot containing all her flour which exploded onto the floor. White puffs fluttered into the air and covered the floor in an impressive starburst.

She cursed and stooped. Her frazzled mind said scoop the flour into her hands and back into the pot. Sorcha dropped to her knees and pulled it all towards her, fruitless in her attempts to clean.

The banging on the door wasn't stopping.

"Who is it?" she called out.

Perhaps the broom would be a more appropriate way to clean this. She looked dubiously over at the straw covered in cobwebs. She'd ruin the flour if she used that. There had to be something cleaner.

Boggart shrieked, bouncing up and down while pointing at the door. Impossibly, the knocking turned thunderous.

Sorcha leaned back, placed her flour covered hands on her thighs, and stared at the ceiling. When had her life turned into babysitting and terrifying moments? She refused to be frightened of someone who couldn't enter the hag's hut, protected by the spell splashed in chicken's blood.

"Boggart, stop screaming."

She didn't listen to Sorcha. Instead, Boggart screamed even louder. Its high-pitched whine dug at Sorcha's ears, a headache blooming inside her skull.

"Please stop knocking!" she shouted. "I'm coming! I just need to take care of this before I—"

The knocking stopped.

Sorcha let out a relieved sigh. She'd taken care of the deep bass. Now she had to make Boggart be quiet.

Leaving the flour for later, she charged towards the panicking Fae. Sorcha knew how to calm children down. In fact, it was one of her better talents. Boggart couldn't be any different from that. She was the same size as one.

Sorcha slid her hands underneath Boggart's armpits and picked her up. Like a child, Boggart wrapped her legs around Sorcha's waist immediately. Panting breaths brushed against her ear, but at least Boggart stopped screaming.

"Shh," Sorcha whispered as she rocked back and forth. "It's all right. Everything is fine. You can stop screaming now, little love."

Although her fur appeared wiry, Boggart was as soft as a rabbit all over her body. Unlike Cian, Boggart wasn't wearing any clothing. One of her feet moved restlessly against Sorcha's stomach.

She only had three toes, Sorcha realized with delight. Three thick, bulbous toes that ended in blunt little black nails.

The pounding started up again. Boggart squeaked and nestled her pointed nose in Sorcha's neck.

"Shh, it's all right," Sorcha repeated as she walked them towards the door. "Nothing is going to happen to you. It's probably Pixie with more food."

She hoped.

With the faerie wrapped around her like a second skin, Sorcha stepped over the massacre of flour and grasped ahold of the door ring. She sent a silent prayer to whatever gods were listening. If this was a will-o'-the-wisp or something equally terrifying, Sorcha would faint dead away.

"Best be safe," she whispered.

She opened the door just a crack, enough to see who was behind it but not let them in.

The dim twilight made it difficult for her to see anything. It was just a blank space on the other side of the door. No walkway, no moon, nothing but black.

Sorcha arched a brow. Now that was unusual.

Something shifted in the darkness, bringing her focus much closer. That wasn't darkness at all, but a black cloth so dark it appeared to be night.

There was only one person on the island who would wear that.

Sorcha nudged the door open the entire way and peered upwards. Outlined by the moon, the master of the isle stared back at her. His cloak made it impossible for her to guess where he was looking, but she could feel the heat of his gaze as if it was a physical touch.

"Good evening," she said. Her words were biting and quick. He was the last person she wanted to see tonight.

"What is that?"

Sorcha blinked. "You must be more specific."

"In your arms."

"Oh," she glanced down at Boggart, who tightened her hold upon Sorcha's neck. "This is Boggart."

"I know who it is, but why isn't she glamoured?"

"You frightened her."

"I frightened her?" he growled.

"That incessant knocking would frighten even the bravest of beasts."

The fire crackled, an ember shooting across the room. Its light cast a brief glow across his features, revealing a glint in his eyes which made Sorcha shiver.

"But not you." His voice was a physical caress, dancing down her spine until it curled her toes.

"I am neither man nor beast, sir. You'll find women are far more difficult to frighten."

She turned away from him. He was ruining all her plans. Now Boggart was too scared for bribery, and Macha knew how long it would take until Sorcha could get her information. The tiny creature was fragile.

Anger coursed through her veins until a flush burned her cheeks. She wanted to fly at him, to scratch at the ugly crystals marring his face and scream that he had no right. The ridiculous, pompous, overbearing ass that he was.

Through all her raging emotions, her hands remained gentle upon Boggart. She soothed the creature with soft circular motions and laid her on the bed.

"There, there," she murmured. "You stay here and I'll make him go away. Will that help?"

Boggart nodded.

"Good. Hide under the covers, and I'll come get you when he's gone."

This would be easy. It was exactly what Sorcha wanted, and now she had an excuse to usher him away. Hopefully, Boggart would then calm down, and Sorcha could sweet-talk her for information about the very man she was forcing to leave.

She wiped her hands against her skirt and marched towards the door with renewed purpose.

"I'm afraid I must ask you to leave," she said.

"No."

He said the word as if it ended the argument. As if just by imperiously inserting himself into her life, he could dictate what he wanted, however he wanted it.

She blinked at him. "Excuse me?"

"No."

"Might I ask why you are refusing to leave my doorstep even though I have requested that your presence no longer darken it?"

"This isle, and everything on it, is under my command. I do as I please."

He moved to step over the threshold. Sorcha ground her teeth, the muscles of her jaw flexing in anger. "If you take one more step, I will activate every protection spell on this cursed hut and expel you from this room."

His foot hovered just above the interior of her home. "You wouldn't dare."

"I would dare much, sir, against a man who seemingly does not understand boundaries. You must ask a woman if you may enter their abode, and when granted approval, you may do so. If they request you leave, then you remove yourself. As far as lording over all who linger on this isle, I must inquire who named you king. They must be sorely lacking in wits."

If he continued, she would figure out how to activate those spells. She was no witch, but he had no way of knowing she was bluffing.

He inclined his head. "You are correct. My apologies, my lady, I was out of line."

Sorcha found herself incapable of words. This man never ceased to surprise her. He was an ass, of that she was certain, but she hadn't expected an apology. Let alone an admission of guilt. Was he capable of self-reflection?

She cocked her head to the side, looking him up and down. "What did you say?"

"I have not been in court for many years. My manners are not what they used to be." He swept his cloak to the side, crossed an arm over his waist, and bowed. "I humbly request your presence at dinner this evening."

"I'm eating here."

"The castle can offer much finer dining."

"Be that as it may," Sorcha gestured towards the fire, "dinner is already cooking."

"Then as forward as it is, I request you allow me to stay. You need not provide food, merely company."

Sorcha panicked. She didn't want him to stay! How was she going to get Boggart to speak? Stammering, she pointed towards the bed. "I'm afraid Boggart is quite frightened of you. It wouldn't be polite to allow you to stay when—"

"Boggart is not afraid of me." The head of his cloak shook. "She's afraid I plan to take you away from her, like I did her hag. Might I come in?"

"I—." She quirked a brow. "Why did you remove the hag?"

"She was dangerous. Her spells were reaching the castle and wreaking havoc among my people."

"You were protecting the faeries?"

"That is my job. They take care of me, and I protect them."

Sorcha breathed in a slow breath, letting it out with a huff. There were no more arguments, no more walls she could erect. He was being polite. It would be rude to refuse him entry now, and he already thought she was little more than a peasant.

It would not do.

She gestured towards the table, "All right then. Come in and seat yourself. There should be enough for all three of us."

He ducked, entering the hut like a storm. He was far too big. Sorcha gaped at his head which nearly touched the ceiling, and the wide spread of his shoulders, which he had to tilt to fit through the door.

It was no wonder his castle doors were two wide. The man wouldn't be able to fit through anything less.

"I'm afraid I do not have a grand palace to offer, or even complete dining services," she said as she walked towards the bed. "But two seats will have to do."

"I've eaten in worse conditions."

"Have you? I was under the impression 'masters' rarely ate outside their splendorous castles." She leaned over the bed and pulled the blankets away from Boggart's face. "He's eating with us, but has promised I can stay."

"I am no king, nor have I always lived here."

Sorcha lifted Boggart into her arms and started towards the table. The faerie clutched at her dress, tiny claws digging through the fabric and into her skin.

"A curiosity I have no desire to satisfy. I will not pity you, sir, if that is your aim."

"I do not ask for pity, but for patience. It is I who am out of line. I remember manners, but they are no longer second nature. I'm afraid I lost them long before I came to this isle." He sat on her chair, the wood creaking ominously for a few moments before silencing.

She hooked her foot around a stool and dragged it towards the table. She must have been a frightening sight, limping towards him with wood screeching, carrying Boggart who looked more monster than beast. He didn't flinch in the slightest, Sorcha noted with disappointment.

Boggart plunked down on the stool and let go of Sorcha's dress hesitantly. She let out a little huff when Sorcha left her side, watching her master with beady eyes.

"I will not call you 'master'," Sorcha said as she pulled the bread from the fire. "Do you have another name?"

"Some call me Cloch Rí."

"The Stone King?" Sorcha quirked a brow.

He reached a hand forward, placing it in full view on the table. The crystals revealed on each peak of knuckle were just as startling as the first time. Violet-toned and ragged-edged, they turned his hand into more rock than fist.

"Ah," she murmured. "Appropriate then."

She set the bread down with a cloth underneath it. Steam rose into the air, the warm comforting scent easing the tension in her neck. She added cheese and fresh strawberries to a plate beside the bread.

"Cian keeps an impressive garden," she said as she sat down. The hut was suddenly too small, the air too close.

The cloak still covered his face, but she could feel his gaze. It lingered upon her hair, following the spirals of her curls across her shoulders and arms. Highly inappropriate. He had said he wasn't a gentleman, and she believed him.

"He wouldn't like you using his name so freely."

"No, I suppose he wouldn't. Perhaps, that is why I use it." She reached forward and broke off a piece of bread, the steam rose into the air in wispy swirls.

"You do so because it might anger him?"

"Annoy him. I would never use his name against him."

"Many humans have said the same thing, and they always use the name."

"Do you think I am like most humans?"

"I have yet to meet one who shatters my perception of your species."

Sorcha popped the bread into her mouth, chewing to give herself time to think. "You think very poorly of humanity."

"I have been given little reason to think otherwise."

"I could say the same about your people."

Boggart reached for a loaf and tucked it underneath her arm. She gave them both a suspicious glance before hopping off her seat and stalking back towards the bed. Her little chirping grumbles suggested she didn't appreciate such tense conversation when she planned to enjoy her dinner.

Sorcha agreed with her. Mealtimes should be peaceful. A time for family to enjoy each other's company after a long day of work. But there was something about this man that pushed all her buttons, and she couldn't help but argue.

"What grievances against the Fae could you possibly have?"

"Abandonment, for a start. You entered this world with full intention of molding it to your will, and then you disappeared."

"Disappeared?" His hand clenched on the table. "Your people ran us out of our lands."

"I find that difficult to believe when you yourself stated that the Fae are far superior to humankind."

She watched his fist tighten until she heard the creaking of stone and crystal. Slowly, he released his hold in tiny movements. When his palm lay flat upon the table once more, the hood of his cloak tilted to the side.

"You are quick-witted for a human. It is…intriguing."

“That sounds like a compliment.” She reached forward for a strawberry and took a large bite. She would count this as a successful battle in their ongoing war. He might have won the first by throwing her into a nightmarish cottage, but she had recovered quite nicely.

The strawberry burst in her mouth. Sweet flavor coated her tongue, filling her senses with the taste of sunshine and summers spent hunting in the fields. For hundreds of years, Sorcha’s family had foraged the land for survival. Her mother had whispered the tales in her ear as they sucked the juice from these red bellied fruits.

Some of the ichor within the strawberry overflowed her lips, dripping syrup down her chin.

Sorcha didn’t see him move, but she felt the touch of his hand as though he branded her. His calloused thumb traced the line of liquid from chin to mouth. It rasped over her sensitive lip, catching every last drop of sticky juice.

One of the crystals on his palm scraped her jaw. Cold to the touch, it was a lightning bolt of sensation against the sudden, flaming heat of her cheeks.

She parted her lips in a silent gasp. The smooth texture of his nail touched her top lip, dipping into the warm breath she expelled before withdrawing.

She was undone, unmade, reborn as something else entirely. Her hands clenched in her lap as she stared in shock at the Fae who dared to touch her without asking, to slice through her stalwart resolve, and stitch the beginnings of attraction into the fiber of her being.

They stared at each other, frozen in time. Moonlight speared through her window and pierced the lining of shadow covering his face. It danced along the deep gashes of crystal, like a stone she had once cracked open to reveal the geode inside.

His eyes held wicked intent that stole the breath from her lungs. Vivid blue, like a crystal clear sky, like the azure waves of the ocean, they saw straight through her.

He wanted her, she realized. He wasn't playing a game; his emotion was too raw and hungry. She had seen the expression upon men at the brothel before, even sometimes cast in her direction, but never had she felt the emotions reflected in herself.

Her stomach clenched. She dug her fingernails into her palms and forced herself to swallow the remaining strawberry.

Sorcha's eyes followed his hand as he lifted it towards his mouth.

The chair screeched as she shoved to her feet. "Boggart, have you finished?"

A squeak from the corner suggested the little faerie still had a long way to go, but Sorcha was quite done with tonight. She looked back towards the massive shadow seated at her table.

"I'm afraid I have to ask you to leave, sir. As you can imagine, my journey has been trying, and I'm finding myself faint."

"From your journey," he repeated as he stood.

She was once again overwhelmed by the sheer size of him. Her head barely reached the center of his chest. She knew his hands were massive, and that she might wrap her arms around his shoulders if she tried very hard.

Sorcha blew out a breath. "Indeed. It was a grueling week-long sail, and then I swam the rest of the way here. Merrow-men are not kind while chasing their prey, so if you would please," she gestured at the door, unable to finish the sentence when the weight of his gaze pressed upon her.

"I have been scolded once tonight on respecting a woman's wishes.

I should not like to experience it again." He swept into a low bow, his cloak spreading across his shoulders like wings.

"Yes, a shrew is not likely to keep her mouth shut."

He chuckled. "The only shrew in this house is the boggart."

Sorcha listened for the angry shriek, but Boggart had nothing to say to the comment. Perhaps she agreed.

Still, it made her cheeks flame all the hotter. She rushed to the door and held it open. "Thank you for the interesting conversation."

He moved like a shadow, silent and smooth, hesitating only briefly in front of her. She inhaled the scent of mint and beeswax.

"It has been an enlightening, albeit short, evening," he said before leaving the hut.

Sorcha sagged against the doorframe. All the energy he carried swept out with him and emptied her body of the adrenaline rush she rode. It had been a brief conversation, but her legs shook and her hands trembled.

A zing of awareness jolted up her spine. Spinning, she leaned out the door and shouted, "Stone!"

He paused, one foot on the dock to her hut and the other on his cursed isle. "Pardon?"

"You said some call you Cloch Rí. I shall call you Stone until you give me your true name."

"You think I'll ever give you that kind of power over me?" His voice wavered with humor.

"I would bet my life on it, Stone."

"I look forward to your attempts, Sunshine."

She hoped he smiled, although it seemed unlikely a man such as him knew how to twist his lips in happiness. There was a certain pleasure to making a man smile. She had forgotten what this was like. The courtship, the laughter, the teasing, everything that made butterflies take flight in her belly.

He started up the hill that led to his castle. The moon rose behind the imperious structure, silhouetting the jagged spires and crumbling peaks. It was a ruin, a relic of a time long ago when this isle might have been a sight to behold.

There was something hauntingly beautiful about this place. The emerald hills glimmered with dew in the silver moonlight. Fireflies danced above the wheat fields looking like magic kissing the land. And its king, the disfigured monster of a man, outlined as a shadow striding across his domain.

"You're being fanciful," she said. "Stop it, Sorcha. Go to bed."

She couldn't. She stayed where she was, pressed against the doorframe, watching him walk away from her.

A small hand tugged her skirt. Sorcha glanced down at Boggart's strange, elongated face. Bread stuffed her cheeks, bulging them to the side and preventing her from squeaking.

Boggart tugged again and pointed towards the bed.

"Yes, it's bedtime. Where are you sleeping, little one?"

The faerie pointed at a small lump of moth-eaten blankets in the corner.

"Is that where you want to sleep? The bed is plenty big enough for the both of us."

Boggart took off for her corner and burrowed underneath the blankets. Her long, whiskered nose poked out of the mound, sniffing for a moment before disappearing again. Sorcha could hear the slight sound of munching.

She must have taken the rest of the bread with her, Sorcha thought with a smile. Shaking her head, she disrobed and hung the velvet dress from the window. It was too nice to leave on the floor or fold into the chest in the corner.

Tomorrow, she promised herself as she got into bed. Tomorrow, she would explore the island and speak with its inhabitants. She would not be distracted by the handsome king. She needed to convince him to come back to the mainland with her and damned if she would fail.

The air vibrated with the sound of wings, wind brushing over her face as she snuggled into the pillows. A raven croaked as it landed on her windowsill.

"There you are, Bran," she murmured quietly, so as not to disturb Boggart. "I wondered where you'd flown off to."

He croaked.

"Of course, I worried. We survived a near-death experience together. And no, I can't seem to sleep."

The raven tilted his head, staring at her with one dark, beady eye.

"It has nothing to do with him!"

He flapped his wings, settled onto the windowsill for the night, and turned his back to her.

"That's just rude," she grumbled. "I'm not lying to you. I slept for a full day when I first arrived here. I'm not tired in the slightest."

Perhaps it had something to do with the master of the isle. His gaze like ice, with molten heat in its depths.

She shivered and pulled the blankets high over her shoulders. Huffing out a breath, she resigned herself to a difficult night with little sleep.

CHAPTER 12

Sorcha crested a hill. Her breath was ragged and dripping sweat stuck long strands of her hair to her brow. She'd wrapped a bedsheet across her body as a makeshift pack. Her own was too large to bring on an adventure across the small isle.

The white sheet was a stark contrast to the old dress she wore. She found the floor length gown in a chest left behind by the hag. Moths had gotten to it, chewing holes through the fabric and leaving the edges ragged, but there was nothing functionally wrong with it. She wouldn't ruin it any further, and who needed fine clothing every day? The velvet was lovely, but not practical.

She prided herself on being a practical woman.

Hiking the sheet higher up her shoulder, she blew out a breath. A curl bounced from its confining tie.

Sorcha groaned. At this rate, by the time she crested the small mountain there wouldn't be any hair left in the tie. The unruly curls demanded freedom.

Gravel crunched under her borrowed boots. There used to be a path here, the ground worn down by centuries of feet. The earth had grown back over the years, smoothing the marred ground, and covering the path to the peak.

She scrambled on hands and knees to the crest. Air sawed from her lungs and her knees wobbled, but she had done it. Plunking down near a cairn, she yanked the wayward curls back into their tie.

Bran cawed overhead, his voice shouting in the air.

"Yes, yes," she muttered as she pulled hard. "You could have done this in half the time. Need I remind you feathers are far faster than flesh?"

He circled above her, dipping and diving as if to mock her exhaustion.

"Must be easy being a raven. Those of us down here have to struggle our way up the mountain. You can soar over and far beyond."

She released the knot across her chest that held the pack with a relieved sigh. Food was only a slight weight, but she was still sore. Her muscles needed to move, to release the tension and stiffness that hindered her movements.

Perhaps a mountain had been a little more than she could handle.

Rubbing her shoulder, Sorcha pulled out the small jug of water and a block of cheese. It wasn't much, but it would do.

She kept a sgian dubh, a knife, strapped to her ankle for moments like this. Dicing the soft cheese, she lifted it to her mouth and glanced down the mountain.

Everything seemed so small from up here. The land stretched out before her, dotted with sheep-like stars in the night sky. Tiny people worked diligently on their land. From here, she could see they had cast aside their glamour. Wings sparkled in the sunlight, warped forms bent over the fields. She knew if she walked within a few feet of them, they would put their glamours up so fast she never would get a peek at what they looked like.

It was the only mountain on the isle. Its peak was even with the top of the castle. Quiet and lonely, this respite gave her moments to think while remaining distant from all the people here.

No one wanted to speak to her about their master. They were as elusive as the man himself, answering her questions in vague responses that weren't quite lies. Perhaps he had warned them away from speaking to her. Perhaps they were loyal to the mysterious man.

Sorcha scowled at the tiny figures. They were equally quiet about their own information. Everyone was polite, kind, and giving, but they didn't trust her.

Glamours were still in place. They brushed her off when she suggested she might help. They whispered behind her back when she left although they likely thought she couldn't hear them.

The master, Stone, remained elusive. She saw him in passing every now and then but didn't feel the weight of his gaze. He didn't repeat the heated experience which had left her dry-mouthed for days.

Her knife slipped in her hand and cut her thumb. Hissing out an angry breath, she sank the blade into the ground.

"Get your head out of the clouds," she scolded herself. "That man is hardly worth your time or effort. Just get him off the isle and to the mainland. And stop hurting yourself while daydreaming."

She ripped a piece of fabric from the bottom of her dress, muttering about foolish, wool gathering girls. Tying it around her thumb, she cinched it tighter than normal as punishment.

Sorcha planned to spend the entire day upon the ridge. She was getting nowhere with the locals. They wouldn't give her any information about their master, which meant she had to go directly to the source.

The source was dangerous. The source burned like fire, with ice cold eyes that made her mind freeze in the wake of his hold. She would have to watch him constantly. There would be no more strawberry incidents, or anything of its ilk.

A voice whispered in the back of her mind that she wanted another such experience. She wanted more than that. For a calloused finger to become a hand, to feel what those crystals felt like against her skin.

"Foolish girl," she muttered.

It was impossible for such thoughts to come to fruition. She'd get herself in trouble, lose focus. Or worse, lose herself.

Stones skittered behind her, cracking together and rolling down the mountain in a great avalanche of sound. She rolled onto her side, peering towards the noise.

Snow white hair blew in the faint breeze. Heavy skirts tangled between Pixie's legs, catching her as she struggled to the top. Her normally calm face was bright red with exertion.

"Pixie!" Sorcha called. She jumped to her feet and ran towards the Fae. "What are you doing up here?"

"Oh, dearie, why do you have to choose such a place to get away from us all? It's awfully far away and my old bones can't take it."

"Somehow, I doubt you're as old as you portray yourself," Sorcha replied with a grin.

"You wouldn't know," Pixie said with a grimace. "Dearie, I hate to ask a favor of you, but something terrible has happened."

Sorcha's smile faded at the worry and anguish in Pixie's voice. "What happened?"

"It's little Doo—I mean—" Pixie caught herself and shook her head. "Pooka! It's little Pooka, he's fallen out of a tree and broken his arm. A terrible thing, nasty break, and he's the only child on the island. It's broken through the skin, dearie, and we don't know how to set the break. He's bleeding something awful."

"Did you put a compress on the wound?" Sorcha scooped up her things and swung them over her shoulder. "How bad is the break? Just how far is the hand pointing away from its usual position?"

"I, I don't know! I didn't look at it closely, in truth. The break was so terrible and the boy was in so much pain…"

"Come on then." A thrill of excitement rushed through her veins. Although Sorcha knew it was likely a terrible thing, she always felt this way before any kind of surgery. Her hands tingled to touch wounded flesh. Her mind fired with ideas on how to solve the problem of pain.

Sorcha's strange mind was both a blessing and a curse. She knew there were countless ways to heal a broken bone, but only a few that worked. If the bone had broken through skin, she would need to set it, then wrap it to encourage healing from the inside out.

She followed Pixie down the mountain at a much faster speed than she'd ascended. Both women rode a wind of anxiety and worry. If the boy bled badly, he might not be alive by the time Sorcha made it to him.

She hoped that wasn't the case.

They reached the hills and ran. Pixie no longer seemed like an aged woman for she flew over the grass.

"I have one thing to ask," Pixie said as they reached the castle. "The boy is young and impressionable. You cannot heal him without seeing his true form."

"Then so be it," Sorcha replied, breathless. "Open the door, Pixie."

"No young man wants to feel scorn from a beautiful woman. I beg you to hide any reactions you might have to his appearance."

"I have already seen both Cian and Boggart, Pixie. There is no reason to worry. Just let me see the boy."

Pixie sighed and swung open the kitchen door.

The room beyond had descended into chaos. The central table was clean of food and utensils. Faeries rushed in wide circles, to and from a small body laid out on the wood. Sorcha saw the faint impression of fur, wings, and scales before everyone erected their glamours.

All but the boy.

He crouched on the table and whined, his face warping through hare, dog, and horse. Pookas imitated animals, but she had never heard of one switching so many times.

Sorcha kept her face steely as she made her way to his side. He opened his mouth with a growl, fanged teeth shining in the candlelight. She had seen animals do that before when they were in pain.

She reached out a hand. "Shh, little master. I will not hurt you."

He growled again, but his lips closed. Again, his features changed. His nose dipped down, his pupils turned to slits, and whiskers grew upon his cheeks.

"Can you control it?" she asked. "I'll need you to pick a form before I can heal your arm."

He turned his face from her, scooting on his butt towards the other side of the table.

There was little time. Blood smeared his front and slicked the table. Red like hers. Red like a human.

She lunged forward and wrapped a hand around his ankle. The other Fae hissed at her movements reminding Sorcha just how dangerous the situation was. These people liked her, but they did not trust her. This was the one youngling they had. They would not tolerate mistakes.

"Easy there," she whispered. "Let me see your arm. I can help."

The boy stared back at her with mistrusting eyes. He had a reason to, she supposed. Sorcha had had very little opportunity to earn his trust.

"I know I'm a stranger," she breathed, turning her voice into a coo. "You are right to be scared. It is a good thing for you to be wary of those you do not know. I can make your arm feel better if you'll let me."

He inched towards her. The movement was slight, but it was there.

Sorcha let out a relieved breath. "That's right, come to me. What a brave boy you must be. To break your arm like this, you must have been doing something terribly heroic."

"No," he grunted through blunted teeth. "I was climbing a tree."

"Oh, well, that is very heroic! There are plenty of heroes who climbed trees. Do you know any of them?"

Pooka shook his head and moved the rest of the way toward her. She gently positioned him so his legs hung off the edge of the table. He moved his hand from the broken arm, stark white standing out amidst all the blood.

"It's hurt real bad," he whimpered.

"Yes. Yes, it is. But I'll help. While I'm working, I'll tell you a story." She gestured over her shoulder, and Pixie leaned in. "Yarrow, as much cloth as you can, and perhaps a little liquid courage. Is there anything different about Fae bodies I should know?"

"Not that I can think of. Is he going to survive?"

"Of course, he is," Sorcha leaned back in shock. "I'm here now."

The collective sigh rocked through Sorcha. Why would they think the boy would die? A severed limb, or perhaps impalement yes, but a broken arm? He hadn't bled out. She could certainly heal him.

She hesitated and asked, "What did you do before?"

"Well," Pixie glanced at the boy and lowered her voice. "Usually, we'd let it be and hope it healed on its own. A wound like this usually festered. We'd do what we could with honey compresses, but most times we'd lose them."

"You don't have to worry about that anymore. I'm here."

Sorcha shouldn't have said the words, but she did. These people needed her strength, her courage, her understanding. They didn't need to know she planned on leaving as soon as possible. Or that she was leaving at all.

She turned back towards the boy and plastered a smile on her face. "Have you heard the story of Macha?"

"Yes," he said with a sniff. Two large tears rolled down his face and dripped onto his bloodied pants.

"Did you hear how she cursed the line of Ulster?"

"No."

"Good. Listen to my voice and nothing else, all right? This will hurt, but I want you to hear the story and not focus on the pain."

They had waited a long time to come get her. The muscles of his arm had wrapped around the bone's new position and did not want to release. Thankfully, it was a clean break. She was gentle with the sensitive bone and ragged edges of flesh.

Sorcha viewed the entire injury before deciding she would need to stretch the muscles before they would allow the bone back in its place. Theoretically, it would be easy. For her.

The boy, she worried about.

She set about the surgery in the best way she could. The entire time she told the story of Macha. How she had married a mortal man and carried his child. How the foolish man had bragged about his wife to a rival king who forced her into a foot race. When she beat him, and lay near dying on the finish line, she cursed nine generations of his family to experience the pain of childbirth.

Although the pain must have been great, he listened. The boy repeated sentences of the story as she made three passes of stretching the muscle. He asked her questions as she snapped the bone back into place with an audible crunch. He bit back tears as she packed the wound with yarrow and wrapped it tightly with cloth.

They were both covered in blood and exhausted by the time she finished. She tugged the knot of his sling and nodded. "That will do. You have been brave enough to claim the title of hero, young Pooka. It's been an honor."

He sniffed hard, but straightened his spine. "It didn't hurt a bit, ma'am."

On impulse, she leaned forward and wrapped an arm around his shoulders. "I couldn't have asked for a better patient, sweet boy. Now ask your mother to tuck you into bed with a full jar of honey."

"I'm not allowed to have that much!"

"I think under the circumstances, you've earned it."

A very tall woman, thin as a birch tree, stepped forward. Sorcha stepped back to give her room and made eye contact.

The woman's glamour shimmered and fell. An adult Pooka looked far different from her son. She was an amalgamation of all mammals. Patches of light and dark fur blended together until she appeared more patchwork quilt than person. Her elongated nose and face were faintly horse-like. This must be his mother.

"Thank you," she said in her deep voice. "I cannot thank you enough."

"You would have done the same for me, if it came to that."

"All the same, you are welcome in my house any time."

Sorcha nodded. She waited until the kitchen emptied, and then sagged against the table. Exhaustion made even breathing difficult, her lungs working overtime. Her hands ached. She held them out, flexing her fingers in and out.

"You did well," Pixie said.

"I must see him every week for at least a full moon. That wound could still become infected."

"I'm sure his mother would appreciate it."

A piece of bread with sliced meat appeared in Sorcha's line of vision. Startled, she glanced up.

"Thank you." She held up her bloody hands. "Perhaps a basin of water first?"

"Come with me."

Sorcha stood on wobbly legs and followed Pixie through the gardens. Cian was absent from his usual post, a blessing she was thankful for. Bantering with the gnome would be difficult when she could hardly see straight.

They crossed a small wooden bridge in the garden and onto another part of the castle grounds Sorcha had yet to see.

It was peaceful here. Water burbled out of an aged fountain. The stone woman inside it poured water from a wound on her chest. She clutched the sword which had plunged between her ribs and held her sword up to continue fighting. Flowers grew wild in this section of the gardens. They tangled with each other, creating walls of roses and thorns.

"I didn't know roses grew this time of year," she mumbled.

"This island differs from what you're used to. Faerie-touched lands bear fruit even in the strangest of times. Why else would we have strawberries this late in the year?"

"Fair point."

"You may wash in this fountain."

"This one?" Sorcha gestured. "This looks far too nice to be a washing fountain."

"Long ago, it was a place of worship." Pixie's expression fell. "No longer."

Sorcha could see it was a sacred place. Blooms of every color stretched as far as she could see. The roses grew with wild abandon, vines stretching all around them. And the woman herself appeared eerily familiar.

She leaned forward to peer at the face. "Is this Macha?"

"It is. I thought it fitting you wash in her waters."

"I won't desecrate sacred ground."

"You're washing innocent blood from your hands. You saved him while telling her stories. Macha will appreciate that."

Sorcha supposed she was correct. The red-headed woman was fierce. Perhaps she would appreciate a little blood in her waters more than she would wine or gold coins.

She leaned down and dunked her hands into the cool stream. It ran over her hands with a soft, trickling sound, easing the aches from her bones. She saw another face in the ripples. A pointed face with wild hair, eyes flashing an unnatural green.

Macha was watching her. The Tuatha dé Danann winked at her, disappearing when Sorcha released the water she held in her cupped hands.

Her purpose burned bright in her mind. These people may be kind, but they should not distract her. Papa needed her. Rosaleen, Briana, and all her sisters needed her to stay focused. A small boy with a broken arm shouldn't so easily sway her.

But he did. They all did. With their thoughtful gifts, their easy going attitudes, and the magical way this isle captivated her. Sorcha had always been an outsider among her family. The witch's child who knew too much. Here? She was just another human girl who could not possibly understand all the wondrous things around her.

If given the choice, she would choose this life over her old one. It wasn't an option, but was entertaining to muse upon at least. She sighed and turned back towards Pixie.

"I am exhausted and my bed sounds like a respite I have earned. If you don't mind, I will take your gracious offer of food."

"Of course, dearie." Pixie handed the sandwich to her wrapped in a cloth.

When had she gotten a cloth? Sorcha stared down at the bundle in her hands. She was missing details so large as this?

She shook her head to clear it. "Perhaps a good sleep will clear my mind."

"Unlikely. It's a rather confusing place for a human such as yourself. I'm impressed you've lasted this long without losing your head."

"Do others?"

"You're the first human who's shown up on our shore," Pixie said with a smile. "You're new to us, although some have experiences with humans. We're all going through some learning."

"I appreciate your patience." Ironic, the words that slipped off her tongue. Hadn't a certain king asked her to do the same for him? And she had mocked him.

"You may wish to walk around the castle to get to the hut."

Sorcha arched a brow. "Why? It's faster to go back through Cian's garden."

"A walk is good for your health."

"I already climbed a mountain today."

"Yes, but the sights one sees on the other side of the castle are rather rare. You won't be seeing it on top of that munro. Eat your food on your walk. I promise you'll feel better if you go the long way."

The strange smile on Pixie's face made Sorcha nervous. The faerie had been kind thus far, but there was still plenty of time for trickery. Narrowing her eyes, she nodded. "All right. There are no games afoot?"

"The Wild Hunt doesn't start for another month yet, dearie. You're safe."

Sorcha continued eating as she rounded the castle. The rose garden didn't stretch very far. Her fingers itched to pull at the weeds, to take on the challenge of taming such a beast. Yet, she also knew that fatigue and roses did not play well together. She was more likely to bleed than succeed.

Once free from the tangled mess of blooms and thorns, the emerald hills stretched in front of her once more. The castle had grown into the landscape. Moss covered the stones at the base of the walls, meshing with the green grass until it was nearly impossible to tell them apart.

She waltzed past a sheep which lifted its head and baa'd.

"Hello," Sorcha nodded. "It's always a pleasure, mistress wool."

The fluffy animal gave her a rather unimpressed look and chewed. She had always liked sheep. Their odd, sideways pupils and all. They enjoyed having their cheeks scratched, and Sorcha loved their pleased expressions.

The bread disappeared by the time she made it halfway around the castle. Pixie had been right. The fresh air was doing wonders for the exhaustion that surged through her body. Each step beat back her drooping eyelids and trembling fingers.

A cracking sound echoed. Too far to cause her to jump—close enough to pique her curiosity.

"What is that?" she muttered as she picked up her pace.

The sound was strangely familiar. Not something she had heard often, but the ping of metal striking metal wasn't easy to forget.

Once, two men had gotten into a duel outside the brothel. Briana had been in the middle of it, rolling her eyes and ignoring the two men fighting over a prostitute. She called them both foolish, slammed the door, and told the girls to pay them no mind.

Sorcha had never been good at that. She had raced up the stairwell, stuck her head out the window, and watched the two men fight. They had been sloppily drunk and incapable of standing straight. Two strikes of sword against sword, and they both gave up.

This didn't sound like that kind of fight.

The closer she came, the more fierce and violent the strikes of metal became. Each clank rang in the air with the resounding quality of a gong. She counted fifteen by the time she reached the top of a hill and stared with open mouth.

This was a new part of the castle. Sturdy wooden fences marked off a section of field, packed down by stamping feet. Straw dummies hung from posts, their guts hanging out from too many hits. Targets lined one end of the fences, painted in circles of red to guide arrows home.

It was the men which caught her attention. A strange dark man stood in the center of the field. Half his head was shaved, dark hair falling nearly to his waist on the other side. There was a smudge of black across the shaved half of his face. He wore little more than breeches. Long and lean, his tanned skin was slicked with glistening sweat. A tapered, wicked spear glimmered in the sunlight, held with ease in his strong hand.

The other was eerily familiar. Sorcha gasped and dropped into the high waving grass, so he wouldn't see her.

So, this was the master of the isle.

Stone, as she now called him, was even more impressive without his cloak. He was massive, easily reaching seven feet tall, although she would've bet her life he was taller than that. Strangely, it didn't make him blocky. His body was as lean as the other man's. Broad shoulders tapered to a trim waist and long muscled legs. He wasn't wearing his cloak. He wasn't wearing anything other than a matching set of brown breeches.

She could count his rippling abdomen muscles even from her great distance. Bulging pectorals and flexing biceps caught her attention as her mouth went dry. He, too, was slicked with sweat. They'd obviously been fighting for some time.

Her gaze caught on the sword in his hand.

"Now, that's a sword," she whispered.

The gold handle sparkled with red stones. The blade itself was clearly well-made, a line down the center hollowed to allow blood to flow freely. It was massive, a broadsword rather than a rapier.

He lifted it as though it weighed less than a feather.

Sorcha's breath caught and her mind went blank. So that's what Pixie meant when she said he was handsome man. In his own way, he was indeed.

The damage to his body was far more extensive than his face or hands. A starburst wound bisected his right shoulder and spread in webs. It looked as if someone had cracked through stone. There were hundreds of small fissures that crawled over his shoulders, across his chest, and down to his stomach. Small scars revealed more parted flesh and burgeoning stone.

Their lips moved though she couldn't hear them from where she hid. Stone lifted his blade and dropped into a fighting stance.

The dark man raced towards him, a grimace on his face that was frightening. He leapt into the air with sword held above his head. Stone shifted at the last second, whirling to keep pace.

They didn't fight in any way she'd ever seen before. Her lips parted as she watched.

It was as if she watched dancers. Although Stone was clearly the larger of the two, he spun in the air and blocked each parry easily. The stones did not seem to hinder his movements. In fact, he used them to his advantage.

The other pivoted off a target and thrust himself high into the air. It was a killing blow if he landed where he wished. Stone kept his sword at his side and grasped the descending blade in a crystal fist. He used the momentum to pound his fist into the other man's face.

Sorcha winced at the cracking sound and forced herself to remain in place when the dark man dropped to the ground. He rolled on his shoulder, ending up on his feet, and shaking his head.

Blood dripped from his nose, but he appeared to be laughing.

"That was where you got the crystals on your knuckles from," she whispered.

Stone had punched so many people, or things, that he had worn the flesh from the crystals underneath. That was the closest thing she could think of, for surely a curse was the cause of his affliction. Stone was clearly Seelie. No one else would be as beautiful, even with such disfigurement.

What did it all mean?

She shook her head and sank deeper into the grass as the two men clapped each other on the shoulders. She could already hear the scolding tone he would use when he realized she had spied on him. Or perhaps he wouldn't scold at all. Perhaps he would draw her into those strong arms, those rock-hard muscles. What would he smell like? Like musk and man? Or like straw and grass?

The unknown man cupped his hands around his mouth and shouted, "Why your highness, I do believe we're being watched!"

Sorcha's cheeks turned bright red. She ducked until her chin touched the ground. Surely, they couldn't see her? The grass was tall enough to cover her twice over if she laid down like this.

There was a grumbling reply she could not quite understand. Peeking up over the grass, she locked eyes with the strange new arrival. She could see his grin all the way from where she was.

He waggled his fingers. "Hello, red-headed lass! You're a long way from home."

Sorcha supposed she could stay laying in the grass until they gave up, but he would still know. She had been spying like a little school girl who didn't know any better. She might as well grit her teeth and be an adult.

Standing, she inhaled a deep breath, ready to accept her punishment. She might enjoy punishment, if Stone would be the deliverer of said punishment. But, the last thing she needed was another repeat of their first night, and his hands on her skin or body.

She didn't look up as she walked towards their practice range. Head down, she counted each step and curled her hands into fists. She could do this without embarrassing herself. She was looking for more yarrow. Pooka would need it, and the stores were low.

Why would Pixie send her all this way if she was only going to embarrass herself? Surely, the faerie had known her master was practicing.

Sorcha almost stopped in her place. That was exactly why the Pixie had sent her here. What was she up to?

By the time she reached the fence, heat flushed up her neck to her face. Sorcha worried her cheeks might be smoking.

She looked up directly into a caramel colored chest. Her gaze traveled farther up, catching on the dark "smudge" on his face that wasn't dirt at all. Tiny dark feathers covered one side of his face, his eye that of a raven, not a man.

She recognized that yellow eye. Full of intelligence, far too human, and watching her with chagrin. The raven had been far more than just a beast after all.

"Bran?"

He swept into a low bow and looked up through the curtain of his hair, grinning. "My lady. It is a rarity to see such bewitching beauty on Hy-brasil."

"If anyone would know, it would be you." She curtseyed in return. "My apologies. I was looking for yarrow."

"Ah, then you had no luck?"

"I'm afraid not."

"I believe there is some directly behind you, fair lady."

She glanced over her shoulder and cursed. "There certainly is."

There went her lie. The Fae could sniff it out anyways. They were incapable of lying. She flicked a glance towards Stone, who stood as still as his namesake with his back to her.

"I had no idea you would be practicing," she began. "I was told a walk would clear my head after dealing with the Pooka. You did hear about the boy, didn't you?"

A droplet of sweat traveled down the valley of Stone's spine. Muscles bunched on either side, stymied only by the protrusion of crystals. "I had not."

"He broke his arm while climbing a tree. I've set the bone and packed the wound with yarrow, but they will need to watch for infection."

"And why are you telling me this?"

Bran cleared his throat. "I'm glad to hear the boy is well. I apologize for lying all this time to you, beautiful thing that you are."

"You've followed me since the MacNara twins," she murmured while casting a curious glance towards Stone, who still hadn't turned.

"I rarely trust the MacNara twins, and when I saw one such as you entering their home? I had to follow you. My honor simply wouldn't allow for anything else."

She wasn't certain he had that much honor. A man who hid himself from a woman in the form of a raven was unlikely to be a gentleman. From the top of his half-shaved head, to the bottom of his taloned feet, this was a man she'd have a hard time trusting.

"You, sir, are surely a rake."

"Me?" He slapped a hand to his chest. "I have never been called such a thing!"

"Bran," Stone's voice cut through the banter. "Enough."

He glanced over his shoulder, revealing the uninjured side of his face. Sorcha noted how he angled his body away from her. As if he were trying to hide. There was no cloak for him to cover the injuries, at least not that she could see.

The man was strange. So easily risen to a challenge when she could not see him, but now he appeared almost frightened. Embarrassed, perhaps? She had placed him in an awkward situation. It was likely he hadn't wanted her to see his disfigurement.

She wouldn't have wanted anyone to know. Sorcha couldn't imagine how he felt knowing that his skin was so severely marred.

She swallowed hard and nodded. "Thank you, Bran, for pointing out the yarrow. I'll take my leave, gentlemen."

Dipping into a curtsy for good measure, she cursed herself for listening to Pixie. With burning red cheeks, she snatched the yarrow and rushed away from the castle. If it took her the rest of the day to get to her hut, so be it. She refused to stay any longer in the presence of a man who so clearly didn't want her there.

CHAPTER 13

Eamonn slammed the door to the castle, hands shaking in anger. How dare she? That woman had no right to walk around the grounds as if she owned the place. All other Fae knew to leave him be when he was in a rage. He would wear himself out with sword and shield, but they were not permitted to view him.

Growling, he swiped a vase from its stand. The shattering crash only eased a small fraction of his anger, but it was something. Shame overwhelmed him.

She had seen him.

When Bran said they were being watched, Eamonn had turned with the expectation that Pixie was coming to announce some other chore he needed to do. But it hadn't been any of the faeries he would have guessed.

She stood in the middle of the field with goldenrod brushing her fingertips. He had named her aptly. Sunshine caressed her hair and shoulders like a lover. Her hair swirled around her like a dust devil made of fire. Her freckles flecked her nose and forehead as if the sun couldn't help but kiss her cheeks.

She was so beautiful. And he?

Eamonn walked past a shattered mirror and growled. He was little more than a monster.

"She's even prettier when in a human form," Bran's voice echoed down the hallway. "I'm surprised you let her stay, considering the circumstances."

"Leave, Unseelie. You have overstayed your welcome."

"I always do. And yet, here I am."

The fluttering of wings buffeted his ears, and Bran materialized down the hallway before him.

Eamonn clenched his fists. "How does she know your name?"

"Jealous?" Bran picked at his fingernails. "Or anxious?"

"No human should know the true name of a Fae."

"Does it make you feel better to know she guessed it?"

"No," he snorted. "But it does speak to your mother's intelligence. Naming her son so predictably will be your downfall."

"My mother is plenty intelligent. She created you, now didn't she?"

Eamonn bared his teeth.

The other Fae hardly seemed intimidated. "Easy there, Stone King. I have no quarrel with you."

"You've done enough." He brushed past the raven and slammed open the door to another abandoned room. There were hundreds in this castle, filled with relics of a time long ago. They held little meaning to him. Which meant they were far more interesting to break.

"Come now, how can I make it up to you?" Bran trailed after him. "I so hate it when you're mad at me."

"The only reason why you are here is to train with the best."

"And you are the best. But we can't train together if you're just trying to kill me."

Eamonn crushed a stone head between his fists. "In my experience, that is the best way to learn."

It was thoroughly satisfying to see the Unseelie Prince's eyes bug out of his head. Bran was whip-quick and wiry, impossible to defeat from a distance. But Eamonn was strong, made even stronger by the crystals that decorated his skin like armor plating.

"What has you all riled up?"

"She saw me." He smashed another piece of a statute, the remaining hand from one of his other rants.

"So?"

"She saw me. I hadn't planned on ever letting her see me."

"That would be impossible anyways. She lives on the isle now."

"She lives in a hut off the isle, specifically so that she would not have the potential to see me."

Bran couldn't understand. Not really. For an Unseelie, he was highly attractive. Most his features were unchanged. Sure, the raven eye in the man's head was unsettling, and he would never have passed for a Seelie Fae, but he was pleasant enough to look at. Handsome for his own people.

Eamonn would never be considered handsome again. Beyond that, he was so flawed that the throne he had coveted for so long had slipped from his grasp. He would never be king and his twin, that treacherous, backstabbing fool, would forever sit upon Eamonn's throne.

"What if I trade you a secret?" Bran's voice danced in the air.

"I don't make deals."

"Not a deal. I've somehow wronged you, although I can't understand why. I'll willingly gift you this secret on a very small condition that you take that poor girl out of the hag's hut."

Eamonn paused. "Why would I do that?"

"Because she deserves to be in the castle. She's lived a tough life, from what I can tell. I'd like to see her pampered."

"She doesn't want to be here. I've offered her dinner every night in the dining room, and she insists upon eating with that boggart in her house."

The raven man hoisted himself onto a cabinet, crouching at the much greater height. "Brownie."

"Excuse me?"

"The boggart is no longer. She's turned back into a brownie."

"That's impossible." He shook his head. "It's only rarely done, and a human girl isn't going to bring a faerie back from the brink of madness."

"Shows how little you know." Bran shrugged. "It's a good secret, too. A shame you don't want to trade for it."

Eamonn shook his head, brought his elbow down upon a stone soldier tipped onto the floor. The satisfying crack echoed so loudly through his own skull that he saw stars. But it helped. Oh, did it help.

He wanted to break more. To wallow in self-pity that she, of all people, Sunshine had seen his true form. He hadn't been able to turn around, for fear of what he'd see in her gaze.

Horror? More than likely. When he had been driven from Seelie that was what their expressions had been. Horror that the king wasn't a man at all.

Beast.

Betrayer.

Secret? His mind drifted towards the tantalizing bit of information Bran held over him. Eamonn, like the rest of his faerie race, had never been able to resist hidden knowledge.

Breathing hard, he glanced over his shoulder. "What kind of secret is it?"

The calculating look in Bran's raven eye made Eamonn shiver.

Bran leaned forward, hands dangling over his bent knees. "I know her true name."

Just the mere thought of Sunshine's name sent him reeling. What would it taste like on his tongue? Likely as distracting as the rest of her. But Eamonn was certain the merest hint would be a droplet of pure honey coating his mouth.

What a deal it was. Moving her from the hag's hut cost little. There were plenty of available rooms, far away in the depths of the castle. He would have someone placed outside her door, to make sure she didn't wander where she was unwelcome.

It was insane. Making deals with Unseelie Fae had never ended well for his family. Look at where he was now! And this was the son of the very Unseelie who had cursed their family for all time.

Still…it was her name.

He scratched the crystals on his jaw, pondering the thought. He could do much with a name. He could compel her to leave the island.

No. He would never do that. Could never do that. She was too intriguing, too interesting, far too strange a human to leave. He wouldn't allow her to wander far from his side, not until he figured her out.

"All I have to do is move her from the hut to the castle?"

Bran leaned forward with a wry grin. "Well, set her up in a nice room at least. I want the girl to be taken care of, not placed on a shelf to gather dust like the rest of your nice things."

"I can't promise to take care of her."

"I didn't ask for that. She's capable of protecting herself. She made the swim across the sea to get to you."

"To get to the isle," Eamonn corrected. "She didn't know I existed."

"And that's where you're wrong, Cloch Rí. She's been looking for you the whole time, and you've been a thorn in her side."

"She wants me to end a plague."

"For now. But who knows. If you let her closer, she might want more."

"Since when do you play matchmaker?"

Bran hopped down from the cabinet, sauntering towards Eamonn on clicking clawed feet. "Do we have a deal?"

Eamonn glanced down at the hand offered. Bran had one human hand, and one beast. He held out the clawed hand, taloned with three fingers like the foot of a raven.

Although his mind screamed he could find out this information on his own, Eamonn reached forward and clasped the talon. For good measure, he dug the crystals of his palm into the leathery flesh. "We have a deal. Now what is her name?"

The wild smile returned to the raven man's face.

"Sorcha."

Chapter 14

"Sorcha." The voice whispered on the winds and tingled in her mind. It swept through her window and through her hair, tangling in the red strands.

She recognized the voice. It belonged to a terrifying woman. Tall, stately, wild red hair matching her own.

Sorcha leaned out the bedroom window and peered across the moors. Will-o'-the-wisps danced merrily above the bog. The scent of peat moss filled the air, earthen and musty. She wrinkled her nose.

Perhaps she only wanted to hear her name. After seeing Macha's face in the fountain, she worried the Tuatha dé Danann had more to say. Was her family all right? She had only made a deal for her father, not her sisters. Had the worst happened, and the faerie come to tell her the bad news?

The thoughts plagued her throughout the evening. Homesickness was a bitter taste in her mouth, leaving bile rolling in her stomach and an empty hole in her chest. She missed them. Briana would know what to do with a man who wouldn't listen. Rosaleen would charm him with her innocent curls and girlish laughter. Papa would give him a pipe and set him down to talk about adventures and traveling.

Sorcha? She would hover in the corner, waiting until someone asked for something. She was far more comfortable taking care of others than she was being the center of attention.

"Sorcha." The wind whispered through her window. "Sorcha, come to me."

Something tugged deep in her belly. The compulsion to move was not a choice, but an order. Her feet slid across the floor even as her mind wailed that she didn't want to move. She didn't know who called out to her.

She watched as if someone else moved her hand, turned the door handle, and pushed the door open.

Macha stood in the midst of swirling white lights. They sparkled upon her shoulders and cast a cold gleam upon her eyes. She lost all color, standing in the moonlight with shadows twining through her hair.

"Lady Fae," Sorcha said. Her feet halted at the edge of the dock. "I had not thought to see you here."

"No, I imagine you didn't. Why else would you have washed your filth in my fountain?"

"It was the blood of a child. One of your children."

"I do not call all faeries my children, nor do I lay claim to a Pooka." She spat the last word as if it were a curse. "The Unseelie can have their animals. Mine are among the Seelie."

"Is that how you would be known? As a mother who cast aside her offspring?"

"You have become daring. That is good. You will need to be strong for this task."

"What more could you possibly ask me to do?" Sorcha's jaw dropped. "I'm already trying to cajole him to come to the mainland."

"Where is your success? I watch you making friends, not convincing the lord of this isle to leave."

Sorcha couldn't argue with that. She hadn't done much. "I'm trying to befriend him so I might convince Stone that—"

"Stone?" Macha raised her eyebrows. "You've named him?"

"Well, yes. How else are we supposed to converse?"

The waters rippled as Macha stepped forward. Will-o'-the-wisps scattered, darting over the lily pads to safety. Ragged-edged clothing revealed glinting weapons strapped to her arms and thighs.

Sorcha swallowed hard. She would accept her death if it came now. There was no honor in forcing a man to leave his home, and she refused to give up that part of herself. Stone deserved to make the choice.

"You are a coward," Macha whispered. She reached out and ghosted her fingertips across Sorcha's throat. "You hesitate, because you wish him to make this decision for you. If you fail, it is not your fault. It is his."

"That's not true," her throat convulsed. "I don't want to force him to make a decision he isn't prepared for."

"While you wait, your people are dying."

"My family?"

"Your father, as promised, is alive. The blood beetle plague is spreading, and you are forgetting your purpose."

"I couldn't forget that."

"It does not matter to me whether you fulfill your deal. But the deal still stands. If you do not bring the master of this isle back to the mainland, then I will release my hold upon your father's health. I need not remind you how poorly he was doing when you left."

Sorcha's entire body shook. "It's only been a few weeks."

"You might not be entirely in the Otherworld, but you are on the border. Time moves differently here."

"What?"

Macha stepped back from her, a tired and knowing smile on her face. "Take care, little human. I will do my best to help you, but time is not on your side."

Sorcha stumbled backwards, barely catching herself on the edge of the dock. What was she saying? Her mind whirled.

"How long have I been gone?" Sorcha cried out. "How long, Macha?"

"That is not for me to say. Hurry, child."

"Macha! Answer my question!"

The water rippled as magic brushed its surface, then the Tuatha dé Danann disappeared.

Tears burned in Sorcha's eyes, streaming down her cheeks as she panicked. Had she been gone for months? Years? How could she have forgotten that time was different here?

But she wasn't in the home of the Faerie. Not really. Hy-brasil straddled the line between Otherworld and her world. She couldn't have been gone more than a few months, could she?

"What must they think of me?" she whispered. "I did not desert you! I would never do that."

But she had. Sorcha had let memories of her family become substitute for the real thing. In doing so, she forgot the warmth of their touch, the sound of their voice, the lingering support of their embrace.

"I'm so sorry. I should never have lost myself in the magic of this place."

Chapter 15

Sorcha paced in front of the kitchen door. She'd spent the entirety of two days mulling over Macha's words, replaying what she might say and how he might react. The problem was she didn't know. Stone was a rather unpredictable person. First he was horrible, then he was kind, then he wouldn't even look at her.

The last thing she needed was to go back to the "toss her out of the castle" route they'd started their relationship with. He had shown an ability to be a gentleman. Now she needed to use that to her advantage.

Her first thought was to dress up. She'd put the green velvet dress back on and twirled around in front of Boggart asking how she looked. Brown patches were showing up all over Boggart's body, and she stroked one on her forearm before clapping.

But that hadn't been right. Sorcha wasn't trying to impress him with her beauty. She needed him to take her seriously. The blood beetle plague was a terrible affliction, and he needed to understand how dire the circumstances were.

She switched to the outfit she usually conducted her midwifery in. Stains decorated the front of the white apron and rips frayed the ends. She thought it rather suited the conversation.

Boggart hated it.

The little faerie then found the perfect dress or at least that's what her chirps sounded like. It had been Sorcha's mother's. Pale yellow with tiny hand-embroidered white daisies along the hem, it snugged tight to her waist while sweeping the ground. Sorcha rarely wore the dress for fear she might harm the delicate fabric.

Still, she tried it on. Worn cotton swayed against her thighs, delicate lace brushing the tops of her feet. The square neckline allowed the wind to brush over her skin, the tight sleeves complimented her strong arms.

Sorcha didn't second guess her choice until she stood outside the kitchens. Now, she paced back and forth wondering what her plan was. Did she think he would say yes just because she wore a yellow dress?

Of course, he wouldn't. He was a man who called himself master. A peasant girl in a pretty dress wouldn't change his mind that easily.

A grumbling voice lifted. "Are you going in or not, girl?"

"I'm thinking."

"What could you have to think about that would make you trample my rutabagas?"

"Hush, Cian."

The click of his jaw snapping together made her flinch. She should know better than to issue an order while using a Fae name.

Sorcha winced, "I'm sorry, Cian. I rescind that order."

His mouth flew open so fast she thought he might unhinge his jaw. "How dare you! This is precisely why humans shouldn't have our names!"

"I agree," she interrupted, stopping him mid-rant. "I never should have used it. That was careless of me."

Cian grumbled but turned back to hoeing the patch of lettuce which she swore had popped up overnight. The man was magic with the garden. Sorcha wished he lived near her sisters. Maybe they wouldn't have given so much money to the marketplace.

Squaring her shoulders, she marched into the bustling kitchen.

Most of the faeries still kept their glamour around her. They feared her reaction to their true form, or worried they might frighten her. Whatever the cause, it irked Sorcha to no end.

Already bristling, she searched through the steam and heat waves to find Pixie. The old woman was one of the Fae who remained glamoured. That little tidbit Sorcha liked least of all.

"Pixie!" she called out.

Everyone paused for a brief second. Sorcha knew what was running through their minds. The human was here. Be more careful than before. Even though they liked her, even though she had saved one of their own, tension appeared where there hadn't been before.

Pixie rushed towards her, wiping her hands on a towel as she went. "What can I do for you, dearie?"

"Where is your master?"

"The throne room, I would imagine."

Sorcha growled. "Why is he always in that damn throne room when I need him?"

"He's expecting company."

"Company?" Sorcha glanced around the room with surprise. "You're preparing a feast?"

"Yes. It's a rarity that we have visitors."

"Who's visiting?"

"I don't think I'm supposed to say," Pixie glanced over her shoulder at the brownies frantically cooking. "You should remain in your home tonight. It would be safer."

"Who's coming?" Sorcha repeated.

Pixie did not respond. Instead, she turned on her heel and hustled back towards the table where she'd been decorating tiny pastries.

Frustration surged through her and gathered in her clenched fists. Sorcha didn't like being left in the dark. Who was coming? This was a cursed isle impossible to even see for another seven years, so who would have the power to find it?

There were so many questions no one would answer. No one in this room, at least.

All the more reason to go bother the master of the isle.

Resolve settled upon her shoulders like a well-worn cloak. She wouldn't be intimidated by visitors who might frighten her. She'd met the terrifying Macha—a woman who rode through battle and cleaved men in two. There were few worse than that.

Her footsteps echoed down the hall as she marched towards the throne room. She vaguely remembered where it was, although she caught herself turning into empty rooms.

One held shattered stone statues. Her foot caught upon a head, empty eyes staring up at her and carved so realistically that she expected it to blink. Unnerved, Sorcha backed out of the room as though the statues might call out for help.

Rounding a cobweb covered corner, she finally saw the grand

entrance. This time, she paused to really look at it.

Carved white marble arched over the double doorway. Tiny flowers, slithering ivy, even beetles crawled from the floor and arched into the ceiling. This wasn't just an intimidating entrance, it was a work of art.

The green double doors stood open, golden rivets and foil outlining each individual plank. It was the only thing in the castle not falling to pieces.

She brushed her hand along the worn wood as she passed. It was clean, much to her surprise. Every tiny piece of the grand ballroom shone as bright as the sun.

Although cracks still traveled through the floor, this was now a place of rare beauty. The chandeliers dripped rubies and emeralds, light striking the gems and casting colored shadows upon the floor.

Sorcha gasped. She hadn't realized paint covered the walls. The Wild Hunt stretched on either side of her. Fae in chariots, armored and terrifying, chased down human and animal alike. Larger than life, they seemed to move on their own as she stared.

All this stretched towards the throne where the king lounged in wait and cast in shadow. New curtains hung from the ceiling, blood-red and so silken they dripped onto the floor. The staircase to reach him was made of pure gold.

"You are early." His grumbling voice raced down her spine in shivers and trembles.

"I hadn't realized I was expected."

"It's you?"

He stood. His great height at once overpowering and overwhelming even though she was still far from him.

Sorcha was intensely aware of her simple appearance. She should've chosen the emerald gown—she might not have looked so out of place. Her mother's dress looked more like a wildflower placed incongruously in a porcelain vase.

Each thunk of his footsteps made her blush burn hotter. What had she been thinking? Of course, he would entertain guests in a finer way than he lived. She was a fool.

Embarrassment did not suit her. Sorcha reminded herself that she was a midwife, not a princess. This was her best dress before Pixie had given her something else to wear. There was nothing to be ashamed of.

She lifted her gaze, and her mouth went dry.

A warrior stood before her. Commander, chief, lord. She sucked in a rasping gasp as he strode towards her across the wide expanse of marble.

He wore elven armor. Each dark silver plate meticulously hammered to fit the movement of his arms. The symbol of a stag embellished the wide leather chest piece. Chainmail swayed against his thighs, knee-high boots striking the floor with hard purpose.

Metallic threads wove through his long braid that was tied off with golden clasps. The sword she had so admired was strapped to his side.

"You should not be here," he growled.

"I see that now."

"I am expecting visitors."

"Yes, yes, it appears so." Sorcha was tongue-tied.

He was so handsome, so overwhelming, so otherworldly that she was incapable of finding her own thoughts. She turned to leave, but paused when he reached out and grasped her arm. Crystals bit through the delicate fabric.

"All is well?"

She shivered. "That depends on your definition of well."

"How can I help?"

"You have to come back to the mainland with me," she whispered while staring at the door. "I cannot linger here any longer."

"You know my answer."

"Then I will have to force you." Sorcha whipped around, her green eyes sparking with anger. "You did not tell me that time passed differently here! My family could be dead in a few days, have you no care for that?"

"Who told you?"

Her heart stopped. His words tumbled over and over in her mind. Sorcha's throat closed as she asked, "Why didn't you?"

"There wasn't an appropriate opportunity."

"The first moment I stepped into this throne room and told you my purpose, you should have let me know that my chances were limited. I cannot give up. My family needs me."

"Family is who you choose, not who is in your blood."

Sorcha wrenched her arm from his grasp. "Then I choose them. A thousand times over, I choose them!"

"You have been given a good home here. In time, I would move you into the castle—"

"In time?" She pressed a hand against her mouth and backed towards the door. "As if it's some kind of reward for good behavior?"

"I had to make sure you were trustworthy."

"Trustworthy? Do you have some kind of initiation people must go through before you lower yourself to call them friend?"

"No, it's not like that."

"Then what is it like, master? What must I do before you consider my family worthy of your attentions?"

She was even with him now, four steps up the stairs. He lifted one foot and placed it on the next step, hesitating in the face of her anger.

"I cannot leave this isle. I cannot help your family, even if I wished to."

A choked sound escaped her lips. "Even if you wished to?"

"That's not how I meant it—"

"I understand perfectly how you meant it. Thank you for making things so clear."

"Wait."

She whirled and raced from the throne room. Sorcha rounded a corner, pushing through back rooms until she recognized where she was. She had to avoid whatever horrific guests he might be entertaining. She didn't want to know what beasts consorted with such a horrible man.

He had no care for her family. And if he had no care for them, then he didn't care what happened to her.

It shouldn't sting as much as it did. She barely knew the man, although he had become a regular figure in her thoughts. She'd even given him a name.

Foolish, she berated herself. Childish. Friendship with him was wishful thinking.

She hurtled down the steps, pushing through the kitchens without pause. Pixie shouted behind her. Stopping would only result in more anger, and Sorcha couldn't deal with any more.

A storm cloud brewed on the edge of the isle. It barreled towards her as she sprinted directly into its electric power. Storms didn't bother her, not when she knew shelter was so close.

The sweet scent of peat filled her lungs. Bleating sheep scattered as she charged through their midst. The tie in her hair loosened in the breeze, flying free to let her hair stream back in a banner of bright red.

Her lungs ached, but she did not slow. She wouldn't stop until she could slam the hut's door behind her. The crash might stop her whirling thoughts.

A tear slid down her cheek. She dashed it away with an angry slap, leaving a mark of red against her freckled jaw. Then another slid free, this time hitting her face so painfully that she realized it wasn't tears at all.

It was rain.

The clouds unleashed their fury. Rain pounded the ground and echoed in her ears. Thunder rumbled in the distance. Lightning cracked far off in the ocean, a bolt zig-zagging from the sky and into the water.

She squinted and kept running. Her mother's dress would be ruined, and it was another thing she could blame on him.

How love-starved was she that she would trust such a monster?

The raging storm echoed the tumultuous emotions beating in her breast. He had no right. He had no right!

She lost her way in the sheets of rain. The hag's hut was barely visible below the small cliff she stood upon, but she would not let that deter her. The rocks were slippery and dangerous. She skidded down, sliding her hands into cracks and crevices, gripping with strong fingers. A small, romantic part of her whispered that this might be what it felt like to touch the geodes of his skin.

She grunted and yanked a stone from the ground. It tumbled down the small cliff side and splashed into the foaming waves. Good riddance. She shouldn't be wondering what he might feel like. She shouldn't be wondering anything about him at all!

Sorcha would leave this isle empty-handed and find another way to save her family. There had to be more she could bargain. She could promise her life to Macha just to get away from this place.

From him.

Lightning cracked and struck the ground above her head. Sorcha flinched, glancing up to see the bolt strike a tree hanging onto the edge of the small cliff. Blinded, she hugged herself close to the rock and whispered a silent prayer.

The tree screamed. Sizzling electricity raced through her, standing her damp hair on end. Then she heard it. The creaking groan, the snapping cracks of roots being pulled from the earth, and the rumbling of stone.

She looked up although she already knew what she would see. The aged tree released its precarious hold on the cliff and plunged towards her.

Sorcha tucked her body closer to the stones, wedging her side into the cliff and shredding the delicate skin of her stomach. The roots slid past, the trunk smashing against the stones but not touching her.

She breathed a sigh of relief. Then, a falling branch whooshed past where she pressed herself into the niche of the cliff. She lifted her head at the wrong moment and shrieked as a flame-red strand of hair wrapped around the slick wood.

It yanked her backwards, tossing her into the deep mire where ocean met bog. Sorcha hit the water with a loud slap. Her back burned, and her mind screamed. She hadn't taken a breath before striking the water, her body sinking like stone.

Bubbles obscured her vision. Air twisted, leaving the tree which dragged her further and further down. She reached her hands for the surface, dark waters swallowing her whole.

The tree hit the muck with a muffled thump. Billowing mud floated up like smoke. Sorcha watched with horror as the surface blurred and disappeared. She twisted—chest aching—and grasped onto the tangled bit of hair.

She tugged, but there was too much for her to yank free. Her fingers felt along the strand until she touched the tree branch. Something slithered through her grasp.

Sorcha flinched backwards in fear, stopped by a yank against the back of her skull which twisted her around. The foggy water was too dark for her to make out more than vague shapes.

But which way was up?

Her heart thudded painfully. She didn't remember which way was up. The branch was attached to her, so directly above it would be the surface? But the tree angled down. Didn't it?

She tugged on her hair again, frantically placing her feet against the branch and pulling hard. She felt more than heard the ripping, but it wasn't enough.

This wasn't how she wanted to die. People didn't often swim in Ui Neill; they were too far away from the selkies to have that bloodline in their midst.

She wanted to die on rolling green hills or in the middle of a field of heather. Why did it have to end like this?

I love you, she thought. I love you so much, Papa and all my sisters. I wish it could have been different.

Black spots blurred the edges of her vision. At some point, she would have to suck in a deep breath. She would breathe in murky water, and that would be the end.

Sorcha had always been a fighter. She wouldn't suck in the salt water until the very last second or until she passed out. Her body convulsed, arguing with her mind that she needed to breathe. She squeezed her eyes shut, so she could forget for one second that she was underwater.

Just a moment longer, she thought. Just one more moment to enjoy being alive. To feel the cold water on my fingertips and remember that she lived.

A warm hand wrapped around her arm. Her eyes snapped open. It was too dark to know whether the shadowy figure was a merrow-man, but she didn't care anymore. She just wanted to breathe.

Heat spread from the gentle touch as it slid down her forearm and found where she still clutched her hair. An odd scrape of scale abraded her skin, slicing through the lock of hair easily.

No, not scale, she realized. Crystal.

She clutched onto his shoulders with clawed hands and desperately kicked. If she could just get to the surface. If she could just inhale.

His hand wrapped around her jaw, forcing her head down. She didn't want to look down into that darkness. Why wasn't he moving? Didn't he understand that she was moments away from inhaling water and—

Warm lips wrapped around hers. He squeezed her jaw and her mouth opened for a moment. He exhaled. She breathed in his air desperately. The pain in her lungs eased.

It wasn't enough, but it would do. Sorcha squeezed her eyes shut and hooked a leg around his waist, anchoring herself to him. She tried not to take too much of his breath, he'd need it to get them back to the surface. But it was addicting.

The crystal running down his upper lip sliced through her own lip. She winced at the pain and drew back. Salt stung the wound.

With her securely held in his arms, Stone pushed off the bottom of the ocean. They shot through the water like an arrow from a bow. She held tight to his broad shoulders, ripples of muscle shifting beneath her fingertips.

They broke the surface, and she gasped in air. It was too much, she choked violently and hung onto him for dear life. He wasn't even breathing hard. He simply waited until she stopped coughing and then rolled onto his back.

When she struggled, he brushed the wet strands of hair from her face. "Easy, relax. Let the ocean take you back to shore."

Sorcha coughed again, "I can swim on my own."

"Let me do the work, Sorcha. Stop fighting me."

She felt as though a bolt of lightning had struck her. That was exactly what she had been doing since the moment she reached this isle. Fighting him, in every conversation, in every rule he made. And yet, he still saved her.

Waves rocked them, white caps growing dangerously high as the storm raged above them.

"I trust you," she whispered and let her body go limp.

He wrapped a strong, bare arm across her shoulders and drew her back against his chest. Crystals bit into her spine from his gaping shoulder wound, but she refused to complain. He swam them back to shore with the grace of a selkie. The waves rocked forward, seaweed brushed her legs, and the wound on her lip bled freely.

"What were you thinking?" he growled.

"I wasn't."

Lightning cracked overhead, casting his face in a grim light. Sorcha turned away from the disappointed expression. She had already disappointed herself, she didn't need him to be, too.

"Obviously."

The wind rushed overhead, pushing waves up and over their heads She shivered violently.

He cursed. "We're almost there. Just a few more moments."

How had she been carried so far out? Sorcha hadn't noticed the tree moving, but it must have slid along the ocean floor.

His feet touched land, and Stone dragged her forward into his arms. The steely bands wrapped around her as if she weighed nothing.

The bulging muscles of his chest were distracting. Not a single hair covered his skin, not even on his arms. Up close, the crystals were so much angrier. The wounds carved into his skin and deep into his flesh. It was a miracle he could even move.

"I can walk," she rasped.

"Enough."

"I'm not so weak as to—"

"I said enough, Sorcha."

She looked up at his severe face, unable to resist tracing the smooth line of his jaw. "That's the second time you've called me by name. I don't remember giving that to you."

The muscles under her fingertips bunched. "I have my ways."

"Obviously."

Shivers rocked her body, and it didn't escape her notice that he tucked her tighter against him. Sorcha shifted until her head was underneath his chin. He was so large she could tuck her knees into his armpits and still be comfortable.

"Why are you so much bigger than me?" she asked, teeth clacking with chills.

"What kind of question is that?"

"I just want to know. All the other Tuatha dé Danann are the same. Y-you're all larger than life."

"I'm not that much bigger."

"You're a veritable giant compared to me."

"We're not human," he grumbled. "That's the only answer I have."

Sorcha glanced over his shoulder, brows furrowing in confusion. "Why aren't we going to the hag's hut?"

"I'm taking you to the castle."

"I was told to stay away from the castle—your guests are dangerous."

"They are."

"I think I've had enough of danger for one night."

Stone jostled her, tossing her up higher against his chest. He was like a furnace, and she couldn't understand how. The water chilled her skin and made her bones ache. Why didn't it affect him in the same way?

"I'm not putting you anywhere they might find you."

"Who are they?"

"That's not for you to know."

Sorcha shook her head. "I might be freezing, but that hasn't changed my curiosity. I thought this isle was only visible every seven years."

"It is."

"Then who are these people who suddenly arrived? Are they shipwrecked, like me?"

"No."

"Do they live on a different part of the isle?"

"No."

"Are they selkies or merrows come to visit?"

"Stop asking questions," he said.

"No," she said, repeating his favorite word. "Why are you shirtless?"

"I'm not foolish enough to attempt swimming in armor. Silence. These visitors can hear very well, and they would be too interested in a human girl. Keep your mouth shut, and trust me to take care of you."

Strangely enough, she did.

Sorcha tucked her hands underneath her chin to conserve what little heat she had left. She had survived many winters, but never had she been this cold. The biting rain washed away the salt water on her skin slicking her body with freezing drops. The wind howled and shoved at their bodies although his steps were sure and steady.

She owed this man her life. Sorcha wasn't sure how she felt about that. Tricking him into coming back to the mainland seemed wrong. He didn't deserve that mistreatment.

If she was being truthful with herself, it was unlikely she ever would have tricked him. Stone was an intelligent man beneath all that brawn. A noble Fae who had taken up the throne in this forgotten place.

They didn't disturb any other faeries along their journey to the castle. Most had sought shelter from the raging storm. Others remained in the castle to wait out the rain. Storms always seemed to keep everyone from their labor, even the faeries.

He rounded the stone castle walls to the place where she'd seen him training with Bran.

Teeth chattering, she bit out, "Is Bran really the raven who has been following me?"

"So it would seem."

"Why would he waste his time following a human?"

"I've asked him the same question."

He entered through a narrow door and slammed it shut behind them, sudden silence and darkness making her heart pound again. "And what was his response?"

"I do not control the Unseelie Fae. No one can."

The darkness made it seem almost as if she were underwater again. Shadows made shapes vaguely familiar, but difficult to piece together.

She recognized this room when lightning struck again, spearing light across the room.

Broken statues littered the floor. The haunting faces stared at her with vacant eyes.

Sorcha shivered and tucked her face against the crystals of his neck. Their jagged edges dug into her cheek but she did not care. The pain anchored her, driving away the fear with knife-sharp points and cold, smooth plains.

His hands clenched on her shoulder and legs. "Not far now."

"Where are you taking me?"

"Somewhere safe."

"There's nowhere safe on this isle," she whispered, her breath whistling through the circular wound on his throat. "Everything is dangerous, and one must decide whether to live in fear, or courage."

"We all know you've chosen courage, little human. Foolishly so."

"I'm not as fragile as you think."

He didn't respond, suggesting he disagreed with her. Sorcha was thankful he didn't argue his point. She couldn't debate him right now, not when her body was shivering so violently she worried she might jolt right out of his arms.

They rounded one last, shadowed corner and reached a dead-end. A carving on the wall caught her attention. A warrior held her sword aloft, driving back creatures of the night which Sorcha could only imagine were the Unseelie. Their twisted and warped forms disappeared into the smooth marble.

Her face was beautiful and hard. Her armor carved so meticulously that Sorcha could see individual links of chainmail. The sword itself appeared so realistic that she might pluck it from the woman's hand and swing it herself.

"It's beautiful," she whispered. "But I don't see a doorway."

"Humans. You look at things so superficially."

Stone jostled her forward, forcing her to grasp onto his neck with a gasp. Their gazes locked for a moment as their noses touched. She felt the warm fan of his breath grazing her mouth. Electric blue eyes burned her flesh and seared her to the bone.

"Look." A crystal brushed against her mouth. "You need to remember this."

She wasn't certain she'd ever forget the cold slide of stone warmed by the heat of his body.

Sorcha ripped herself from his captivating gaze and glanced over her shoulder. He pressed his thumb into the grooved pommel of the sword. She heard a soft click, the rasp of sliding stone, and then he pushed.

It wasn't just a carving; it was a door.

He wrapped his arm around her again, and she kept one arm looped around his neck. She wanted to be upright for this hidden secret. She wanted to remember.

Darkness lay within the room, not with tendrils of fear but a soft quiet that eased the soul. The slight burble of water reached her ears trickling from some unknown stream. Heat brushed against her skin in an almost physical touch.

Sorcha released a slow breath. "I can't see anything."

"I'm going to put you down," he said at the same time. She heard the creaking of crystals. "Patience, little human."

He set her down on a smooth bench. Sorcha couldn't see the color, but she could feel the texture as soft as velvet. She ran her palms over the edges, the bumps of carvings, dipping into hollows and valleys.

Impulsively, she toed off her sodden shoes. Soft moss cushioned the arches of her feet as she placed them back onto the floor. It was not wet with rain as she'd expected.

Sorcha tilted her head, listening for the pattering sound. It was there, but far away, as if she was in the very belly of the castle. She couldn't believe they were in a dungeon. No dungeon had a door so fine nor moss so soft.

Where were they?

Yellow light flashed, blurring her vision in bright sparks of color. The beautiful room before her couldn't be in the castle! Lush moss carpeted the circular room and ivy covered the walls, making it seem more forest than room. A canopy of blushing roses hung in tendrils over a bed piled high with furs. In the center, a carved woman stretched towards the ceiling atop a still pool studded with white flowers. Her wings spread wide for flight and were so detailed that Sorcha could see the veins stretched across them.

"This place is too fine for me," she said.

"There's no such place."

Her jaw dropped. What did he mean by that? He couldn't be saying she was worthy of such a room? This was fit for royalty or a high-born Fae gifted in the arts.

Sorcha glanced down at her calloused palms and shorn fingernails feeling well and truly out of place.

"I can't—" he paused and glanced at her then down at his chest. "I have to ready myself for these pests. I trust you can warm yourself?"

"Is there a place for a fire?"

He gestured towards one of the ivy-covered walls. "Everything you need should be in the room beyond."

"Oh." She didn't know what else to say. He'd saved her, brought her to this haven, and then…was leaving? Who did that? "It's very difficult to understand you."

"I don't know if that's a compliment."

"Neither do I."

He stood surrounded by green, and she couldn't help but wonder who this man truly was. She caught glimpses of him, but never the full portrait.

He held his hands limp at his sides. Drops of water dripped from the strands of his hair, running down the shaven sides, and disappearing into the crevices filled with gems. He couldn't meet her gaze, and as she watched, his hands clenched and relaxed.

"You aren't comfortable with me looking at you," she said. "That's why you didn't wish to speak when I saw you training."

"I know what I look like."

"What do you liken yourself to?"

"A monster. These," he gestured towards the shoulder wound and his throat, "are unnatural. Marks of disfigurement that make me less Fae, less of a man."

"I don't see how something such as that could make you less of anything. They are startling at first, but the shock fades, and I hardly even notice them now."

"It is a beautiful lie." He swept into a low bow. "I'd forgotten how refreshing it is to hear such words. Thank you for not telling me the truth."

"What?"

He swept out of the room so quickly she felt only the breeze of his passing.

Sorcha was left with the trickling water, the soft movement of roses, and complete silence. She sat upon the bench and stared at the ceiling, at the surrounding splendor. She was utterly alone for the first time since arriving.

Drawing her knees to her chest, she blew out a quiet breath. When had she last been alone? Surely it must have happened, but she couldn't think of a time. Her sisters had always been home. She'd traveled to the MacNara's with Agatha, had left with the Dullahan, spent days upon the ship. Even in the ocean there had been merrow-men and the Guardian.

She refused to let her thoughts turn dark. Heat should be her first task. She needed to get out of these wet clothes or she would catch cold.

The healing thoughts helped. She could diagnose herself like a patient, the segmented thoughts easy to follow.

Sorcha stumbled to her feet and brushed the ivy aside. She'd never seen a washroom such as this. More vines covered the walls, blue flowers unfurling their petals and filling the air with a heady floral scent. A large circle cut into the ground, warm water constantly pouring from a small hole in the wall.

"A hot spring," she murmured.

There was a small chamber pot in the corner, along with a vanity table filled to the brim with hairbrushes and pastes she did not recognize.

None of this was for her, she reminded herself. She should warm her shivering body and then jump into bed. There was no need for pampering, nor did she have any idea what those faerie treats would do to her.

She stripped the sodden fabric away, pausing a moment to stare down at her mother's dress. Seawater was likely to stain it, but she could at least try to save it. Tears pricked in the corners of her eyes.

"I miss you," she whispered. It was the same feeling every time. She missed her pagan rites, Beltane, the whispered faerie stories her mother had been so good at telling.

Steam rose into the air in wispy tendrils, begging Sorcha to warm herself. She turned and dipped a toe into the water. The shocking warmth made her gasp, then moan as she sank into the water to her shoulders.

Her shivers ceased immediately, coaxed to stillness by the gentle lapping waves of water. She could stand in this pool, and it would only come up to her breasts. This was safe water.

Curious, Sorcha scooped a handful and touched it to her tongue. Fresh water. Not a hint of salt tainted the taste, nor was it sulfuric as many hot springs could be.

"This place continues to grow stranger by the hour," she whispered.

Tipping her head back against the stone lip, she let her mind quiet until her skin pruned. Even then, she took a while to leave the comfort of the bath. It was as if she was the last person on earth. Silence calmed her anxious thoughts, steam whisked away old aches and pains, and the water held her in a gentle embrace.

She could spend the rest of her life like this.

When her eyelids drifted shut more than they stayed open, Sorcha dragged herself out of the warm bath. Blearily glancing around the room, she realized there was no drying cloth available.

She sighed. Hopefully, Eamonn wouldn't come waltzing back in while she stood stark naked in the center of the room. She dunked her mother's dress in the water and wrung it out a few times.

Leaving the yellow fabric on the edge of the bath, she peeked through the ivy to make sure no one was in the room. Of course, faeries could glamour themselves. She narrowed her eyes.

"Hello?"

No one responded.

"If there are any servants in here, I'm going to come out and I have nothing else to put on. Please don't...stare."

She chided herself as she dashed across the moss. Who was going to stare at her? They probably thought she looked as ugly as she found them.

Leaping into the large bed and snuggling beneath the furs, she hummed contentedly as the softness brushed her skin. The furs dried the water away and trapped the heat until she was in a cocoon of warmth and comfort.

She sighed happily, but took stock of her body just in case. The shivers had left, but she could already feel her nose clogging. She would have a slight cold, but hopefully nothing would settle in her chest.

If she was lucky, she would escape this entire ordeal unscathed. If she wasn't, she would need to make compresses and drink as much tea as she could.

Sorcha could hope that her body wouldn't have any adverse reactions. There wasn't time for her to fall ill.

Chapter 16

Eamonn sat in the shadows of her room, berating himself for returning here. He hadn't planned on this. Especially not on this night.

The emissaries from the Seelie court rarely came to visit. He found it curious they chose now, of all times, to show their faces. Was there a spy in his court of fools? He couldn't think of anyone who would pass secrets to his brother, but it wouldn't be the first time. He would need to interrogate a few to ensure his safety. For the good of everyone, his brother could not know what happened on this isle.

They always made him angry. These glittery giants, women and men, dressed in full armor under the pretense that they wished to visit an old friend. None of them cared how he lived before his banishment, and they didn't care now.

He thought the entire thing suspect, always had, but it was not within his power to deny them. If his brother wanted to keep an eye on him, then he could. But Eamonn wouldn't make it easy on him.

Armored and silent, he stared them down. The throne room changed to ballroom, a slap in the face to the brother who was not king. They brought their own musicians, their own people, everything that they thought he didn't have. The only thing Eamonn did was have the room cleaned.

Let them think he lived in splendor and enjoyed his life here on Hy-brasil. Eamonn enjoyed the thought of his brother's anger.

And when it was all done, he had meant to go back to his room. To break whatever he could in an attempt to cool his anger and embarrassment.

But he found himself here.

Staring at her.

Her hair fanned out around her head like the petals of a red rose. Streaks of sun-kissed skin paled to milk white, beautiful and unique like the rest of her. She was soft in sleep. Softer than he'd ever seen her.

There was always a hard edge riding on her shoulders. Lines formed between her brows, expressive with all her emotions. She was an open book.

His lips quirked. She wouldn't like how easily he read her.

One hand tucked beneath her cheek, pale lashes spread out and casting shadows. He sat himself in the darkness and counted every freckle on her face. It was the first time in years he had calmed down without crushing marble, shattering pottery, or snapping wooden frames.

He didn't know how she did it. Even while asleep, there was something infinitely calming about her mere existence.

Should that frighten him? He felt as though it should.

She stirred in her sleep, yawning, and slowly opened her eyes.

He waited for the flinch, the jump, the terrified shriek that would make his ears rings for days. So many Fae women had reacted in a similar way.

She did none of that. Sunshine, Sorcha, did none of those things. She blinked a few times, focusing on his form in the shadows, and then a soft smile spread across her face.

In that moment, she gutted him. No one had looked at him like a person in such a long time, without pity or fear. She just opened her eyes and smiled at him. As if he was finally where he belonged.

"I had a feeling you might come back tonight." Her voice was raspy as if water filled her lungs. Right on cue, she coughed into her fist.

"It's not unusual to fall ill after attempting to take your life." Why did he say that? Eamonn dug his fingers into the crystals on his opposite wrist. Always picking a fight, especially when worried.

"Oh, hush, you know that's not what it was. I need my things," she said when she stopped coughing. "I have a tea for this."

Eamonn gestured towards the small table he had set next to the pile of furs. "Anise, honey, and mulled wine."

She glanced over at the steam rising from the porcelain cup and back to him. "Yes. Thank you. That's exactly what I needed."

"Don't look so surprised. Healing humans is not so different from the Fae."

"I guess it isn't." She pulled herself up, catching the furs against her chest and shoving the heavy mass of her hair back. "You know the healing arts?"

"A small amount. I watched my nursemaid as a child."

"Clever."

"I never claimed otherwise." He watched her sip the tea, her face scrunching up. "Bitter?"

"I just don't like the taste of anise. Never have."

"It will help."

That soft expression returned to her face, eyes half-lidded and lips quirked to the side. "Yes, it will."

He didn't know what to say when she stared at him as if he brought all the stars in the sky to her. It was tea. Nothing more, nothing less.

They stared at each other until his heart raced. Eamonn couldn't piece together why he was so affected. Then his eyes traced the line of her shoulders. Bare and pale as the moon. Tiny freckles dotted her skin, more than he had counted on her face. He hadn't seen those.

How badly did he want to connect those dots? Enough to clench his fists and lock the muscles of his legs, restraining himself from leaning forward and tugging the furs away. He had forgotten to bring her anything to wear.

Bless his forgetfulness.

"Are your visitors gone?" she asked.

"Excuse me?" His mind had been elsewhere. There were freckles dotting her arms, so it would make sense if they spread to her legs as well. Was she freckled everywhere?

"Your guests, the dangerous ones. Have they left?"

"Yes."

"Is it safe for me to wander your halls again?"

"I—" he shook his head to clear it. "No, it's never safe to wander the castle halls. There are many hidden secrets and spirits who keep them."

"I haven't met a spirit yet, just faeries."

"Then you are lucky."

"This place is one of the strangest I have ever seen. Spirits wandering the castle at night. Faeries in the kitchen. You do keep strange company, Stone."

His name hovered on the tip of his tongue. Just once, he wanted to hear her say his name. His given name. But he knew how dangerous it would be to tell her. A human in possession of a faerie's name was bound to use it.

Even that danger would be worth hearing her lilting voice caress the syllables of his born name.

If he was any other man, he might have told her, but he buried the desire for the safety of his people. Eamonn was a creature bred for war and destruction. He could not take the risk.

She leaned forward and coughed again. He clenched his fists, reminding himself that she could take care of herself. She was human and not worthy of his instinctual reaction. To protect. To care.

His father's voice echoed in his mind. She was beneath him. A base creature on par with the lesser Fae. Ignore her struggles, but use her as a servant or slave when the time was right.

He'd never believed those words.

Eamonn stood and settled next to her on the bed. Her bare back shook, ribs expanding until he could see the bumping lines before hacking out air in the next second.

His hand was so large against her skin. It spanned the entirety of her back, rubbing gently back and forth. He did not pound—that wouldn't help—just tried to comfort as his nursemaid used to do.

"Thank you," she said on a sigh. "I'm sorry. I didn't expect a simple dip in the sea to affect me so."

"That was more than a dip."

"Venture?"

"Mistake." He caught himself again. Why was he so cruel to her? He couldn't understand why he tried to make it an argument every time she spoke. Other than to see the red peaks of color on her cheekbones that he so thoroughly enjoyed.

Eamonn didn't clench his fists this time. He reached and ran a finger over the high arches of her cheeks, tracing the spaces between freckles.

"What are you doing?" she whispered.

"I haven't the faintest idea."

He could get lost in those eyes. Green like ivy leaves, like moss when the sun first strikes after days of rainfall. How was she holding him captive? Had she cast a spell on him?

Or maybe he was simply so starved for attention he couldn't help himself. She was the first person to see him as a man, not a monster.

How could he stop?

Eamonn leaned down, eyes darting between her wide gaze and pouting lips. He'd never noticed her lips before. Berry red, thinner than most but still pleasing. Would she taste like the raspberry color staining her mouth?

"Master?" Cian's voice cut through the silence, jolting him to his feet and back to reality. "I'm sorry to interrupt, but there's been an unexpected complication."

"How so?"

"It's the visiting Unseelie, sir. He's requesting an audience, demanding really, and said he won't take no for an answer." Cian rubbed the side of his head. "He nearly took my ear off pulling at it."

"Bran," Eamonn grumbled. He glanced back at Sorcha, who clutched the furs to her chest. Her eyes were wide, her chest heaving.

That was the fear he'd expected. He should've known that although she may someday trust him, she was unlikely to ever want him. What a fool he was.

Eamonn nodded, and then eased off the bed and away from her. Without glancing back, he ducked out of the room. He'd made enough of a scene to want to hide from her for the rest of his existence. Bran had done the right thing by causing a mess only Eamonn could fix.

Damned Unseelie usually ended up being right.

Chapter 17

Sorcha moved permanently into the green room after her incident at the cliff. Boggart panicked, rushing around the hut and shattering plates until Sorcha caught her and explained the faerie was coming with her. That soothed her troubled mind although she didn't let go of Sorcha's leg for a few hours.

The faeries helped get all her things to her new room. She insisted everything go in the bathroom. The clothes remained in the drier bedroom. She didn't want to ruin the pristine image by filling it with wardrobes.

Thankfully, the faeries agreed.

Sorcha spent hours in the room, enjoying the quiet solitude. Boggart mostly stayed with the other brownies in the kitchen, having found a new appreciation for a large space to work with. She brought every meal to Sorcha and spent time listening to her talk. She still didn't speak.

The warning Macha had issued rang in Sorcha's ears more often than not. She'd tried to find Stone for several days, but he'd disappeared. She suspected he was in one of the castle towers. Pixie had whispered the suggestion a few times, but no one would tell her which tower.

Time was ticking. Every day passing by felt like a nail in her father's coffin. She had to do something! But there wasn't anything to do—not as long as the master of the isle hid himself from everything and everyone.

She sat on the edge of the faerie fountain, watching minnows dart towards each other. Every tiny movement flashed their silver bellies as they playfully zipped away from her fingers.

It was late, and she should be sleeping. The longer she stayed on this isle, the less she felt the need for rest. Energy sparked in the air. It made the hair on her arms stand up and her body yearn to move, to dance, to do anything other than fall asleep. Again.

There was so much more she could be doing.

"But they won't let me," Sorcha breathed with a sigh. "They think I'm some well-to-do lady with no need to be in the garden."

She snorted. She had mucked stalls, pulled weeds, and stuck her hands where they shouldn't be. The scars on her arms and legs were proof enough.

They'd heard it all. Every time she argued with them, the faeries shook their glamoured heads and sent her back to her room, or for a walk in the fresh air, or heavens forbid suggest she might need something else to eat.

Sorcha ran a hand over her soft stomach. She'd eaten enough in the past month to feed three people, and still they said she was too skinny.

A minnow swam towards her swirling finger, tapping it before dashing away.

Sorcha smiled. At least the animals were welcoming. Even a few of the sheep had taken a liking to her, and they didn't mind when she trudged through the fields with a dirty hem. The faeries would not make her a lady. She had no use for being a lady.

All she needed was their master to agree to return to the mainland.

"Sorcha," a voice whispered on the wind. "Sooorchaaa."

It exhaled her name, elongating the syllables until it sounded like a long drawn out moan. Frowning, Sorcha peered into the shadows. No eyes blinked back at her, no faeries stood in her doorways.

"Hello?" she called out. "Is anyone there?"

"Sorcha."

"Yes?"

A soft breeze brushed against her face and stirred the hair hanging around her cheeks. This room was closed in the depths of the castles, with no windows or cracks where the wind might sneak through. A breeze was impossible.

And yet, there was one.

She reached out her hand, fully expecting to meet a solid invisible body. It was not a solid beast, nor was it a faerie hiding in plain sight. This was truly air tangling around her.

Again, her name whispered through the room. This time it was accompanied by movement on the wall furthest from her. Ivy shifted in a waterfall of movement as if a hand brushed against the other side.

Sorcha rose from the fountain and gingerly made her way to the wall. She was certain there was nothing behind that wall. She'd checked a hundred times, running her hands over the plain stone as she checked for secrets the faeries may have hidden.

The ivy shifted again.

She held her breath and reached forward. The leaves were cold to the touch, far colder than the room.

"Sorcha," the voice whispered. "Come to me."

Magic swirled through the room. The ivy rustled, then suddenly blasted the greenery away from its surface. A burning white light grew so bright that Sorcha tossed an arm over her eyes. The sound of ringing bells filled her ears.

Then all was silent.

Sorcha dropped her arms, blinking at the swirling wall of darkness before her. The wall had turned into water. Dark water, like the bottom of the ocean that had nearly killed her.

She shivered. What kind of magic was this?

"Sorcha," the voice warped as it passed through the liquid portal. "Sorcha, come to me."

Her stomach dropped, but she couldn't quell her own curiosity. Someone was calling for her. Were they hurt? Was it someone she knew?

She reached out and touched the wall. It quivered and quaked. A small piece of it broke off, floated over her shoulder, and popped in the center of her bedroom.

"Strange," she whispered.

Everything here was strange, and she found that it didn't shock her anymore. Watery portals, faeries in kitchens, boys made up of a menagerie of beasts. What else could happen in this strange and unusual place?

"Sorcha, there is not much time."

She glanced over her shoulder. No faeries stood in her doorway. No whispers suggested they were listening. Would anyone know if she disappeared?

Someone would have an opinion about this. The angry lord of the castle would notice she had disappeared without his say-so. A rebellious part of her wanted to plunge through the portal just to anger him.

"Why is that considered rebellious, Sorcha?" she asked herself. Her voice bounced back through the portal, echoing her words. "You're curious. Go through the portal."

"Yes," the whisper repeated. "Go through the portal."

"It could be dangerous."

"It is dangerous."

"But that has never stopped me before."

"You are brave."

"What if this is an Unseelie?" she peered through the waters, trying to see if anyone stood beyond.

"It's definitely Unseelie."

"They're unpredictable."

"They're everything you ever desired."

"How so?"

Apparently, the voice didn't want to answer questions, as it didn't respond. She waited to see if it would speak again.

It didn't.

Sorcha understood what it was doing. The voice, or owner of the voice, wanted her to go through the portal, and it wanted to convince her to do so. This couldn't end well. She had read countless tales where faeries lured humans into their worlds. The Unseelie were not kind to humans.

"This is a terrible idea," she whispered. "You're going to end up hurting me, or trapping me in the otherworld forever."

"We wouldn't do such a thing."

"You want to do harm."

"We want to provide knowledge."

"What could you know that I do not?"

The wind coiled around her ankles and wrists. "We know much, little human. Your beast is not what he says he is."

"My beast?"

"Stone." The voice moaned the word, dragging out the syllables as it had her name. "He is not who he seems to be."

"Then who is he?"

"Come to me, Sorcha. I will explain all you desire to know."

Her scalp tingled.

This was a trap. This was an Unseelie who wanted to lure her into the Otherworld and toy with her.

How did the stories always end? The human would lose their minds in the depths of the Unseelie kingdom. They would find themselves slaves, left to the mercy of the hideous creatures crawling through the muck and mire.

But so many of these creatures were different than the stories. The Seelies weren't what she thought. Could it be that the Unseelie were also not how the myths portrayed?

Taking a deep breath, she plunged into the portal.

The liquid clung to her body, sticking to her hair and clothing. It pulled at her. Did it want to drown her? The sticky fluid clawed at her lips and eyes, but never sank into the wide gape of her scream.

Cold sank into her body until she was certain it would freeze her. She would die here, and the Unseelie would win. Her toes curled, her fingers grew numb, and the coils of her curls solidified.

What a fool she was.

The bubble of portal popped and threw her out. She gasped, tumbling onto a stone floor, air whooshing from her lungs on impact.

Laying on the ground, she tried to find her bearings. Dim, grey light revealed shadows but no solid forms. The floor was solid stone, so she wasn't outside. The air was stale. It tasted like dust and something she couldn't quite name. Rotten, but sweet. She could hear a soft sound above. A dull shush, a scrape of something heavy brushing against stone.

That was impossible. There couldn't be anything above her, not something that weighed enough to make that sound.

Curling her hands into fists, she squeezed her eyes shut and counted to ten. She was brave. She was strong. Fear would not force her to curl into a ball and weep.

Sorcha's fingers began to shake.

"Sorcha," the voice called out to her again. This time it wasn't through the portal, but echoing from above. "Look at me."

"I wish not to."

"Look at me!" The voice boomed so loud that Sorcha flattened herself against the floor in fear.

Cold seeped through the front of her dress. She blew out a breath and wondered what Macha would do. Would she draw her sword and threaten the Unseelie's life?

Probably, but Sorcha was not Macha. She couldn't condemn anyone when she hadn't spoken to them, judged their character, heard their story. There was no reason for her to be frightened of this creature who commanded her gaze. She placed her hand flat against the floor and pushed herself onto her back.

A monster anchored herself to the ceiling above Sorcha. At first, she couldn't make out the shape hovering in the air. It was too large, too much of a blob made of shadow.

Then she made out the bulbous stomach, bloated and larger than three horses combined. Eight legs stuck out from the wide belly. They shifted as she watched, smoothing across the stone ceiling, and creating the sound she had heard.

Attached to the body was the torso of a woman. Heavily muscled, so pale she was almost blue, with long lanky hair that hung down towards Sorcha. The smile spread across the creature's face split from ear to ear.

"Hello, Sorcha of Ui Neill," the monster murmured. "Welcome to Caisleán dorcha."

Not just Unseelie then, Sorcha realized. This was their castle, the home to the royal family of Unseelie beasts. The family who were kings and queens of monsters.

She swallowed the scream rising in her throat, and instead stared in horror at the dead body trapped in a white blanket of webbing. "Lovely to meet you."

"Is it?" The woman cocked her head to the side. "You look positively terrified."

"I am."

"Then why don't you scream?"

"I do not wish to offend."

"A scream is a gift." Thin legs scraped the ceiling as she untangled herself. Muffled thumps echoed, one leg striking the ground near Sorcha's legs. More followed, thumping again and again until the creature was looming over her. "It is an agreement that I am a terrifying creature whom you respect and fear."

Sorcha swallowed hard.

The woman leaned down, until she nearly touched Sorcha's face with her own. A hairy leg balanced her right next to Sorcha's ear. "I wish to hear you scream."

She couldn't contain it. Sorcha squeezed her eyes shut and screamed out her fear and terror. This beast wasn't just going to scare her, she would devour her whole.

No stories whispered this creature's name. Nothing had hinted to the little midwife from Ui Neill that something like this ever existed. Faeries were strange, yes, but they were never so deformed as this.

A leg stroked Sorcha's stomach. She pushed backwards but knocked her head against a thick leg. The tiny fibers of hairs brushed the back of her neck. Trapped. Sorcha was trapped. There was nothing she could do but scream and scream.

"Enough!" The booming shout splintered through her skull in tiny points of pain. "You have done me a great honor with such terror."

She traversed over Sorcha, heavy belly brushing against Sorcha's side. She swallowed the gorge that rose in her throat. The stomach was smooth, not hairy like her legs. A red splotch of color resembled an hourglass on her belly, but Sorcha had never seen the arachnids in Ui Neill.

The creature pressed her hands against Sorcha's chest, forcing her to stare up at the ceiling. Shock tied her tongue in knots. The creature only wanted to hear her scream? What other purpose did she have for dragging Sorcha here?

Of course, there might not be a purpose at all. The Unseelie might have found herself bored and merely wanted a plaything. But how had she known where Sorcha was?

The cobwebs on the ceiling moved.

"Please, don't let there be another," she whispered.

"There isn't." The creature's voice lifted in amusement. "It's my dinner."

Sorcha narrowed her eyes and cried out. There was a man tangled in the webs. At least, she thought it was a man. The spider woman had wrapped him up so tight, she could only see the outlines of pectoral muscles and the bulging thigh muscles that strained against his ties.

"He'll quiet down eventually."

The webs covered his face, preventing him from breathing. "He's going to suffocate."

"Yes, he will. That is the point."

"What a cruel way to die."

"It is better than poison that travels slowly through the blood. At least now he will calm down then drift off into sleep."

"Why not just snap his neck and be done with it?"

The movement of the woman paused, and Sorcha felt the weight of her gaze like a physical touch. "Would that be your preference?"

"If you plan to eat me, I would like not to be alive at all."

"I don't plan on eating you. Little girls like you make terrible meals. Not enough meat on your bones. Besides, humans are always so bitter."

Sorcha lifted a hand and pointed. "That's not human?"

"No, that's Seelie. I prefer a lighter diet while I'm watching my figure."

"You're watching your figure?"

"Isn't every woman?"

Sorcha couldn't imagine what figure the creature was talking about. It was hard to force a ball into sensuous curves.

"Why have you brought me here?" she asked.

"All in good time. Get up, girl."

She looked back up at the man who was tangled in the creature's web. His struggles were slowing, a few twitches here and there were the only way she knew he was still alive.

"I think I'll stay here."

"You want to watch him die?"

"No."

"Then get up."

Sorcha couldn't find an argument. Sighing, she rolled onto her knees and told herself to forget about the man in the ceiling. He was beyond her help, no matter how much she wanted to cut him down and breathe air back into his lungs. She, too, was at the mercy of the monstrous woman.

"What shall I call you?" Sorcha asked.

"You may call me Your Queen."

"Queen?" Sorcha gasped. "Are you—"

"Yes.

The queen of the Unseelie Fae stood before her, and Sorcha was acting as if she were some beast she needed to squash beneath her heel. She was lucky to still be alive.

Falling onto her knees, she pressed her thumbs to her forehead. "Forgive me, Your Majesty. I am a lowly beast indeed to not recognize royalty."

"I asked you to get up. Do not make me ask again."

Sorcha scrambled to her feet again. What did this creature want of her? The darkness stirred, casting out mist in great billows that swirled around the Queen's legs.

Her legs moved in synchronization Sorcha realized. Not like a real spider which sometimes could seem jerky in their movements. This woman moved with a natural grace. Each leg lifted and was placed so gently that the sound they made was quiet and dull.

"Are you done staring?"

"What?" Sorcha looked up to see that the Queen was staring back. She was immensely tall. Easily two of Stone's great height. "My apologies."

"Stop apologizing."

"I—" she cleared her throat. "I understand."

"Good. Now, follow me."

She didn't want to follow this creature deeper into the darkness. Who knew what waited for her there?

The Queen saw her hesitate. "I'm not going to kill you, child."

"You have yet to answer why I am here."

"Because I bade you come."

"That's not an answer."

The Queen sighed. "There is much at play here. You have stepped into a world where you will make a decision that will ultimately affect all the players on the board. I will not leave the fate of the Fae in the hands of an uneducated human. Follow me."

"What do I have to do with that?"

"All will be revealed in time. The web is large, and there is much to explain."

Sorcha watched the spider woman disappear into the darkness with her jaw open. There was much to explain? She was just a midwife. What did she have to do with the fate of the Fae?

She wouldn't go with the Queen. They had obviously coaxed the wrong person through the portal.

Giggles echoed behind her, coming closer and closer through the fog and darkness. Shivers danced up her spine. What manner of Unseelie stood behind her? Was that the wind on the back of her neck, or was it the breath of yet another monster?

She bolted after the Queen, steps loud and uncontrolled.

The entirety of the castle was dark. Some small sconces decorated the walls, lit with green fire that did little to cast light in any direction.

She couldn't see, but she could hear the queen.

Thump. Thump. Shhh. Thump. Thump. Shhh.

It was a horrible sound. The dragging of a thick body by legs too thin and hairy. Sorcha shivered again, knowing nightmares would plague her for years to come.

The Queen's chuckle bounced from ceiling to floor. "Good, you are smart enough to follow."

"I'm smart enough to not be left behind."

"Ah, yes. My children are far too curious for their own good."

"Your children?" Sorcha glanced into the shadows. "How many do you have?"

"Seventeen Tuatha dé Danann children, and hundreds of lesser Fae."

That alone was intriguing, and went against everything Sorcha knew. "You have children who are both Tuatha dé Danann and not?"

"We are not the Seelie Fae. There is value in lives which are not human in appearance."

"Do the Seelie Fae not agree?"

"No."

She had suspected as much. The legends always spoke of creatures that looked like humans as kings and queens. So few people saw any kind of faerie that didn't look like a human.

A stairwell appeared before them, the stones swept clean and glistening in the green light. Sorcha blinked, trying to bring everything into focus. It was difficult here, where magic was so thick that she could see it like a fog.

"Do you not wear glamour?" Sorcha asked. "All the faeries I have met thus far have worn a glamour."

"Seelie, I take it?"

"Most."

"All. An Unseelie would never hide their true form. The Seelie hide to protect human's delicate sensibilities when the reality is that we are all beautiful, powerful beings. Humans should run in fear."

"You would give them nightmares for the rest of their lives."

"Will your dreams be troubled?"

"Without a doubt," Sorcha shivered. "I will never sleep again for fear you will hover above my bed."

"You flatter me."

That was not her intention, although she was relieved her words had complimented the Queen. Sorcha merely told the truth.

A scrying pool on a large altar stood in the center of the room they entered. Shards of black glass made up the floor. Sorcha stared at it and swore she saw dark fire reflected beneath. Wind brushed across her ears bringing with it the screams of tortured souls.

The Queen skittered towards it, hunching over the bowl, and rocking back and forth. Sorcha wasn't certain she had ever seen a spider move like that. Was the queen even part spider? Was she merely wearing the skin of one?

The Ballad of Tam Lin burst into her mind. The Queen in that story had turned his lover into a spider. He held onto her great abdomen, her legs, her great eyes. For days, he hung on as she changed into dozens of creatures.

Sorcha couldn't help but wonder if this chosen form was symbolic.

"Come," the Queen said. "Gaze into my pool, and I will show you all you desire."

"I desire very little."

"Humans lie every day. You desire so many things that you cannot even breathe for the wanting."

"I want health and happiness for my family. That is all."

"Oh, little human. You desire so much more than that. It is healthy to want."

"I care for others."

"You care for yourself. The desire to heal others builds your confidence, solidifies your reason for being. You have yet to discover who you are. Come."

Sorcha stared at the Queen's strong hands gripping the edge of the stone bowl. "I'm afraid to know what I want."

"Everyone is."

She stood on the precipice of something great, but she didn't know what she would find. The Queen offered something without cost.

"What do I have to do?" Sorcha asked.

"Listen and learn."

Small, black dots appeared on the Queen's forehead from her eyebrows to her temples. At the same time, every dot blinked.

A whimper escaped Sorcha's mouth as she realized the dots were eyes. The Queen, like many spiders, had multiple eyes that all stared with expectation at the human on the stairs.

What did she have to lose? Thoroughly uncomfortable, Sorcha stepped towards the scrying pool.

"What would you have me learn?"

"Everything."

The Queen leaned forward and dunked a finger into the clear water. It swirled, dark magic dropping like ink and spreading rapidly. Black swallowed the bowl of water and wisps of white smoke rose into the air.

"You are entangled in the most important plot of this millennia, and there is so much you need to see."

"Why?"

"The Fae are a tricky lot. Our legends speak of so many beautiful stories. Of heroes who swing blades that cleave giants in two. Of heroines who seduce a man with one glance and drag them to the bottom of the ocean. But we are not a group of people who enjoy death and destruction. There are as many species of Fae as there are stars in the sky."

Whispers echoed her words, three voices overlaying the Queen's.

"Who are they?" Sorcha asked.

"My children."

"Where?"

The Queen glanced over her shoulder and nodded. Three women stepped forward, lashed to the ceiling by thin threads of web. They had rings pierced down their arms where the threads looped through. Pale as snow, their eyes were blind. No color lived on their bodies at all. White hair, white eyes, white skin so pale it was blue.

"Three daughters," Sorcha nodded. "You are blessed."

A smile spread across the Queen's face. "Blessed? You don't have children, do you?"

"No, your highness."

"Children suck the lives out of their mothers. They drain them until they are little more than husks. But they are good for the soul."

One of the wraith-like women stepped forward. The Queen petted her head and pushed her towards the scrying bowl. "What secrets do you have to share with the little human?"

The pale woman cocked her head to the side, unseeing eyes blinking slowly. "I share the state of the Seelie Fae."

"Why?" the Queen asked.

"It is important she know the situation in Tír na nÓg. She must know what the people do and how they suffer."

The daughter stepped forward and reached out her arm. The Queen looked at her with no emotion, wrapped her strong around the limb, and snapped it in half.

Sorcha cried out as blood poured into the scrying pool. White bones poked through torn flesh and fragments of hanging muscle dipped into the water. Through it all, the daughter did not flinch nor cry out.

"What are you doing?" Sorcha screamed. "Stop!"

"You do not understand our ways. Watch and learn. That was what you promised me." The Queen patted her daughter on the head again. "Thank you. Go back to your sisters for healing."

She stepped back into the fold. The other two reached for the thick threads of webbing and pulled hard. They lifted the injured woman into the air by the rings on her arms. She dangled for a moment, suspended above the ceiling before a long spider leg reached out and pulled her through the webbed ceiling.

"What was that?" Sorcha whispered.

"My husband."

"There are more of you?"

"It takes two to make children."

"What manner of Fae are you?"

"Do not waste the blood of my children. Look into the scrying pool, and see the truth of the Seelie Fae."

Sorcha wanted to follow the injured woman to insist that she might help. Of all people, she could set a broken bone, wrap the injury, pack it with herbs so it didn't get infected. But these were Unseelie Fae. They would not want her help.

Swallowing hard, she nodded.

Black water swirled with blood. She placed her hands on the side and leaned over until she could peer into the depths.

"What am I looking for?" she asked.

"There are images even in the darkest of places." The Queen placed her large hands on top of Sorcha's. Her flesh was frigid. "See the truth."

A dwarf appeared in the water. His beard tangled around his ankles, and he fell onto the ground. He reached out to stop himself, but a whip cracked through the air before he touched the ground. His face twisted in pain, then he lay still.

Another man walked towards him, golden hair swinging at his waist. The golden newcomer was perfect in every way. His skin glittered in the sun, his eyes strikingly green. He held the whip coiled around his wrist and nudged the fallen dwarf with a look of disgust.

"What is he doing?" she asked.

"They use the dwarves to mine for copper and gold. When anyone tries to leave, they whip them until they either return or die."

"Why?"

"They want the gold but are not willing to work for themselves."

The image shuddered, shifting to reveal a beautiful pixie. Her forehead arched up into points, looking very like an autumn leaf. Blushing colors painted her skin, furthering her autumnal look. Black eyes swallowed any white that might have existed on a human, but still seemed kind.

The pixie winced and rubbed her hand over the opposite wrist. Skin burned red around a brand in the mark of a trinity knot.

"What is that?" Sorcha asked.

"The faeries are branded depending upon who they call master. Each of the lesser Fae are born with this mark, but it can stretch and distort as they grow. It will be burned again into their bodies if it is difficult to tell who's mark it is."

"Why brand them? Why not simply know who works for you?"

"So that the faeries can't slip away in the dead of night and disappear."

Sorcha's mind raced. She knew what that meant, what darkness the Unseelie suggested brewed in the Seelie lands. "They're slaves?"

"They most certainly are. Their king has turned them into little more than beasts to trade. They are born, bought, and worked to death long before they see their families grow."

"It doesn't make any sense," she muttered. "Why force your people to be unhealthy? It isn't the mark of a good king if he cannot provide a good life for all his people."

"Were you under the impression that the wise king is a good one?"

"Wise king?"

The Queen snorted, retreating from the altar with great thudding steps. "It is the name he has given himself. Wise, for his knowledge is vast."

"Knowledge does not mean intelligence."

"Astute for a human child."

"You are not the first to say so."

"One last vision especially for you, Sorcha of Ui Neill."

Brows furrowed, Sorcha leaned over the pool and stared into the dark waters.

A woman appeared, painfully beautiful and holding her hand over her belly. Her waist-length blonde hair swept nearly to the floor. Silver silk fabric poured from her shoulders to sweep the crystal floor.

"Who is she?" Sorcha asked.

"Elva, the most prized concubine of the king. Her mother was one of my most prized followers." The Queen tapped the water with her nail. "She has just realized that she may be pregnant."

"Isn't that a good thing?"

"That is not up to me to decide. You will need to know her name. You say you are a good person, midwife. This is one who you could save."

Sorcha looked up. "Why would you want me to save any of the Seelie?"

"I am not a heartless creature. There are some who deserve to live, and others who I would relish crushing their skulls beneath my hands. Elva is one whose true name I give to you in full confidence you will use it well."

Another of the Queen's daughters stepped forward, and Sorcha winced in preparation for the next dark deed. She couldn't take much more of this. The Unseelie were always rumored to be twisted and depraved, but how far did that insanity travel?

Did they feast upon it rather than food?

"Peace," the Queen whispered. "You have seen enough bloodshed."

The Princess reached up and held a mirror towards her mother. Vines tangled around the handle. It was as large as Sorcha was tall, and the Queen held it as if it were nothing more than a handheld mirror.

"Do you know our history?" the Queen asked. "Do you know the difference between Seelie and Unseelie?"

"Your kind gave up honor and law to live wild and free."

"Yes. And do you think we made the wrong choice?"

Sorcha didn't know. She shrugged, frowning in concentration as she mulled the question over in her mind. "Who am I to judge others for the choices they make? If a soul is born to be wild, it will only grow angry with a leash wrapped around its neck. If a soul prefers order, then it will shrivel with too many choices. Neither is wrong."

"You do not see darkness as evil?"

"Nothing is evil. The very idea was created by those who won wars and wished to paint their poor choices as the right thing. No one goes into war or battle thinking they are evil."

"You speak with the tongue of a philosopher."

"I am just a midwife."

The Queen's face split open in that jagged edged smile again. "Come closer, Sorcha. This mirror will show you the future."

"I do not wish to see my future."

"I wish to see it."

Sorcha frowned and remained where she was. "You want to see my future? Why am I so important to the Queen of the Unseelie Court?"

"Look."

She wanted to. Every fiber of her being screamed for Sorcha to look into the future and see what would happen. Who didn't want to know what their end would look like? How much time she had left?

But what would she find? If she stayed on Hy-brasil her family would die, and she would've done nothing to prevent it. If she returned home without Stone, it was likely she would die from the beetle plague. There was only one suitable ending, and it was slowly slipping out of reach.

Sorcha shook her head. "I have no wish to see my future. I will stand before the mirror if you need to see it, but I will not look."

"You have no desire to see the end of your life?"

"Of course I do," she said. "I want it more than anything, but I am also frightened of it. I make my own choices, and I would rather believe they have not already been destined."

The Queen's expression softened, a strange look on such a monstrous being. She lifted a hand and beckoned Sorcha forward. "Then I will look for you, child."

Sorcha's footsteps echoed in the altar room. Each steady sound beat in tune with the pounding of her heart. She closed her eyes as the mirror began to move, then turned her back.

Even the air seemed to hold its breath. The Queen was silent as she watched the images casting light on the floor. They twirled and moved at Sorcha's feet and she watched them with rapt attention, but could not make out what they meant.

One of the daughters gasped, and a thick body moved above them. Sorcha held still until the cold sank into her bones. Her toes ached, her fingers trembled, and her breath fogged the air.

"So that is your choice," the Queen said. "You are an interesting woman, Sorcha of Ui Neill."

"Is it an agreeable choice?" She wanted to ask why she was making a choice at all. Thousands of reasons danced through her mind, but none seemed important enough to tempt a Queen. Of course, even the wing-beat of a butterfly could change time.

"It is agreeable to me."

"And to me?"

"I do not know you, human child. How should I know what you will find agreeable?"

Sorcha licked her lips. "May I turn around?"

"Do you wish to?"

"No."

"Then why are you asking?"

"I have never flinched away from something I was afraid of."

Thumping from the ceiling made the cobwebs twang. They vibrated as the great king of the Unseelie Court descended from his throne. He was so much louder than his wife. She prayed it was because he did not care to be quiet or dainty. She had a feeling she was wrong.

Sorcha slowly turned, holding her breath so hard her lungs hurt. She would not scream again. These creatures could try to frighten her time and time again, but she would not scream.

He stepped from the ceiling, long legs clacking as they struck the ground. Armor covered the hairy appendages that rubbed together with a grating sound. Like his wife, the king was too muscular to be attractive. His body bulged, swollen with meat and strength.

"This is the girl?" he grumbled. His eighth leg touched the ground and he lurched towards his wife, rubbing a leg against hers. "Did you find out what you need to know?"

"I found out enough."

"If I may," Sorcha asked. Her voice wobbled. "Will you now tell me why you summoned me here?"

"You're going to find out soon enough. You are welcome to leave now, human girl."

Sorcha wasn't sure if she should. The entire situation was scarring and terrifying, but there was something strange about the faeries.

"You aren't telling me everything," she murmured. "Why are you meddling in my life?"

"The master of your isle does not know there are Unseelie living in his household. You must be careful, for you do care for them."

"Who?"

"Oona is her given name, and as she is of my Court, I gift her name to you."

"Who is she?"

"Your Pixie."

So, her name was Oona. It was a beautiful name for a beautiful creature, and Sorcha was honored that the Queen thought her trustworthy enough to gift it.

"That still doesn't answer my question."

"I have no intention of answering."

"Fair enough," Sorcha murmured. "I'll have to ask Bran if he has any idea."

The Queen froze, and the King stiffened. He cocked his head to the side and lifted a long finger to point at her. "What does this Bran look like?"

Sorcha gestured at her face. "Half raven, half man. He has feathers, a raven eye, and the leg of a bird."

Echoes of laughter came from all directions of the room. They bounced atop the ceiling and shook the webs.

The Queen shook her head, still chuckling. "Ah, you have met my ugliest son then."

Ugly? The royals in front of her were anything but pretty. How could Bran be considered the ugly one?

The King shook his head. "Unseelie do not value beauty in the same way the Seelie do. He is too human, too weak, and can only change his form into a raven. Pathetic excuse for a child, but then, he is the youngest. We do not have to worry about him taking the throne any time soon. Be gone, human. Tell my boy to come home soon. His sisters miss him."

One of the albino daughters lifted her hands as if she were pleading. Were these creatures even capable of such emotions? Did they miss their family, or did they miss the way they might torture them?

Sorcha didn't plan to stay and find out. Bowing so low that her forehead nearly touched the floor, she whispered, "It was an honor,

Your Majesties."

"An honor?" The Queen tsked. "Oh dearie, the Unseelie do not like lies. You may want to run, for my children are hungry and your fear tastes sweeter than wine."

Sorcha did not have to be told twice. She'd counted each step as she followed the Queen and knew the way back to the portal.

Spinning, she raced down the stairs taking them two at a time. It didn't matter that she might trip and fall. Breaking her neck would be a blessing if it meant freedom from this hellish castle.

Breath sawed in and out of her lungs until she tasted blood. Screaming laughter chased her, goblins and trolls whooping and hollering as they tracked her. Down the corridors she flew until she couldn't hear them anymore.

She slowed to a walk, holding her ribs as they ached from overuse. Why did she ever wear the dresses Pixie gave her? They were too tight!

Oona, she corrected herself. Pixie's name was Oona.

She smiled at the thought. Oona might not be pleased, but it was a beautiful name, and Sorcha would never use it without permission. It was the third Fae name she held. How lucky a woman was she?

The portal room remained untouched. Fog swirled across the ground, lifting in tendrils that looked like hands reaching for help. Sorcha walked through them. She had to remember that these were Unseelie Lands and did not live by the same laws.

She couldn't help those who were suffering without condemning herself to the same fate.

Sorcha pulled her cloak around her when cold air drifted underneath its folds. She shivered and peered into the darkness to find the watery portal, or even the barest hint of leaves.

There. In the deepest shadows between leaves and branches, she recognized a familiar stone wall.

Brushing aside ivy and moss, she placed her hands against its cold stone surface.

"There you are," she said. "It's time to go home."

Nothing happened. She scraped her hands all over the edges, but couldn't open the portal. Nothing seemed to work. No gemstone in a sword that she could push, no whispered words.

"Oh, what have you done?" she whispered into the night. "How am I supposed to go home now?"

"Portals are magic, you know," a familiar voice echoed. Deep and baritone, she had only heard it once before.

Sorcha turned on her heel, pivoting to glare at the Unseelie Fae who stood behind her. "Bran."

"Sorcha."

"What are you doing here?"

"I should ask you the same question. Don't you know that the Otherworld is dangerous for humans?"

"I could say the same for Unseelie. It's worse here, so I've heard."

"Ah, there are so many bad stories about my kind." He grinned, his raven eye dancing to and fro while the human eye remained locked on her. "Not all stories are true, little human."

"You've been kind thus far." She pressed her spine against the wall. "I would ask you continue to do the same."

"I hear you met my parents."

"And some of your siblings as well. I would never have guessed you came from such parentage."

"Where did you think I came from? A bird?"

"Certainly something that suggests the same species," she gritted through clenched teeth. "You lied to me. You didn't tell me you were an Unseelie prince!"

"I was not aware that you were privy to such knowledge."

Sorcha blinked in shock, her jaw falling open. "How dare you even say such a thing? You traveled across the sea with me! You followed me from the MacNara's, and you teased me in front of Stone. I would even go so far as to muse that you were behind him moving me into the castle."

"Do you think I'm looking out for you, I wonder?"

"Why else would you be following me?"

"Because the MacNara twins paid me to? Perhaps I wished to infiltrate your 'Stone's' castle. Or maybe I wanted to drag you here to be my slave." He cocked his head to the side. "There are plenty of reasons and none of them kind."

"And none that I believe."

"Is that so?"

"You are far too smart a man to be bought, even by the MacNara twins who appear to be intelligent and manipulative people. You don't want to harm Stone; you practiced with him like an old friend and teased him quite mercilessly. And if you wanted to drag me back to Unseelie with you, why haven't you? Why wait until your mother summoned me?" She tilted her chin up, refusing to be cowed by this dark man.

"Ever so brave," he whispered. "You are a remarkable little human. Did you know that? There are few who would dare stand up to me in such a way, but you didn't even flinch. You are quite the match for him."

"For who?"

"No one."

She arched a brow. "Really? That's what you have to say?"

"No one, everyone, someone." He shrugged. "There are plenty of people of whom I could be speaking. The long and short of it is that you need to go back home before he finds out where you've gone."

"Stone?"

"Yes."

"You—" she bit her lip. "You know him?"

"No one knows him."

"But you know him more than most."

"Yes."

"Perhaps you might answer a few questions for me."

Bran's raven eye narrowed. He crossed his arms over his chest and the bird eye looked her up and down. He was measuring her or trying to see a way through her lies. Finally, he waved a hand for her to continue.

"Your mother made me look in the scrying bowl. There were faeries that the Seelies used for slaves. Branded, mistreated, living out their lives as if they were not worth even the slightest of things. Is this true, or was this some kind of Unseelie trick?"

He snorted. "The Seelie like to make their people labor until they break. They believe in bloodlines and power more than respect. Don't let them fool you. They preach honor and then stab each other in the back."

"Is Stone treating the faeries on the isle like slaves?"

"Do you think he is?"

She pondered the question before shaking her head. "I don't think so. I've seen no behavior that might support such an accusation. But I do not see him often, and secrets hide in the shadows."

"I know Stone well enough to say that he's not treating them like anything. He's a solitary creature. Rare for a Fae."

"Is it?"

"We're creatures who like the company of others. Even the Unseelie enjoy each other's company. Stone has never been like that. They say he used to tent away from his men on the battlefield. He was the first to reach enemy lines, and the first the enemy found if they came looking in the night."

"And now?"

Bran cocked his head to the side. "Ask a more direct question."

"Is he the same man now as he was back then?"

"No, but not in the way you think. He has become harder and softer with time."

"How is that possible?" She wanted to know the answer so much it burned in her belly.

He shook his head. "That's a story I can't tell you. You must ask him if you want to know that badly."

"How can I ask him? I rarely see him!"

"That might change soon." Mischief and hidden knowledge sparkled in his eyes.

"You know something I don't know."

"I always know something humans don't know. You're a lucky little thing to be living in a time of such burgeoning change."

Sorcha's mind raced to keep up with the Unseelie Fae. His words made little sense, but she knew he mostly spoke in riddles. There was something he didn't want to tell her. Something she needed to figure out for herself.

"Are you lying?"

"I cannot lie."

"Are you hiding the truth?"

Bran's face split in a jagged-edged smile. His raven eye locked upon her gaze while the other glanced away. "Faeries always hide the truth. It's too easy if we don't."

"I would argue it's much better if you don't hide the truth. You might get the results you want."

"Where's the fun in that? It's better if the ending is chosen by free will rather than our own design."

"Why get involved if you don't have a specific ending you want to see?" Sorcha shook her head, knowing he wouldn't answer her question. "Can you open the portal, Bran? I'd like to go home."

"Home?" He tilted his head to the side again. "Curious choice of words."

"Slip of the tongue. My home is with my sisters."

"Perhaps now, but not for long." He nodded at the portal. "All you have to do is see through the glamour, and you can go home."

"How am I supposed to—ah." She pulled the hag stone from between her breasts and placed it against her eye.

The stone turned to a watery portal through the small hole in the hag stone. Light shimmered from its surface. The ivy beyond had not been pulled back, leaving the room obscured and difficult to see, but it was there.

She knew it was.

"Thank you," she said as she turned.

Bran had disappeared. There wasn't time to figure out what he was hiding. She took a deep breath, stilled the disquieting sadness in her heart, and left the Unseelie lands behind.

Chapter 18

Leaving the Unseelie castle was more difficult than entering. The cold touch of the portal sent gooseflesh across Sorcha's skin. Magic such as this should never touch a human. It slid along her body like the foreign touch of an unseen person.

Sorcha shuddered, unnerved by the cold, clammy sensation. It was over soon, or would be as soon as her left foot slid free. Ivy brushed against her face until she blew out a breath that stirred the greenery.

She fluttered a hand in front of her face, parting the curtain of ivy and entering the enchanting bedroom.

Nothing had changed. All her things were exactly where she had placed them. The blue flowers glowed with a soft light emanating from their petals on the far wall. The faerie fountain stared placidly off into the distance, hardly comparable to the real thing.

How could she ever look at this place with the same eyes? This island was beautiful, but the shadows now moved, and the bed looked like a prison.

She sighed and unhooked the clasp of her cloak. It fell to the ground with a wet thump although she didn't remember getting it wet.

Exhaustion overwhelmed her. She couldn't remember a time when it wasn't hovering in the corners of her mind like an unwelcome house guest. She never remembered inviting the bone biting feeling, but it never seemed to leave.

A soft sound interrupted her thoughts. Sorcha couldn't pinpoint where it came from in the room. Everything was how she left it, right down to the emerald leaves overlaying the walls.

Again, the shushing noise echoed in her ears. It was the distinct sound of fabric sliding against fabric. The movement of a human body.

Or perhaps that of a Fae.

She sucked in her breath and froze, shifting until the portal was no longer at her back. The air was too still, laced with violence and aggression. She'd never felt danger so powerfully.

Her heart beat. She breathed so quietly she hardly inhaled at all. Darting eyes searched for the cause of the sound as she wondered what had followed her onto the isle.

A shadow peeled away from the wall, rushing towards her so fast that Sorcha didn't have time to react. A pillar of darkness surrounded her. She slammed back into the stone wall, ivy tangling in her hair and around her shoulders.

Sorcha turned her head to the side and squeezed her eyes shut. She couldn't, wouldn't, look death in the eye. Taking one last deep breath, she caught the scent of lemons, mint, and whiskey.

Stone?

His shaking hand brushed a coiled red curl away from her face, tucking it gently behind her ear.

"Where were you?"

The question reverberated in her mind, but she couldn't find the words to answer. Questions of her own overpowered her tongue. How had he realized she left? Why was he here? What had happened while she traversed the Otherworld?

Was he drunk?

He stumbled, rocking sideways before catching himself with a forearm slammed against the wall above her. "Where were you?"

Again, he asked the same question. Anger made his words harsh, but she caught the distinct tones of worry underneath the growl. Why would he worry about her? She added the question to all the others she would never give voice.

"Unseelie lands," she whispered.

"And why wouldn't you ask me?"

"For what?"

"Guidance. Protection. An answer to whether or not it was too dangerous for an unarmed, weak, human woman in the Otherworld?"

Sorcha gulped. "I was unaware I might need any protection. There was no point when I felt like I was in danger. Until now."

"You think you are in danger from me?" His head tilted and a spear of light slashed across his eyes. Twin lines wrinkled between his eyes, vibrant blue nearly glowing with anger.

She couldn't respond. Her fear spiked the air with static electricity, making the hair on her arms raise. Of course, she was frightened of Stone. He loomed over her until all she could breathe was his scent, and all she could see was the powerful set of his barreled chest.

"Sorcha." He said her name as if it was a prayer. "You never have to be afraid of me."

He lifted a hand and traced the outline of her face. Crystals scraped across her forehead, past the sensitive skin of her temple, down the soft curves of her cheeks. She couldn't breathe as he thumbed the plump rise of her lips.

He swayed again, eyes squinting in concentration. "You are so flawed. So unlike my people who would have scrubbed these markings from their skin long ago."

"Markings?"

"These," he touched the peaks of her cheeks, her forehead, and the dip of her upper lip.

"Freckles," she whispered. "We call them freckles."

"I've never seen them before, though I know their name. The Fae have smooth skin, like porcelain, as if an artist had painted them with one tone. But you…you have so many colors."

"Colors?"

"Your hair, your skin, even your eyes have flecks of green, blue, yellow."

"You've noticed all of that?" She couldn't stop asking questions. Shock twisted her tongue, asking questions she didn't mean to voice.

"I notice everything you do. You haunt my steps and my dreams. You've bewitched me, Sorcha, and I want my soul back."

"I don't know how to give it back to you."

He leaned closer, his breath fanning over her lips. "I wonder if you taste like the sun."

"You're drunk."

"Yes, I am."

She didn't move as he leaned down and devoured her.

He tasted like whiskey and peppermint. Her eyes fluttered shut as the textures of his mouth slid against hers. Soft lips, like velvet, nibbled at her own. She couldn't breathe, didn't want to, even as his arms slid down the wall and slipped around her shoulders.

Teeth nibbled at her full bottom lip. No, she realized, not teeth. The harsh edge of crystal biting into her swollen flesh as he pressed harder.

She inhaled in surprise, and he took advantage of the opportunity. His warm tongue swept into her mouth, bringing with it an explosion of flavor. Spices, foreign to her senses, made her drunk as their tongues tangled.

Strange, she hadn't thought it would be like this. And then she didn't think at all.

He tasted her, unmade her, whispered endearments she didn't understand against her mouth. The crystals sliced at her skin, splitting open her lip, and pouring the metallic taste of blood into her mouth.

He didn't stop. She didn't want him to.

Warmth poured over her like a wave. She couldn't think. He was everything and nothing, tying her to the ground by the electric heat of his mouth. His hands slid over her shoulders and massaged her muscles until she relaxed against the wall.

"I knew you would taste like sunshine," he whispered against her lips. "I knew it from the moment I first set eyes on you."

"Another flaw?"

"Entirely."

He dedicated his attention to sipping from her lips. To licking, and sucking, and tasting every inch she would allow him. Hot breath slid across her cheeks, crystals cold and scraping, a sharp contrast to the soft flesh of his skin.

Teeth worried at the sensitive peaks of her ears. Her knees went weak, mouth dropped open in pleasure even as her eyes snapped open. Her nerve endings came alive. Heat rippled through her from the points all the way to her belly.

"What—" she gasped.

A pleased, masculine growl rumbled in her ear.

His hands traveled down her arms, smoothing across the skin he found so flawed. Somehow, she didn't think he meant it as an insult. She'd seen the Fae for herself, so perfect they looked like stone. Perhaps he saw something alive in her. Something real.

She arched her back as one of his hands trailed across her collarbone. He nibbled at her ear, scraping both teeth and crystal against the sensitive flesh. His hands traveled farther, fingers trailing along the gaping, oversized neckline of her dress. She thought surely her mind would fracture from the pleasure as his hands ghosted over the soft swells of her breasts.

Until the air went cold.

His breathing changed. The hot gusts of breath stilled to calm, measured inhalations. He pulled a long strand of web from her shoulder, the sticky filaments stretching out across his fingers.

"What is this?" he growled. "And you say you had no need for protection?"

"It's not what you think."

"You lie." His eyes narrowed further, an entirely different beast staring at her through the windows of his soul.

"I didn't speak with anyone," she whispered, cowering against the ivy. "Stop looking at me like that."

"Like what?"

"Like you want to hurt me."

"I promised I wouldn't hurt you, and I will hold true to that vow. No more lies, little human. Why were you in Unseelie lands?"

She swallowed. How much should she tell him? The Queen wouldn't want her running her mouth, and the information she held was a secret. Sorcha still didn't know who had opened the portal from this side or if it was entirely the Queen's doing.

But he would know if she lied. She wasn't certain how the Fae knew, if they tasted it in the air or could read body language. If he knew, then he would continue to push until she told the truth.

Sorcha had never been a good liar. "I don't know why I was there. The portal opened from this side, and there was information the Unseelie Queen wished to share with me."

"That portal can't open on its own."

"I don't think there are any Unseelie here."

His eyes darkened, storm clouds brewing in the vivid blue. "Oona."

"What?"

He didn't answer. The heat of his body disappeared, leaving her shivering and alone in the room.

"It's probably better he left," she finally said with a shaking sigh. But she didn't believe the words. How could she when her body was quivering with unfulfilled pleasure?

Was that how it felt for her sisters? Surely, it couldn't; they had no attachment to the men who came to the brothel.

A memory surfaced of a blond man with his arms wrapped around Briana. Sorcha had caught them in an alcove outside the brothel, whispering words of endearments, the likes of which she'd never heard before. The soft press of lips to skin, the sound of gasps and sighs.

Maybe they did know what this felt like, Sorcha thought. Maybe they'd had it ripped away from them so many times they forgot to tell her.

Or they didn't want to share. The moment felt so infinitely private that Sorcha wasn't sure she could breathe a word of it. She tucked the memory into a hidden part of her soul for a time when she felt lost or discouraged.

For a single moment in time, she had felt what it meant to be cherished.

Her mind flared to life as the heat in her body disappeared.

"Oona!" She gasped.

He'd left this bedroom with clear intent in his eyes. Anger had radiated from his skin like a physical being, his crystals glowing and shimmering with rage. Stone had promised he would never hurt her, but Sorcha had no way of knowing whether he promised the same to the faeries under his protection.

She burst into motion, rushing from the room, and swinging herself over the bannister and down the stairs. There was no time for exhaustion, no hesitation, nor second thoughts. Sorcha had to warn Oona, to rush her from the castle until she could figure out a way to calm him down if possible.

As much as Stone knew his people's families, he didn't know them well enough to guess where they were. Most of the pixies on the isle slept with each other in Macha's garden. They said it kept them safe and protected.

Oona wasn't like the others. She slept in the kitchens with the brownies, to make sure that her domain was clean every night.

If Sorcha had observed Stone correctly, he would go to the pixie grotto first. Then he would go to the kitchens.

She ran shoulder first into a door, busting through it so she could shorten her path to the kitchens. Stone's legs were longer. He would be much faster, but he was operating through rage and nothing else. Sorcha was still thinking clearly.

Rooms filled with covered furniture and shattered wood flickered through her vision as she ran through each long dead room. Spider webs tangled in her hair and dust covered her shoulders as she made the last jump and threw open the door to the glowing warmth of the kitchens.

"Oona," she frantically called. "Oona! Wake up!"

A small mound in the corner shifted, and the pixie sat up. She didn't don her glamour immediately. The round face didn't match the persona Oona had chosen for herself. The high peaks of her forehead resembled an oak leaf, violet tinges blushing the high tips and trailing down her shoulders onto her wings.

"What? Who is it?"

"Get up, Oona! He's coming!"

"What?" The pixie burst into movement, throwing blankets into the air and rushing towards Sorcha. "Where is he coming from?"

"I'd assumed he would go to the grotto first."

A roar shook the door, coming from Macha's fountain.

Oona glanced over her shoulder. "You are correct. And now you know I am Unseelie."

"Yes."

"I did not mean to lie, but there are so many secrets in our world. The Queen wanted to see you, and I could not refuse."

"Oona, he's almost here!" Sorcha wrapped her hand around Oona's forearm and tugged. "You're coming with me. I know where to put you until he calms down."

"I won't put you in harm's way."

"I'm the only person in this castle that has nothing to fear from him. He gave me his word. Come with me!"

Oona glanced at her in shock. "He promised what?"

"If you don't come with me now, I will carry you. Get moving."

"The master has never given anyone a promise of protection. Explain yourself, dearie."

Sorcha blew a breath at her hair. "Oona, I order you to follow me now."

Using the faerie's name was harsh, but Sorcha could hear his footsteps pounding towards the kitchen. Their time was short.

Oona's spine straightened, and fire flashed in her eyes. But she followed Sorcha when she turned and raced back the way she came.

Sorcha tried to make their trail difficult to follow. She took them through different sections of the castle, hoping a long chase would quell some of his head. They passed broken statues, scuttling spiders, and ripped paintings of faeries she would never meet.

"We're almost there," her harsh whisper barely audible over the pounding of their feet. "So close, Oona. Keep up."

The faerie ran faster.

Sorcha slid around a corner, skidding until her spine hit the wall with a harsh thunk. The air whooshed from her lungs, but she forced herself to keep going. She didn't know what Stone planned on doing. The fear in Oona's eyes spoke volumes, and it was enough for her to steal the faerie away.

Her gut said Stone would regret any judgement he made in anger. These faeries had dedicated their lives to him. They weren't slaves, they weren't servants, and he had no right to harm them. Even if they made mistakes.

She slammed into the carved wall and pressed the stone in the sword's pommel. The grating grind echoed. Stone's enraged shout was far closer than she hoped.

Sorcha grabbed Oona's shoulders and shook her. "You listen to me. There's a bathroom in the back corner with a hot spring. Get into the springs and do not come out until I come get you. Do you hear me?"

"You're putting yourself in danger for no reason, dearie. Don't worry yourself with me. I've lived a full life."

"And I would have you live more. Oona, I order you to hide in the hot springs."

The faerie's spine stiffened, and she disappeared into Sorcha's bedroom.

"Now that's taken care of." She stepped farther away from the carving and the groaning stone slid back into place. "Let's deal with the last bit."

She slid her fingers around the sword pommel, wiggling and gripping until she felt it give away. The tiny nub of stone slid into her hand with little complaint.

"And you're coming with me." Sorcha stuck it between her breasts for safe keeping.

Then she turned, pressed her spine against the carving, and waited.

She didn't have to wait long. He came barreling around the corner like a bull, sides heaving and crystals casting violet light onto the floors and walls.

He pointed a finger and shouted, "You defy me?"

"I do."

Stone walked towards her, each step a deliberate movement filled with aggression and power. She likened the movement to the first night she'd seen him. Intimidation was his purpose, and the first night she had been frightened.

She refused to be this time. Sorcha tilted her head back and met his gaze with a set jaw. "I'm not letting you get to her."

"She is mine to punish. An Unseelie living under my roof has no right to live."

"She is no one's but her own. You have no right to punish her for begging my help. If you want to punish someone, then punish me."

He hesitated. "You?"

"I walked into that portal without anyone telling me to. If you require someone to scream and shout your anger at, then it should be me."

"You didn't know what you were doing."

"I knew precisely what I was doing! I was raised with stories of the Fae. I left offerings and sacrifices to your people since I was a child. Unseelie lands are legend, and I assure you, I know all its dangers. I did not eat or drink. I spoke to as few people as possible—"

"You spoke to unknown Fae?" he interrupted.

"I spoke to those who were necessary, and Bran helped me back. What more do you want, Stone?"

Angry breaths expelled from his body in short huffs. "You should have asked for my help."

"Which you couldn't have provided. You are stuck here with the rest of them."

"I would have given you a weapon to take with you!" he shouted

Sorcha matched his tone and screamed back, "I wouldn't have used it! I heal people, I don't attack them, Stone."

"My name is not Stone!"

The walls creaked as his thunderous shout struck the walls. The carvings behind her quaked, and the floor shook with the force of his rage. He turned from her, his shoulders shaking with anger.

And fear, she realized as the light of his crystals dimmed. He had been frightened for her and waiting for her to return had only caused the fear to fester.

Sorcha's own anger dimmed.

"Then what would you have me call you?" she whispered quietly as she stepped forward. "Master? King? Lord? There is nothing else for me to say."

"I would have you call me by name, if it were possible."

"And why isn't it possible?" Daring to reach forward, she placed her hand against his back. Though fabric covered his skin, the dips of crystal gashes were easy to find. She slid her fingers into the wounded valley to hold him in place. "You already know my given name."

"A human in possession of a Tuatha dé Danann's name is far too powerful."

"Why? Do you fear I might order you to kill someone for me? To steal?"

"I fear that you would ask me to lay the world at your feet." He glanced over his shoulder, blue eyes searing through her calm resolve. "And it would be all too easy to do."

He stepped forward, her hand sliding from his back, out of the grooves of crystals that bit at her fingers. Then he walked away from her, each footstep measured as if he were trying not to run.

She did not stop him, nor was she certain that she could. The sheer force of his power frightened her. But it was the blunt terror of his words that held her in place.

Would she ask for the world?

Sorcha didn't know.

It was some time before she walked back into her bedroom. Sorcha's mind whirled with the possibilities of what he had meant, what that meant for their relationship. Was that a declaration of intent?

Did he feel something for her? Did she feel something for him?

She wasn't certain. She knew that his eyes haunted her dreams, that his tortured body was intriguing rather than fearsome. Did she want him? The violent reaction of her body to his suggested she might.

How would that even work? He was so much larger than her, surely he would crush her if she even attempted to have relations with him. And a part of her questioned whether she wanted him or the protection he could provide.

Would that make her a whore like her sisters? Was payment the requirement that divided easy women and business women?

Sorcha feared she would never know. And did it matter? Her sisters gave pleasure and reassurance to those who might not have it in any other way. If they derived pleasure from their job, then they should continue it. She would not judge them.

She pulled the small stone from between her breasts, staring down at the carved marble gemstone. Her mind stilled, thoughts narrowing down to one question which loomed above all others.

Would he have hurt Oona?

The stone slid easily back into place, and the heavy door receded into the wall. Sorcha longed for the day when the grinding of stone against stone would cease. When it had been used so much that the passage was smooth and silent.

She toed off her shoes, moss soft against her aching feet. She hadn't run this much in ages, between her bolting steps in the dark castle and then the rush through the portal. Her body wasn't certain how to handle the rush of adrenaline followed by bone-deep exhaustion.

Along the way to the bathroom, she pulled off each piece of her clothing. The outer kirtle dropped to the ground, the heavy skirts and belts holding each piece in place. Underclothing stuck to her skin where blood and fluid had leaked through each layer of fabric.

Sighing, she brushed aside the ivy and found Oona waiting by the door with a brush in her hand.

"Relax," Sorcha said. "It's just me."

"Oh, thank heavens," the pixie dropped the brush to the ground. "I wouldn't have hit him, dearie. I just…I just—"

Sorcha lifted a hand. "If his intent was to hurt you, then you have every right to protect yourself. Now if you don't mind, I'm very tired."

"Of course, dear."

Oona reached for the final ties of Sorcha's underclothes, quickly untangling the strings, and stripping the heavy weight from Sorcha's body. Sorcha stepped into the hot spring, sighing as her muscles eased.

"Did you bring the water from here?" she asked as Oona turned to put her underthings away. "The first day?"

"No. No, this is a royal room. These rooms are off limits for lesser Fae. Not without permission or company."

"But I'm not a high Fae."

"Perhaps you are," Oona looked at her intently. "You've the pointed ears, although far smaller than any I've ever seen. Are you sure you aren't a changeling?"

"My mother would have told me. She was a friend to the Fae and would have raised their child with pride." As much as she wanted to be Fae, Sorcha doubted there was the barest hint of it in her bloodline.

"And you have no ancestors who came from Underhill?"

"Not that I know of, and I've never had any sway with the elements.

The earth is just earth, the air just air."

"Then you must not be Fae." Oona shook her head. "I don't know what you are child, but you aren't entirely human. This room was not meant for creatures such as me. It's said that all living things would grow ill and shrivel if they weren't meant for such a room."

"Are you certain it's not just a myth?"

"Most things are myths, but there's a shred of truth in every story. The magic here has deemed you worthy of staying within its walls. How, or why, I have no way of knowing."

Neither did Sorcha. It didn't seem right that she stayed in a room like this. It was too fine, too beautiful, and she had never lived in beauty like this before. Why should she start now?

Oona bustled out of the room, muttering about masters and faeries, and Sorcha could hear her opening chests for sleep clothing.

Sorcha's fingers ghosted over the tips of her ears, wondering if perhaps she had a bit of Fae in her, after all. But wouldn't they know?

Perhaps it was something she would never know or understand. Sorcha scrubbed her skin with a brush, the thick bristles turning her skin bright red and digging out all the crust underneath her nails. The water hardly changed color at all. It seemed to clean itself, replenishing from the free flowing spring.

Oona brushed aside the ivy that acted as a bathing screen, a light silk nightgown in her hands. "Come on then. You've had a busy day."

"I'm sorry." Sorcha looked up at her, wet hair tangled at her shoulders and spread out in the water like a fan. "I'm so sorry that I used your name without permission. I didn't want you to get hurt, but it's no excuse for treating you like that. I keep using faerie names even when I know how powerful they can be."

"There's no harm done, child." Oona's lips quirked to the side. "You saved my life."

"Still, I would like to give my name in apology. I trust you to use it well."

Oona's eyes nearly bugged out of her head. The nightgown fell from her hands and landed on the floor like a dying butterfly. "Why ever would you do that? Dearie, that is a dangerous thing to do. You should not give any Fae your name! Ever!"

Sorcha stood from the water, wrapped a cloth around her body, and held out her hand. "It's nice to meet you, Oona. My name is Sorcha of Ui Neill. And it would please me greatly if you would refer to me by name from now on."

Tears slid down Oona's cheeks. "I couldn't. It's not right."

"Please. I'm so far away from family and friends, and I consider you as close to me now as any other. I would like to hear you call me Sorcha, for it is my given name and should be spoken often."

"Sorcha," the faerie whispered. "You are the first human to ever give me their name."

"Use it wisely."

"And only with love," Oona said. She stepped forward and wrapped another cloth around Sorcha's shoulders, rubbing briskly. "Now let's get you dried off and into bed."

"Do you want to talk about the Queen?"

"Let me take care of you. I have no wish for nightmares, my dear."

Sorcha could almost feel the aching pain of loss. Oona was banished here, and likely would never see her family again. The resolve set inside Sorcha grew all the more strong. She would find a way to send Oona back home. To send all of them home.

They deserved to see their families. They deserved to be free.

Chapter 19

Eamonn stormed into the highest tower of the castle, rage simmering underneath his skin. How dare she? How dare she defy him, in his own castle, without even a hint of fear in her eyes?

She should worry that he might snap her pretty little neck. And he could!

He held his hands out, staring down at the palms that had taken so many lives in his long life. He could feel the shifting of flesh, the crack that echoed through his fingers when a spine gave way. There was not a gentle bone in his body.

At least, that was what he had believed.

But even with the multiple bottles of whiskey clouding his mind and judgement, he had been gentle with her. The crystals on his hands hadn't broken through her speckled skin.

He tossed his head, shaking the long braid down his spine. Speckled wasn't the word. Flawed, as he had told her, wasn't the word either. Those freckles were captivating little stars decorating her skin like the splatter of a painter's brush. She was the most unusual creature he had met.

The voice of his twin brother, Fionn, echoed in his mind.

"But you always loved the humans, brother."

Eamonn growled. "You have no place here."

"You'll hurt her, like the rest of them. Those hands weren't capable of preserving such delicate bodies even before you broke. Ruined, maimed, beast that you are."

The old doubt filtered into his conscience. He wanted to be the kind of man who was capable of touching a woman and not worrying that she might break. He wanted to stroke soft skin, to squeeze and pet, but he knew what dangers lay down that path.

And it infuriated him.

Roaring out a frustrated call, he swung a heavy fist at the newest chair in his living quarters. The wood splintered beneath the weight of crystal and bone. Small shards burst into the air, slicing through his forearms.

The now familiar ache forced him to pause and tilt his hand. Meaty flesh split farther and crystals grew through muscle and skin. They glimmered, reflecting the light as if to mock him. They were beautiful, yes, but they were ugly at the same time.

He dropped his hand in disgust.

"That temper tends to get you in trouble."

Eamonn's jaw ticked at the familiar voice.

"Why were you in Unseelie lands, Bran?"

"Am I not supposed to be looking after your newest lady conquest?"

"Why?" Eamonn added steel to his voice, not allowing the other Fae a chance to argue further. Bran would talk around a subject until he was blue in the face.

"I had business there."

"You should not be following her."

"Why not?" Bran stepped out of the shadows, a sly grin on his face. "I do what I want, Prince. Just as you do."

"You should have been protecting her if you were there."

"She was fine. Managed well if you ask me. The only thing that caught her up was the portal." Bran's raven eye winked. "And if we're being honest, opening that on her own was an impossible task. She wouldn't have gotten it open without any Fae blood."

"You don't think she has any?" Eamonn wasn't so sure.

"Dry as a bone, that one. I thought perhaps she might, but any power would have surfaced on that ship we came over here on. She's not Fae."

"Then what is your explanation for the ears?"

Bran shrugged. "Physical deformation. She is strange though, I'll give you that. She knows how to manage the Fae and always says 'thank you.' I haven't had a human thank me in what feels like centuries."

"They forgot about us. That's why we left."

"All but her." Bran nodded towards the now broken furniture. "I'd hazard a guess you did something you're regretting?"

"Go away, Bran."

"I'm here now. I don't think I want to leave until the end of this story. What do you plan on doing with her?" Bran walked towards one of the lounge chairs, splaying his body across it without a care in the world. He pointed towards the comfortable seat. "This one is off limits. Break the others."

Eamonn sighed, tension and anger giving way to annoyance. "I'm finished."

"You say that, but then you always end up flipping the chair I'm seated in."

"That's because you annoy me so much."

"I don't follow your rules, Seelie. It's just the way I live my life."

"And you waste your time annoying me?"

Bran kicked his feet in the air, holding his hand out for a drink he knew Eamonn would share. "It's not like there's much going on back in my court. And here you are, on the brink of making the next step towards your future."

Eamonn lifted a glass and the bottle of whiskey from his desk, pouring a healthy amount into the crystal. "You think I'm on the brink of something? What other future do I have than rotting away on this isle?"

"Well, you don't have to stay here." Bran leaned out and grabbed the drink. "You're just choosing to."

"That's not true."

The raven eye rolled in its socket. "If you haven't put that piece of the puzzle together, then there's not much I can do to help you, brother."

Eamonn narrowed his eyes, glaring down at the reclining faerie. "Do you know something?"

"I know a lot of things." Bran sipped the whiskey. "This is quite good."

"And you will not share?"

"You already know it, Eamonn. You're just refusing to admit that you know it. Use that brain of yours. If the crystals haven't affected your head yet that is."

Eamonn stared for a moment, his mind whirling with possibilities until it settled on the information Bran was using. He shook his head.

"That was a long time ago, and I am no longer king."

"Ah, but you are the oldest son."

"And unfit for the Seelie throne." Eamonn held his arms out, crystals sparkling in the dim candlelight. "Do I look like a Seelie Fae? Do you really think they'd follow me?"

"I think all the things you used to say were compelling to the faeries who only knew slavery. If you kept whispering in their ears of freedom, they might just follow you rather than your brother who treats his subjects like cattle rather than people."

"There is still the matter of the Tuatha dé Danann."

Bran drained the rest of the glass. "Do you think that's an issue? They always chose you, Eamonn. You were the favored son from day one. Or did you think your brother hated you simply because he was born with darkness in his heart? Hatred is learned, Eamonn, and it festered inside Fionn for years before he stabbed you in the back."

"I would have been a good king," Eamonn said. "But I never would have been a great king."

"Times change." Bran hopped onto his feet, circling the room, and eyeing the crystal decanters on Eamonn's desk with a calculating raven eye. "What are you going to do about the girl?"

Eamonn slumped onto the remaining chair. "I haven't a clue."

"Send her home?"

The glass in Eamonn's hand shattered.

Bran cocked his head to the side. "Unlikely then. Well, if you will not send her home, then just what do you plan on doing with her?"

"I have yet to decide."

"I have an idea."

"Do you?" Eamonn's head thumped against the back of the chair, and he stared up at the ceiling. "Please, advise me Unseelie Prince."

"Remind yourself what it feels like when a woman wants you. It might do you a world of good."

"She doesn't want me. She's frightened of me, yes. But any other emotion has never passed through her at the sight of me."

"Curious. It didn't look like that when you tried to consume her."

"I what?" Eamonn's face flamed with embarrassment and anger. "You were watching."

"I'm always watching," Bran tapped the black feathers circling his eye. "But more importantly, I could see what you did not. Alcohol may cloud your mind, but it does not mine. She wants you, my friend. Almost as much as you want her."

"And what do I do with that? You ask me to plan for war, and then to distract myself with a woman." Eamonn tossed the remaining shards of glass onto the floor. "A man can only do so much, Bran."

"I can help if you want. However, I'd much prefer the task of distracting your lady."

Eamonn growled.

"Calm yourself." Bran lifted his hands in surrender. "I jest. You need to wait for your brother to make the first move, and trust me, he will. Why do you think I was in Unseelie?"

Eamonn wanted to throw something at him. "Was this entire conversation a way for you to circle around to what you found out in Unseelie? Out with it, Fae!"

"Not yet. I want to know what you're doing with Sorcha first."

"I don't like you using her name so freely."

"I think she's hardier than you give her credit for. No faerie blood runs in her veins, but there's something else there that gives her a spine of steel. What are you going to do with her?"

"I don't know," Eamonn groaned. "Give me peace and perhaps I will find out!"

"You gave her the queen's room, yet you do not know what you want her for." Bran tsked. "You're a confusing man, my friend. A supple woman, willing no less, just floors away from you, and yet, you hide in a tower."

"Are you quite done commenting on my love life?"

"That will never stop."

Eamonn stared at the ripped portrait of his mother and prayed for patience. He'd never been good at waiting. The battlefield wasn't a good training ground for patience. "Bran."

"Fine. Your brother has been keeping track of you, you know, and this girl worries him. He thinks a happy life might coerce you into returning."

"He is a fool."

Bran snorted. "A fool who is correct."

"She has no sway over my actions or decisions."

"You've left this tower more since she arrived than you had in your entire time here on Hy-brasil, and you are considering going to war with your brother."

"I considered that before she showed up."

"And now you have meaning behind the action. She would look pretty with a crown atop her head." Bran mimed placing a tiara on top of his half-shaved head.

"She's human."

"What's that got to do with anything? For once in your life, give up that stalwart honor and foolish sense of right and wrong! War is coming whether you choose it or not. Enjoy your last days of freedom.

The bloodshed will begin soon."

The feathers on Bran's face ruffled and spread across his skin. His form shifted, morphing from man to beast. He let out one croaking scream before lifting into the air and flying out the window.

Good riddance, Eamonn thought. He couldn't handle one more minute of the Unseelie's constant suggestion he go back home.

What was left for him? A stolen throne, a twin who hated him, a kingdom who assumed he'd abandoned them. At least here there were people to take care of.

He clenched his fists as the pit of his stomach clenched. He missed home. It was a strange thing, to miss a place so profoundly that his heart ached. But this place held none of the beauty that Tír na nÓg could offer.

Standing, he paced in front of his mother's portrait. "Even you wouldn't want me home. You, who did nothing when Fionn hanged me in the square. Our own people cheered for days as I dangled, unable to die because the crystals on my throat protected me." He jabbed a finger towards her. "You didn't even cut me down."

The memory was a jagged thing, harsh and cutting even after a hundred years. She had tears her in eyes when their gazes met, but she had not helped her son. Her first born. Her beloved warlord prince who had cut down the world for her.

His mother had shown her true colors. As had his father, who hadn't even looked as his son hung from a fraying rope. Three days. Three days he swung in the breeze and endured the never-ending pecks of crows, the cries of vultures waiting to feast.

He had defied them all.

Death would not come for him. He would not submit to those who had betrayed him. Eamonn survived. He had always been good at that.

Fionn hated him, of that he was certain. Something festered deep within his twin's gut, and there was nothing Eamonn could do to change it. What brotherly love there once might have been, was long gone.

Eamonn braced his arms against the wall next to his mother and let his forehead touch the cool stone. What choice did he have?

The faces of the isle's Fae danced behind his lids. They had been banished for many things. Stealing from a Tuatha dé Danann. Worshiping a different ancestor than their master. Going home to visit family when they should have been working.

Nothing as serious as murder. They would've swung next to him on the gallows if they'd done such a thing.

There was no purpose to this place, other than a punishment worse than death. Fionn's voice echoed in his mind.

"Let him rot."

And that was exactly what he was doing. He might as well grow barnacles rather than crystals. Eamonn was doing nothing other than sitting and waiting for time to pass.

He glanced over and met his mother's cold gaze. "I'm coming home, Máthair."

Chapter 20

Sorcha wound through the hallways, twisting the armful of lavender she carried into a purple crown. The brownies were busy cooking and had little time to entertain her. She'd tried to talk with one of the selkies, but he had to go fishing to replenish their stocks.

Every day that passed brought new frustrations and new boredom. Blowing out a breath, she stuck her tongue out in concentration as she finished the very end. Lavender made a beautiful flower crown, but the tiny buds sometimes fell off before she could finish.

She'd smelled the patch before she saw it. Rosaleen had always been searching for more lavender to hang in her room. She said it took away some of the more unpleasant scents.

Sorcha didn't have the heart to say that even lavender couldn't take away the scent of death. It wasn't what Rosaleen had been talking about, but Sorcha's struggles had been far different.

Crown finished, she placed it atop her head and let her red curls coil around it.

Soft slippers on her feet rendered her footsteps silent. If she came across anyone, Sorcha planned on telling them that she'd gotten lost. In reality, she was looking for the master of this isle. He had disappeared after one drunken, angry night.

Again.

She was growing tired of having to find him. Stone should be accessible for all his people, herself included. She had to convince him to come back to the mainland with her.

Every time she saw him, her tongue tied itself into a knot. She hadn't even asked the question again!

One part of the castle was off limits. The faeries said she was forbidden from entering the western tower. It was the master's and the master's alone.

But she had seen Oona slip into the shadows. She had carried food in her arms, for the master himself, but she had still gone into the western tower. That meant it wasn't off limits for them.

Just off limits for her.

She placed her palm on the cracked wooden door and glanced around. She couldn't see any faeries, and no one cried out for her to stop.

"Hello?" Sorcha said.

No one responded.

"Good enough," she whispered as she pushed open the door.

A blast of cold air pushed her backward. Purple petals tangled in her waist length hair and fell onto the floor. The blanket of cobwebs on the ceiling stirred. They bounced with the weight of the musty air and shadows danced upon the walls as spiders fled the light.

Sorcha blew out a breath. "There is nothing to be afraid of. Shadows are just that. Shadows."

Her own voice echoed, distorted and warped. She shivered, but pushed on.

She wandered for a while. The western tower was far larger than she expected. There were many doors down the long hallway into darkness. None of them opened, no matter how hard she pushed.

Eventually, she gave up trying. She stayed close to the wall and squinted in the darkness to make out where she might go next.

There, up ahead, was a light. Dim and with no source she could distinguish.

Sorcha squared her shoulders and crept down the hallway until she could press her palm against the door. The light was yellow. Candlelight?

A smile spread across her face.

"Got you," she whispered. "Let's see what you've been up to."

She tested the door, one hand on the handle and the other firmly against the wood grain. Unlike the others, this door was well oiled. Silent, it hid her presence as she slid it open inch by inch.

Sorcha peeked through the small crack. A candelabra glowed with the light of a dozen candles placed atop a sconce on the wall nearest her. There was a nice blanket of shadows behind a pillar. If she could sneak over to that, he wouldn't be able to see her.

Bravery, foolish bravery perhaps, was her middle name. Holding her breath, she darted through the door and ducked into the shadows.

Her heart pounded so forcefully she was certain he would hear it. He'd be so angry if he found her sneaking. Even his servants would berate her for hours if they discovered she had stolen into this forbidden place.

Sorcha furrowed her brows. She listened for some kind of sound. The movement of fabric, the exhale of a breath, the murmuring of voices.

Was he here?

She leaned around the pillar. The room was small, quaint even. Blue glowing flowers grew up from the floor, stretching their vines into the ceiling. Leaves larger than her entire body folded over the thick tendrils and swept the ground.

At the end of the room, a large stone loomed in the shadows. She had seen its ilk before. A sacred stone, the triskele carved into its surface marking it as a holy object.

He knelt before it wearing nothing but a small loincloth. His back was broad, sliced so many times that he glimmered in the weak blue light. Even his feet were broken, she noticed. The sole of one gaped open and a valley of violet crystals danced down it.

Her cheeks burned. He held his hands folded before him, long braid trailing down his back and completely still.

She should leave. This was a holy place, and her intrusion was not welcome.

Shame made her palms sweat. She had always been a curious creature, but she'd never waltzed into a church just to watch. This was sacrilege.

"Grandfather," he murmured. His voice was deep, like the shifting of the earth in the middle of the night. "Nuada Airgetlám, I beseech your help."

Grandfather? She ducked behind the pillar again and pressed her hands against her chest. He was the grandson of Nuada Silverhand, ancient king of the Seelie Fae, long thought dead? It wasn't possible!

"I am lost. I have followed your paths, listened to your wisdom, and still I am here."

The pain in his voice made her ache. Sorcha had never heard him speak in such a way. He was a private person, and she wasn't surprised that he kept his secrets close.

Her eyes locked upon the cracked door. He fell silent and her opportunity to do the right thing was now. She could slip out, forget that she had intruded, and tell herself she had eased the curiosity eating at her.

But now, here, she could satisfy that curiosity. It burned so brightly her thoughts burst into flame.

She gritted her teeth and twisted her fingers together. She would regret this.

A few moments more, she told herself. He had to leave eventually. Sorcha peered around the pillar again, watching as Stone leaned forward and pressed his forehead against the ground.

The strong muscles of his thighs bunched. His back flexed, tightening into a valley following the ridge of his spine.

"They know where I am. I have always said that if they find the courage to fight me, then let them come. My brother must find the man within if he wishes to wipe me from the Otherworld. And I have remained alone."

She pressed her chest against the pillar. Her fingers were freezing, but she couldn't pull away from the shadows. Her eyes stayed locked upon his prostrate figure.

"You raised me to be a weapon. I was untouchable with your sword at my side, and then you allowed me to be cut down by my own blood. Through all this, I endured. I existed. But now, I do not know what path you wish me to take.

"There is another here. A woman who survived the journey from Ui

Neill to Hy-brasil. I thought such a thing impossible for one so frail, and surely the mark of your children is upon her."

Sorcha held her breath. She wanted to know what secrets he held regarding her presence.

"She is a distraction I do not need. If I wish to be prepared for my brother's attack, then I should ignore her. Or perhaps send her away."

He sighed, as if the thought pained him.

"He sent more men. I entertained them for a time in the throne room, but their eyes wandered. They searched for the best place to attack. The easiest way to draw blood and strike at my heart. I'm confident they found nothing."

He hesitated, and she leaned forward to hear his quiet words.

"I have no fear of pain. My hands are stained with the blood of kings and the ashes of old gods. But I fear what my brother might do to her, should he find out about her existence."

His head dipped forward in thought.

"She is strange. Unlike the creatures I am used to, or the ones remember from Seelie. Breakable and yet strong. Flawed, yet somehow perfect and uncommonly kind. I don't know what it is you would tell me to do, Grandfather."

Sorcha knew what she wanted Nuada to tell him. Try anything you want, for our time is fleeting.

Her heart raced as her mind played through the possibilities. He was not an ugly man. The crystals were unusual and dangerous, but they didn't detract from the harsh angles of his face. Her sisters would run from him in fear.

His height alone would be a problem. And if he was so tall, there may be issues with fitting together…in more intimate ways.

She cocked her head to the side and looked him up and down. It was worth taking a chance. He was a beautiful man.

Stone sat up, his back and shoulders flexing. Shadows danced across the imposing muscles, flickering to life only to disappear as he shifted.

"I fear touching her with my hands. I am an unyielding man, created to do violent things. Laying with a woman, being kind to a woman, is not in my nature."

Her heart shattered all over again. Did he truly believe he was incapable of being gentle?

Green light trickled from the top of the triskele to the bottom. Great drops of emerald fluid leaked from the edges of the stone and slid to the ground.

"Peace, grandson." The voice was smooth honey wine, the comforting voice of the wind after a long journey home. "The course of love is no easy path to tread. The sky may tremble, and the wind may howl, but the only person who can sway your decisions is yourself. What do you feel when you look at this girl?"

"It is like nothing I have ever felt before."

"Do you like the way it feels?"

"It makes me feel weak," Stone growled. "One look from her, and I am ashamed of myself, of my decisions, of the path I walk."

"And what path is that?"

"I walk towards my death. My birthright was taken, and I will not allow another to take what should be mine."

The green light flared so bright that Sorcha had to duck behind the pillar.

Nuada's voice rose, "And whose choice is that, grandson?"

"My own."

"Do you wish to die?"

"No."

"Then my suggestion is for you to live. As much as you can. Experience life, experience courage and honor in ways you were never given as a young man. You are still a being capable of brutality, but that does not define you. The Fae are infinite creatures, capricious and volatile. It is far past time for you to discover other purposes for yourself."

"You approve?"

Nuada's chuckle echoed in the room, and the green light faded. She watched the nearest pillar until the light completely disappeared from its gray stone. Only then did Sorcha peek from her hiding spot and glance towards Stone.

He remained kneeling in the same spot, head heavy. His hands flexed upon his thighs but he did not move. He did not speak.

He did not know she was there.

Sorcha turned and let herself out of the altar room. She wasn't certain she breathed a single breath as she raced down the hallway and out of the western tower.

What had she heard?

She pressed her spine against the wall and leaned her head back until her hair caught in the cracks of stone. She didn't know how to take this new information. What would she do now that she knew of his affections?

His words rang through her skull over and over again. She made him weak.

Was that a good thing?

CHAPTER 21

Sorcha rubbed her eyes, yawning as Oona dragged her down the hallway.

"Where are we going?"

"The master has asked for you, dearie."

"The master?" Sorcha asked. "Why would he be asking for me this early in the morning?"

"It's not for me to say."

"Do you know?"

"Haven't the faintest idea! It's just a lovely thing that he's asked for you. He doesn't ask for anyone."

"And here I thought that might be just the tiniest bit frightening."

Sorcha didn't know what to think as she walked through the hallways in nothing but her faded cotton nightgown. Her hair stuck out in all directions, curls creating a nest of hair that hardly bounced as she moved.

She spent more hours than she could count taming the wild beast of her curls before bed. Even so, she always awoke the next morning with the wild mane tumbling in all directions.

"Wait, hang on," Sorcha grumbled as she twisted her arm. "I'm hardly dressed for meeting with Stone."

"Stone, is it? You've given him a nickname?"

The sparkle in Oona's eyes made her uneasy. "I won't call him master. But it's hardly proper to meet him in my nightclothes."

"Oh, faeries don't have the same delicate sensibilities as humans. You're fine as you are."

"I most certainly am not!"

"No matter, if we go back now, we'll be late. And I can promise you, the master won't appreciate us being late."

Sorcha blew out a breath to stir the curl in front of her eyes. "Why should I care what upsets the master?"

"He's been so nice to you lately, dearie. You should be kind in return."

"He's been kind?" She wracked her brain, trying to remember even the slightest bit of kindness he had shown to her lately. But try as she might, she couldn't remember even seeing him. "I hadn't noticed."

"You didn't notice the daisies on your bedside?"

"Those were from Boggart."

"Nor the sweetmeats that are far better than the kitchen has ever made before?"

"You were trying new recipes. I watched you bake them."

"There were far more dresses in your clothing chests than I remember."

Sorcha shrugged her shoulders. "I found another dress in the hag's hut that were my size. I'm failing to see how the master has been kind. You aren't helping, Oona."

"If you just looked, you could see that he had a hand in all of that."

"I see just fine," she ducked underneath a low hanging beam that Oona could fit underneath easily. "But he's been hiding again."

"Oh dearie, he's never hiding. He's just making sure you're comfortable in every way he can."

"Somehow, I doubt that," she grumbled, a flash of guilt heating her cheeks for a moment. She was being ungrateful, perhaps even childish, but knowing his emotions for her somehow made this all so much more difficult.

Oona shoved her around a corner, through a room she didn't recognize, and out a side door of the castle. Sorcha spun around, hands on her hips.

"I didn't even know that door existed." How could she? Once closed, it blended into the worn stone. "Strange."

"Is it?" Stone's deep voice traveled like a physical touch down her spine.

"Oh!" Sorcha spun, pressing her spine against the cold wall of the castle. "I didn't know you were there."

"Obviously," he said as he stepped from the shadows. Black breeches covered his legs, his ever-present dark cloak covering his form and blending into the shadows. "Although one begs to understand why you wouldn't be looking for me? Oona must have told you I requested your presence."

"She said you summoned me." Sorcha stuck her chin into the air. "I don't like being summoned and dragged out of bed."

His gaze lowered. The burning touch of such a bright look made her knees weak and her hands clutch at the wall for support. He looked as if he could see straight through the thick cotton nightgown. It showed her ankles, which was more than enough, but somehow it felt as though he could see all of her.

Sorcha tugged it higher up her neck. "Why did you want to see me?"

"I thought perhaps we could share breakfast."

"Breakfast? And I couldn't get dressed to do that?" She shivered. "It's nearly time for the first snow fall."

"I would gladly take the blame for your shivers, if only it was my decision to not allow you further clothing." Sorcha watched with wide eyes as he swept the cloak from his shoulders and held it out to her. "If I may."

"So chivalrous," she commented.

The crystals marring his face had lost most of their strangeness. She now saw him, the man beneath the scars and cruel curse. Still, she wanted to wince when she saw the new cut along his jaw.

She swept the cloak over her shoulders, his lingering warmth enveloping her. She inhaled and without thinking blurted, "Why do you always smell like mint?"

His startled laugh was a balm to her homesick soul. "Why do you ask?"

"I didn't think it was a Tuatha dé Danann trait. Bran does not smell like mint although I believe he is the same species as you."

"You think Bran and I are the same?" The brow not held still by crystals arched.

"Well, yes. Although he has more physical deformities, it does appear that you are similar in structure and build. You are not just any Tuatha de Danann."

"Astute. You notice things most humans would not."

"Why do you smell like mint?"

He chuckled again. "You aren't letting that go, are you?"

"I must have my curiosity satisfied."

She watched as he held out an arm for her to take. Strange, she thought, that he could swing so quickly from raging bull to well-bred gentleman. Sorcha arched her own brow.

"I will give you your answer," he acquiesced, "if you walk with me."

"What happened to breakfast?" she asked as she slid her hand over his forearm. Crystals bumped underneath the fabric of his flowing white shirt.

"You seem less inclined to eat."

"I rarely miss a meal. I would not say no to good food, even if the company may yet sour my appetite."

A hearty laugh rang in her ears as he guided her from the castle. "You think very little of me, don't you?"

"On the contrary. I think very highly of you and become disappointed when you do not live up to my standards."

"Ah, and what standards are those?"

They stepped onto a dirt pathway leading them towards the ocean. The cold, autumn air bit at her cheeks and turned her nose bright red. This had always been her favorite season in Ui Neill. The grass would eventually turn brown, the leaves flaming the same color as her hair. Although she would miss the summer, autumn always had a special place in her heart.

How long had she been gone now?

She blinked away the sudden tears in her eyes and forced a grin. "If I told you my standards, you would certainly try your hardest to meet them. And then, however would I meet the real you?"

"The real me?"

"You are not the terrifying man you portray yourself as."

The muscles under her hand bunched. "Why do you say that?"

"Oona says you've been leaving me gifts." It was the only excuse she could think of to say. Sorcha didn't believe he was the one who had left them in the first place. Boggart and the other brownies were far too kind. They liked any excuse to see her happy.

"Yes, the daisies were difficult to obtain this time of year."

She stopped, so startled that her feet forgot how to move. Sorcha stared up at him, mouth agape. He paused when her hand slid off his arm, glancing down at her with a questioning expression.

"That was you?" she whispered.

He flushed. "Come on. If we're late, you'll miss it."

"Miss what?"

"Your surprise."

"I thought this was just breakfast."

"It's a little more than that." He shook his head and held his arm out again. Obviously impatient, he waited for her to decide.

"I—" she glanced down at his arm and back up at his face. "Why are you doing this?"

"I thought that would be rather obvious." His gazed dipped towards her mouth, blue eyes flashing with an emotion she couldn't—wouldn't—name.

Sorcha couldn't reply. Instead, she reached out and held onto his arm again. Her fingers slid over the craggy bumps and valleys, callouses whispering over the silken fabric. They both shivered at the contact. If he asked, she would say it was the cold.

He didn't ask.

They wandered across the fields as the sun turned pink on the horizon. The birds awoke, singing their morning songs to each other. Though chilly, it was a clear morning with not a single cloud in the sky.

"Hurry," he murmured.

They picked up speed, clambering over rocks and across seaweed. He held her steady over every bit of their journey, never letting her slip or tumble to the sand.

His handprints burned into her sides, even when he wasn't touching her. Sorcha marveled at his strength. He could lift her without appearing tired or showing any strain. Both his hands could span her waist.

How was it possible that such a creature existed, and yet so many humans didn't know they were there?

She shook her head and pulled herself up onto a rocky incline. Catching her breath, she turned back to look at him as he hefted his bulk over the stone to join her.

"Where now?"

He pointed behind her. Tilting her head, Sorcha turned and gasped.

A waterfall tumbled from a rocky cliff into a vast pool of water. Glamour hid it from her view until she nearly fell into its edge. She hadn't even heard the crashing thunder of water striking the ground. White foam bubbled where the waterfall met still pond.

Great stones jutted towards the sky, moss growing upon their granite surfaces. It stretched as far as her eye could see. And at the base, white horses stamped their feet in the ripples of water and tossed their heads.

She had never seen anything like it before.

"It's beautiful," she whispered.

"I thought you might like it."

"I do. It's a rare gem in a world that could use so much more beauty."

"It gets better," he murmured in her ear. "How much do you trust me, Sorcha?"

"Very little."

His chuckle danced across her skin in bubbles of sensation. "Ah, you must do better than that, lass. How much do you trust me?"

"Enough."

"Close your eyes."

She stiffened, but complied. Curiosity had always gotten her in trouble, and she wouldn't back away now. Besides, it seemed as though he was far more interesting than he let on.

Strange, but she hadn't thought that a Fae could capture her attention so wholly. There had been many men in her town, but none of them so intriguing. So odd. So unusual.

The words rang in her ears. Of course the strange witch's daughter, the midwife who thought she was more, fell in love with an impossible man. In love. The words burned even thinking them.

His arms reached around her, chest pressed against her spine. She moved forward and back with each great inhalation, rocking on the waves of his own making.

She gasped as his fingers traced the outline of her chin. Delicately, oh so delicately, he touched her. As if she might shatter with just the mere breath from his lips.

His fingers lingered at the stubborn thrust of her chin, joining together to spread across her full bottom lip. The butterfly touch trailed up her cheeks, his thumbs anchoring at her jaw.

The slightest graze whispered over her eyelids.

"Your eyelashes feel like feathers," he whispered in her ear. "I have very little poetry for women such as you. I cannot ever compare your body to artwork, or sing you songs of lovers in a hidden grove. My experiences limit my words and talents."

"I never wanted poetry," she said on a soft sigh. "I only wanted a man who could see me for who I am."

"Then open your eyes, Sorcha of Ui Neill. And see the world as it truly is."

She blinked, opening her eyes as if she had never seen the sun. And, had she ever seen it?

The veil of the world shattered through the ointment he pressed against her closed lids. Colors were suddenly so much more. The white horses grew long manes and water dripped from their foaming snouts. Webbed toes stamped the ground, their tails flicked back and forth.

His arm around her waist was suddenly more solid. More real. The crystals were more than just stone, they were imbued with magic that she could see as sparkling light dancing atop his skin.

"Oh," she whispered. "What did you do?"

"I opened your eyes." He nudged her backward, holding her against his chest and letting her stare without worry of balance or fear of falling. He had opened her eyes to the world she had never seen.

"I had no idea all this was here."

"Glamour is a strange thing. Faeries place it upon everyday objects without even realizing what they do."

One of the horses tossed its head, glancing at them with dark green eyes.

"Kelpies?" she asked.

"Yes."

"Aren't they dangerous?"

"Not to me."

"And to me?" She tilted her head back, looking up to catch his expression.

He stared back at her. His brows smoothed. and his lips curved into a soft smile. The crystals marring his eyes, lips, and skull were made more beautiful by her new sight.

"Never to you. Not as long as I stand by your side."

She felt his low hum against her spine. It wasn't quite a song, nor did she think he had the voice to sustain such a melody, but a rumble that came from deep within his belly. The kelpie nearest to them lifted its head.

It ambled closer, shaking its wet and dripping head. Seaweed tangled in its mane, and foam erupted from its nostrils every time it snorted.

"Have you ever wanted to touch a kelpie?" he asked.

"It's dangerous. They'll drag humans down into the bottom of the ocean and drown them."

"But, have you ever wanted to touch one?"

"Yes," she answered. "Without question, I have always wondered what they felt like."

He stepped forward, sliding his feet under hers until he walked for the both of them. His arm around her waist was comforting and strong. "Then let us fulfill that wish."

The kelpie tossed its head as they moved, watching every twitch, every step, every breath that Sorcha took. It ignored Eamonn, perhaps the only creature in existence that was able to ignore the crystals and jagged edges. Its head swayed as she walked closer, a strange translucent glimmer spreading across its body.

"What was that?"

"That is what a glamour looks like to a Fae."

"That?" It looked like a bubble stretched across the kelpie's skin. Light reflected off the surface in rainbows. "But it's so beautiful."

"Did you think it wouldn't be?" His hand slid under her arm, guiding it up into the air. "Deceitful things are not always ugly."

"Shouldn't they be?"

"Not necessarily. Sometimes, we hide our true selves to spare humans the grievous injury of our appearance."

Sorcha looked over the kelpie, seeing the strange webbed feet, the scaled skin, the seaweed hair and did not flinch. She could understand how some humans might be afraid of it. The legends said it was dangerous, and it likely was. It was different, uncomfortable to even be around.

But that was what made it so lovely. Sorcha had been the oddity in her town, and she knew how deceiving appearances could be.

She stepped out of Stone's comforting warmth. Her nightgown stuck to her skin as mist clung to the sodden fabric. The cloak felt heavy upon her shoulders, but did not slow her determined pace.

Her palm met the cold, wet snout of the kelpie. It huffed, bubbles foaming between her fingers.

"Hello," she whispered.

It cocked its head to stare up at her. A strand of seaweed fell across its forehead. Sorcha didn't hesitate. She brushed it aside and stroked her hand across damp scales.

"There. Now you can see me."

Stone's voice rumbled, "I've never seen a human treat faeries so kindly."

"I've never seen a human treat faeries like anything at all." Her heart clenched. "We have forgotten what it means to be connected to the earth, to the waves, to the creatures who care for all of those things."

"It is why we faded from your world."

"And I hope you know that your kind is dearly missed." The kelpie's skin was faintly like that of a snake, albeit a cold, wet one. Sorcha couldn't stop petting the creature nor did it seem to want her to stop. Every time she pulled her hand away, it would bounce its head.

"Is that so?" Sand suctioned to his feet as he walked away. Sorcha tracked the slurping sounds to the rocks where he settled. "I see no signs that humans even remember us."

"Myths and legends teach us lessons. Tales of your kind frighten children, and I can't say how many people have thought their babe to be a changeling. They remember you, and they blame many things upon faeries that are their own fault."

Sorcha could not change the minds of people who were so set in their ways. She wanted to, but she also wanted to remain free of fire.

"And you stayed true to the old ways?"

The kelpie snorted on her hand and turned to provide its back. She knew what it wanted and shook her head. "No, my friend. I have no wish to visit the land beneath the waves. Go back with the others."

Sorcha patted the broad back and made her way towards the flat rocks Stone sat upon. The water had yet to splash them although it wouldn't have mattered. Water already weighed her dress down from mist gathering at the hem.

Shivering, she tucked the edges of his cloak underneath her legs. "My mother followed the old ways. She taught me how important it was to leave milk on the windowsill, offerings at the hidden forest shrines, and to always respect the way of the Fae."

"Smart woman," Stone said. His eyes remained trained upon the kelpies rooting through the pool's still waters. "Would that others listened to her wisdom."

"They thought she was a witch, because strange things happened around her. Faeries helped when they could. I don't think they meant to make her seem suspicious or strange. They just wanted to help."

"What happened to her?"

Sorcha shivered again, placed her chin onto her knees, and sighed. "They burned her at the stake for worshiping devils. It took her nearly an hour to burn, because it was so misty that they had to keep lighting the pyre over and over again. I was lucky they didn't feel like burning a child that day."

His bright eyes locked upon hers. "They burned a favored of the Fae?"

"I don't think she was favored. Just one who recognized that our world would never be the same if she gave up on her beliefs."

"And for that, they burned her." Stone shook his head. "Your people are barbarians."

"There is kindness in even the darkest of places. My father plucked me from my village and brought me home. He took me as a daughter, told his children that I was their equal. People such as him exist, but it is so easy to focus on the bad."

Stone grunted. "You have a unique way of looking at the world."

"How so?"

"You twist even negative things into positives. You refuse to think ill of anyone, even those who have wronged you. I have never seen such a creature."

Sorcha shifted, mist playing across her face in small ice cold pricks. "And you? How would you have dealt with a dead mother and a people who betrayed you?"

He reacted as if struck. His gaze snapped away from hers, fists clenching in sudden anger. The muscles of his jaw worked. "Revenge."

"Revenge?" Sorcha shook her head. "What good would that do?"

"I find wiping out those who have wronged you tends to soothe the soul."

"It cannot soothe the soul in the slightest and even suggesting so is cruel. The implications of revenge are that no mercy will be shown."

"Would you show mercy to those who killed your mother?"

"You have experience with this," she said. Her eyes searched his for the truth and found a lingering pain she recognized. "What happened to you?"

"The Fae are not kind creatures. We do not allow for weakness to show among our people."

"The brownies accepted Boggart back into their family with arms open wide. Even after she fell from their ranks and returned with her tail, quite literally, between her legs. Tell me again, Stone, that your people do not allow for weakness."

The ragged sigh that rocked his shoulders tugged at her heartstrings. "The Tuatha dé Danann do not allow for weakness. The lesser Fae are far more…" He paused, seeming to struggle for the words.

"Kind."

"Kind," he repeated with a nod. "Yes, they are capable of forgiveness, which is more than I can say of my people."

"Can they really not forgive? Or do they choose not to?"

His hand touched the angry wound of crystals that wrapped around his neck. "I do not have an answer for that question, Sorcha."

She couldn't stop staring at his throat. The markings were too familiar, yet she couldn't pinpoint what might have caused such a wound. She had seen a man nearly decapitated once, his family had brought him to her in hopes that she might help. There hadn't been any possible way for her to bring him back. But these markings weren't that.

A memory surfaced of bright red skin, bruises spread in spidery tendrils, and the vacant eyes of a thief who had been in the wrong place at the wrong time.

Sorcha had been too young to understand that the hanged man was dead. She ran through the crowd and tried to help him stand up. The gasps of the crowd would always haunt her, even more so than the dead eyes of the man.

She rose onto her knees, turning towards Stone with her gaze locked upon his neck. She gave him time to back away, to brush her hand aside, to tell her to stop.

He didn't.

Her fingers settled upon the cool surface of the crystals. The ones here were smoother than the others, like the polished gems of a crown. She dipped her fingers into the crevice. Magic, so cold it burned, tingled underneath her nails as she followed the angry line to the back of his neck.

"This was among the first," she whispered.

"How did you know?"

"The stones feel old."

"Worn down by time and the elements."

"They hanged you," she observed. "I recognize these marks, although I didn't piece it together until now. How did you survive?"

His massive hand touched just below hers, fingering where skin met rock. "I didn't think I would. The crystals prevent anything from killing me. I hung there for three days before they finally cut me down."

"What did you do?"

"I existed."

Sorcha shook her head. "Surely it was more than that? Living isn't a reason to kill someone."

"It was for my family."

"Family?" Shock jolted through her body until she thumped back onto her heels. "Your family did this?"

"I told you, the Tuatha dé Danann do not forgive weakness."

"What weakness? The crystals? How are they a weakness?"

Suddenly enraged, she surged forward again. Her fingers traced the ragged edges of crystal that bisected his face. She touched the top line at the edge of his shaved skull. "This is the mark of a brave man who has endured much hardship."

Her finger traveled down to rest just above his brow, "And this is the beginning of a journey." She trailed over his eye and hesitated at the high rise of his cheekbone. "The mark of self-discovery." To his lip where the crystal made it difficult to him to smile or speak. "Of bravery." Her thumb touched his chin, "Of stubborn pride."

He chuckled, "Stubborn?"

"I recognize familiar flaws."

"Yes, you are certainly stubborn, little human."

"So much so that I refuse to give up on bringing you back with me. I have to save my family, Stone."

He growled, and she shrieked as his arms wrapped around her and lifted her into his lap. Encircling her with crystal and the scent of mint, he stared. "You refuse to give up on this cursed adventure?"

"It's not cursed. Macha sent me herself. I made a deal, Stone. And I don't think she'll let me give up any time soon."

"Macha," he grumbled. "She is ever meddlesome. Far too interested in humankind if you ask me."

"I didn't ask for this."

"You shouldn't have made a deal with Macha."

"It was the only way to save my family." She reached up and cupped the good side of his face, leaving the raw edges free to her gaze. "I will not regret making this deal, because it led me to meet the most magical people, a wondrous land, an enchanted place filled with all the delights I never would have seen otherwise."

He tilted his face in her palm. Light sparked off the edges of crystals and nearly blinded her. "I am glad you will remember this place fondly."

"And she brought me to you."

Stone stiffened in her arms, his eyes snapping open, burning into her soul. "Why would you say that?"

"You are the most intriguing man I have ever met."

"Monster."

"Man." She pulled him closer, pressing her forehead against his and tasting mint upon the air. He had endured so much, had survived it, and all she could think was that she'd finally met someone who could understand her.

This was a man who had seen what perceived differences could do, in the most drastic of terms. His own family had condemned him for his appearance and had disregarded his suffering.

She wanted to fix him so much, her heart ached.

"I am sorry life has been so cruel. You should never have suffered, but you are strong and kind underneath all those layers of stone and gem."

"It made me strong," he growled, his breath fanning over her lips.

"Oh, yes. You are very strong."

She heard the creaking of his teeth grinding against each other.

"You should flee this isle and tuck yourself back into bed."

"Why?"

"I am not the kind of man you want to fall in love with, Sorcha."

"Who said anything about love?" She surged up, pressing her nose against his and her chest flush to his crystal shoulder. "My time here is finite, unlike your long-lived kind, love only makes this more difficult. All I can ask is for memories that will fill my thoughts with magic. You've done that for me already, Stone."

He growled. "My name is not Stone."

"Then would you tell me what it is?"

Her heart stopped as his broad hand pressed against the small of her back. He cupped her head and slanted his lips across hers, pulling the breath from her lungs as his tongue tangled with hers. Heat spread across her skin like a powerful desert wind.

She wrapped her legs around his waist, knees tucked against his ribs. It didn't matter that the crystals dug into her thighs or that her lungs screamed for air. The taste of mint, lemon, and man coated her tongue and made her lips tingle with new desires.

He groaned, clenching his fist at the back of her head. Her hair tugged, little needles of crystal biting the back of her skull. She should tell him it hurt, but the warmth of his kiss was overwhelming. He didn't just kiss or taste.

He claimed.

Sorcha gripped his crystal shoulders and let her mind free. She focused upon the feather-light touches stroking the dip of her spine. The lingering pass of sharp crystal and velvet-soft lips. The hypnotic rhythm of his darting tongue.

He pulled back, and they both gasped in air. His hands fisted in the material of his cloak wrapped around her, but he did not pull or rip. She thought he might, considering how his hands were shaking.

"I thought I had imagined that first kiss," he whispered.

"Did you?"

"I was drunk."

"You smelled of whiskey."

"I wasn't entirely in my right mind."

"I noticed," she smiled. It was impossible not to touch his face, now that she knew he wouldn't flinch away. The crystals were a tantalizing texture against the heat of his skin. "Would you have hurt Oona?"

"I have no way of knowing. The Fae are…precipitous at the best of times."

"Easily angered?"

"Emotions do not come naturally to us, and when we do feel, it is a thousand times stronger than any other species."

"Ah," she whispered as he pressed his lips against her fingers. "That is why Boggart changed so much when she lost the hag."

"And when she met you."

"I am no paragon nor miracle maker."

"No, but you are infinitely kind, and you always remember to thank us for our services. Do you know how much that means to a faerie?"

"It's what I would want them to do for me," she replied. "They have given me no reason to not be kind. Their hearts are good and their intentions pure, no matter the cause. This has been my dream since I was a child, to sit here on the edges of a pool with kelpies and faeries surrounding me."

"Then I am glad I could make your dreams come true." He said the words as if she had given him a gift.

She rolled off him, planting her butt back on the cold rocks with a small smile on her face. "Did you say something about breakfast?"

"In truth, I forgot it at the castle."

"Did you?" Sorcha burst into bright peals of laughter. "Stone, that was the entire point of this trip!"

“The entire point was introducing you to the kelpies,” he grumbled. But he smiled that sideways smile she recognized.

She pressed a hand to her stomach. “It was a magical experience I’m not likely to forget. Can I come back and see them again?”

“As long as you are with one of the Fae.”

“Why?”

“Kelpies serve their purpose. They are not good at resisting temptation.” He stood and held out a hand for her to take. “And you are most certainly tempting.”

She grasped his hand and did her best not to wince as the crystals on his palm dug into her skin. “But they aren’t dangerous to the Fae?”

“Not at all. They recognize us as one of their own. You, however, are human.”

Sorcha tucked a strand of hair behind her pointed ears. “My father used to jest that I had faerie blood, because of these.”

“If you had faerie blood, the kelpie would have known it. He tried to get you to climb atop his back.”

“It didn’t feel like he was trying to kill me.” She glanced over at the male kelpie who flicked his seaweed tail in their direction. “It felt different from that.”

“They have their purpose, and they know it well. He would have pulled you underneath the waves if you’d let him.”

Sorcha didn’t respond, but placed her hand on top of Stone’s forearm and let him draw her from the magical place. Her mind stayed with the kelpies, wondering if he would have harmed her after all. It didn’t seem like that was the intention.

Those dark green eyes had seemed almost sad. Sorcha couldn’t believe it wanted to hurt her.

Rather more that it simply wanted to show her something remarkable.

Chapter 22

Flour burst into the air in great white clouds. The brownie it struck stared in horror at the mess covering her apron, then narrowed her mouse-like eyes and twitched her elongated snout.

"M'lady!"

Sorcha covered her mouth with a giggle and let the remaining flour drop back into its bag. "Sorry." She shrugged.

"You are not sorry! I watched you pick it up and throw it right at me."

"You said you needed flour."

"I said I needed help cooking. You're making a mess." The brownie tsked. "Whatever are we going to do with you, child?"

"Perhaps give me something to do rather than bother you."

"Is that your game?" The brownie sniffed. "Working around the kitchens is no place for a lady."

"I'm not a lady. I'm a street rat turned midwife who lives above a brothel. How many times do I have to tell you? Give me something to do with my hands!"

"I most certainly will not."

"You could use the help," Sorcha trailed the brownie around the table, tapping her soft head as she went. "I can bake bread, I can peel potatoes, I even used to make soup for the entire family. I think I could figure out how to make even more than that."

"I'm not doing it."

"Why are you so stubborn?"

The brownie whirled and brandished a wooden spoon. "Why are you so persistent? Go make yourself useful somewhere else, child!"

"Where? In the gardens? Cian's already chased me out three times today."

"Did he use the pitchfork?"

Sorcha rubbed her behind. "Yes."

"Good. That's the only way to get nasty little things like you to stay where they're told."

Sorcha groaned and plopped down on a chair. "What am I supposed to do then? Wait around until someone gets hurt? That's dangerous you know. I'll just start causing accidents to ease my own boredom."

"You wouldn't dare," the brownie said as she slipped off the apron and beat it with the spoon. "You're too kind for that."

"Yes, I am. But I have given it a good hard thought."

"Thoughts aren't actions, love. Now would you get out of my kitchen? I've got to make a day's worth of meals for all the faeries, and you aren't helping."

"But I want to help!"

Steam rose in the air from the big pot of soup the brownie was working on. She waved a hand and knives chopped the vegetables, measuring cups scooped up milk and salt, even the dish cloths Sorcha had ripped down rose back into their place.

Magic made everything so much easier. It felt almost like cheating.

Sorcha sighed and banged her forehead down on the center table.

"You're getting my table dirty."

"I'm resting," she murmured against the grain. "Isn't that what you all keep telling me to do?"

Oona's voice joined them, thoroughly amused. "Resting is what you're supposed to be doing regularly. Somehow you forget that."

"I've rested so much that I don't even want to sleep at night."

"Well, dearie, that's the life of a lady."

"Then lady's lives are boring, and I want my old one back."

Oona rubbed her back as she passed, leaning down to whisper in her ear, "We need to go back to your room. Now. But you cannot seem suspicious. No one can know."

Now that was exactly what Sorcha needed to spice up the day. She sat up straight and plastered a fake smile on her face. "Oona, I think I have a new idea for decorating my room. Would you come with me and suggest plants that might grow?"

"You want to plant things?"

"Of course, but I'll need your opinions. I can't understand what would grow here and what wouldn't."

The brownie turned and gave them both a suspicious glance. "What are you up to?"

"Nothing," Sorcha said. "I just want to redecorate."

"Oona, you be careful with that little human. She's a menace!"

Oona smiled, "Oh, she's a dear little thing. Just bored is all. I'll take her out of your hair, if it pleases you."

"It does," the brownie grumbled. "And make sure she doesn't come back any time soon!"

As if she would go back into that kitchen run by a stuck-up mouse.

Oona hustled her from the room with a hand on her back. Sorcha should have been alarmed at the speed they raced towards the portal, but excitement coursed through her veins.

"Don't you run the kitchens?"

"Not anymore. The master said that's only for people he can trust to not put poison in his meals."

"Rude!" Sorcha blurted. "He knows you're loyal."

"He does, but I betrayed him, dearie. It was the right thing to do. Now, open this wall so we can get inside. It's of the utmost importance."

The fear in Oona's voice rattled Sorcha. This wasn't an exciting trip, or even something that she would speak of again. Her brows furrowed, and she pressed the stone pommel hard.

"Is everything all right?" she asked as they raced into her bedroom. "Did something happen to one of the faeries?"

"They're fine. It's you I'm worried about. You've been summoned."

"Summoned?" Sorcha snorted. "By who? The master again?"

"By the king."

Her ears stopped working. All she could hear was a painful ringing sound. The crashing of bells and funeral dirges.

"The king?" she repeated. "How does the king know I exist?"

"I don't know, my dear. But he knows and you cannot refuse him"

"Who is the king of the Seelie now?"

"His Highness the Wise." Oona spit on the floor. "And may he rot forever in his castle. He does not respect the lesser Fae, and I wouldn't trust him as far as I could throw him. Pathetic excuse for a man. And dangerous. You must be careful with your words."

"I won't go." Sorcha shook her head. "He's not my king; I don't have to answer."

"He is everyone's king. If you don't go, he will send someone to hunt you down. The Wild Hunt is nothing compared to the creatures the king can call down upon you."

Then she had to go. There were no other options, but Sorcha still wracked her mind trying to figure out a way to escape.

"The king?" she repeated. "What would he want with me?"

"Midwives are scarce, and rumor has it his most favored concubine is pregnant."

"Concubine?" Sorcha repeated. "Does he not have a Queen?"

"Not this king," Oona muttered. "He has chosen to rule alone."

"Isn't that a bad idea?"

"It's a terrible idea! The Seelie queen has always tempered the king. She is the kindness to his justice, the heart of the people. She is giving and just. That has always been the way of it until His Highness the Wise took the throne."

Oona swung a cloak over Sorcha's shoulders, smoothing the fabric until it settled just right. Worry furrowed her leaf-like brow.

"You're making me worried," Sorcha said with a soft smile. She touched Oona's brow gently. "I won't do anything rash. And, as you remember, I'm a knowledgeable midwife."

"Don't say a thing about living on Hy-brasil," Oona advised. "He won't like that information very much. All we can do is hope his informants don't tell him how they found you."

"Why shouldn't I tell him about Hy-brasil?"

Oona guided her towards the carved portal and lifted her hands into the air. Delicate, twig fingers swung in the air as she called magic to life. "No matter what you do, do not mention the master."

"Why can't I mention Stone? Or Hy-brasil?" Sorcha backed towards the portal and stared Oona down. "I need to know before I make a mistake!"

The cold touch of the portal slid up her ankle and calf before Oona bowed her head. "You'll figure it out when you get there, dearie. Just keep us all, and yourself, safe."

The pixie reached forward and shoved Sorcha's shoulder. She tumbled onto a cold marble floor, worry spinning her head.

She would know when she got there? What in the world did that mean?

"Ah," the cold voice made her freeze. "You must be the midwife."

It was so inhuman that she had no difficulty pinpointing to whom the voice belonged. The king himself waited on the other end of the portal, and Oona hadn't even mentioned that.

She placed her hands firmly on the floor, following the lines of gold in the polished stone all the way to the most extravagant throne she had ever seen. It was so tall it touched the ceilings, feathers and fairy wings turning it into a testament of Fae. Red billowing curtains stretched from the top all the way to the ground like theater curtains.

A man reclined in its center. This was all far too much show for a midwife, but the silver cape he wore trailed three men's length onto the floor. His white blond hair reached his waist, just touching the embroidered waistcoat he wore. Not a single stitch was out of place.

Guards stood at attention all around, their golden armor gleamed in the sunlight pouring from the open ceiling, nearly blinding her. They clutched swords the same height as Sorcha in their hands.

"Your Majesty," she said and bowed her head again. "I am the midwife."

"Good. I have use for your skills. Come with me, human." His voice was as cold as the bitter blizzards in the dead of winter.

She shivered and rose to her feet. "It is always a pleasure to provide services to those who require them."

"I'll keep that in mind when I need a new concubine." His feet entered her line of vision. Perfectly manicured shell-pale toes framed by his golden sandals. "Who can say no to a king?"

He lifted a hand, and her gaze locked upon his fingertips. Stained black as night, his nails were pointed. She had seen the cause before in a previous patient. By the time she arrived, the woman had already been comatose.

Opium addiction was a dangerous beast to tame.

The stained fingers slid underneath her chin and tilted her face to the light. She was hesitant to look him in the eye—kings could be quite strange—but Sorcha had never been cowed before.

She looked up and her world ended.

Stone stared back at her. Or not Stone, but what he might have been if crystals hadn't cracked through his skull.

Perfect cheekbones, flawless skin, full lips that she had seen quirk to the side so many times she knew each line and fold. His eyes frightened her most. Vivid blue, like the sky after a violent lightning storm and so familiar her heart hurt. Now, she saw cruelty reflected in those eyes. She missed the flawed fissures and frown lines surrounding them.

"You'll do," he said as if she wasn't about to faint. "Come with me."

Her feet stuck to the floor. He turned away from her with a flourish of his cape, and still she didn't move.

The king? How did he look exactly like Stone?

The Seelie King glanced over his shoulder and arched a perfect brow. "Are you so foolish that you do not understand an order when you hear one?"

Her Stone. Her kind, disfigured Stone was not reflected in this strange apparition before her. She suddenly understood why Stone reacted so violently when she mentioned family.

This man hadn't just stolen Stone's birthright. He'd taken a kingdom, a throne, mother, father, brother.

Even his face.

Oona's voice echoed in her mind. Do not let the king know where she came from. Do not mention the master. No wonder the pixie had been terrified.

Tears pricked her eyes. She had so misjudged Stone as a cruel man who saw no other solution than revenge for those who wronged him. This wasn't just a family squabble. His twin had ripped away his life and inserted himself into what was rightfully Stone's.

She wanted to smack the perfect face of the king. She wanted to drag her nails across his cheek, so he too might feel the pain and anguish he had caused.

But she couldn't. Sorcha needed to keep a cool mind to get through this alive. Under no circumstances would she risk Stone's life.

"My apologies, Your Majesty." She dipped into a curtsey, hiding her angry tears and red flush. "Please, lead me to the lady I might assist."

"You are far too presumptuous." He reached forward and fingered a lock of her hair. "I wonder what Fae calls you slave?"

It was too close. "No one, Your Majesty. I came from the human realm."

"And who let you into my kingdom?"

"I have always been close to the faeries. My mother left her offerings every week and passed along the respect in her bloodline."

"Respect." He let her hair drop as his lip curled in disgust. "Your kind has little understanding of the word."

The king turned, lifted an imperious hand, and walked away.

The air rang with clanging metal as the guards slammed their swords against their chest plates and followed their king. Sorcha tucked her arms against her sides and tried not to trip. The guards were so close to her that she could feel the cold air radiating from their armor.

It all seemed to be far more fanfare than necessary. They were all over two feet taller than Sorcha. Why did they need so many guards for just her? She wasn't likely to be able to fight one of them, let alone fifteen.

She caught glimpses of the Seelie castle from between the soldiers. It was as if the entire palace was made of light. White floors, golden ceilings, rays of sunshine that bounced until it hurt her eyes to look into some of the rooms.

How did they live like this? Everything was too perfect, too pristine. Her fingers itched to leave a smudged print on the glistening floor. Anything to prove that this place was real and lived in.

Sorcha glanced over her shoulder and caught sight of the faeries trailing after them. Brownies and hobgoblins, dressed in little more than burlap sacks. They held brooms and dustbins, sweeping up any dirt that might have fallen from their feet. More trailed after them with hand rags and water. Their gaunt faces were haunting and hungry.

His Highness the Wise, indeed.

Clenching her fists, Sorcha reminded herself where she was. This was his land, his palace, his kingdom. Although she wanted to free every faerie she found, she would only get herself killed. Or worse, reveal where Stone hid.

She didn't even know if he was hiding. Stone had spoken of revenge. Did he have a plan she didn't know about? Were the other faeries privy to such information?

Questions whirled through her mind until she could hardly think or breathe.

There were no answers in the pristine walls and sun-flooded rooms. She would have to wait until she returned home. Then she would corner Stone and force him to answer all the things he had not shared.

They marched through a pavilion, giant stone arches outlining the square. Flowers bloomed, larger than life and vibrantly colored, filling the air with a sticky sweet scent.

"Would you like a drink?" the king asked. "The honey from these flowers are said to be the most rare and exotic treat."

"No, thank you. I am not thirsty." She would not take any chances.

"Food? We have many things you may never have dreamed of before."

"No. I ate before I arrived."

A grin spread across his sculpted lips. "As smart as you are brave. You are an intriguing little human."

"I know the ways of the Fae," she said. "It is an honor to serve when I can, but I do not wish to linger here."

"You have someone to go home to?"

"No."

"You're lying." He licked his lips as if she had provided a most delicious delicacy.

"I rarely lie."

"I can taste it in the air. Humans are so easy to read. Your eyes dilate, your chest heaves with your guilty breath. You are a book that I can peel open and read every word."

She hated him. She hated every dark word that dripped from his tongue, because she knew he was right. He was nothing like his brother and that frightened her more than anything else.

They walked through the pavilion, and he rapped his knuckles against a marble door.

"My love," he called out. "I have brought you a gift."

"I do not wish for a gift!"

"You will want this one."

"Please, my king. I do not feel well today."

"Precisely." He shoved the door open and nodded towards Sorcha. "Enter."

"She does not seem to wish for visitors."

"It is not her choice. My concubines obey to my every whim and fulfil my every desire. I wish for her to be seen, and you will ensure she is healthy."

Sorcha curtseyed. "Then your wish is my command."

As she passed, he reached out and grabbed her chin. "If she becomes ill after you touch her, no one will be able to hide you from my wrath. I will peel your skin back inch by inch, and I will keep you alive through it all."

"I wouldn't dare harm someone who needed my help."

Sorcha glared at him, meeting his gaze without flinching. This man could threaten her all he wished. She refused to bow to a man who treated his loved ones like slaves.

The king dropped his hand, chuckling. "I will leave three guards by the door. If they hear anything unusual, even the slightest of sounds, they will bring your head to me on a platter."

"I am doubtful my head would satisfy your pallet," she growled. "Might I suggest a more tasteful organ?"

The grin on his face was as feral as her words. The king turned, snapped his fingers, and left with half of his guards. More than three remained standing at attention.

Good. Perhaps the king realized just how dangerous a little human midwife could be.

"At ease, gentlemen," she muttered to the guards. "I wouldn't want you to faint in all that hot armor."

Sorcha didn't wait to see what kind of startled expressions they tossed her way. She stepped into Elva's room and slammed the door behind her. Let them rot while they waited to see what she might do. Sorcha didn't care. If they served such a horrible king, then they deserved the same fate.

Smoke curled around her waist like tendrils of fingers. Frowning, Sorcha turned and peered into the bright, sunlit room.

She had never been inside an opium den and had never desired to do so. Now, she knew what they looked like.

Red velvet hung in great sheets from their ceiling, tangling with golden wire twisted into leaves. Gemstones hung in sparkling tendrils from above. From floor to ceiling, smoke coiled around all the opulence.

Hookahs littered the floor, laying atop mountains of pillows and spilling liquid to the floor. Three faerie attendants lay stretched across the ground. Bark skin made them blend into the ground, their lips and fingers stained black by opium tea.

"Elva?" Sorcha whispered, using the faerie's true name on a whim. "I am a midwife."

"Midwife?" The bed rustled. The faerie woman pulled the curtains aside. "What are you doing here?"

"Your king summoned me."

Elva ripped the curtains to the floor. Her grace disappeared under the haze of drugs. "You are in grave danger."

"I am here to help you."

"If he invited you here, then he knows precisely who you are. And he knows where you come from."

The words made Sorcha freeze. The faerie had so many drugs in her system, that surely she wasn't revealing she knew about Hy-brasil. Or did she?

"I come from the human realm," Sorcha said. "I am here to make certain you are healthy. It is what your king wishes."

The faerie fell against Sorcha. "You do not understand. You do not know him. He wants to hurt me, so he brought you here. You need to go."

"What is wrong? Elva, you need to speak to me. If there is something I might do to help you—"

Black-tipped fingers pressed against Sorcha's mouth. The faerie's eyes were wild. "No. No, there is nothing you can do to save me."

"Save you?" Sorcha repeated. "Do you need saving?"

"What could be done for me was lost long ago, little human."

The panic made Sorcha nervous. She held the much larger woman in her arms and pressed Elva's head into her shoulders. Tears soaked through the fabric on her shoulder.

Squeezing her eyes shut, Sorcha pressed closer until their bellies touched. It had been nearly a month since she had seen Elva.

Smooth stomach met smooth stomach.

"Are you not pregnant?" Sorcha whispered.

"He wrapped me in silk and velvet. He called me his love and tore me from everything I loved."

"Where is your child, Elva?"

"Gone. With everything else."

"What happened?"

"Life." The faerie woman pulled back, swiping at her tears in anger. "Life for a Tuatha dé Danann royal. There is nothing you can do to help me, midwife. I made a deal with a devil and take a snake to bed each night."

"Elva—"

"I can help you."

"What?" Sorcha shook her head. "I do not need help. I need to make sure you are healthy, and perhaps that is why your king brought me here."

"He did not bring you here for me. He brought you here for a lesson to be learned. He does not believe that me losing the child was merely because it was my first and because faeries do not carry children well. You are his scapegoat. His reasoning behind the loss of his child."

"I will not give you anything to prevent childbirth." Fear twisted around Sorcha's tongue, slowing her words into a slur.

"We both know that is the truth. But he has never cared for the truth."

What a sad existence this woman lived. Sorcha tucked her arm around Elva's side and nudged her back towards the bed. It was unclear whether the woman was speaking from the heart or a drug-induced panic.

Either way, Sorcha's job was to heal. She couldn't mend the rift between Elva and her king. She couldn't even touch the pain that stained the woman's soul. All she could do was get her settled in bed and quiet her mind.

She tucked the faerie into bed and smoothed her hair from her sweat slicked forehead. "Where are you from, Elva?"

"Cathair an Tsolas."

"The city of light?" Sorcha smiled. "I've heard of the legends. It is a place constantly filled with the sun."

"It sparkles when you look upon it."

"Tell me of your city, Elva. I dearly love stories."

Elva whispered tales of a magical city filled with Tuatha dé Danann and faerie subjects. She laced legends Sorcha recognized with truths that spoke of pristine streets and people wearing the most outlandish costumes.

All the while, Sorcha cleaned. She lifted the dryads from their stupor and handed them out the door to the guards. The men seemed surprised that she would dare lay a hand upon any faerie.

"Not a word," she growled at them. "Take these ladies back to their quarters, or where ever you put them."

"They stay with the concubine."

"And I say they go. If you wish to argue, please tell your king to meet me here. Otherwise, put those women where they can sleep off the opium."

The guards stared at each other, shrugged, and two left with the faeries tucked under their arms.

Sorcha closed the door once more. Elva's privacy could be contained within these walls. No guards needed to gossip any more than they already were going to. The king and his favored concubine both relied upon opium. Enough that their fingers were stained with its poison.

The story of a beautiful city filled the air. It twisted in the smoke and filtered out the windows as Sorcha threw them open. Fresh air would do a world of good for this room.

She piled the pillows against the far wall and placed her fists upon her hips. There wasn't much else she could do in such a fine room. This wasn't built to be a comfortable living place, but a feast for the senses.

"You don't live in a very practical bedroom," she murmured. "Pretty it might be, but useful it is not."

Elva didn't stop mumbling her story. The words seemed to ground her. The opiates were slowly filtering out of her system as Sorcha puttered about.

She stuck her finger in a small groove in the wall. A door popped open, revealing what looked to be all the items she would need to clean.

"Convenient," Sorcha said. A bucket of water waited for her, along with a mop that looked as though it had never been used before. Why keep something in a closet if it would not be used?

Faeries. They would never make sense to her.

She poured the water onto the floor and scrubbed stains and smells. "Elva. Enough with the story, my dear, I think I know enough to believe I lived there."

"Humans can't live there."

"No? That's a shame. We're not all that bad."

"I'm beginning to see that." The fog had cleared from Elva's voice. Now, she sounded more ashamed than babbling. "What are you doing?"

"Cleaning."

"Yes, but why?"

"Because there is hookah oil smudged into your floor, and the entire place reeks of opium." Sorcha paused to blow a red curl from her forehead. "Don't you ever have anyone scrub the floors?"

"None other than you."

"Hmph. If you aren't going to do it yourself, you should have someone clean at least every once and a while."

"Why not you?"

"I'm not for hire." Nor would she ever be. The longer she was in this place, the less Sorcha liked it. How had Stone grown up in this place?

The thought filled her mind until it was all she could think of. Stone had lived here. He had grown up here. The king was his brother. And the king's concubine sat only a few feet from her.

Moving the mop once more, Sorcha stared down at her work. "Elva?"

"Yes?"

"Did you know that the king has a twin brother?"

"It's blasphemy to even mention that the king has a sibling."

"Does that mean you won't tell me about him?"

Elva rolled onto her side to watch Sorcha work. "I knew him."

"The king?"

"His twin."

"What was he like?" For once, she could speak about Stone with someone who wouldn't hide the truth from her. There were enough opiates in Elva's system to loosen her tongue. This might be the moment when she finally figured out his story.

"He was an impressive man. The king and queen took different routes to raising their sons. The eldest boy tended towards the wild and feral faeries. They feared he might turn Unseelie, so they convinced him to train his mind and body as a warrior. He was the most fearsome creature who ever lived."

"You speak as if he no longer exists." Sorcha couldn't clean and listen at the same time. She leaned the mop against the wall and sat down on a stool. "Is he dead?"

"Gone. And if you're lost to this world, you're as good as dead."

"Where?"

"Banished. Some say he still lives on Hy-brasil, but I have many contacts there. If he lived, I would know."

"Do you think he was murdered?"

"I wouldn't put it past the king to do everything in his power to keep the throne. His twin was the favored son. He was perfect until his brother destroyed him."

"So I've heard," Sorcha murmured. "You said you knew him?"

"As best as anyone could. He was older than I and always fighting the Unseelie. There was something wild in him that could not be tamed. He frightened me. He frightened most of the faerie women, but we all wanted him. You know, we used to call him the red stag?"

"The red stag? Why?"

"There was something in him that wasn't faerie at all. Something that spoke of beasts in the wood, whispers on the wind, magic in his blood that didn't come from the Tuatha dé Danann. He was dangerous, and I think his brother saw that in him."

Sorcha hung on every word. She leaned forward until she perched on the very edge of the stool. "What did the king think his brother would do?"

"He would change everything," Elva whispered. "He didn't see the lesser Fae as creatures made to work. He saw them as people, valued them as soldiers and friends. That is not the Seelie way."

"Is change such a bad thing?"

"I wouldn't know."

Sorcha's heart broke for this shell of a woman. Her feet carried her to the other woman's side. With as much gentleness as she could muster,

Sorcha tucked her back underneath the covers.

"Try to sleep," she murmured.

"Will it help?"

"I don't know if anything will help. But I find that a good night's rest and quiet dreams always seem to ease the soul."

"My dreams are all nightmares." Elva turned onto her side, away from Sorcha's kind hands. "But at least I know that nightmares aren't happening, no matter how tragic they are to experience."

Sorcha stayed until Elva's breathing slowed into the steady rhythm of sleep.

What had this woman endured? What had they all endured?

She stood slowly, taking care to not shake the bed. They all had such tragic stories, such heartbreaking lives where hardships did not end.

Humans struggled throughout their entire existence. Poverty, death, illness, were all things that humans understood came with their humanity. Sorcha had never thought that faeries would also struggle. They were spirits of nature. Surely, they would live better lives?

She had been wrong.

"You got her to sleep?" The king's voice was quiet as he entered. "I don't remember the last time she laid herself down without a fight."

"She needed comfort."

"And you think I'm incapable of providing that," he murmured as he sat on the edge of her bed.

"It is not my place to judge, Your Majesty." But they both heard the hidden words beneath her quiet tones. Yes, she blamed him. She blamed him for a lot more than just Elva's unhappiness.

He stared down at the beautiful faerie he called concubine. There was something about his expression that made Sorcha feel as though she were intruding. He didn't glare, or grasp at her flesh. He simply stared at her with a soft expression and followed the line of her cheek with his gaze.

"I love her," he said. "I love her so much it hurts to breathe. But that is one of the hardest things about being king. If I marry her, I put her in harm's way. If I leave her as concubine, she stays safe, but she hates me."

Sorcha's tongue got ahead of her mind, words slipping from between her lips without permission. "I don't think it is the title that offends her."

"No," he chuckled. "No, it's everything. I am not my brother. I do not see the lesser Fae as creatures capable of having positions of power. I do not believe giving them free will benefits our people. The old ways have worked for a very long time. Changing things leads to unanticipated endings, and I will not risk the future of our people on the dreams of others."

"I asked her if change was a bad thing, and she said she didn't know. Now I ask you the same, King of the Seelie Fae. Do you believe change is bad?"

He looked at her with a troubled expression wrinkling his brow. "The Fae are unused to change. Perhaps you would be better suited to answer such a question."

"I think controlling the future with an iron grasp only limits the possibilities of tolerance and positive change."

"You are far too wise to be human."

"I am not Fae," she said.

"You are something else entirely." He looked back down at Elva, fingering the edge of her blanket before standing. "I owe you a boon."

"A boon? From the King of the Seelie? That does not seem a wise choice to offer."

"And yet I offer it freely. Easing her troubled soul is worth more than just a boon, but I do not believe you will use such a gift in a way I will agree with."

He held out his hand for her to take. Sorcha raised a brow and hesitantly grasped his hand in hers.

She wanted to trust him if only because he looked like Eamonn. His palm was smooth against her calloused fingers. No crystals bit into her skin. No scars abraded the sensitive flesh of her wrist. He was perfect. Everything Stone was not.

Sorcha shivered. "Then I accept your boon with the understanding that I do not agree with your choices, King."

"You are not the first to disagree with me and you will not be the last. Know that I am grateful for your assistance, and will not forget it."

"I hope someday that is useful." She pulled away from him and scooped up her cloak.

"As do I, little midwife," he said. "For I fear you and I will face each other on different sides of a battlefield someday."

Sorcha glanced over her shoulder, hand on the door to her freedom. "Have you consulted with anyone to see your future?"

"I know my future without having to ask any of the Unseelie their opinions. Both of my endings result in killing myself. Either this flesh, or that of my mirror."

Something inside her clicked like a key turning in a lock.

He knew.

He knew she lived with Stone. He knew where she came from, and still he ordered her here.

And now he was letting her go.

"Why?" she whispered.

"The end will come whether you are involved in this story or not, midwife. I believe it will be far more interesting with your intervention."

"Why is it that all Fae seem to think that their own future is a story?" Sorcha said. "There is no story here. No one will sing of two brothers who destroyed each other!"

"How can you know that for certain?" The king waved a bejeweled hand. "There are stranger stories told to this day. Keep your head up, little midwife. Your journey has only just begun."

"I want no part in this story."

"You're already in it. War is coming. Tell my brother to enjoy his last few days of life."

CHAPTER 23

"Where are we going?" Sorcha asked. A blindfold covered her face, the velvet soft against her skin.

Stone had walked into her bedroom with it in his hands, a sheepish grin on his face. He refused to tell her where they were going, but she also refused to stop asking.

"Sorcha, just let it be a surprise."

"I can't do that. I want to know."

"You'll find out!" he said with a chuckle.

"But not soon enough!"

She didn't think he knew about her recent escapade into Seelie. He certainly hadn't mentioned it.

Sorcha had scrubbed her skin for an hour before she saw him. Clean water and lemon verbena washed away the scent of faeries and anything else he might have recognized from home.

Weeks passed. Sorcha took to begging him every night to return to the mainland with her. Sometimes, she thought he might bend. Other times, all she did was anger him.

He grew angry so easily.

But tonight, he was happy. Pleased, almost. The surprise he planned obviously meant something to him.

"Stone," she begged, "I want to know!"

"And you will, little human. Just not yet."

Sorcha tried to figure out where they were going. She knew each turn of the castle by heart, but got lost when he spun her in circles.

"What are you doing?" she asked with a laugh. "You'll make me dizzy."

"I don't want you to guess what direction we're going."

"I wasn't tracking our steps."

"You most certainly were. I could hear you mumbling under your breath." He leaned close, breath tickling her ear and sending shivers down her spine. "I refuse to let you ruin this surprise."

"I don't like surprises."

"You'll like this one."

He placed his hands on her shoulders and guided her down the hallways. Each step felt more and more unfamiliar until he finally tugged her to a stop.

His hands were so big. They covered her shoulders and dipped into the hollows of her collarbone. She was intensely aware of the soft circles he drew just beneath the winged bones. He seemed to stroke her skin without thought.

"You have been so kind to my people. And you have made a lasting impression upon all of us. I wanted to do something for you."

"Thank you," she said. "I don't deserve anything special though. I hope you didn't go out of your way."

"We only spent a few nights on it."

"A few nights? Stone!"

"My name is not Stone."

"I refuse to call you master."

He chuckled, hands sliding across her shoulders and tangling in the heavy weight of her hair. "Someday, I would like to hear the word cross your lips just to see how unnatural it sounds."

"You won't like it if I ever called you master."

"No, I wouldn't. I've come to expect you to surprise me, Sorcha. It would be a shame for you to fall in line like the rest."

The knot at the back of her head pulled, and the velvet fell free.

She gasped in delight. The throne room glimmered with light. The ceiling, free from cobwebs and dust, had a mirrored finish that reflected the candlelight. Smooth marble and great swaths of red fabric made the room seem fit for royalty.

Sorcha couldn't care less for the grand appearance of the room. It was the people her eyes locked upon and the sight of them that made her knees weak.

Every faerie on the isle had dressed in their finest. They did not decorate themselves with silk or velvet, but clean clothing and woolen cloaks. Their faces scrubbed clean, they had tied their hair in intricate braids.

They were not a people of royalty. They were not kings and queens, but men and women who lived on the land.

"They look out of place," she said with a chuckle. "And they are the most beautiful things I've ever seen."

"Good. You'll be seeing a lot of them tonight."

"Not for me," Sorcha turned with a worried expression. "You didn't bring them all together for me, did you, Stone?"

He winked. "You have lost your memory coming here, haven't you, Sorcha? As much as I would love to force my people to bend a knee to your beauty, that is not why they are here. It's Samhain."

"Already?"

She'd left home in spring, and it was Samhain already? Sorcha felt as though she'd only just washed up on the shore, and now autumn knocked upon the door of the human world.

The tangled mass of people parted, and Oona marched towards them. Her wings were on full display, red markings painted from her lip to chin.

"Child of the human world, would you do the honors?"

"The honors?" Sorcha tilted her head. "Do you celebrate the same way my people do?"

"Your people? Or your mother's people?"

She grinned. "My mother's people. My father and siblings were never ones to celebrate the old ways."

"Then light the fires for us, child, and honor the dead."

Sorcha tangled her fingers with Stone's for a moment, squeezing his hand. She looked over her shoulder as she descended the stairs. His gaze caught hers, pride and honor reflected in their depths.

"Thank you," Sorcha said.

"I knew it would be important to you."

"How?"

He shrugged. "I just knew."

Her fingers slid from his, trailing along the crystals of his palm and whispering across their twin callouses. She walked backwards down the stairs with a soft smile on her face. "And will you be partaking in the festivities, my king?"

Stone's jaw dropped and Sorcha reveled in his surprise. He seemed unable to speak. A state she found surprisingly suitable to her tastes. With a wicked grin on her face, she turned to Oona and followed her to the altar.

"The Wild Hunt is tonight?" Sorcha asked. "Are we safe here?"

"This is not the Otherworld, but it is not the human world either. The Wild Hunt does not touch upon these shores," Oona replied. "But we still honor the ride and dream of seeing their might once again."

"We won't even see them?" Sorcha had hoped to catch a glimpse. Now that the ointment had cleared her eyes of glamour, it would be a treat to see what the faeries saw. The Wild Hunt, led by their great horned king, had always been fascinating.

Her disappointment was great, but it was also a blessing. She didn't know what Cernunnos, the leader of the Wild Hunt, would do if he saw a human in the faerie prison.

Thick branches with green leaves still clinging on their twigs created an altar where Eamonn's throne usually sat. The roots of the tree wrapped in a circle on the floor, creating a base that was strong and steady. Offerings piled near to overflowing all around it. Milk, honey, and more food than any Tuatha dé Danann could devour.

"It is a good offering," she said.

"This year has been better than most. We have much to be thankful for."

"As do I." She reached for a goblet filled to the brim with wine and poured it on the roots. "To many years with family and friends, may we all last the night without nightmares and the next year without pain or strife. I thank my ancestors, the gods above, and the gods below. We come to this place to celebrate Samhain and seek shelter from the Wild Hunt."

Something stirred within her breast. A memory, or an age-old knowledge passed down through generations. She remembered the words as if her mother whispered them in her ear.

Sorcha lifted a finger and traced runes into the air. "Spirits of the East and Air, I welcome you into our circle and bid you well tidings. On this sacred night of Samhain, come dance with us."

Faeries stirred behind her, pixies lifting into the air and buffeting her spine with their breeze. Her curls blew over her shoulders. Blue light lifted from the runes she drew. She gasped. Never before had she seen a Samhain ritual like this before.

Leaning forward, she struck flint and steel to light the candle at the base of the altar. "Spirits of the South and Fire, I welcome you to feast with us on this sacred night."

The candle flared, and the air turned hot. She told herself not to wipe at the sweat on her brow, that it would insult the faeries who enjoyed the heat.

She dipped her fingers into the goblet to her left and flicked the droplets of water. "Spirits of the West and Water, I welcome you to drink and be merry with us tonight. Join our revelries on this sacred Samhain eve."

The air turned muggy. Her dress stuck to her back, and her hair felt heavy with the weight of water in the air. A kelpie snorted although she had not seen any in the crowd.

A small pot of dirt was the last and final piece of her ritual. She rubbed the dirt between her fingers, feeling the ancient knowledge it held.

"Spirits of the North and Earth, I welcome you to this hall and ask that you tell us stories from ages past. Speak easy and loosen thy tongue on this sacred night."

She felt the powerful cheer of the faeries before it made her ears ache. Sorcha grinned, unable to keep her own happiness from bubbling forth. This was a good night. A blessed night. A peaceful night.

Her chest squeezed tight and her eyes lost focus. There was one more candle that should be at this altar.

She reached forward, traced the outline of leaves that died and withered as she watched. She struck the flint and steel one more time, lighting the dead tree on fire.

The faeries fell silent.

"I welcome thee, Morrighan, and your sisters to our fold. Lady of Fate, War, and Fear, you are welcome within these walls." Sorcha lifted a goblet of wine, tilted her head back, and closed her eyes. "Morrighan—hail and welcome!"

A deafening cheer followed her words, but she did not hear it. Instead, Sorcha heard a pleased chuckle and smelled the wheatgrass scent of horses.

"Well done," Macha murmured. "Feast and stay safe from the Wild Hunt."

Oona wrapped an arm around Sorcha's shoulders and gave her a shake. "Well done! It's almost as if you were born a druid priestess!"

"A what?" Sorcha opened her eyes in shock. "What did you call me?"

"Oh, dearie, you have druid in you. I knew there was something strange about you. Only a priestess would know that ritual. And someday I'll ask who taught it to you, but for now, drink!"

Another goblet of wine pressed into her hand. Holding two, she watched Oona dance a merry jig towards Cian who watched with a sour expression. When the pixie reached him, he sighed and held up his arms. They spun in wild circles around other Fae until everyone in the hall was dancing.

Sorcha stood with her hands full, watching the merriment with shock. A bubble of laughter escaped her lips, effervescing until she couldn't contain it any longer.

A crystal hand plucked one of the goblets from her grasp. "Well met, priestess."

"I am no priestess," she shook her head. "My mother may have been, I'm realizing now. It was from her book that I gathered that knowledge."

"That kind of precision comes from years of practice."

"I can honestly say that I have never performed a Samhain ritual quite like that. Do you think it's because we're closer to the Otherworld?" She gulped a mouthful of wine as if that might help clear her head.

"No. I think it's because druids pass knowledge through maternal lines. And because you were born a priestess."

"My mother always wished I was a changeling, that faerie blood would have been something to be proud of."

"Your mother wouldn't wish you to be a changeling, they have sad lives. We've already confirmed you're not Fae. Perhaps there are a few things we might consider."

"We?" Sorcha glanced up.

His ocean eyes stared down at her, curiosity and kindness reflected in their depths. "If you are so inclined to find out who you are, I offer my services."

"What help can you provide?"

"There is a library."

"Here?"

"Yes."

Sorcha placed her hands on her hips. "When were you going to tell me?"

"When you asked."

"And if I never asked?"

Stone's lips quirked to the side. "Then you would never know."

"You are a cruel man," she said as she handed her goblet to a passing faerie. "Do you dance?"

"I did."

"That sounds as if you no longer dance."

"It is no longer graceful," he patted his hip. "The crystals prevent much movement. Fighting is one thing, grace is innate when you're fighting for your life. Dancing does not come naturally."

"Good," she said. Sorcha lifted her skirts high enough to show her feet and pointed. "I have two left feet. I cannot dance well at all, and it's very likely that you will be thankful for the crystals because otherwise I might crush your toes."

"I don't have crystals on my toes."

"Then you will when I'm done with you." She winked. "Perhaps you would care to look at your dance card for a free space where I might write my name?"

He arched a brow. "Can you even pen your name?"

"Not all humans are illiterate." She shook her head. "You know I can read, Stone."

The growl that rumbled from his throat sent shivers down her spine.

Sorcha gasped as broad hands slid around her waist and pulled her against his chest. She splayed her fingers against his heat. His legs framed hers, inner thighs pressed against her hips. Her stomach was flush against his—crystals biting through the thin fabric.

"This is hardly proper," she whispered.

"Humans do not dance as the Fae do."

"This is how you dance?"

"Well, not particularly."

She glanced up and caught the sparkling laughter that danced in his eyes. He cocked his head to the side, lifted a hand, and gently tucked a strand of hair behind her ear. His fingertips were feather-light against her skin. He traced a circle against her neck, trailed down the slope of her shoulder and arm, lifted her hand until it rested against his bicep.

She couldn't breathe, couldn't even think as he followed the same path on the other side of her body and curled his fingers around her hand. His other palm flexed against her spine.

"This is the proper way to dance with a woman," he said.

"Is it?" Sorcha heard the breathless quality to her voice, the sultry notes that dripped from her tongue.

Heat flashed in his gaze, a blush spreading across his cheeks. "Perhaps you have never danced with a man."

"Boys, yes. A man?" Sorcha's eyes followed the ragged edge of crystals, the barbaric braid swaying from the peak of his head to his waist, the linen tunic belted by sheep skin. "Never a man such as you."

He pressed gently against her spine, and they spun into the crowd. Faeries waltzed around them as a band struck up a tune.

Sorcha would remember none of the fluttering colors and magic sparking in the air. How could she? He stared at her as if she were the world. As if she plucked the stars from the sky and wove them into the strands of her hair.

Stone used his body like a weapon. He spun her in circles until she didn't know which way was up and which way was down. He only stopped when she stumbled, falling into his arms.

She liked being pressed against his chest far too much. He was safe, and broad, and so much more than any man she had ever met before.

She said something, it could have been anything, she didn't know what. But he tilted his head back and laughed so hard that the corded muscles of his neck stood out in stark relief. The crystals gaped at the wound caused by his hanging, and she couldn't see the disfigurement anymore.

He was beautiful. An instrument of power and symbol of strength.

Stone spun her into his arms, pressing his cheek against the top of her head before unraveling her. He pressed her spine against his chest, dipping until he could whisper in her ear, "How did you know I was to be king?"

"You carry yourself as if you were meant to rule."

"And Oona told you."

He would taste the lie, so she said nothing and glanced over her shoulder. "Does it really matter how I know, Stone?"

His expression turned so fierce that she thought he might crush her. Instead, he traced his finger down her cheek and pressed his forehead to hers. "Eamonn."

"What?" she gasped.

"My name is Eamonn."

Before she could comment on such a gift, he spun them in wide circles around the room until she tossed her head back and laughed. This was perfect. Every single moment was perfect and sweet.

And he was perfect. Every broken bit of him was perfect for her.

He had brought together all the people who meant something to her. Every faerie who had given her gifts, kindness, laughter, peace. They were all here in their finest outfits, and it didn't matter that they had no silk nor velvet to share.

Their hearts beat as one. Samhain had never been celebrated by such a strong family of people.

They passed the day in each other's arms. Every now and then, they would stop for food and drink. Sorcha's feet ached, but she didn't want to stop dancing. So she would stuff her face, tease the faeries she saw along the way, but she never strayed far from his side.

There was an impending sense of doom, something she couldn't explain or understand. Although this night felt as though they found each other for the very first time, tomorrow was uncertain.

Her siblings' voices whispered in her mind. This was how a woman became a mistress. Fall in love with the wrong man, and disaster was sure to follow. He should be a king! And Sorcha? She was a midwife from so far away that he wouldn't even know the name of her town.

Sorcha brushed the voices aside, not wanting to worry about the future tonight.

Another voice joined her siblings. Tell my brother to enjoy his last few days. She couldn't tell Stone—Eamonn, she reminded herself—that she'd met his twin. She refused to issue a warning she wasn't certain held any weight.

She had a boon from the king of the Seelie Fae. If he wanted to kill his brother, then she would use her boon against that. Eamonn would live. They could stay on this isle until the end of time.

And then the blood beetles would devour her family.

It was so easy to forget reality here. She understood the many stories of men and women who spent centuries in the Otherworld only to return and find everything gone. Life was so easy here. There were no responsibilities, no people to take care of, only herself and her own whims.

Perhaps someday she would forget the echoes of her family. Tonight, she certainly would. But tomorrow morning, Sorcha knew she would remember every bit of the guilt she sewed into her bones.

The music quieted as the sun dipped below the horizon. Her dress stuck to her skin, and her hair billowed around her like a red cloud. She leaned against Eamonn's side and stood at the window staring at the bright streaks of colored clouds.

"Have you enjoyed your Samhain, m'lady?" he asked.

"I believe this was the most enjoyable celebration I have had the pleasure of joining."

"What was your favorite part?"

"The company."

"Ah," he chuckled and scratched the back of his neck. "Present company excluded, I would hope."

"Hope? Why would you hope for exclusion from that grouping?"

Eamonn spread his hands wide. The pink light of the sunset played off the crystals. "I'm hardly fit to grace the halls of lords and ladies. The dogs may enter, but the wolves must stay beyond the door."

She hated hearing him speak of himself like that. So many years of torment and disapproval from family and friend led to self-hatred. She had seen it in herself.

It was so much easier to say he was wrong and ignore the emotions reflected in herself.

Sorcha reached forward and intertwined her fingers with his. "Even wolves can be tender, loyal, and brave-hearted. I would rather run with them in the wild than paint my face and try to blend into the walls."

He squeezed her fingers. "I forget who I speak with."

"A midwife?"

"A druid priestess with far more power than she admits." He pressed his lips against the backs of her knuckles. "I'd like to show you something."

"Another surprise? Eamonn, I might faint away if you keep up with this. I'm convinced someone has stolen your body and masquerades as a gentleman in your flesh."

His eyes flashed. "I enjoy the sound of my name upon your lips far too much."

A shiver trailed down her spine. "Then I shall endeavor to use it upon every occasion."

"Come with me."

She trailed after him into the depths of the castle. Past cobwebbed corners, stained glass windows dimming with the sun, and hidden alcoves where mist gathered. Up a stairwell she didn't recognize that curved dangerously with no railing. Out onto a catwalk so high that the clouds tangled in her skirts.

"Where are we?" she shouted into the wind.

"Are you afraid?"

"No! This is beautiful!"

His grin flashed as the stars blinked to life behind him. "Wild thing that you are, fear has no name for you, does it?"

"Fear is an enemy to battle. I know her well."

"Do not fall."

"Will you catch me if I do?"

"I will fly upon the wings of the Wild Hunt if need be."

She burst into laughter. "I thought faeries couldn't lie?"

He tugged her off the edge of the catwalk and into a hidden corner. The heat of his chest seared through the fabric of her dress. "I do not lie. If I had to call the Wild Hunt to save you, I would."

"I think I would fall to my death before you could manage."

"I'd find another way."

Sorcha grinned and shook her head. "What do you want to show me?"

Eamonn pressed his back against the wall and pushed. The sparkle in his eyes caught her attention before she noticed the wall had turned into a door. A warm glow lit the frame with orange light.

He pushed harder to reveal the fur rugs and walls lined with books.

"Oh," she whispered. "Is this the library?"

"No. These are my quarters."

"Yours?" Sorcha arched a brow. "Just what kind of woman do you think I am, Eamonn?"

She knew he would growl at her use of his name. She wanted to hear it again and again.

The deep baritone rumbled from deep within his chest. It was the call of a lion to its mate, the quiet huff of a stag in the forest, the gurgle of water underneath ice.

He reached for her, yanking her into his chest until her hands splayed against him. "Say it again."

"I have no need to call you by name."

"Say it."

"You brought me here for a reason, Eamonn." Sorcha grinned at the quake she felt behind her palms. "Why are we here?"

The disappointed breath that blew across her face smelled of mint. "You are temptation, little priestess."

"Hardly. I wasn't raised a druid."

"You don't need to be. Druid is in your blood, and I'm curious to see what you think of this surprise."

He didn't let go of her entirely. Eamonn slid his hands down her arms and tangled his fingers with hers. Silent, he guided her towards a bookcase and released his hold.

The tome he pulled from the shelf sparkled in the light. Its deep green cover and gold threaded words wavered under her gaze.

"Is it glamoured?" she asked.

"Not that I know of."

It was changing in front of her eyes. The green dappled as if sunlight was striking it through leaves. The letters shifted and moved until she couldn't read what the title was, let alone who had written it.

Eamonn held it out for her to take.

She stroked the spine, something inside her calling out to treat it like a beloved pet. It creaked as she opened the pages. Ink blots stained most of them, hand drawn pictures of herbs and instructions filling the parchment paper.

"Who wrote this?"

"I don't know. There's nothing on the pages."

"What?" Sorcha glanced up. "There's plenty on the pages. There's just no signature."

"I can't see anything written in that book. I have tried for years, but no matter how much I try, the pages remain blank."

"Interesting." With her nose buried, she meandered towards the chairs. "There's much here I've never considered. Mugwort, for example, is rarely used to cure nightmares. It's curious that it suggests using it while chanting… something. I can't read that part."

"You aren't quite ready for it yet, I imagine."

"Why?" Sorcha wrinkled her nose. "Why wouldn't I be ready for knowledge?"

"For the same reason I was not ready to be king." He plucked the book from her grasp and set it down on a small table. "We all must grow before we take on responsibility."

"You would make a good king."

"So you say, but I was not ready as a young man."

He circled her. Sorcha knew the expression in his eyes. The darkened edges, the attention to detail, the hunger that she had only seen in a wolf. She was being hunted, and she didn't know whether she wanted to flee or embrace the danger.

"I see many qualities in you that would make a good king. I don't know if anyone is ever ready to take on such a daunting task."

"How did you know I was meant to be king?"

"That's my little secret."

She felt his breath fan across the back of her neck. "I don't like secrets."

"Would you prefer that I lie?"

"I never prefer lies."

"Then I am afraid you must resolve yourself to be disappointed, Eamonn."

Sorcha stood perfectly still, fear locking her knees and curiosity stilling her breath. At the sound of his name, a single finger touched her throat. Her breath caught.

His fingernail scratched just enough to leave a mark as he trailed it down her neck and to her shoulder. He hesitated for a brief moment before hooking it underneath the yellow fabric of her dress.

He was giving her time to tell him to stop, she realized. A voice in her head screamed to leave, to run, that a faerie could not be trusted. But her heart knew what she wanted.

Him.

Sorcha sighed as the fabric of her dress slipped down her shoulder, baring milky white skin dotted with freckles. He groaned and traced patterns between the beauty marks.

"Do you know what they used to call me, Sorcha?"

"No." She couldn't think, let alone decipher what his words meant. Not when he was stroking the bare skin of her shoulder and the cold breeze brushed past her sensitive arms.

"The Red Stag. I used my blade like the antlers of the beast, leaving wounds dotting across my enemies' flesh. I carved my namesake in skin more times than I can count."

"Is that supposed to frighten me?"

"It is a warning."

"That you are dangerous?" She glanced over her shoulder, the fabric of her dress slipping even further. "I know that, Eamonn. You are the sword, the weapon, the soldier of the Seelie Fae."

He traced circles on her neck. "And the sword is far mightier than the pen for a time. But eventually a sword loses its weight, becomes a symbol more than a weapon. All warriors turn to the pen once they win their wars."

"Precisely why I believe you would make a good king."

His breath feathered over her arm. Crystals pressed into soft flesh, surrounded by the velvet heat of his mouth. A soft flick of his tongue stroked between freckles.

"Why does your whole body taste like sunshine?" he asked. "It's intoxicating."

"Does my whole body? I wasn't aware you had tasted every inch."

"There is no going back from this Sorcha. If you make this choice, I cannot stop."

"You are a large man, Eamonn, but you are not my first."

Sorcha reminded herself to breathe as his hands curled around her waist. He yanked her against him, pressed her spine against his stomach. "Who dares touch what is mine?"

"I am my own before I am any other's. But if you must know, I grew up in a brothel. A girl gets curious."

"A girl toes the line between right and wrong."

"Is there such a thing?" She spun in his arms, eyes sparking with anger. "Right and wrong suggests that there is only black and white. I refute that belief and instead replace it with my own. If I desire a man, I shall take one."

An answering anger sparked in his own eyes. Crystals lit with the fires of his passion. "And what do you desire?"

Every fiber of her being yearned for him to touch her. She wanted his fingers in her hair, his body pressed against hers—in hers—until she didn't know where he started and where she ended.

Sorcha wanted him. It didn't matter he was larger than her, or that he was Fae. She might regret it in the morning, but now she would enjoy every second of this poor decision.

She slid her hands up the wide plane of his chest, tangled her fingers around his braid and pulled him down. Their foreheads pressed together. She inhaled his air and breathed into him new life.

"I desire a king."

"Then a king you shall have."

He lifted her into his arms as if she weighed nothing. Sorcha had seen him swing a sword taller than her, perhaps she felt like a feather to him. She might have pondered such thoughts if he hadn't swooped down and devoured her lips.

Her body glowed with passion and desire so great that she feared it would never be satisfied. Something, or someone, uncurled deep within her soul. A woman she barely recognized, who knew how to take what she wanted and asked for the world.

Candlelight disappeared in curls of smoke as he laid her across a feather down bed. Inky darkness obscured him from her vision.

His hands trailed down her sides, following the indents of her waist and the flare of her hips. Cold crystal pressed against the smooth column of her neck. The highest points dug into her skin, not quite painful and sending shivers racing from each touch.

The tight bodice of her dress eased. Her lungs expanded and her back arched, pushing her chest into his waiting hands. He slipped his fingers under the gaping fabric, smoothing his fingers around her waist and pulling her into his chest.

Stones pressed against bare flesh. She sighed, the sound almost too loud as he surged up and captured her lips again. The erotic scrape of crystal mingling with his guttural groan sent shudders rocking through her body. He smoothed his hand over her bare spine, hand shaking as he held himself in check.

"Eamonn," she whispered. "I want to see you."

"No one wants to see this face."

"I desire to see nothing but you."

Candles flared to life all around the decimated room. Shattered furniture, shards of stone statues, and broken mirrors created a battlefield. The bed was all that survived unscathed.

Eamonn did not look at her. He turned the scarred half of his face away from her as if she might be insulted by the mere sight of him.

Sorcha reached out and sunk her fingers into the hollows of his cheek. She whispered fierce and hoarse, "How dare you hide from me, my king."

"Your king?"

"You hide from no one."

The words struck a fire deep within her belly. She would tear apart anyone who dared say this man was not a king. She had met the imposter who wore a stolen crown. No man could ever live up to the goliath who hovered above her and dimmed the lights for fear his face would lessen her passion.

Her heart beat like a pounding drum. She gentled her grip on his face, sliding down the well-known dip of throat and collarbone. Her fingers curled around the edge of his shirt and lifted it.

All the while, Eamonn's eyes watched her movements. So many emotions played across his face. Shame. Embarrassment. Wonder.

"What manner of creature are you?" he asked. "Fearless in your ability to see past this gruesome figure, and so selfless that you would allow a beast to lay hands upon you."

"You are not a beast," she said as she flung his shirt to the floor.

The caverns of geodes followed the lines of his ribs. She traced their edges, daring to dip into the crevices until crystals bit at her fingers. Sorcha outlined each wound, each grievous injury until she was certain she had marked each with her scent and her touch.

She sat up, pressing her chest against his and her mouth against his shoulder. She traced the mangled flesh and stone with lips and tongue.

"I claim you as mine, rightful king of the Seelie Fae." Sorcha sank her teeth into his skin, biting through flesh until the harsh edge of stone cracked her lips.

Blood smeared his shoulder. Marking him for all eternity.

He roared out in anger, or perhaps something far more dangerous. His hand flexed beneath the fabric of her dress and ripped. Crystals and warm skin traced the delicate line of her spine in apology.

"You toy with fire," he growled. "Once wounded, I never heal."

"Good. Perhaps any other woman who dares touch you will think twice."

The feral grin on his face beckoned the creature inside her, the woman who wanted to feast upon the Fae. "And you say you are not a druid."

"I like you better with your mouth shut."

"Shall I find something to keep it busy then?"

Sorcha couldn't respond. A fire burned in her blood, and need swelled until it crashed over her mind. She straddled his waist and arched her spine, offering her body as a banquet upon which he could feast.

Candlelight made her skin glow. He lifted shaking hands, gliding over the bumps of her ribs until he could take her in hand. She tilted her head back, unable to maintain eye contact when the crystals flared to life. Violet glowed behind her closed eyes.

She gasped as crystals slid over the tips of her breasts, cold and strangely hard. Her spine curved further, and she pressed into his hand. A long sigh hollowed her belly as he teased a silken tip between his fingers.

He followed the line of her throat with his nose. Teeth closed around her ear, his hot breath vibrating in her ear. She clenched her legs against his sides as wet heat rushed through her.

"Lie down," he drawled.

"No."

"Sorcha."

"I said no."

"Now is not the time to argue with me."

"What did I say about keeping your mouth shut?" she asked.

Sorcha locked her ankles and twisted her body. His brows drew down in surprise, but he obliged her request. Eamonn rolled.

He stretched his body across the bed and settled her hips over his. Cocking his head to the side, he asked "What now?"

A wicked grin spread across her lips. Sorcha smoothed her hands over his shoulders, pushing his arms away from her and onto the bed. She stroked across the bulges of his biceps, over the crystals on his forearms, and locked her fingers with his.

Her hips rocked, playing back and forth across his hardness. He was incredibly large, far more than a human man could ever dream of being. A small moment of worry made her wonder if he would fit.

She'd have to make him.

Sorcha whispered her lips over the mangled mess of his shoulder. The crystals scratched into the surface of his chest nipped at her mouth. She danced her fingers across his ribs, smiling at his gasp as she trailed her fingers across his stomach.

She lingered at the band of muscles arching over his hip bone. Tiny nibbles sent gooseflesh raising before her eyes.

"Sorcha," he moaned. "Have pity on a man."

Hardly. She looked up at him, flicking a brow before biting down hard.

He clenched his fists in the sheets and threw his head to the side.

"Pity is for the weak," she whispered, "and you underestimated the woman you took to bed."

She slid her fingers beneath his breeches, brushing her cheek over his throbbing heat. The sheets whispered as he arched against her touch. He lifted himself so she might free him from the confines of clothing.

He was glorious. Sorcha was thoroughly pleased to see that faeries were built entirely similarly to men.

She pressed a kiss against his shaft and made her way back up his body. She straddled his waist and took hold of his hands.

"You have been on this isle for a long time. It would be careless if I did not ask how long it has been."

Blue eyes blistered with heat as she tucked his fingers against her ribs. "Too long."

"How long is that?"

"Long enough that I'm not putting a number to it."

"Then I'll be gentle this time," she whispered.

In truth, she wasn't certain she could wait. Her wet heat already slicked across him, and she couldn't stop the rhythmic canting of her hips. His arms flexed, and he pulled the dress over her shoulders.

Hands roamed down her shoulders, lingering upon the curves of her breasts and sliding across her thighs.

"Gentle?" he asked. "When have I ever asked for gentle?"

She had never felt like this before. He willingly gave her full control over the situation, and she wanted to devour him. She wanted to mark him for all eternity. To shred him until all he could do was whisper her name.

The newly discovered part of herself, the animal, the beast, wanted to see him on his knees. She understood what men felt like when they came to the brothel. She could order him to do whatever she wanted.

Sorcha leaned forward, sank her teeth into the lobe of his ear, then soothed the ache with her tongue. "What do you want, Eamonn?"

He growled and lifted his hips.

"Oh," she whispered. "Is that all?"

She reached between them and wrapped her hand around his hard length. He pulsed between her fingers, eager and wanting. As a reward, she slid her hand up and down until he was breathing so fast that he rocked the bed.

But not yet. She wasn't done with him yet. She paused, waited for him to catch his breath, then notched him at her opening. He was broad, too large, too thick, and far too enticing.

She wanted to see him as he entered her. She wanted to watch his eyes and brand herself into his soul.

"Eamonn," she whispered, knowing how much he liked to hear his name on her lips.

"Now, Sorcha."

A rush of heat tensed her belly, and she groaned. Throwing herself down, she seated him all the way to her core.

They both gasped, arched, ached for each other as two became one. The candles blew out as a gust of magic rushed through the room.

He filled her to the brink of pain. She stung, but the needles of sensation eased from pain into pleasure. Erotic tingles danced down her spine, multiplying as he groaned in appreciation.

Sorcha leaned forward. His breath feathered over her lips, and she couldn't bring herself to move. Not yet. She wanted to savor each moment that passed. Each clench of muscle that dragged him ever deeper.

A drop of sweat dripped down his temple.

"You feel like coming home," he whispered. The words tasted sweet against her lips.

She knew how long it had been since he felt like he had a home.

He'd been the outcast for centuries. And now, he admitted that sliding into her body fulfilled that piece of himself.

The earth could have split open, and Sorcha would not have been able to stop. She lifted up and drove back down. She gasped, clenching hard as she set a rhythm that made him grip the sheets again.

He didn't touch her until she picked his hands back up. He gave her all the power, all the freedom to use his body as she saw fit. She pressed his palms against her breasts, dragged his hands to her mound and encouraged him to touch, to learn her body as she learned his.

Slow movements became frustrating. She braced her hands on his chest and sped up but her thighs were quivering and her mind fractured.

He growled and lifted her away. He spread her across the bed, her hair a wildfire of curls, as he plunged back into her.

The time for tenderness had passed. The animals inside them clawed to the forefront. They fought beneath the sheets, twisting for power and control. She sank her teeth into his shoulder again, fitting them into the marks she had already left. The howling in her soul grew louder as he reached between them and slid his thumb across her molten heat.

"Eamonn!" she shouted.

She tensed, her whole body reaching for the stars. Higher and higher he brought her, forcing her further than she had ever gone until she arched her back and cried out in release.

Her eyes opened wide to watch as he threw his head back and groaned. The crystals that wrapped around his throat pulsed, his arms shook, and his hips stilled.

They had battled, drawn blood, and in the end, they lifted each other towards the stars and emerged victorious. Both alive, and undone.

Eamonn fell onto the bed next to her, chest heaving.

He tucked her against him, a wide hand spread across her spine. Sorcha hid the smile blooming across her lips. It was strange how easily he lost the self-conscious way he carried himself. First, he stopped wearing the hooded cloak, then he grew comfortable with her seeing his scars, and now he didn't flinch when they were pressed against her skin.

A woman could get used to this. Even the stones on his hands didn't bother her. They had heated in their passions and warmed her back. She was cocooned—safe within his arms.

The sheets rustled as he shifted his legs closer to hers. His lips pressed against her brow, gentle so that he did not break her skin with the crystals. "Stay with me."

Sorcha shivered. "There's far too many meanings for me to guess what you mean."

"Stay with me here on Hy-brasil, for as long as you live."

"It's a bold command for a faerie. Your kind despise humans."

"You aren't human. You're druid, and beyond that, you are mine. They will love you, or I will bring them to their knees."

She sighed and pressed her lips against his collarbone. "You can't force people to accept change. And as much as I love this place, the faeries, this world you've shown me, I have to go back."

"Why? To save the small amount of people who care for you?"

"It's not just about my family, but everyone. The blood beetle plague is horrific, and I will not allow it to spread any further."

"And they promised to give you a cure, if you brought me back," he grunted. "They twisted the truth, Sorcha. They'll send you on another impossible quest as soon as we return to your land. And another after that. Faeries, especially the MacNara twins, cannot be trusted."

She rose onto an elbow, searching his gaze for the truth of his words.

"You don't think they have the cure."

"I think they know of the cure, but they have been trying to meet with me for centuries. They toy with their puppets, force them to dance, and they do not care whether they snap the strings."

"I will break those strings," Sorcha growled. "How am I to save my people?"

"I don't know." He lifted a hand and tucked her wild hair behind her ear. "I don't know if it's even possible for you to save them. Plagues come and go, but humanity always survives them."

"People are in pain. I can't stay knowing that they're suffering and I might help."

"You have too large a heart for your body," he murmured.

She caught the hand he pressed against her chest, holding it tight enough that the crystals pricked her skin. "I can't, Eamonn. They're my family, my people, I can't let them live a life they don't deserve."

"Every time you open your mouth, it's as if you are plucking words from my soul. Promise to stay here, and I will return to your world with you. I will help you in your journey to find the cure for your people."

"You will?" Sorcha hadn't thought he would so readily agree. "Staying here is the easiest choice I have ever had to make. I will remain by your side gladly."

"It stings that I have to bribe you to remain here."

She had heard the words before. Men said to them to her sisters every day of the week. They paid women for favors and hoped that they loved them in return. Sorcha knew none of her sisters loved those men, but the way her heart hurt when she saw Eamonn told her this was different. This was true.

Laying back down, Sorcha tucked her head into the hollow of his throat and breathed in his earthy scent. "I stay because I choose to, not because you have agreed to save my people with me. You spared me the difficulty of deciding between you and my people. For that, I thank you."

He hesitantly wrapped his arms back around her. He pulled her closer to him until she couldn't tell where he began and where she ended. "No one should have to choose between their people and those they love."

"Speaking from experience?" She knew he was. She had seen the place he had grown up, the glistening palace walls and the silk draperies. His people needed him, missed him, desired to have a king worthy of their affection. Even the royals, Elva came to mind, wanted him to return.

"Yes."

Someday she would convince him to go back to Seelie. She would convince him to take his stolen throne, to place a crown atop his head, and become the man she saw inside him. His people would rejoice and cheer out his name.

But not until she saved her people. Only then would she convince the Seelie prince to return. Perhaps it was selfish, and likely the wrong choice, but Sorcha couldn't bear it any longer. Her people needed her. The guilt tore at her soul and their imagined screams of pain ate at her mind. This place, although beautiful, was not hers. She would willingly give up her old life if she knew that her family and people were happy.

Closing her eyes, she snuggled closer to his heat and resolved herself to sleep. He pressed a kiss against her head. She stayed awake until his breathing evened into the steady rhythm of dreams.

Chapter 24

Sorcha rolled onto her side and reached for Eamonn. She hadn't slept well—a new bed was always difficult the first night. She kept rolling over to find him, worried that he might disappear into the night.

The Wild Hunt was afoot, and she feared he would be taken by Cernunnos and his bride.

Her fingers smoothed over the empty bed, sheets cold from the absence of his body. The spike of fear made her breath catch in her throat. Where was he?

It couldn't be the Wild Hunt. Moonlight filtered through the windows, mocking her thoughts. Surely no other Tuatha dé Danann would take him from this prison?

Mind catching up to the fear, Sorcha sat up and dragged her fingers through the tangled mass of her hair. She was thinking irrationally. This was the place they banished people. No one would remove them.

She took a took breath and forced her muscles to relax. She focused on the tips of her toes, willing relaxation to travel from the ends of her feet all the way up her body. Once her muscles released their tension, she felt significantly better.

There was still no answer to what had happened to Eamonn. Where he was? Perhaps he had gone to bathe himself.

She couldn't imagine why. A grin spread across her features in the twilight. He had proven himself quite a worthy man.

Her body ached in places she hadn't realized she had. Each throb of muscle and quake of limb reminded her that she had been well and truly claimed, and that she had laid claim to him as well.

Sorcha bit her lip and pulled the blankets up to her chest. Curls fell across her naked body, slipping on the silken sheets.

"Where is he?" she muttered. "I would like to repeat last night."

Clattering echoed from outside the door. On the stairs? She couldn't imagine why Oona would bring food or tea up. It was far too late, and if Eamonn asked her to make the trek up those stairs in the middle of the night, then Sorcha had words to stay to him. The man wouldn't learn a thing about his people.

Oona was an old woman! No matter that her body appeared young, she had enough years on her to deserve a bit more respect.

She slid her legs over the edge of the bed and hissed when her toes touched the cold stone.

"Eamonn," she growled. "Everywhere else in the entire castle has sheepskin so we don't freeze our toes off in the morning. Yet you insist upon punishing yourself even this early."

Dim light made it difficult to find her dress. The yellow fabric was ruined. He had ripped all the buttons off the back. But it would have to do for now. Oona wouldn't mind if a bit of her skin was showing.

The faerie had already seen every bit of Sorcha anyways.

She snorted. How strange it was to no longer worry about who saw her nudity. She had been frightened of revealing even the smallest bit of ankle when she first arrived. Now, she wasn't worried about waltzing around with her entire back unclothed.

The mind was a strange and wondrous thing, she mused. She slid the fabric up and over her shoulders, pressing it against her chest and maneuvering a makeshift tie around her waist.

Clattering became clanging, growing louder and louder as it reached the door of Eamonn's quarters. Sorcha's brow furrowed. She knew that sound, and yet she didn't.

It wasn't the sound of pottery or plates.

The door to the bedroom burst open, slammed against the wall with a thunderous bang, and fell off its top hinge. She shrieked and held her arm up.

"Sorcha!" Eamonn's shout was a welcome, if concerning, sound to hear.

"Eamonn!"

"Where are you, woman?"

He couldn't see her in the darkness. She ran towards him, wrapping her arms around the frame outlined by candle glow.

"I'm here," she whispered. "I'm here. What's wrong?"

Metal dug into her ribs. Her biceps met cold armor and the pommel of his sword pressed against her belly. He was dressed for war.

Eamonn wrapped his arms around her, pressing his lips against her hair. "Thank the gods. You're safe."

"I'm fine, what's happening?"

"When did you see my brother?"

The question chilled her to the bone. "What?"

"You saw my twin, Fionn, and you did not tell me. When was this?"

"Eamonn, I'm sorry. I should have told you. He summoned me and I knew it would cause problems if I didn't go. I didn't want to—"

He held her an arm's length away and mashed a finger against her lips. "I'm not angry with you. I just need to know what was said between the two of you."

"Nothing I thought you needed to know, or I would have told you immediately."

"He tried to convince you he would be a good king."

"Yes," she nodded. "He tried very hard."

"And he didn't succeed."

"No. I still believe you would be the better king, and it pained me to see an imposter sitting on your throne, wearing your face."

He tilted his face, wincing at her words. "You may regret saying that."

"He offered me a boon. He wouldn't dare harm me, not when I can command him."

"Dangerous for a king to offer such a thing."

"That's exactly what I said."

Eamonn tapped her chin with an armored finger. "Precisely why I find you so interesting, Sorcha. You think like a soldier."

"I think like someone who wants to survive. Why have you donned your armor?"

She watched him carefully as he pulled away. The armor creaked with his movements, groaning and shrieking plates scratching against each other. His spine stiffened, and he took a deep controlling breath.

"I always knew it would come to this. My brother has wanted me dead for centuries. I threaten his right to sit on that throne, even though I have been disgraced and banished. As long as I am alive, the people will always call for the High King of Seelie to sit upon the golden throne."

"As they should."

"It's not my choice, Sorcha," he said. "The world has made this decision for me. I am ruined, therefore, I am unfit to be king."

"Don't you believe change is worth considering? Perhaps the people who choose to be Seelie Fae no longer wish to have a perfect king."

"You say blasphemous words you could not hope to understand."

"I understand more than you know." She reached for his face, framing his cheeks with her hands. "Your people are dying under the control of a tyrant who shows them little kindness. They want you to come home. Even the Tuatha dé Danann."

"What do you know of such things?" A spear of candlelight spread across his face.

No, not candlelight, she realized. Fire from outside the window of the castle's tallest tower. Something was burning outside. She could smell the smoke now, acrid and burning her nose until she wanted to sneeze. She would not look.

"Elva was the faerie Oona wanted me to help. She said she was raised with you and your brother. She spoke very highly of you and the good things you might have done if you became king."

"Elva," he whispered. "That is a name I have not heard in a long time."

"The king made her his concubine."

"He had no right." The sudden anger in Eamonn's voice startled Sorcha.

"Was she yours?"

"No. She was another's, but he would not have claim over a Seelie woman if the Seelie king wanted her." He cursed. "How dare he meddle in such things? No wonder he is so hated."

Sorcha swallowed. "Eamonn, why are you in armor?"

"The king is here."

Of course. She should have guessed, but she hadn't wanted to think the worst had happened.

"Why?"

"You know why."

And she did. The king wanted to kill his brother once and for all. Sorcha ducked her head, stroked her hand across the smooth plates of his armor, and nodded.

"What do you need me to do?"

"Stay safe and out of the way."

"How?" She looked up at him for guidance. "I've never been in a battle before."

"Follow me. I will bring you somewhere I know you won't be harmed."

"And if you fall?" She didn't want to ask the question. The thought of him bleeding out on the battlefield without her assistance made a scream rise in the back of her throat. "I can help the wounded."

"I need you to stay out of the way. Follow me as closely as you can, and if we come across any of Fionn's men, do not interfere."

Sorcha nodded and followed as he rushed from the room. The weight of his armor must have been great, but he moved as if he wore nothing. It differed from the metal armor she had seen before. Interlocking pieces slid easily against each other and did not hinder his movements. No adornments made the armor "pretty." It was functional. Practical. Like him.

She held her skirts high as they raced through his chambers and out onto the dangerous parapet hanging above the ground. It was then that she saw the army.

Spread out across the isle she loved so dearly, men and women in golden armor lifted their swords and spears. The Fae who lived in the castle and served their true master stood around the castle in a weak line.

There were so few of them.

Sorcha stopped running, fisting her hands in the fabric of her skirts as tears dripped down her cheeks. They would die. Under no circumstances could such a small amount of Lesser Fae stand a chance against an army in full battle gear.

The faeries she knew and loved held kitchen pottery in their hands. Pots, pans, garden hoes.

A choked sob rocked her forward. "They don't even have weapons," she whispered. "Please have mercy on them. They don't even have weapons."

"Sorcha!"

She flinched at Eamonn's shout, rocking forward dangerously near the edge.

"Sorcha, get down!"

A man climbed over the edge of the parapet. Twin blades glinted in the moonlight. He used them as hand holds, puncturing wounds into the side of the castle. They knew where Eamonn was.

The gilded edge of his armor was sharp as a knife. He spun towards her, not Eamonn, and grinned at her look of fear.

"You're getting in the way," the faerie grunted. "Off you go."

He lunged, and she spun away. His hands caught in the fabric of her dress, and she fell onto her hands and knees. Stone bit into her palms. Hair fell in front of her face, obscuring her vision. His hands gripped her ankles, and she screamed.

Then he disappeared. Ripped away from her legs with a panicked shout of his own. She looked over her shoulder to see Eamonn lift the faerie over his head. Too easy. Too simple. His expression was cold and heartless as he threw the man over the edge.

The echoing scream sounded like the wail of a bean sidhe.

"Come." Eamonn reached out a hand for her to take. "We have to go."

"That man—"

"One of my brother's and not worth your guilt. Get up."

She wanted to vomit. Sorcha had seen death many times over, but never so carelessly handled.

For the first time since meeting him, she looked at Eamonn with new eyes. Somehow, she had fantasized about him as the hero in a fairytale, but he was a flesh and blood warrior whose hands and body were stained with death and war.

She fit her hand into his, knowing full well what it meant. She could not support death. But she would not turn from him either.

He pulled her to standing and nodded. "That's not the last of them, Sorcha. There will be more."

"I know."

"You didn't."

"I do now."

He gave her one last, lingering glance before racing towards the door to the main part of the castle. Sorcha followed, her heart thudding hard in her ears.

The clattering of his armor echoed in the winding stairwell. It bounced up the circular tower, growing louder and louder. The slamming gong of church bells. Funeral bells.

A body fell silently down the middle shaft of the stairs. Sorcha wouldn't have noticed it, for the female faerie did not even shout in fear, but air whistled through her armor and the thudding weight charged the air with electricity.

"They are following us," she said. Her words seemed too loud, disrespectful of the deaths she had just seen.

"Of course, they are. Stay close."

As they neared the bottom, Eamonn drew his broadsword. The rubies in the handle suddenly made more sense. The blade feasted upon the blood of its enemies, and thousands of souls were caught there.

Though the thought was fanciful, Sorcha still edged away from his sword.

"Are you frightened of me?" he asked. He did not look at her, instead he stared down the hallway and waited for her answer.

"Not of you, but of your weapon."

"You should be afraid of Ocras."

"The sword's name is Hunger?"

"It devours my foes and cleaves flesh and bone. She does not desire you."

"She?"

Eamonn flashed a feral grin. "Of course. Women are capable of both beauty and pain."

"There are many who would argue with you on that."

"They would have to argue with Ocras."

"Are we running?"

"Not yet."

"Why are we waiting?" She didn't look down the hallway, not wanting to see what they would run towards until the last second.

"Just a bit more," he murmured. "Just long enough to give them time."

"For what?"

"Now."

He rounded the wall and charged down the hallway with a piercing shout. His roar made the walls shake and the ground quake with the force of his rage. As promised, Sorcha followed close behind but gave him enough room to swing his sword.

And swing he did.

Four soldiers waited for them. Two men, two women, golden armor molded to their bodies. Helms topped with bright feathers hid their species and made them appear all the more otherworldly.

They attacked all at once, and it was as if they struck a bull. Eamonn ducked into the first one, slamming his shoulder into the man's stomach. Metal crunched as he lifted an arm to block a sword slicing towards him. It struck his forearm and snapped in half as it cut through his armor and met crystal underneath.

Ocras sang as she swung through the air and sliced through the neck of a male faerie. It stopped halfway through, blood dripping down his armor as Eamonn placed a foot on his chest and shoved him away.

He didn't hesitate. He turned and lashed out, plunging the sword into another soldier's chest cavity. She shrieked and fell to the ground while holding her stomach.

Eamonn wrenched her sword out of her dying grip and caught the next attack on its blade. The weapons shrieked their fury into the air. The muscles on Eamonn's neck bulged, veins pulsing as he pushed the other back. Step by step.

Unlocking their swords by swinging his to the side, Eamonn sank the blade through the crevice where thigh met pelvis. The man fell with a cry, holding onto his leg.

The last woman ran. She raced down the hallway as if it might contain a new escape. Eamonn growled and pulled the stolen faerie sword from the man's leg, ducked his head, and calmly walked down the hallway.

Sorcha didn't know whether to be terrified or angry. The metallic scent burned her nostrils. Blood welled into the air until she thought she could see it hanging above her like a curtain of guilt.

She couldn't stand by and watch this happen.

Eamonn wasn't looking, so he couldn't stop her. She rushed forward and placed her hands on the faerie man's shoulders.

"Easy," she whispered. "I will drag you back to the wall. Do not make a sound, or he will turn around."

The man grunted and pressed his hands harder against his wound.

Sorcha, though small, had grown strong from manipulating the human body and hiking all across the isle. He was larger than her but small for a Fae. She tucked her hands under his armpits and dragged him a few feet until he could lean against stone.

She dropped to her knees next to him and brushed his hands out of the way.

"No," he grumbled.

"Let me. I'm a healer."

The wound was deep and cut through muscle. If he was lucky, he would live, but he would never walk again.

Sorcha would not be the one who told him that. Perhaps faerie healers knew more than she did about their bodies. The only thing she could do was stop him from bleeding out.

The tearing sound of her dress made Eamonn pause. She could feel the heat of his stare, his anger burning through her flesh.

Quickly, she wrapped the cloth underneath his thigh and cinched it as tight as possible. She knotted the fabric, ignored his pained whimper, and turned towards Eamonn glaring daggers at her actions.

"I won't let him die."

"Why? Some strange affection towards my twin?"

"Because he's just doing a job. I won't stand by when I can help, no matter what side he fights for."

"Soft heart."

Eamonn turned and flung the sword in his hand. It whistled through the air and embedded in the faerie woman's back who scrabbled at the door, then hung limp.

"Let's go," Eamonn said. He turned and yanked Ocras out of the other woman, holding out a bloodied hand for her to take.

Sorcha stood slowly, measuring him with a weighted stare. "You're angry at me."

"I am."

"Why?"

"He doesn't deserve your help."

"He's alive. That means he deserves my help. I will never stop wanting to heal people, and if you want me to then we can end this now. I help others. That's what I do."

She watched a muscle jump on his jaw. His eyes canted away from hers, staring at the wall until he finally nodded. "So be it. Come with me."

He did not reach out a hand, and she did not take his arm. They stood still in the hallway filled with blood, looking away from each other. A rift between them grew, splintering and splitting, a canyon tearing apart their tenuous alliance.

Sorcha should have been heartbroken. She should have been sad, but she was angry. How dare he be angry at her for trying to save another life?

Her heart whispered to be gentle. That the man standing before her needed as much healing as the man behind. His brother was here to kill him. Eamonn likely would not be looking for those who were just doing a job compared to those who wanted him dead.

Maybe they all wanted him dead. She had no way of knowing.

He glanced at her. She met his gaze as his eyes widened in fear.

"Sorcha!"

She heard the crunching sound of armor moving before she turned. The faerie she'd saved stood behind her. She saw nothing but cold determination in his gaze and a knife that seemed to glow in his hands.

Time slowed. She heard her own exhalation and his hand began to descend. Sorcha ducked, her palms dragging across the plates of his armor. Her fingers slid across metal and gripped a sharpened piece.

She gasped as he fell against her, staggering in pain. She squeezed her eyes shut as hot blood poured over her hands. The jagged edge of armor bit into her fingers, but sliced into his chest even farther when she tried to move.

Her hands trembled, but she couldn't make them move. He gasped in her ear, the rattling wheeze of a dying breath. She knew it well. Sorcha had heard it many times, but never so close.

Eamonn might have killed the others, but she had killed this one.

"Sorcha." Eamonn's armored hands pulled her away from the body. It fell to the ground with a wet thud. "Sorcha, I'm sorry you had to do that."

"I didn't mean to kill him."

"You had to protect yourself, mo chroí."

"I didn't know what to do."

"The first one is always the hardest. But we do not have time for this."

"I should check for a heartbeat," she said. She tried to turn but he wouldn't even let her look at the body.

"No. No, we leave now, Sorcha. I need to hide you from him."

"From who?" Her mind felt foggy. All she could feel was blood on her hands, and she should have been comfortable with the feeling. How many times had she felt blood on her hands? Pouring from between a woman's legs. It was life.

But this was death.

"Sorcha."

"I thought you and Bran looked like you were dancing. It was beautiful to watch you spar. I was so impressed. I thought real battle would look like that, but it doesn't."

"Practicing is one thing. It's easy to make the movements look graceful when there is no blade striking at your throat. Real battle is gritty, messy, brutal. I'm sorry you had to see it."

"Mo chroí," she whispered. "You called me your heart."

He gripped her hand and did not answer. They raced through the halls, ducking around soldiers. The castle rang with the screams of Fae who had not gone to the forefront to fight the king's army.

Sorcha couldn't handle any more death. She squeezed her eyes shut and let Eamonn guide her across the floors. Perhaps he knew that she wouldn't look. Eventually, he swung her into his arms and charged through the endless doors and hidden rooms.

He burst through a side door. She curled against his chest and whimpered, wanting nothing more than for this battle to end. For her life to be back to normal. To wake up in her own bed and have this be nothing more than a wondrous tale for her sisters.

Wind brushed her hair across her face, cool and calming.

On the breeze, she heard a haunting song. A cry that trembled from a woman's lips, speaking of lost love and a death that came too soon.

Eamonn stood still.

"Bean sidhe," he said. "I have no quarrel with the Unseelie."

"Where is my brother?"

"I had assumed he returned to you."

"No twisted truths, Seelie king. I want my brother returned safely."

Sorcha felt his nod against the top of her head. "I have use for him yet."

"He will not fight for you. We do not need another war with the Seelie Fae on top of everything else which has happened. Bran wants a war. He does not speak for the Unseelie council."

"I have never thought he did. He gave up that life long ago."

"Good." The banshee wailed, and the wind picked up again. "See that my brother returns home safely."

"After he assists me."

"The deal is struck."

The cold touch of the wind felt like a woman's hand. It slid across her brow and down her arms. Sorcha heard a quiet whisper on the breeze.

"Hello, priestess."

What did the Unseelie woman know that Sorcha did not? The words weren't merely an observation. As if she had seen her before, or perhaps her likeness.

Eamonn touched her chin. "You must walk from here, mo chroí."

She touched her toes to the ground and balanced herself on his arm.

"What are you going to do?"

"What I should have done a long time ago."

"You're going to fight him?" Sorcha shook her head. "Eamonn, more bloodshed will not fix this. You need to talk to your brother."

"You think he wants to share the throne? It's not possible for the Seelie Fae to have two kings."

"Surely, your parents had thought of this? You're twins, Eamonn! They must have known there would either be two kings, or you would sit upon the throne."

A shadow passed over his face. "They had always intended for us to share the kingdom. Fionn made his choice."

Another faerie name she had in her collection, although this one she did not want. The name of the king danced upon her tongue and tasted like soured milk.

She did not want this responsibility. She did not want this name that branded itself into her mind because she knew this was the first faerie name she wanted to use.

This was the only power a human had over a Fae. She had his name, and now she could command him to do whatever she pleased. Sorcha could walk into the fields of battle and scream for him to stop and he would.

But such responsibility meant she chose a side. It meant she trusted that Eamonn would make a better king, and now that she had seen him in battle she was no longer sure of that. He had changed much. All she knew for certain was that he was not his brother.

She could not decide if that made him worthy of a throne.

Eamonn stared down at her. "You have chosen?"

"I will not choose. I came here to save my people, my family. Not to become entangled in the faerie courts and their wars."

"I don't think you have a choice," he said. He traced a line from her forehead, down her nose, and across her lips. "You're here, Sorcha. That means you're involved."

"I don't wish to be."

"Wishes mean nothing to the Fae."

"I know." The words caught around the thick knot of a sob.

"I never meant to hurt you."

"Eamonn, tell me what is going on. Where are you taking me?"

"I'm not taking you anywhere, mo chroí."

He leaned down and caught her lips in a searing kiss. He poured himself into her, sinking tongue and taste until she felt the essence of him crawling underneath her skin. Their memories pulsed in her heart, and she knew this was goodbye.

Sorcha tangled her fingers in the long tail of his braid and pulled him towards her. She dug her nails into his skull, marking him as hers even further than she already had. Their teeth clacked together, blood welled at her lips, but she did not want to stop. If she stopped, her heart would break, and her being should shatter into a thousand pieces.

He pulled away.

"No," she whispered and squeezed her eyes shut. "No, Eamonn don't do this. You promised to come back with me."

"If you stayed." His thumb traced a line over her bottom lip. "And you aren't staying."

Taloned feet gripped her waist. Her eyes snapped open, and the ground dropped away.

"No!" she screamed. "No! Please, no!"

Her soul splintered, shouting that she didn't want to leave him. He shouldn't be alone when he faced the battlefield.

Great wings buffeted air against her head. She struggled, to no avail. The beastly bird did not release its hold upon her waist. Soon they were too high for her to escape.

The highest peak of the castle was nearly within her reach. Everything looked so small, even the armored faeries who attacked the front door and beat back those she loved. She could still hear the screams.

Eamonn stared up at her. Once she was too high and fell limp in the bird's claws, he turned and walked onto the battlefield.

The faeries of the isle parted like a sea in front of him. His tarnished and aged armor looked like stone as he moved through the crowd. The golden army stood in front of him, a wall of power and clear intent.

Sorcha wondered which one was Oona. From so high, she couldn't make out faces or traits she might recognize.

Eamonn's people were short and squat. Their forms warped and stretched with animal features, strange skin, oddly shaped bodies. They looked so different compared to the perfection Fionn brought with him. These were the Tuatha dé Danann, the great faeries who enslaved those who did not deserve it.

The twins mirrored each other, standing at the forefront of their armies. Fionn sat upon a great white steed. The long tail of his hair whipped in the breeze. Eamonn stood with his legs rooted in the earth, his braid thin and still. They stared across a sea of blood and did not move.

"Bran?" she whispered into the wind.

A booming caw echoed all around her. She glanced down at the talons wrapped around her waist. Each claw was as big as her forearm. Rough grey skin covered them. She hadn't realized he could turn into such a massive beast. Another secret revealed, another to store away in her memory.

"Are they going to kill each other?"

The wind whistled past her ears, and she couldn't tell if the croak was for her or simply a grumble.

"Am I ever going to see him again?"

The Unseelie Prince didn't answer. He turned them both away from the battlefield and soared over the ocean.

Too far away for anyone to hear her sobs.

Chapter 25

They traveled across the sea with great speed. Bran took them high over the storm's edge, moonlight giving way to sunrise.

Sorcha wanted to take in the beauty. She wanted to appreciate the world, because she would never see it this way again. Merrows jumped from the waves and called out to them. The Guardian swam through the depths as a shadow drifting aimlessly.

She took it all in, but her heart felt empty. Drained. She wasn't certain if it was even there anymore.

Her faerie prince was likely dead. If he wasn't dead, then he'd killed the mirror image of himself. Who could be the same after that?

Was killing a twin like killing oneself?

Bran's claws dug into her skin, shredding the waist of her dress. The pain was dull compared to the ache of her heart. She'd always thought she would grieve like Rosaleen did when she lost a lover she liked.

The blonde waif of a girl would wail and scream. Her cheeks would burn with the salt of her tears. The house would ring with the anger of her cries, the disappointment in herself, and the man who had left.

Sorcha was numb. There was nothing inside her at all. Just a dull throb where her heart used to be.

Bran's toes shifted. "I'm bringing you home."

She nodded, although he couldn't see her response.

He jostled her. "Did you hear me, midwife? I'm bringing you home. Wasn't that what you've wanted this whole time? To go home?"

Sorcha did not respond. Instead, she stared down at the waves and wondered how much it would hurt if he let her go. She had heard the higher one was, the more solid the surface of water became. If he let her go, she might strike hard enough that she wouldn't even feel it.

His toes clenched hard, squeezing the breath out of her. "It's not the end of the world, you idiot. You have a purpose, remember?"

"Excuse me?"

"I can tell you're moping!"

"I think I have a right to."

"You didn't even fall in love with him. You've lost a good friend. That means nothing."

"He has become a part of me."

The faint outline of houses appeared on the horizon. A familiar city. It felt like such a long time ago that she had stared across the table at humans. How long had it been?

Time moved differently in the Otherworld, and Macha had said it was the same in Hy-brasil. How much had her world changed?

Sorcha wasn't certain she would survive it.

Bran soared over the tops of buildings, past ships and sailors. No one looked up at the great winged bird carrying its human cargo. He took them to a small hut. Abandoned and falling down, it may have once been a home.

No longer. Sorcha listened to the soft sound of feathers as he brought them down to the ground. He placed her gently on the roof of the hut and hopped down to the dirt where he shifted forms.

Feathers melted into caramel skin. Black clothing formed over his body. Talons shrank into fingernails until only small points remained. A dusting of tiny black feathers still decorated his face, and the single raven eye glared up at her.

Bran held his arms out. "Time to get off."

"I can't feel my body," she whispered. "It's the strangest feeling. I never thought losing someone I loved could actually hurt my physical form."

"Come, Sorcha. I will tell you a story."

She didn't want to hear a story. She wanted him to take her back to Hy-brasil, so she could look after the survivors of Fionn's war. The hard look in his eye suggested he wouldn't take no for an answer.

Perhaps it was better in the long run. She scooted to the edge of the thatched roof and tumbled into his arms.

He set her down carefully, then placed a hand on her back and pushed her towards two fallen logs. She sat down hard. Her hands didn't feel right. They didn't seem to be placed on the ends of her arms in a way she could control. They almost felt backwards, but that wasn't right at all. She had used these hands thousands of times.

Bran reached forward and cupped the backs of her trembling fingers.

"I lost someone very dear to me. I spent my entire existence wooing her. Sticking twigs in her hair until she had to cut it to get them out.

Putting frogs in her bed and mice in her slippers. I teased her endlessly, and still she loved me."

He sighed heavily.

"And then one night, someone took her away. There was nothing I could do, and I was promised she would be happy, but I would never see her again."

He squeezed her hand to bring her attention to his story.

"I thought piecing myself back together would be impossible. It certainly felt like it in the first few months. But I found a different purpose as someone other than the man who loved her. I found my freedom, respect for myself, and I realized that even without her I was still a good man. I could still do great things, and that she was just a reward for working hard."

He lifted her hands and pressed his lips into her palms. "You will find yourself again, Sorcha. And I believe it will be in healing your people with these hands."

"How am I supposed to heal them?" Her eyes were so dry she couldn't even blink. "He was the answer to finding a cure, and now he's gone."

"I'm certain you will find a way. You always have."

"Is he really gone? Am I never going back to that wondrous isle full of faeries that I love dearly?"

"Do you think they'll still be there?"

"I want them to be. I don't want there to be a war and all that death. Bran, how can I stop it?"

The hands holding hers disappeared. Cold air rushed around her body, stealing the breath from her lungs. She glanced up and found that she was alone.

The sun rose into the sky far above her by the time she found the courage to stand. Her knees shook. Her body trembled. Her lungs gasped for air, and still she did not feel like a person.

Pain should ground her body. It should remind her that she was alive. It didn't.

"Home," she breathed. "I want to go home."

She didn't know where home was anymore.

The landscape became more recognizable the more she stared. These fields were ones she knew like the back of her hand. Sorcha stumbled as she moved, but at least she was moving.

Each step brought her closer and closer towards the haven she remembered in her mind. A small home. Quaint, three stories of stone and wood and laughter.

Gods, how she needed the laughter.

Stones crunched beneath her feet, digging into the calloused flesh until she bled. She remembered vividly another time when her feet were aching. Sorcha had dragged herself throughout the known world, only to return to this place.

Chickens clucked. The air smelled sweet, like fresh baked bread and sticky honey. Sorcha stood on the rise of the hill beyond the brothel.

She inhaled again and trembled. The smell of bread turned stale, honey turned sickly sweet, and the scent of death made her vision blur.

There were boards over the windows of the brothel. Nailed crudely from the outside, locking her family within. The side door that led to the chicken coop was also boarded shut, and the chickens were living out in the wild.

"No," she moaned on a trembling wheeze. "No, please no more."

The tears came like a wave crashing over her head. She fell onto her knees and crawled to her family home, unable to stand but needing to help them.

She knew the painted markers on the windows. A red beetle, haphazardly painted as if the artist wanted to flee the area as fast as he could. Smart man. The blood beetle plague was apt to spread if they took to the air.

Sorcha didn't care. She didn't want her family to die alone, and she would not allow them to die if she could.

Like an old woman, she pulled herself up onto the fencing and stared at the stone walls. Flashes of anger, old and buried deep, fueled her.

She stepped forward. Each simple movement so difficult that she seemed to have forgotten how to walk. Step by step, shift by shift, she lifted foot and flexed thigh until she pressed her hands against the boards covering the door.

The wood bit into her forehead as she leaned against it, but she did not feel the pain. They were in there. The beat of their hearts called out to her.

"Rosaleen," she whispered. "Briana, Papa…anyone."

She didn't know how long she stayed there, hovering between life and death, choice and silence. Heat spread over her body, wrapping around her waist. It almost felt like arms holding her against a solid chest and breathing life into her body.

Healing would take time. But courage, strength, honor, these were things that had always been deeply embedded in her soul.

Sorcha lifted her head and yanked hard at the boards.

"Briana!" she shouted. "Let me in!"

She threw her weight against the door and began pulling at the hammered boards. Each harsh jerk wrenched her shoulders but the first board tore free. She continued to screech and shout, banging against the barrier that kept her from her family.

Finally, a voice came from the other side. Weak, but wonderful to hear. "Sorcha?"

"Yes, yes, Rosaleen! It's me! I'm coming in."

"Don't come in!" Her sister coughed. "It's not safe."

"I'm coming in whether you want me to or not. What happened?"

"We're sick."

"Is Papa alive?"

"Barely."

"Is anyone dead?"

"No."

Sorcha sobbed out a breath of relief. "Good. That's very good. Now, I'm going to pull at this last board and then I'm going to come in."

"You can't. You'll get sick too."

"Are the beetles still flying?"

"No."

"Then I won't get sick. I won't let you or anyone else die."

She wrenched the last board free and grasped the door knob. It wouldn't turn.

"Rosaleen," she groaned. "Unlock the door."

"I'm not letting you die for me."

"I won't die for anyone."

"You left us."

"I didn't have a choice. I was trying to find a cure and failed." Sorcha's throat closed and her voice turned hoarse. "Let me help you. Please, give me a purpose again. I promise that I will do nothing other than heal you."

Silence rang louder than screams. Sorcha held her breath and counted the seconds that passed by until she heard the click of a lock.

Rosaleen opened the door and peeked through the crack. "It's not pretty in here."

"I know."

"We're not pretty anymore."

"You will always be beautiful. Even when you are old and grey and wrinkled."

The door opened completely. Open sores spread across Rosaleen's body where they had tried to extract the beetles. Burn marks scarred her cheeks and circular brands traveled her arms like chains.

Sorcha ghosted her fingers over one. "What are these?"

"The healers said they knew how to stop the beetles for good. It didn't work."

Resolve straightened Sorcha's spine. A beetle moved underneath her sister's skin, traveling across the high plane of her clavicle. She could stop this. She could help, and Bran was right.

She had found her purpose, and she refused to give up.

Sorcha pulled her sister into her arms, hugging her tight. "I'm here, little sister. I'm going to keep you alive."

"Where were you?"

"The Otherworld."

"With the faeries?"

"Yes."

"We always thought you were a changeling."

Sorcha smiled. "I'm not. I'm a druid."

"Are you going back?"

Sorcha stared into the darkness of the brothel. Shadows moved, clung to bodies, and her sisters entered the room. Her father shuffled from his bedroom and leaned against the door frame.

Their clothing hung on their skeletal frames. Hollow cheeks and haunted gazes stared at her as if she were their salvation. Sorcha knew that she was. She would expend every bit of her energy healing them.

She kissed the top of Rosaleen's head.

"Yes. Yes, I am going back."

Acknowledgements

There are so many people to thank for this book that I couldn't possibly write them all down. If I forget you, I am sincerely sorry and yell at me later.

Nata - This cover made the book what it is today. Your artwork inspires me to be a better writer and helped bring this story completely to life. I cannot thank you enough.

Amy - Your editing skills have no limit! Thank you for looking over this whopper of a book and for putting up with my constant changes. You were immensely helpful and I look forward to collaborating even more!

Emily - Thank you for the constant support, the jokes that made me laugh, and talking me off cliff edges. I'm not really sure I would have put this book out into the public. Not to mention the knitwear that you've created based off this book series (www.withlovefrommaine.com)

Mom and Dad - From green hair, to constant complaining and stress, you've been there from day one. I am so thankful that I have family who supports me through every bad decision, every knee scrape, and every resounding success.

To my Readers - Every book you buy, every review you leave, every message you send means the world.

This is for you.

ABOUT THE AUTHOR

Emma Hamm is a small town girl on a blueberry field in Maine. She writes stories that remind her of home, of fairytales, and of myths and legends that make her mind wander.

She can be found by the fireplace with a cup of tea, her dog, her fiance, and her two Maine Coon cats dipping their paws into the water without her knowing.

For more updates, join my newsletter!

www.emmahamm.